MIDNIGHT AT NOON

ARDAIN ISMA

Table of Contents

Praise for Ardain Isma 1

Ardain Isma 3

Acknowledgments 4

Author's Note 7

Prologue.. 10

Chapter 1 16

Chapter 2 27

Chapter 3 43

Chapter 4 57

Chapter 5 69

Chapter 6 83

Chapter 7 91

Chapter 8 106

Chapter 9 112

Chapter 10 130

Chapter 11 135

Chapter 12 146

Chapter 13 161

Chapter 14 178

Chapter 15 193

Chapter 16 200

Chapter 17 213

Chapter 18 221

Chapter 19 230

Chapter 20 241

Chapter 21 256

Chapter 22 268

Chapter 23 280

Chapter 24 287

Chapter 25 293

Chapter 26 311

Chapter 27 325

Chapter 28 341

Chapter 29 354

Chapter 30 369

Chapter 31 388

Chapter 32 394

Chapter 33 403

Chapter 34 416

Chapter 35 433

Chapter 36 441

Glossary of Haitian /
Other Non-English Terms 461

Praise for Ardain Isma

"As I read Midnight at Noon, I felt a profound connection to the community of peasants and merchants in northern Haiti. Ardain Isma masterfully weaves recent social upheavals and historical realities into the geography of the Northwest, creating a gripping narrative of Haiti's ongoing struggle to establish democratic governance and infrastructure. He is truly a master storyteller."

— Carrol Coates, distinguished professor of Comparative Literature at Binghamton University, New York, and translator of Jacques Stéphen Alexis's *Compère Général Soleil.*

"Author Ardain Isma paints a precise picture of the havoc such civil strife generates, with civilians trapped between the forces of established government and revolutionaries with a desire for reform"

- Saint Augustine Record

"MIDNIGHT AT NOON is not only the tragic and compelling story of modern-day Haiti, it is also a powerful plea on behalf of the downtrodden, the disenfranchised ANYWHERE in the world. Thanks, Ardain, for your meticulousness in crafting this beautiful story of love and hope for the 'hopeless.'"

- Bobbie Hart O'Neill, career journalist of *Native Unity*.

"MIDNIGHT AT NOON" is an impeccable tale that vividly portrays the stark divide between the haves and the have-nots. At its heart, it is a dazzling story of a young peasant man and a maid, whose moral heroism enables them to navigate the chaos of war and its harrowing consequences. Ardain, I commend you for crafting such a powerful narrative."

- Jacob Davis, editorialist for CSMS Magazine.

"A poignant tale of the common's man fight for social justice, *Midnight at Noon* takes you on a mental excursion through the streets and alleys of Haiti. Dr. Ardain Isma draws inspiration from a tumultuous history to craft this gripping, thought-provoking masterpiece."

- Rashmi Bora Das, author and essayist

"This is a heartfelt story that captures the essence of the universal human experience. Beautifully written, it takes readers on a journey through the heroic struggles of Haiti's marginalized people as they yearn for social justice."

- Gabriel Constans, author and screenwriter

Ardain Isma

Ardain Isma, born in Saint Louis du Nord, Haiti, spent his formative years on the island before immigrating to the United States. A celebrated essayist and novelist, he is the author of several critically acclaimed works, including *Bittersweet Memories of Last Spring* and *Last Spring was Bittersweet*. Ardain now resides in Saint Augustine, Florida, with his wife, Maryse.

Acknowledgments

Special thanks to my wife, Maryse, for her patience and understanding during the countless hours I spent writing and revising. Their steadfast support was essential to bringing this project to fruition.

Gwo kout chapo pou manman mwen Anne-Rose Isma kite ede-m anpil pou tout sa ke-m te bezwen sou Anwodo.

Heartfelt thanks to my loving mom, Anne-Rose Isma, whose invaluable knowledge of the historic village of Anwodo greatly enriched this project. I am deeply grateful for her unwavering support and love.

In memory of Bobbie Hart O'Neill, a dear friend and fervent supporter, whose unwavering encouragement remains cherished, though she did not live to see the release of Midnight at Noon.

In loving memory of my late cousin, Loubert Desmangles, whose unwavering passion for the village of Anwodo deeply touched the hearts and minds of all who knew and cherished him.

MIDNIGHT
AT NOON

(2nd Edition)

Author's Note

This book was first published in 2015 and received critical acclaim at the time. However, I have long felt the need for a second edition, a sentiment echoed by several academic colleagues. They encouraged me to pursue a new edition and relaunch, believing it would give "Midnight at Noon" a fresh opportunity to reach a broader audience. In this new publication, while I have made some minor stylistic changes, I have neither added to nor omitted the fundamental ideas that guided the first edition.

Since my college years, I have wanted to write a story that reflects the struggle of people around the world for better living conditions, particularly those in war-torn regions and impoverished nations like Haiti. In societies where opportunities are scarce, a small fraction of the population often controls a significant portion of the wealth. This reality was starkly evident in Haiti in the early 1980s when the Haitian people finally overcame their fear and began to protest against the 29-year Duvalier dictatorship. These protests grew and ultimately led to the downfall of one of the most brutal regimes in the country's history.

However, the fall of Duvalier did not bring the economic prosperity for which so many Haitians had sacrificed their lives. The partisans of the old regime remained in control and resisted allowing the masses—yearning for participatory democracy—to be part of the political process. Faced with this reality, it didn't take long for the disenfranchised Haitians to return to the streets, demanding true sociopolitical reforms and the removal of the Duvalierists and their allies from power.

What followed was a protracted struggle for social justice that resulted in the 1990 election of Jean-Bertrand Aristide, who won a decisive victory. But nine months later, he was overthrown in a bloody coup that shattered the hope for a better future cherished by millions of Haitians. Aristide was sent into exile but later returned to complete his presidential mandate after a compromise with the coup leaders. Unfortunately, he became a conformist politician, adhering to the old rules, leaving many Haitians feeling betrayed.

Since then, attempts to restore democratic rule in Haiti have consistently failed. The impoverished Haitians and their genuine representatives are rarely, if ever, included in the decision-making process, and their grievances have been persistently ignored. Most Haitians believe their country's misery is largely due to foreign interference.

Every nation has the inherent right to self-determination, including the ability to choose its political system, make its own decisions, and determine its future without external coercion or influence. Foreign interference undermines this right by imposing outside agendas, manipulating local politics, and subverting the will of the people. Haiti is a classic example.

Sovereignty is a foundational principle of the international system, affirming the independence and autonomy of states to govern their own affairs without external interference. When foreign powers intervene in the internal affairs of another country, they violate this principle, destabilizing the global order and setting dangerous precedents that could justify further interventions elsewhere. Such actions can breed resentment, conflict, and undermine the legitimacy of both the interfering state and the government it supports. The contemporary history of Haiti clearly illustrates this.

Over the last thirty years, foreign intervention in Haitian politics—whether direct or indirect—has exacerbated existing tensions, fueled internal divisions, and perpetuated Haiti's humiliation under the guise of aid.

Before writing this book, I conducted extensive research on contemporary Haitian literature, reviewing many fictional and non-fictional works dating back to the Haitian independence war. This helped me understand the issue of class antagonisms, which lies at the root of Haiti's problems. In writing this book, I also wanted to pay homage to the forgotten heroes of Northwest Haiti—figures like Jean-Baptiste Cataboix, Jean-Louis Grand-Maison, Etienne Bauvoir, Pourcely, Bodin, Poitevien, and the Louis brothers from Saint-Louis du Nord (Nicolas, Alain, Jacques, and Vincent)—and many others whose names must forever remain in our collective memory. They were the brave, romantic fighters in General Capois' army, the hero of the Battle of Vertières in November of 1803, the final battle that paved the way for Haiti's independence and the defeat of Napoleon Bonaparte in Saint-Domingue (as Haiti was known during its colonial era).

Though written from the unique perspective of a revolution, this book attempts to shed greater light on what seems to be an enduring problem. Had it been written under different circumstances, the story might have been different, but not necessarily better.

Ardain Isma
Saint Augustine, Florida
August 12, 2024

Prologue

Dusk fell. This was the mad magic of day shifting to night. The sun made its fleeting stand before melting into the horizon. From the yucca fields and banana plantations, the first few notes of the cricket prelude floated, and in nearby bogs, the peeper frogs tuned up. In the evening twilight, the hibiscuses shut their blossoms, while night-blooming jasmines embalmed the air—shooting out a fragrance strong enough to tenderize all sadistic hearts hidden in the foliage. The first rooster ordered his hens to hit the mango branches for another long, fearsome night. Days in the tropics always closed with a *slam*!

Ordinarily Odilon, a shabbily-dressed Haitian plantation worker, stiff with aches and old far beyond his twenty-five years, would scuttle home in this last fading light. Today, his plodding was hesitant. He faced a daunting task—telling his aging mother, whose heart condition was terminal, that he had witnessed his younger brother Avisène being arrested and hauled off to the police station for a crime Odilon knew he hadn't committed.

Pausing on the hilltop overlooking his village, he dropped into a familiar crouch, longing to pick up and cradle in his palm the clay homes thatched with dry palm fronds nestled in the valley below. It seemed so small and distant. Maybe this was how he wanted to see it—as his heart pounded hard, ready to explode. He stood up, fear buckling his legs. He fell to the ground, tears streaming down his cheeks. Surely, he was not a coward. Men are not born cowards, and yet years of living under a merciless dictatorship can transform them into timid souls.

How was he going to tell his mother about her "baby" son without wounding her fragile soul? It tore him in half: upset his mother with sadness and break her heart into a million pieces, or bring good news by securing his brother's release? He sighed with a dreadful foreboding, for he knew too well the ways of the local police.

Odilon's thoughts raced in rhythm with his heart. Life could be so unfair! Why was it that poor, defenseless people always suffered the most injustices? The district chief of police, M. Anakreyon, wanted to placate his domineering wife who had threatened to leave him if the police did not arrest the vandal who had ravaged her banana crop. That made his brother a handy target. A curse upon that wretched woman!

Struggling to regain his footing, he muttered through his teeth, "I've never been a coward—and I will not be one now!"

Odilon guessed his brother was singled out because he was considered by the local authorities to be an unknown peasant. Who would listen to a peon crying out that he had been wrongfully accused? The true culprits were likely thieves from the mountains. They could easily be mistaken for the local poor folk. They dressed and talked the same. They danced and slept the same. A curse upon them, too!

Hate and anger boiled over his youthful soul, bolstering his courage. He lifted his solemn face to the heavens. He shouted at the sky, not caring if he was heard, he swore, "Tonight, I will join my brother in prison—or do whatever it takes to regain his freedom."

Night's curtain dropped like iron rods. Odilon hurried down the hill along the pathway leading to his house, navigating between the yucca fields where the cricket symphony was in full swing singing in a dramatic crescendo. Other local worthies came alive in the looming darkness. Massive mango trees transformed into sleeping giants, hiding monsters within. Assassins lurked, ready to strike. Beneath the spreading branches, werewolves performed their ancient ceremonies, while day-creatures huddled together, frightened and silent.

Odilon reached the ravine—etched in local rampant rumor, the place where a *simbi* was often seen combing her long, shining raven tresses in the moonlight. Here he was quick to make an extra-powerful sign of the cross, laying it in broad strokes across his pulsating chest as he flew like a bat out of hell to his front door.

Safe! But the dreadful fear that overcame him on the hill returned with a vengeance. Trembling, rattling the door, he found himself unable to open it!

Odilon's house was a carbon copy of all the other homes in his small community. With its dirt floor, one bunk bed for his mother, one little *nat*, and a small table with four wooden chairs, it was the dwelling of peasants. Houses were tied together by a network of walkways strung throughout the village of Anwodo, a small plot of the third rural district of the town of Saint Louis du Nord in Haiti's Northwest Department.

Unlike the harsh reality of the people living in the barren landscape of the far western section of the province, this part of Haiti was abundant in flora, which could mask any squalid poverty. This made the whole area appear as a picturesque setting in a tropical paradise. Bright green banana trees supported with maize stalks and lima bean poles enhanced Odilon's house. Flowering star apples, mango, cashew, and avocado trees shed their delicate blossoms on a plush carpet of tall guinea green grass. The dazzling colors and fragrant blooms were the veneer painted over the squalor of poverty.

Odilon's mother, Cécile, age sixty-two, was the village elder. She commanded a wealth of much-deserved respect: playing the role of soothsayer, predicting the future of every newborn, and forecasting every natural disaster. Vast and motherly, deep and mysterious, her supernal presence alone generated an aura of constant mystery. Every evening, when the village children gathered by her front door, they listened to her prophecies, and her breathless tales of witches and werewolves, leaving with eyes as big as saucers. Each of their tiny hearts overflowed with a wonderful dread, loving every moment of these spirit-filled adventures, eager to pass on their stories to family, friends, and neighbors, or anyone who would listen.

Tonight was an exception, there were no children in sight. The faint light from his mother's gas lamp was extinguished. An eerie breeze darted through nearby trees. An omen! Odilon, suddenly fearing for the life of his brother, grabbed a machete from its peg by the front door, and hurried down the main pathway leading to the rural chief compound.

Determination transformed Odilon from a fragile human being into a dynamic fighting machine. Any energy subdued by his oppression was resurrected in full force. Odilon glided through the jungle. He was a determined soldier weighing the machete in his right hand with a palm frond sack strapped around his neck and a sombrero planted on his head. He had become a *Benoit Batraville*, a *Pancho Villa*, and a *jistisye*— not to be deterred from his mission until justice was served. *"No hay un paso atras,"* there'd be no stepping back.

The darkness plaguing Odilon earlier in the evening succumbed to a bold, bone-white full moon rising behind the towering mountains. Heavy grey clouds with glowing edges hung overhead in a solemn atmosphere. In this ghostly moonscape of silence, Odilon's shadow became his sole companion. Crickets and peeper frogs all went still.

Passing several houses on the valley floor, he crossed a slit of a river that split the valley in two, separating the squalid homes from the fertile fields. A quiet sigh escaped his chest as he reached the outskirts of town where the chief compound held his captive brother.

As he neared the edge of the chief's estate, Odilon's surge of bravado unraveled. The imposing brick mansion was guarded by high concrete walls topped with broken glass and huge shards of razor-sharp metal. His determination, passion, and unconditional love for his brother might not be enough to release him.

Behind the front gate, two uniformed guards stood at attention at their posts. Each one cradled an assault rifle, ready to pull the trigger at the first sign of an intruder. Fearing the noisy fallen crunchy mango leaves and palm fronds, Odilon discarded his sandals, tossed his white t-shirt, and crept to the rear of the compound to a shack where he thought his brother might be imprisoned. Loud voices floated in the air, an argument in progress—increasing in intensity as he neared the shack.

"I *told* you not to hit him too hard!" roared the commanding voice of the chief.

"It was self-defense," a second voice protested. "If I didn't knock him down, I could've been killed."

"Well, what do we do, now? This is a fine mess you've gotten me into."

"I really don't know, sir. But you know I always follow your orders. Tell me exactly what you want me to do, and I will do it."

Odilon's soul filled with anguish. He clung to the hope that the ugly conversation was not about Avisène. The Haitian "order of life" in the peasantry under a police state meant that a simple mistake could get Odilon, or his little brother, killed on the spot.

He could see nothing from his position outside the wall. So, Odilon crept into the jungle and climbed a tall avocado tree adjacent to the back of the compound. He crawled up onto the main branch of the tree where he could get a full view through the open door of the shack.

A solitary bare lightbulb dangled from the thatched ceiling, illuminating most of the room. The chief was ensconced in a comfortable armchair, but his shaking leg revealed his anger. M. Dieujuste, a rural policeman, stood next to the chief, glaring down at the lifeless body of Avisène, who was sprawled in a puddle of congealed blood.

Another man sat veiled in the shadows next to the chief. He seemed familiar to Odilon but could not place where he knew him from. He was certain this man was an accessory to the murder. But who was he?

The weather sighed in protest. All moonlight vanished as the angry heavens broke open, unleashing a monsoon that washed away the tears flowing down Odilon's time-worn face. It was as if Mother Nature herself lifted him in the torrential arms of water and off to the outstretched branch. He slid him down the trunk of the avocado tree and delivered him to the safety of the jungle below.

Chapter 1

C'est en vain camarade que j'épelle le folklore quotidien de mon people…
Frère Camarade maintenant je le sais
Tu lis par-dessus mon épaule
Car on ne tue pas la fleur à coup de mitraillette….
S'ils ont volé ta vie, ta mort nous reste.
Et c'est à partir d'elle que j'écrirai la légende des hommes de granit
et des femmes de marbre qui naissent de toi pour libérer….
En un combat joyeux de fleurs and the panthères….

Anthony Phelps dans "La lettre à Raymond Jean-Francois."

In vain, comrade, I spell out the daily folklore of my people...
Brother Comrade, now I know
You read over my shoulder
Because one does not kill the flower with the weapon of war....
If they stole your life, your death remains with us.
And it is from it that I will write the legend of the men of granite
and the women of marble who are born from you to liberate……
In a joyful fight of flowers and panthers....

Anthony Phelps in "The letter to Raymond Jean-Francois."

Although Avisène was not well known in his district, his mother was quite famous. The news of her son's murder was broadcast throughout the area, and their family's small courtyard was soon packed tight with mourners. They came from Ti-Riviyè, Nan-Vyekay,

Bwa Chandèl, Mòn Méris, Barlatier, Bassin Joseph, Desrouvray, and Nan-Banman. The tiny village of Anwodo was filled to overflowing with a sea of people coming to pay their respects to Odilon and his mother.

The cool sea breezes that caressed the swaying tree branches of the village were still that sad day. Not one leaf could be seen floating in the air. No colorful hummingbirds hovered in view. The voice of the *kolobri*, that beloved Haitian songbird, was silent. Heavy grey clouds acted as a giant umbrella to block the sun and protect mourners from the stifling heat.

Odilon and Cécile were huddled in misery on the edge of a small bunk inside their house. Avisène's body was wrapped from head to toe in a clean, coarse, and wrinkled white sheet. He lay in a rough-hewn pine coffin lined with a little *nat* on the floor. This presentation was a sharp contrast to Haiti's peasant tradition of full viewing for mourners. The sight of Avisène's mutilated corpse was too gruesome to expose to such a group of people already plagued by deep fear and anger. Two men hugged Cécile tight to prevent her from smashing her fragile head on the packed dirt floor in her intense grief.

Odilon wasn't crying. His thin, dry hands rested between his trembling knees, as he sat lost in thought. He hadn't told anyone what he'd seen the night before at the chief's compound—not to protect just himself, but his mother too—from the looming threat of interrogations by the district and State. How could he ever prove what he had witnessed? And to make matters worse, he had only seen it because he'd broken the law by trespassing on the chief's property.

The crowd outside was not asking for *kleren*, the rum served at rural wakes. No one was playing dominoes to pass the time. Instead, they were gathering into small groups, wondering "Who committed such a horrible crime, and why?" Some of the mourners were certain that Avisène was killed because he was a goat herder. He raised a special type of goat that resembled the African gazelle. Many folks in this rural section kept an eye on his goats, including their region's only agronomist. The goats were swift and graceful with high shoulders, long necks, and soft, gleaming eyes. But their short, solid, branching horns were forked and curved skyward, proving them to be goats and not antelopes. Nonetheless, no one believed Avisène deserved such a harsh fate, regardless of who may have coveted his prized goats.

By mid-morning, some of the women mourners took the initiative and began to make, pour, and serve strong cups of coffee and tea. These quiet local women understood that the presence of alcohol could inflame the tense, angry crowd.

Alphonse Jean-Baptiste appeared out of nowhere as if by magic. He was the most feared and respected male elder in that rural section. He went inside Odilon's house and pulled him outside as the mourners looked on with growing suspicion.

"When did they find the body?" Jean-Baptiste demanded.

Odilon stammered, "Around six o'clock this morning."

"How did you learn about the murder?" Jean-Baptiste clutched Odilon's stained and torn clothing, threatening him with the other, a clenched fist.

"I was asleep…there was a knock on the door," Odilon whispered—the beginning of many necessary lies. "My mother was already awake and went to the door. I woke up to her anguished voice, crying out for my brother."

"Where was he last night?" Jean-Baptiste didn't look at all convinced.

Groping for his courage, Odilon lied outright. "I don't know. I came home late, and he was still out."

"Did he have a habit of going out at night?" he asked.

"No, he usually came home from work around five p.m. In fact, he always came home earlier than I did. He was the one who fed the cows, pigs, and the herd of goats you see outside under the cacao tree."

Jean-Baptiste threw a menacing glare at the animals tethered to one tree in a small enclosure while he gnawed on an unlit pipe. The shameless interrogation and his indifference to the deceased made it clear that the man was an informant to the chief. Odilon was scared spitless, trembling as he fought to keep the truth quiet. He burned to tell someone, anyone, he knew exactly what had happened that night. But he also knew Jean-Baptiste was not a person to trust with that story.

"Your brother must've been doing well for himself and your family. This is a fine, expensive-looking herd of many cows, pigs, and goats."

"M. Jean-Baptiste, you know that no one here has enough money to own large animals like these. This small herd is only part of the usual cooperative share-raising system, where the rich people buy and farm them out to the poor people – to raise them for a small fee."

"I understand clearly, Odilon," the man sighed while still glowering. "But remember the old proverb, 'People get killed for boiling water.' Obviously, not everyone in this village has the privilege of raising so many animals. His death could've resulted from someone's major bout of jealousy."

"I understand what you mean, sir, but I'm afraid no one in this village or the district is capable of committing such a horrible crime. If you will excuse me, I must talk with the people who have come to mourn the death of my brother." Turning to the gawking onlookers, Odilon made as if to stand before them.

Jean-Baptiste released him from his iron-like grasp. "Yes, go ahead and talk with your people. My apologies, I truly feel sorry for what happened to your brother."

Gathering himself, Odilon soothed his frayed nerves by meeting with the mourners. His mother was in no condition to talk or host. She was unable to stand alone and unsupported, so great was her all-consuming grief.

Shoving his way through, M. Jean-Baptiste forced himself into the crowd gathering beneath the mango trees. Though the people were lost in mourning, they still drank plenty of coffee or tea, seeking refuge from the oppressive midday tropical heat. The rugged, authoritative man marched down the path toward town, disappearing into the nearby yucca field.

#

The one thing that set M. Jean-Baptiste apart from the rest of the community's elders was the fact that he was an informant for the chief. A short, muscular man about five-and-a-half feet tall, his wavy, shiny black hair glittered as he walked beneath the intense rays of the sun. He never wore a hat, and villagers believed this was his way to show off his distinct biological traits.

He appeared more Ethiopian than he did Haitian and seemed to be very proud of his formidably dark and handsome aquiline looks. He always sported a dark khaki military jacket, strutting with his chest thrust forward, encompassing all his territory – with the odd contrast of a pair of reading glasses perched on the tip of his nose. In a display of pride, and, perhaps vanity, he would preach to the people on how to be a good citizen, telling them they must forever bow to the blatant authority of the State.

He stopped to relight his mahogany pipe. It was given to his grandfather by a *bracero* from Cuba in the early 1950s. He was smug in leading the superstitious peasants into believing that the pipe held deep, powerful magic. That it could transform anyone who held it into a mighty wizard. Jean-Baptiste maintained that he got the pipe from his grandfather before he died. He crowed that it made him the most important wise man in the community. The peasants feared his magical powers, and therefore, no one dared to contest the validity of his claims.

As well as being a political mouthpiece for the chief, Jean-Baptiste controlled most of the *houngan* and *manbo* in the region. He never masked his role. In fact, he often bragged about it. It was well known to everyone that he was a steadfast, major part of the current fascistic regime. It was obvious he went to Odilon only to question him about his brother's murder, so he could report his findings to the chief. But one thing puzzled Jean-Baptiste, Odilon was on the scene when his brother was arrested, but never mentioned it. Jean-Baptiste surmised that maybe Odilon knew more about his brother's death than he would care to have admitted.

The chief was waiting for M. Jean-Baptiste, known to them informally as Alphonse. At the first hard-knuckled rap, a servant cracked open the door.

"Is Chief Anakreyon here?" Alphonse asked, his face breaking into a broad grin.

"He is in his quarters, trimming his beard. Would you come into the living room to sit down while I inform the Chief you have arrived?" The household servant was a tallish boy with bone-white cheeks, sporting a giant, purple-pink pimple on the tip of his upthrust broad nose.

"No thanks, I'll stand." he sighed. He hated waiting.

The boy left Alphonse in the vestibule. He goose-stepped to the chief's chamber, where he found him wrapped in a plush cotton bathrobe. He was lounging around on his favorite divan with his black beard freshly trimmed. He clenched a lit pipe between his yellow teeth. It wafted curls of awful-smelling smoke into the room.

"M. Jean-Baptiste," said the young lad, not daring to call such an important man Alphonse, "requests to speak with you." The boy lowered his head in deference, avoiding eye contact with the chief.

"Tell him to come here, Dieudacé."

Being only seventeen years of age, Dieudacé was "forever" obedient, as he was supposed to be. He was about to return to the vestibule to fetch Alphonse, when the chief spoke again.

"Dieudacé, after you summon M. Jean-Baptiste," the chief frowned, "take my horse to the ravine for plenty of water. On your way back, stop by the garden and bring me *malangas* and yams. Since we already have smoked fish, we'll make some *roy* for dinner tonight. And shut the door as you leave. You hear me?"

"Yes, sir."

The chief wanted no one around to hear the conversation about to take place. After Alphonse entered and the servant left, the chief got up from the divan and locked the door. Standing erect, his scruffy head nearly touching the ceiling, he towered over M. Jean-Baptiste, well-suiting his position of vast authority.

"Alphonse, what is the situation over there?" Frowning, the chief returned to his comfy brown leather divan, shaking his crossed legs.

"It doesn't look good, my Chief," Alphonse replied, biting his thumbnail.

"What do you mean, 'it doesn't look good'?"

"I mean what I just said. I walked into a mob of people who were upset and ready to explode! They want to know who could've killed the man. He and his family are highly popular in their area. Those who knew him stated that he was courageous, faithful to the State, and respectful."

"Did you hear anyone talking about how the body was found?"

"No, Chief, they seemed more interested in asking why anyone would want to kill a fine young man like him. But something still bothers me—why didn't Odilon mention his brother's arrest when I questioned him? We know he was there when his brother was taken. I saw him crying when Avisène was tied up and led away. I know this peasant, and he's no fool. I don't think he believes his brother was murdered by thieves on his way home from a *djouba*."

This infuriated the chief. He thrust his feet into his slippers and leapt up, light on his toes from the divan. He grabbed an expensive, razor-sharp sword that hung in a corner of the room.

"You're mistaken, Alphonse, if you think for one minute that a nasty little peasant like Odilon presents a challenge to my authority or dares to accuse me of being the murderer of his precious brother.

We'll close his mouth once and for all! We must act swiftly, before he creates more problems."

Alphonse was stunned – but he had witnessed his boss in action. He knew the vain, power-hungry chief harbored a cruel, gigantic streak. He had watched the chief enjoy taking part in the grisly torture of screaming, shredded-up prisoners, but never before with such anger.

"Chief, what has Odilon ever done to upset you?"

"He lied to you! He didn't tell you he was present when I had his brother taken! This tells me he is conniving and must be dealt with. He's now stirring up trouble amongst our people. He is a dangerous man!"

Knowing the chief bore no respect for his superiors and certainly had no fear of his inferiors, Alphonse did his best to try and calm the chief.

"I honestly believe Odilon didn't state that Avisène was arrested for fear that his brother might lose his dignity. Even in death, people have no respect for anyone accused of stealing. He's simply too ashamed to have people know that his brother was taken into custody. I think it's best to let the matter go."

The chief scratched at his beard. "Maybe you're right, Alphonse."

"Chief, I think we shouldn't even reveal to the ignorant masses that Avisène was ever arrested. For one thing, you'd be named as the prime suspect in his murder. Second, I don't think you have the manpower to overcome a rebellion of that size if the people believed you to be the killer. You'd be helpless, unable to protect your home and fields. I think you're overreacting. Odilon is just a poor peasant. Why turn him into a martyr?"

"Yes, I guess I'm overreacting a little," the chief sighed, easing back down onto his divan. "I'm sorry for what happened last night. That young man may have been right in resisting his arrest. He kept insisting he was innocent, but he was also disobeying my authority. I ordered that he be struck down only to subdue him, but my assistants hit him too hard. They got carried away. Once they started, I couldn't stop them."

"I understand perfectly, Chief Ana." Alphonse was pleased that he was able to smooth things over. Perhaps his mahogany pipe had worked its wizardly magic!

"What happened last night was," the chief continued, "a situation that simply got out of control. All of this is because of my henpecking wife, Fosia. Last week, she kept after me. She threatened to leave me if I couldn't find the thief who was stealing her bananas! As you can see, I had to do something to shut her up – so I had this young man arrested. I never meant to harm him! I was even going to release him, but things got out of hand."

"There's no need to explain. I know your wife can be tough to deal with. You did what you had to do. I'll go back to the wake now and continue monitoring the situation." Alphonse nodded his head in respect, then, sauntered out, leaving the soothed chief to suck on his pipe.

#

While Alphonse was known somewhat affectionately within the district as being the "little man to the chief," Chief Anakreyon himself was feared and hated by all the grumbling peasants. Though he was in his mid-fifties, his six-foot-tall frame made him tower over the average folk in his village, striking fear into their hearts. To top it off, no one ever saw him smile. He was by all accounts, a stone of a man.

Marked by long, ugly scars, all of unknown origins, his sun-dried ebony face broke open into another ugly scar, his unsmiling mouth. This unspeakably scary gap was reinforced by several protruding buck and vampire teeth, which made Anakreyon, with his triangular jaws and sharp cheekbones, look like a fearsome venomous snake. At home he always wore a thick, plush bathrobe – nothing more – to keep cool in the ninety-degree, suffocating heat of the Haitian tropics.

Rumors circulated in the village that he was an aficionado of *Playboy*. Outside his compound, he wore a dark khaki uniform, riding his giant roan horse and sporting expensive ebony-dark sunglasses. He knew he commanded the public's strict attention at all times. With a silver-fringed sombrero, the chief projected the image of a true Spanish don—a man of property in this once-paradise of the Caribbean.

Anakreyon was the highest government official of the rural section, the most powerful *houngan*. His small army of rural police carried both machetes and WWI army rifles. The mythical powers he flaunted, combined with real political power, allowed the chief to rule with a terrible iron fist.

The only person he truly feared was his own wife, Fosia. She was an unpleasant and strident woman in her early fifties, who a day before the murder left home to go visiting her two daughters at their boarding schools in Port-au-Prince. Her swollen, clammy face and greyish eyelashes exposed a pair of enormously round eyes, in which wiggly lines of wormy blood could be visibly spotted whenever she was screaming during her most reprehensible moments. Her unusual neck appeared far too thin to hold up her humongous and expertly coifed curly head. It seemed to have been designed by her Maker to enhance her despicable and nefarious nature.

The peasants called her *Metrès Ezili Je wouj* after an African spirit from the Dahomeyan tribe known for her vile sorceries and evil ways. As fate would have it, she managed the village's only grocery store and bakery, selling gasoline, second-hand clothes, cooking oil, and household items. Not being one to skimp on enjoying her meals, she weighed more than three-hundred pounds. With every step, her bowling-ball breasts thumped against her ribcage like beating *tom toms*.

Amongst most other rural chiefs in Haiti, Anakreyon belonged to the "Dinosaurs' Clique," owning hundreds of acres of farmland where his peasants worked as sharecroppers. At the end of each harvest, however, there were no crops to share. Most of the peasants were too poor and were always in debt to the bitter Fosia for their basic needs.

Chief Ana's domain was an irresponsible, outdated feudal system operating in the 20th century. A vicious cycle, his system reduced the sharecroppers into living like virtual slaves, true serfs to the house of their greedy lord and master.

As Anakreyon's horse galloped down the small country roads, the scattered playing children of the village ran helter-skelter for cover. The rumor mill had it that the chief was a werewolf, always hungry and on the hunt for small children.

Unknown to most, his real name was Yvon Mercier. He had adopted the name of "Anakreyon" after a 19th century notorious *houngan;* a sorcerer who had lived in the town of Anse-à-Foleur, about ten kilometers north of Saint Louis.

Chapter 2

Like David against Goliath, Odilon did not have a chance against the mighty Anakreyon. He wanted revenge, but how was he to get it when no one but him knew how his brother was murdered? He had no proof but his own peasant word, which in this case was worthless.

Back at Odilon's village by mid-afternoon, a short, hunched and nut-brown peasant woman in her mid-forties emerged from inside the little house. Her owlish face, swamped with freckles coating her cheeks and forehead, hovered under a hatband that kept the sweat from pouring down her forehead. Her bunched-up dress was long and white, with faded black pinstripes all around. Mincing forward in halting steps as if possessed, she was swathed in a blue, scruffy kerchief loosely tangled about her neck. In spite of her diminutive size, she instructed the crowd with a booming, commanding voice to gather closer.

Her name was Manzè Rosa, Cécile's distant cousin living in the valley of Ti-Riviyè. Her husband Digamon, a lop-eared, tall, sturdy man with greyish-white hair, followed her, waving around an old, rusty saber sword in his right hand. Digamon seemed to be a buffoon to some, but to most, he was one of the most respected male peasants in the valley. He stood tall and proud next to Rosa smoking a pipe. He wore knee-length wrinkled pants and a crisp white polo shirt.

His face contorted, red-rimmed eyes filled with sorrow, as he gripped a grilled corn-head in his left hand. He looked, for all the world, as if he were about to make a noble speech. Before he could speak, Odilon burst from his family's house and grabbed a position next to his relatives. Together, they took charge of the memorial service. Most of the people there had moved under the welcoming shade of a gigantic, spreading mango tree in order to listen to any speeches with the utmost attention. Silence now replaced the idle gossiping, as Odilon lit a giant, colorful candle while Rosa spoke to the crowd.

"I know everyone would like to see Avisène's face for the last time. But this is impossible, for he is gruesomely mutilated. His murderer shall pay!"

"Oh yes!" the crowd shouted in unison.

"We are only prey in that predator's territory," Rosa continued.

"Oh yes, we are!" responded the crowd in a Haitian version of the African call-and-response technique.

But turning toward Odilon, Rosa stepped back to give him a chance to speak. After all, his brother was the murdered man. For a moment, Odilon quivered with visible fear and horrible trepidation – but only for a moment. He knew what he needed to say, and how deeply he needed to say it.

"Let us not forget that the dew reigns only before sunrise, and it's only in treacherous pathways that wild horses are captured," boomed out the little peasant man, speaking his words in a clear, powerful voice that captivated everyone. "So, I'm asking everyone to stay calm. We don't want to have any excuses for breaking the law of the land, at least not for right now. Our time will surely come!"

At the far edge of the crowd, M. Jean-Baptiste stood in the shade of the yucca field, monitoring every gesture and word with the eagle eyes and ears of an informant. His gut was starting to tell him that this wasn't going to end well.

"We may never find justice on this earth for my brother," Odilon continued. "But I know there is one justice the killer, or killers, will never be able to escape: the justice of Papa Bondye, Papa Danmbala, Papa Ogou Feray, Mèt Agwe, Ezili Dantò, Bosou Twa Kòn, and all the other *lwa* from *Lafrik Ginen*," he declared, invoking the African spirits with so much emotion that all four of his limbs shook as if he were in a sorcerer's trance.

The audience was mesmerized. Observing this, Jean-Baptiste realized that the chief had been right: Odilon was dangerous – a threat to the State.

Rosa took two steps forward with her head bowed in reverence. "I need four strong men to come and help carry the coffin."

A wave of more than twenty men surged forward. Odilon instructed four of them to follow him inside the house. A man exited the house, assisting Cécile. Odilon and three men carried the coffin. As these men took the lead, the crowd followed behind like a solemn church procession to the cemetery on the edge of town. All along the route, people stood in silence in front of their doors, staring in deep respect and sympathy for Cécile, who struggled to walk.

As they reached the gates of the cemetery, a harsh westward wind swept through. It was soon followed by a steady drizzle, one that lasted half an hour. Everyone clung to each other, pinned down by the intensity of the sudden rain. Emotions ran high. A short, barefoot woman with hazel eyes and brownish hair, stuffed inside a red head kerchief, surged forward from the very back of the crowd. She was dressed in a blue *karako* and carried a clear plastic sheet. Traces of soggy hair slipped through her kerchief to sag down over her shoulders as she walked backward, until she reached the edge of the correct headstone, where the grave had been dug.

At the foot of the coffin, she stood facing east while invoking Ezili Mapyang, the most dangerous of the *Ezilis*, seven times before she wrapped the simple wooden coffin tight with the plastic bag. A sprightly assortment of flowers and small branches of *pert lauriers* made up the simple wreaths adorning the grave site.

The grave diggers, who had just finished digging, rested their shovels on top of the fresh mound piled to one side of the grave. All eyes were glued on the barefoot woman, who grabbed several handfuls of dirt from the mound and sprinkled it over the coffin, while intoning African liturgies that few people in the crowd understood.

The gathering throng moved in silence to the coffin. Some women, overwhelmed by their emotions, let loose their anger by launching waves of outbursts that spilled over the borders of the cemetery, perforating the murmurs of the nearby hills. Two men cradled Cécile by the arms, leading her near the headstone where the coffin was being laid.

"Before we put my brother in his final resting place, let's take a moment to invoke the spirits of our ancestors, so they will intervene to protect his soul," Odilon pleaded with the milling, anxious crowd. His eyes turned moist and red, like fire dropped on dry leaves ready to burst into flames.

Rosa stepped forward with the invocation. "Oh Pa Louisius, Grann Fevrinya, Anacile, Tant Anelie, Grann Asie, Teyo, Capi, Manka, Tant Menmen, and all the other dead from this village, I'm asking you to protect Avisène's spirit so that his soul will live on forever."

Everyone now circled the edge of the mound. Some of them had their lower arms crossed over their shoulders, while others intertwined their long fingers with each other. They all stood erect in complete silence out of respect for the dead young man.

Utter motionlessness reigned, intruded upon by the shriek of a few hummingbirds chirping in the distance. Odilon and the three others lowered the coffin to the bottom of the grave, as everyone looked on in bereavement and broken-heartedness. The mound around the grave site dwindled as the grave diggers filled the hollowness of the grave with shovelfuls of earth that fell like rumbling thunder over the resting coffin. Once the grave was filled, the diggers dabbed the surface flat before the flowers were laid on top. Finally, Avisène's name was written on the headstone as proof of his burial. The crowd now dispersed, laden with the heavy cries of the grieving peasant women.

M. Jean-Baptiste had listened to the invocation with overwhelming dismay. He trembled in fear as he glanced at the eyes of the people, witnessing their never-before-seen rage and their taste for revenge tearing through his small, authority-worshiping body. Bolting in a hasty retreat from the cemetery, he headed for the chief's compound, banging on the front door with great urgency.

"Who is it?" the servant boy asked.

"It's me, Alphonse. I must speak to the Chief immediately!" His voice was shaking, almost out of breath.

"Come in. Chief Ana is in a meeting right now. Wait here, and I'll ask him if he wants to speak with you."

Less than a minute later, the servant returned to the vestibule and escorted Jean-Baptiste to the meeting room, where he found the chief in the midst of a serious discussion with some of his top lieutenants on how to take care of the strange situation.

"Alphonse, what is going on with Odilon and his brother's corpse?" one of the chief lieutenants asked.

"Shut up!" roared the chief. "Let's hear what the man has to say!"

After the frightened informant gave his chief the latest details, their discussion took a serious turn. Should the rural police take the body, disperse the crowd, and arrest Odilon, Rosa, and Digamon for disturbing the peace?

"I have it on good authority," said the chief, "there's going to be a massive demonstration, demanding justice for the dead. I'm afraid if we don't stop the funeral, the results could be devastating. What do you say, Alphonse? You were there! You know exactly what's going on." The chief crashed his fist into a lamp table anchored in the corner of the room, smashing it into pieces.

Alphonse cleared his throat to temp down his nerves. "It's too late now to stop the funeral procession. Chief, I know the people are extremely angry, but I believe maintaining a wait-and-see attitude is the wisest possible course of action."

"Are you *sure*?" The chief looked more ready for murder than patience.

"You can do anything you want; you're the chief. But what could be more devastating than a confrontation with a large group of angry people? The last thing we need is to escalate things further. I've lived here all my life, and I've never seen such a public display of rage—except for this afternoon. Remember, they've called on the gods and spirits of their ancestors for help. The potential magic of their rituals, whether real or imagined, should never be underestimated."

Some of the lieutenants groaned, leered, and hooted; but they all made the sign of the cross. Calling on their ancestors was a serious sign that trouble was afoot.

"I saw the great passion of the mourners manifested in their eyes, though Odilon was urging them to be calm and wait for justice. I don't think we have the means to confront them now. It would be impossible to do so."

"What do you mean by 'impossible'?"

"I'm saying we don't have the manpower to subdue a large crowd. We can send security forces to restore order, but I fear they will be overwhelmed by the size of the group. More will likely join them if trouble breaks out. You can't send all your personnel. Some will have to stay behind to protect you and your property."

"Then, what should be our course of action?" Frowning as usual, which he did even when happy, the chief had to acknowledge this bitter fact.

"Wait and see how things develop," Alphonse responded, tendering his voice to shed some calmness into the room. "What could be worse for you? What if you do something to attract the attention of our superiors in the district? Ti-Jean likes you, but you know the man has no friend but his own power. In the face of American pressure, if trouble should break out, he'll dump you in a heartbeat. He's already done it to his top people in Gonaives and Port-au-Prince."

This stopped the chief in his tracks. He plopped down on his chair, crossing and uncrossing his legs. "What if I arrest some people with criminal records and accuse them of the murder of Avisène? Would that be enough?"

"It could be a good idea if it doesn't backfire on you. I watched Odilon, Chief, and you were right – he can become a dangerous man. He's not just a stupid peasant. He has a commanding voice that holds everybody's attention, including mine! And yet I'm puzzled by the fact that he keeps insisting on justice without it seeming to be directed at any common criminals."

"What do you mean, Alphonse? Do you think he knows we are the ones who killed his brother?" The chief thought he should be plotting his next move. They were wasting their time on deciding what to do instead.

"No, I don't mean it in that sense. How could he know? It was in the middle of the night around two a.m. when the body was dropped off on the roadside. What I think is that something is telling him that we may know who the killer is, and that you are protecting him for some reason. I'm still surprised that he's never mentioned that he was present when his brother was arrested. That may have been the last time he saw his brother alive, and he can't possibly have forgotten the incident."

The pipe dropped from the chief's gaping hole of a mouth in slow motion, as if in a dream, or a nightmare. He began to sweat bullets, and stood up to shed his plush robes, exposing his naked body to the startled group.

"Well, what do we do?" he demanded.

"Just what I suggested before," Alphonse answered, undeterred by the chief's sudden nudity. "We develop a wait-and-see attitude. I will keep Odilon under close surveillance."

Most of the uncomfortable lieutenants nodded in agreement as the chief settled back onto his now uncomfortable divan, mumbling to himself.

#

Even though Odilon had weathered the death and burial of his brother, his search for justice would not subside. It had, in fact, increased. It was coming in like the ebbing tide. Meanwhile, his mother withdrew further from her already limited world. Her only meal was a tiny bowl of barley that she ate every day at noon.

There was no one to talk to at home, now that Avisène was gone. Avisène had been Cécile's main caretaker, and it had been his job to tend the animals. He had seldom traveled with Odilon when he was working or looking for work. Odilon knew that he was alone and must handle things alone, waiting for the wind to blow his way. He was a confused, scared little man. The day Avisène had gone out with Odilon was the fateful day he was arrested, and later murdered. Because of this, Odilon felt responsible for his brother's death. If only he had stayed home.

As time wore on, Odilon slipped into a somber daily routine; but his family obligations had doubled. He was now the sole breadwinner. Roaming their rural section, he offered his cheap labor to anyone who wanted his services, soon finding that this only opened him to greater exploitation. He barely earned three to five *goud* per day. Other times, he agreed to work for food—*malanga*, yams, bananas, and breadfruits—which he carried home and cooked for dinner. He also took over his brother's task of caring for the family's animals—two emaciated cows, three muddy pigs, a half dozen goats, and one lonesome donkey.

One Friday afternoon when he was done feeding the animals, he returned home to find his mother missing. "Oh my God!" he shrieked. "Where is she?"

"*Ma Konmè Anasé!*" he called out to a neighbor. "Did you see my mother this afternoon?" He paced the ground in his scruffy sandals.

"Yes, I did." The neighbor wondered at Odilon's respect for his mother.

"I came home from feeding the animals, and she isn't here! I looked for her everywhere, in the garden, under the mango trees, and in the open fields. Where is she? She's never done this before!"

"I remember," the neighbor said. "She was going to Mrs. Saint-Facile's house to ask her to sew up a piece of fabric she bought yesterday at the flea market in Ti-Riviyè."

Odilon heaved a sigh of relief through his thin-walled chest.

"Be happy that she's getting better, Odilon, more like her old self!"

"Yes, she's finally eating better, but I worry about her."

As the neighbor stood nearby, Odilon saw his mother coming home with a sack full of avocados perched on her head. He rushed over to her, yelling.

"*Manman*, you had me scared! Where've you been?"

"Didn't I tell you this morning that I was going to see Mrs. Saint-Facile to have her sew two pieces of cloth for me? Here, have some avocados. Take them and put them in the attic. These are the purple ones, your favorites."

"Yes, you did *Manman*," Odilon said, greatly comforted. "But I forgot. I'm happy to see you getting better and going out, but it's getting late. It's not safe to travel around here at dusk—there are werewolves nearby."

Odilon grinned. He took the sack of avocados from his mother with great care so as not to damage the fruit. He clambered up a ladder, carrying dry banana fronds with him to stuff around the avocados and hasten the ripening process.

"I know, my son, but I'm old. And when one is old, it's easy to be fearless."

Anasé, who was listening to the conversation between Odilon and his mother, laughed. "I think you're right, Aunt Cécile! My mother always says that about old age. It makes you forget about fear."

Anasé then went back into her house. Odilon wrapped his bare brown arms around his mother's loving neck and embraced her. He nudged her into the house to her bunk, while he sat perched on the small *biyòt* near the table. He shoved back the weathered, broad-rimmed box-top hat he wore in the fields to shield his scalp, face, and neck from the intense tropical sun rays.

He crowed softly, "I'm happy *Manman*. Tomorrow is Saturday."

"My son, I can imagine it. But I always feel the same on Friday afternoon, and every other day as well. Now that your brother is gone, the days are long and lonely. Still, it's always a great joy for me when you come home every afternoon."

"I think of you while I'm at work. I feel guilty leaving you alone. I tell people 'no' when they ask me to stay longer. I always say that I need to be with my mother. Today, I left early. I was at a day-job for Mr. Laurin, the coffee exporter over in Nan Banman. He owns ten acres and was having a *konbit* to plant bananas."

Cécile replied, "Yes, my son. Nan Banman is very far away. I can't remember the last time I was there. I may never get there again before I die—I'm too old for that long walk. I can no longer climb mountains. Next time you go, don't forget to bring me some sweet mango *monben* and *menvil*."

She stood up and went outside, followed by Odilon. "Since I was little, I was never a big fan of long walks. I used to hide at my grandmother's house each time my mother wanted to make those weary, dizzying trips over the mountains. They say that *La diablesse* and *Mèt Minuit* walk there at noon in the thick of the coffee and banana plantations, but Nan Banman was different for me. I was always ready to face the most fearful ghosts in the forest for my delicious mango *monben!*"

Odilon smiled and nodded. His mouth watered as he dreamed of the spectacular, magical taste of the *monben*. "*Manman*, didn't you say we have relatives in Nan Banman?"

"Yes, my son, but we shouldn't confuse them with our relatives here. They're from my mother's first husband, a womanizer with children all over this section. This is why Patekrè, Misyèl, and Jean

Noel are your uncles. Here in this village, apart from Chief Anakreyon and his own, we're one single happy family, all descended from the same bloodline. We are the grandchildren of Pa Lisis and Fevrigna."

"*What?* We're all related?" Odilon was astonished by this revelation. "How could that be? Some of the people in our village fall in love and have children with each other! How can they possibly be blood relatives?"

She brandished her traditional wooden spoon with a gentle smile. Cécile stirred the vegetable stew over the cookfire she tended right outside the front door. "Unbelievable, but it's true. Listen to me."

"Yes *Manman*, I am listening." Awestruck, Odilon edged closer.

"Pa Lisis married Fevrigna, a woman from the sixth rural section of Saint Louis, around 1889 – during the time of President Flovil Hyppolite. They ran a windmill business and grew cacao, coffee, sugarcane, and bananas. They weren't wealthy, but lived fairly well from their big estate, which stretched from Ti-Riviyè all the way to the edge of town."

Odilon inched closer, leaning on the rickety side of the aging house. He had never heard of this side of the family before. Cécile seldom talked in depth with him, at least not when Avisène was still alive.

"They bore several children: Anelie, Anacile, Louiner, Premise, Majette, and Man Pèpè. Over the years, the children grew up and made their own families in the village. We came from Anacile's branch of the family. She is the mother of my mother, Amazile. Louiner is the father of Berno, Sonson, Linia, Lamine, Dieuseul, Dius, and Lifèt. Premise had Paulema, Dieudonné, Constantin, and Gaston. When Elie Lescot was president, Gaston traveled to Cuba.

"He only returned home once. Everybody was happy to see him. He'd become a giant, the greatest boxer in Cuba! One Sunday morning after church, he met ten men pumping air into the wheels of an old Ford, struggling and sweating profusely under the hot, red-swollen sun. Gaston simply pushed them aside, rolled up his sleeves and filled the wheels with plenty of air in less than five minutes."

Odilon had taken the spoon from his mother's hand to stir the pot, and his jaw dropped upon hearing about Gaston. "Our family tree is very interesting!" admitted Odilon.

Pleased and grateful to hear about his family, he smiled for the first time since his brother was killed. "But *Manman,* whatever happened to him, over time?"

"God only knows. Two weeks after he helped those men, he went back to Cuba. That was the last time we saw or heard of him. People say he is still in Cuba. Who knows? He was tall, strong, handsome, and a womanizer. They say he had plenty of children all over Cuba."

"But what happened to the rest of our family?"

"Oh yes," Cécile continued. "Majette had Lekè and Théo. Mrs. Pèpè had Ms. Eliska, Likfè, Jorame, Afari, and Julien. Anelie had Rosita, Simeon, Tèsyis, and Excellence. So, you see…we all have the same bloodline."

Smacking his thin lips, Odilon tasted the stew as he was stirring the pot. "This is delicious!" he exclaimed, taking another large spoonful.

"Oh, my son, you will never change! Why don't you wait for me to put the food on your plate?"

"The food smells so good and is so tasty. It's too hard to wait. This is the only real meal of the day for me…and you know I'm hungry."

Cécile patted Odilon with a gentle tap on the side of his smiling face, for his skin was stretched tight over his cheekbones. At times when he smiled, it looked like his poor face would crack open. "I know, son. I was joking with you. I'm praying to God for the day when you don't have to work so hard. You already look twice your age. My mother used to say that poverty is mankind's greatest enemy."

In respectful response, Odilon refrained from grabbing the plate – but soon he was wolfing down his food.

"I see you're enjoying your meal tonight."

"I haven't had wonderful food like this in a long time." Odilon was beaming. He leaned over and kissed his mother's wrinkled face. "*Manman*, you've added new ingredients to the *roy*. I'm so happy you're feeling better."

"You are your old self again, like be-" He had started to say *"before Avisène was murdered"* but caught himself just in time.

Cécile did not hear this last part. "Yes, I put in your favorite smoked fish, some *kalalou gombo* and lima beans."

"No wonder it's so tasty. Listen *Manman*, tomorrow I'm going to town to sell eggs and breadfruit to raise money so you can see the nurse at the clinic."

"Yes, I do want to see the nurse. The clinic is free, but I have to pay for any medications."

"God is great!" Odilon breathed a deep sigh of relief. "I'll make decent money at the open market. And Mr. Jerome owes me twenty *goud* for a job I did last week. He promised to pay me tomorrow after the market is closed."

"I hope he pays you," Cécile said. "But I don't trust him. He's a good friend of Anakreyon. And you know what that means."

"Yes, *Manman*," Odilon's tone was grave, "I know exactly what you mean."

"Speaking of Anakreyon, I forgot to tell you that this morning after you left, two men came here looking for you. They said they were workers from Anakreyon's house."

"What did they want?" Odilon began to tremble, petrified. "*Manman*, how could you forget to tell me something like this until now?"

"I'm sorry, son. It just slipped my mind. Anyway, they wanted to speak to you about a job offer."

"They said 'a job offer'?" This was most puzzling.

"Yes, I was surprised to hear that. But I told them you weren't home. Then, they asked if I knew when you'd be back. I told them I didn't know when you'd be home, nor did I know where you worked today. I hope I said the right thing."

"Nothing is wrong, *Manman*. You did well."

Cécile threw back her shaggy grey head, guffawing. "I didn't know where you were – even if I did, do you think I would've told them? I may be old, but I'm not stupid! My mother used to say that the person who holds a machete and chops off the head of the snake is not always the true killer—it's the one who points out its location!"

What had started as a carefree conversation learning about his relatives, darkened fast. It felt cloudy from the utmost terror at the news of the two men. It was clear that Anakreyon sensed he knew more about his brother's death than he had let on to M. Alphonse Jean-Baptiste. He realized now that he should have told the informant that he had been on the scene when his brother was arrested. The authorities were growing suspicious. That was a serious mistake on his part.

Grasping his belly, overcome by nausea, he was going to lose that wonderful meal. He needed to get out of the house, and away from *Manman*.

"I have to feed the pigs. I got carried away with your stories and completely forgot about them. I must go outside, right now!"

"Be careful, son," *Manman* called out. Her filtered, commanding voice sounded like a tropical bird of paradise's trills to him. "You know that if werewolves can walk in broad daylight, they'll surely be out after nightfall."

Waving her words away, moving like a jungle cat in the shadows, Odilon slunk over to the biggest of the mango trees, feeling as though he left half his guts under its cooling shade. There went the wonderful stew. The thought of confronting a werewolf did not seem nearly as frightening as being caught by one of Anakreyon's ruthless, machete-wielding henchmen.

By the time he got back to the house, his mother was sound asleep. Odilon laid out his sleep mat without a sound. It was made of loosely braided banana fronds. He layered it with a couple of cotton sheets to use as a buffer between him and the dirt floor. His fear-frazzled body was exhausted as he curled up on the makeshift bed. Stomach growling and mind churning, he rolled over to lie on his back with his long, thin fingers entwined beneath his head. Odilon listened to the musical refrain of his mother's snoring as he watched the bright moonlight play through the cracks of his humble cottage. She was never loud, so this often gave him a sense of tranquility. He thought they were safe, at least for the time being. Magical images of the werewolves and Anakreyon's men blended into the disappearing moonlight as he lapsed into a much-deserved night's sleep.

The morning dew lingered on the muddy ground and verdant foliage, giving the world a fresh, new face. Odilon woke up and shook the sleep and stiffness from his limbs. The droplets of dew framed the breathtaking beauty of the wild roses and blooming hibiscus plants. The soft, fragrant scent of jasmine, eglantine, and citronella blossoms was more than enough to give him a positive start to the day. Grabbing fruit from the table and scarfing down a portion of last night's stew, he felt refreshed and ready to tackle the day's worst challenges—or so he thought.

"*Manman*, I can't believe it's Saturday already! It's a long, busy day ahead. I have to hurry into town and get a good spot to sell my goods. The last time I went to the marketplace, it was too late. I spent the day selling only half of what I brought with me. I don't want that to happen again."

"I hear you, my son. You only do what I did. I learned from my mother that the earlier you arrive, the better chance you have of selling your goods. The competition is less intense, and the buyers get there early to find the best bargains, so you can leave early with your pockets filled with *goud*."

"*Manman*, I have to get going," Odilon said, anxious to leave. "I got the donkey ready last night when I fed the animals. I just need to fill the sacks with breadfruit and avocados. I'll put the eggs in the brown canister and pack them with newspaper to keep them from breaking. Everything's as usual, just like before—nothing to worry about. You have a good day, *Manman*, and I'll see you late this afternoon."

Within minutes, he was on his way, glancing around to see if anyone was watching or following. The swollen orange orb of the miserable sun struggled to climb up behind the mountains. The young man doubted if anyone in Anakreyon's compound was awake this early in the morning.

Odilon felt at peace with the world as his morning meal settled in his stomach and he bobbed up and down on his scruffy, greyish-white donkey. He felt jaunty in his traditional thin cotton khaki shirt, brown knee-length sewn-up trousers, a loosely wrapped white handkerchief around his neck, and his favorite brown cow-skin sandals, topped off with a sombrero. A cool breeze gently licked his careworn, weather-beaten face. Despite it all, he felt strong, energized, and ready to face whatever the day had in store.

Chapter 3

Odilon stayed off the main road, taking an old country backroad leading into town. He wanted to avoid passing the chief's compound in case they were up and about. Few people ventured out in these early morning hours.

"I'm not afraid," he mumbled to himself. "After all, my real bogeyman is only Anakreyon, and I'm certain he wouldn't be caught without his bathrobe on out here at this hour!"

After ten minutes of teeth-rattling jogging on the donkey down the narrow trail, the village of Anwodo faded away behind them as they entered a canopy of green foliage. Odilon had forgotten to bring a water bottle with him. But the small drops of moisture that condensed overnight made the morning dew impossible to ignore, so he stopped to drink from a huge, curled-up plant frond. When they exited the canopy, the trail meandered down to the bed of a shallow ravine, leading toward a steep hill covered with tidy banana groves. The hill was truncated by long lines of towering breadfruit trees and bushy mango *djon* on both sides of the trail.

As soon as they crossed and readied to climb upward, the donkey began to bray in shrill defiance. He displayed an unexpected stubbornness, kicking his front feet far up into the air while zigzagging and stiffening his tail.

Odilon struck several lashes into the startled beast's bony behind, forcing him to stop braying and stay the course. "What's up with you, boy?" he growled, exerting his strong will against the animal. "Today is too important for me to tolerate such misbehavior."

Seconds later, total obedience returned, and they started to climb upward into a silent jungle. No leaves rustled overhead; no crickets chirped. In the midst of this undisturbed quietness, only a timid breeze swept through the giant banana leaves. The still of the night had yet to be vanquished, until a swallow flew to a nearby tree. Odilon's heart leapt at the sudden noise. He lurched sideways, nearly slipping off his donkey as he tried to pinpoint the bird's direction. But it had already vanished behind the giant, bushy leaves. With a few more light lashes, Odilon urged his beast onward, quickening their pace toward the summit.

The intense rays of sunlight cast a yellow glow on Odilon's squinting face when they reached the hilltop. The cloudless, clear-blue sky seemed endless over the distant horizon. Raising one hand above his forehead, he gained a glimpse of the valley below. He paused for a minute to catch his breath while turning around to rediscover the striking scene of this picturesque valley – a lush, green paradise, with a breathtaking décor of tropical wildflowers along the foothills. To the north was Moulen Ti Toto, a sugar mill that bore the name of its owner, Toto, a wealthy farmer in town that everyone called Mr. Kanson-Fè-Never-There. This was due to his aloof demeanor, and his brutal, sneaky ways of dealing with his employees at the mill.

The screeching sounds of the machines crushing the sugarcane down below echoed their way to Bwa Chandèl, the next village on the other side of the valley. To the east lay a vast, dormant yucca field extending to the west bank of Bassin Joseph, a deep river valley that ran upstream to the village of Desrouvrays, nestled between the mountain gorges of Nan Banman. A lone, massive farmhouse stood in the middle of the sleepy field, disturbing the laid-back monotony with its majestic presence. A woman named Isiana, a good friend of Anakreyon, owned the house. That was enough to make Odilon quiver as the faces of his henchmen flashed across his mind.

To the west was the town of Saint Louis, about a mile from the foothills and sitting adjacent to the eastern shores of the Caribbean

Sea. Far beyond the seaside was the island of La Tortue. It looked like an ancient crocodile with age-old scaly skin sleeping further in the distance. The turquoise water between La Tortue and Saint Louis was at low tide in the early morning hours. The low, calm waters attracted dozens of fishermen. They perched on canoes or sat in makeshift rafts to catch the fresh salmon to sell later at the marketplace.

To get to Saint Louis, Odilon had to circumvent a dangerous scarp – a rocky, steep slope on the hillside – by following the trail that ran south to reach the neighborhood of Sou Fò, on the southeastern entrance of town. Odilon felt reenergized as the donkey began its descent down the slope. A few meters away from the foothills, the landscape began to change. Scattered huts and occasional small farmhouses began to line both sides of the trail.

"Bonjou Manzè Rosalie. E lè nouvèl?"

Odilon greeted a young woman. She was wearing a crinkly nightgown while sweeping the dust from the steppingstones that led to her front porch. A flock of hungry, clucking hens and roosters stood ready to devour her feet for their morning maize.

She waved at Odilon, crying, *"Bonjou mon frè!"*

Brimming with curiosity, her sleepy eyes awakened as she squinted, pausing with both hands resting on her homemade, sorrel broom. Slowly, she gave 'the puppy eye' to Odilon. She let the spaghetti-straps of her nightgown roll off her shoulders and hang atop her exposed breasts. Her see-through nightgown did nothing to camouflage her muscular legs, and her stiff brown buttocks that flexed under her butterfly-printed panties.

Coughing, Odilon closed his eyes in embarrassment. Not intending to get trapped into a seductive conversation, his only plans were to sell his goods. That was his focus that morning. So, he pressed on. But the more he advanced, the less sporadic and more intense the houses became as the trail widened at the southern fringes of town.

Odilon was listening to the blaring sounds of passing vehicles in the distance with glee. "I'm finally in Saint Louis," he muttered, greeting the passing farmers with a confident smile as his donkey steadily jogged down the widening, dusty road.

While he neared the edge of town, the peaceful mood of the country turned into the hustle-bustle of a thriving community. Odilon thought, "I'd never want to live here. How do people deal with the constant noise and activity?" He dabbed at the dirt crusting on his forehead with the loose edge of his kerchief. The dust was rising from the *tap-tap* and motorcycles racing along the unpaved streets.

It was eight a.m., and the city was fully awake. Street vendors were everywhere, hauling things while looking for a spot to sell goods at the marketplace. Peasants streamed in from the countryside. Street corner vagabonds roamed the streets in search of their next prey. The *restavèk* were everywhere—those children who seemed eerily determined to be slaves for the rest of their lives. They were younger and older, boys and girls. All of them were carrying water jugs on their heads, or buying household goods for their masters, or babysitting their master's children. Odilon shook his head in disgust while the donkey trotted through the milling crowd of bright, but exhausted-looking faces. He preferred the free life of a sharecropper, poor as he may be.

The marketplace faced the town's main Catholic church. The *konpradò* merchants had already set up their shops, ready for their first victims. Each price would be doubled, even tripled in some cases. These merchants were greedy predators and knew the peasants had no choice but to pay whatever price was demanded.

Church bells tolled loud, deep, and sonorous, announcing it was time for another dose of Papist brainwashing. Odilon and his family had long ago left the altar of the Catholic Church, preferring the Voodoo magic of their African ancestry. But every now and then, like most Haitian peasants, he made the sign of the cross to ward off any oncoming evil spirits.

It had been nearly six-hundred years since the first French buccaneers set foot in this corner of *Ayiti Kiskeya*. The town of Saint

Louis had changed in many ways, though not always for the better. There were no paved streets, no sewer system, and no land fields on the edge of town. The city had the aura of an American Western mining town of the 1800s —wild, crazy, and dusty. Signs of new construction could be seen on the outskirts. There, primitive life collided with new civilization. When the expatriates returned to the Motherland, their pockets lined with cash, they brought the luxuries of modern living with them. Mules competed with BMWs. Square dancing, *konpa*, *zouk*, *troubadours*, even hip-hop could be heard pouring from the open doors of at least one bar or nightclub.

On wet, rainy days, people became stuck in muddy pools like vultures on sap-covered gum-trees. There were two main arteries framed by narrow alleyways around the downtown district. The sprawl of the new demographic was the result of the peasants leaving the rural sections in search of jobs and city life.

Burgeoning suburbs were sprouting up on the hillsides, and around the northern fringes of town. These extravagant two-story homes were built by the expatriates who came home to seek a place of their own in this tropical paradise after living overseas. On Main Street, the traffic was the most congested. A bird's eye view from the hilltops gave a stunning glimpse of the colonial architecture embalmed in the corrugated and rusty metal roofs of the dust-caked houses down below.

It was a staunch Catholic community. Every year, Saint Louis du Nord became the interim capital of Haiti for three days, from August twenty-third to the twenty-fifth. This was when the residents would celebrate the patron saint of the town—Saint Louis Roi De France. (Saint Louis, the King of France). It was a holdover from the French colonization. During that time, celebrants poured in like rain. They hailed from New York to Miami, Nassau to San Francisco, and Paris to Montreal. The pilgrims mixed freely with the locals and *émigrés* to savor delicious Haitian fried pork, partying hard from dusk until dawn.

Despite such festivities, Saint Louis was like other towns in Haiti. It could not escape the iron grip of the Ti-Jean government. In any given day, the government would send its mythical monsters to roam the streets and terrorize the population at will, giving its secret police *carte blanche* to enforce law and order at all costs, including killing innocent civilians. These government watchdogs were under the direct control of Bèbè Le Tyran. He was the delegate representative of the Northwest province. He worked in close collaboration with all the rural section chiefs, including Anakreyon and his henchmen.

Ti-Jean came to power under false promises after twenty-nine long years of the brutal Duvalier dynasty. The Haitian people were in full control of their political strength at long last. After all, they were the ones who engineered the downfall of that regime. They were now in no mood for political blackmailing by the Ti-Jean government. At first, Ti-jean promised democracy and economic prosperity. Instead, he delivered nothing but lies, intimidation, and economic stagnation.

For weeks there were rumors flying of massive anti-government demonstrations that would be taking place all over the country. The Haitian security forces were balanced on a razor-sharp edge. That very Saturday morning as Odilon tried to sell his meager but worthwhile goods in the crowded marketplace, the first signs of the long-awaited anti-government revolt were about to take place.

Two hours after Odilon arrived at the market, around ten a.m., frantic reports were blaring on radio stations. They announced the country was on the verge of civil war. The oppressed masses of Haiti were uniting into one voice, demanding the immediate downfall of President Ti-Jean's reactionary, bourgeois-led regime.

The news spread from Jacmel to Les Cayes, from Jérémie to Gonaives, from Port-de-Paix to St. Marc, and from Cap-Haitien to Port-au-Prince. An armed organization active in the mountains of the Northwest known as the Revolutionary Resistance Front emerged from the underground and began to mobilize the people. As always, Le Tyran sent his forces out to squash and quell the rebellion. But something in the air told the people that this time, things would be different.

Odilon was pleased he had met his goal and finished selling his merchandise. He was on his way to the town square, where he had left his donkey tied up, when the sharp crack of gunfire shattered the warm chatter of the marketplace.

"What the *hell* is going on?" he yelped. His terror rooted him to the spot as he strained to get away.

"Bèbè is trying to wipe out the population again!" a woman vendor spat. She was enraged as she packed up her merchandise.

Moments later, two explosions sent shockwaves barreling through the marketplace and town square. White smoke wafted skyward and dead bodies were strewn about.

"It can't be! Oh my God!" Odilon screamed.

"What's going on?" a horrified woman cried out.

"Can't you see?" he hollered, "There are ten people on the ground, dead and bleeding!"

Odilon fled with his arms outstretched like a frightened bird. He lunged toward where he had left his donkey tied earlier that morning. But the desperate, screaming people blocked his view as they struggled to find refuge from the explosions and gunfire. The crowd surged, submerging him in a wave of humanity. Odilon staggered sideways in the violent crush of pushing and shoving. He was unable to keep his balance. His face was smeared with dusty sweat, caking into mud and blurring his vision. He trembled as his stomach climbed into his throat.

His legs buckled and he collapsed near a makeshift stand that had been abandoned. It was filled with scattered rice and red beans. His cries for help were ignored, lost in the thunderous echo of bullets scattering in the air. Odilon braced for the worst. He clenched his teeth and called upon the last vestiges of his energy to steady himself. But shockwaves heaved through the loose, rocky ground. They pitched him feet first into the cloudy air, jarring every bone in his already fragile body. Unable to fight the unstable pavement and the waves of fleeing humans tossing him about, he sprawled face-down onto the ground and closed his eyes.

When facing death, people tend to lose their fear, and group together as one. All of a sudden, a small knot of gatherers began to chant in unison, "Liberty or Death - Liberty or Death - Liberty or Death!" Other people starting to converge on the town square, joined the voices: "Liberty or Death!"

Emotions ran high. At last, Odilon managed to stand up and pushed his way to his little grey donkey. Bullets were flying dangerously close. He was desperate to untie the animal, when he was startled by a voice.

"What d'you think you are doing, young man? Do you want to be killed? Do just like me. Lie on the ground!"

The voice was that of an older man. He had a large walrus mustache and looked like one of the Haitian-Arabs, a merchant from the coast, who had lost his fortune. His broad face was red from the dust blowing all around. He was trembling as he lay on the ground. Odilon had seen him hiding behind the church compound, and thought he was a secular priest.

"I'm sorry," Odilon yelled above the explosions, "but I have to go…want to make it safely home with my donkey!"

"No! Wait for things to settle before you get your beast and yourself killed! Watch me…we're going to crawl until we get behind the wall."

They crawled to the refuge behind the building wall. With bullets zooming overhead, it felt as if they crawled forever. The voices became louder as the sounds of gunfire diminished. Not long after, the clattering of gunshots subsided and replaced by cries of joy.

"Do you think it's safe now?" Odilon asked the older man.

"I don't think it's safe to leave yet, but if you must go-"

"I'm not staying here a minute longer! I don't want to die, but I've never been a coward." Pointing to the crowd, he could hear many people chanting. "If these brave souls have the courage to face death with their bare hands, it would be a betrayal not to join them. Goodbye, sir, I give you my thanks."

"Wait a moment. What's your name, young man?" the old priest asked, bending over and panting from the exhaustion of crawling and hiding.

"Odilon Joseph. I come from the second section in the village of Anwodo, near Ti-Riviyè."

"Be careful, my son," wheezed the old man as Odilon picked his way through large chunks of rubble and joined the crowd in the town square. As he approached the group, hideous visions of his brother lying sprawled in the chief's compound pounded in his head with a *tom-tom* beat of fierce vengeance. All at once, Odilon was dying of his bottomless thirst for revenge.

Pulling his short body erect, he began shouting with all his might: "*Abas, abas, abas Ti-Jean…Abas!*"

The crowd cheered a heart response, "*Liberté, vive Haiti!*"

Although Odilon did not know it, he had just become a revolutionary.

"What happened to the *Zenglendo?*" he asked a teenage boy, who was on a drum to the cries of "*Vive Haiti! Vive liberté!*"

"They fled like rats to the mountains. The RRF fighters are after them, so we're in power now…the people's power!"

"How did our people gain this amazing power?"

"Bèbè Le Tyran sent his henchmen to suppress the demonstrators. They shot at close range to scare us off and kill us. But we were ready this time! The RRF fighters protected us; they returned fire with greater force. There are dead on both sides – but this time our people did not retreat! Overwhelmed, the filthy police fled!"

"I see people with hands tied behind their backs. Do you know them?"

"They're prisoners taken by the RRF fighters."

A moment later, a mighty, potent male voice boomed from a microphone. "We need to bury our dead with dignity!" The shout blared and the loudspeaker's bass succumbed to the uproar, almost squelching that powerful voice.

Odilon leaned into the crowd to catch a view. He spied a gigantic, looming black form sporting an olive-drab uniform. He was cradling a Kalashnikov assault rifle in his muscular right arm. Odilon moved closer to get a better glimpse of this impressive giant. The crowd was mesmerized by his authoritative presence.

The commanding man was tall, stocky, and held a proud air about him. His imposing gaze captured Odilon's attention. He had an oval face with a goatee and long angled sideburns. They hid his dark, high cheekbones. A pale, military-green beret completed his sharp visage. His olive-khaki uniform was overstretched, ready to burst open under the pressure of his bulging, meaty biceps and triceps. His powerful shoulders were squared, and his trunk-like legs were solid and stoic, holding up his erect frame.

He wore a patched pair of khakis held in place by a silverfish buckled belt, thicker than even the cinch of a mule. He looked not mulatto, not Arab, and not entirely darkish. For sure he was a *sang mêlé*. His grey eyes radiated through his rimless spectacles in that hazy, midday heat. They made him appear as strange as anyone could look in this part of Haiti. His salt and pepper hair pegged him as being in his late forties or early fifties. His balloon khaki pants were tucked inside mud-smeared ebony, leather boots that crackled thunderclaps at every step he took on the wooden stand.

In an instant, Odilon dreamed this giant of a man was Gaston, his stray great-uncle that was lost in Cuba many years ago. Gaston was a giant who had become a legend after beating Papacito, the once-greatest boxer of the Caribbean. But Odilon pushed aside his dreams. A crowd of men and women in uniform, wielding a display of weaponry, stood at complete attention with rapt respect for the speaker. Once again, the powerful speaker dominated his booming microphone, readying to speak to the revolutionary crowd. The strap of his AK-47 was wrapped around his thick neck, allowing him to release his death-grip on the weapon.

"I've never seen this man before! He must be an RRF leader," the astonished Odilon mumbled to himself.

"Comrades," he began. "Let us remember that this war is far from over. This small victory is a bittersweet interlude in our long struggle to eradicate misery, humiliation, oppression, and exploitation from our country.

"This heroic and glorious battle we've just won is only one of many more to come in our rightful quest to rid our country of foreign domination and neo-colonialism. This is going to be a long, protracted struggle. One that must be directed at all enemies of the people. It must especially be directed at the traditional politicians who are competing against one another over who is best qualified to represent the strategic interests of the imperialist countries.

"It must be directed at all the *bourgeois konpradò*, Haitians in name only, whose sole vocation is to oppress and exploit the masses. It must be directed at the dinosaur *latifondistas*, who swear to maintain the status quo at all costs.

"You see, this is not an easy task. Even after we eliminate all these obstacles, our struggles will not be over. We will have to fight the military, malnutrition, deforestation, and the other forms of ecological and social problems facing our country. There will be a constant struggle against corruption within the state bureaucracy.

"We in the RRF strongly believe that honesty in public affairs must be the norm, rather than the exception. We need to join forces with the compatriots who harbor the same desires for our beloved Haiti. Let's make no mistakes about it! In this long and painful struggle, some of us will die before we reach the finish line. Some of us will become traitors, as their convictions were only skin-deep. Let's keep in mind that I may not get to see the Promised Land with you. But we should never forget our fallen comrades. Despite all of these obstacles, these worries and uncertainties, Haiti will not only survive but will be free at last. A people united around a great and just cause will never be defeated. *Vive Haiti! Vive Liberté!*"

The enigmatic man then passed the microphone over to the other speakers, and strutted away into the roaring, applauding crowd with the magnificence of a mythical leader.

"Who is this man?" Odilon asked a heavy-set woman standing nearby.

"Olivier Zebeda, leader of the RRF," the woman responded, giving Odilon a strange look. "Where are you from that you don't know who he is?"

"I'm from Anwondo, near Ti-Riviyè." Embarrassed, Odilon did not know of Zebeda – but he had at least guessed the nature of his mission.

"You mean Anwondo near Bwa Chandèl?"

"Yes," he replied. "I'm sorry for asking such a stupid question."

"I don't think your question is stupid! A lot of people know of him, but I think many are seeing Zebeda for the first time."

"You see," Odilon continued, "that's the thing! I've never heard of him before. But he has the kind of magic that shakes your soul. He's passionate, and he clearly believes in what he's saying. I can tell. He chooses his words carefully and appears to be quite well-educated."

"He is also…very charming," tittered the lady, a sexy twinkle in her eye.

"There are many things he said that I don't understand. But I felt as if he was talking directly to me. My family is the victim of the kind of injustice Mr. Zebeda was speaking about."

"How is your family a victim? What injustice was done to you?"

"I lost my only brother to the *zenglendo* Zebeda was referring to. They murdered him in cold blood…he had no chance to fight back at all."

"How would you know that? Were you there when it happened? Was he a political activist?"

"No, my brother was a man who only wanted to work humbly and go on living, and they took his life. It's a long story, which I don't wish to recount; but somehow, I think today is a day to rejoice. After hearing this man, I have renewed hope. Look over there! The bodies are being collected. This is the painful part! Freedom is not cheap, is it? Zebeda was right. There is a price to pay," he sighed, resting his hand on the lady's wide shoulder, "but I must get my donkey and be on my way."

Once the crowd began to disperse, several of them decided to follow Bèbè Le Tyran and his police troops to the mountains. Others headed toward his home to gleefully loot and pillage—signs that the revolution had begun. Odilon rode in the middle of the crowd, bouncing along atop his little donkey. But as they reached the front gate of Le Tyran's compound, they found no signs of anyone there. Enraged, the people decided not to retreat. Several angry men surged forward, a knot of killer violence. Within minutes, the metal front door was torn off its complaining hinges, and the mob poured in. They destroyed everything they could lay their hands on. They found coffers filled with thousands of American dollars. They looted expensive furniture, clothing, vintage wines, and raided a food depot. But the discovery of something so heinous struck their hearts with pure violence – a torture chamber. It was hidden behind the master bedroom. It was small, but sickening. The walls were coated in rotting blood and guts and smelled of hell and death.

Odilon joined the surging rage over the assassin escaping their vengeance. "I hope other Haitians will give him the hard justice he deserves!"

Tying his donkey to a thick mango tree outside Le Tyran's house, Odilon told the mob to go after rural chief, Anakreyon.

"His house is located not far, over the hill in Anwodo. Even if he hides in a hole, we'll find him. We'll pour hot water in and force him out like how we catch wild *touloulou*. And then we'll pour chili peppers mixed with boiling hot water down his throat!" Odilon shouted as the angry crowd followed him.

More peasants joined them. "*Fòk nou pran Anakreyon! Fòk nou pran Anakreyon!*" They chanted. But by the time the mob reached the chief's compound, he had fled with his men. His house was ransacked. Nothing was left but the blank walls.

Chapter 4

Pillaging, death, and destruction were over for the time being. The mob was dispersing, one by one, in a trickle, each carrying loot home to their families. The night struggled to overtake what was left of the day. Odilon and his donkey followed the main road. His longing to get his hands on the men who had killed his brother was sharp in his chest. As he heard the birds fighting for their spots in the mango trees above, he murmured with a wan smile, "Tomorrow is another day."

It was early evening by the time he and his donkey reached the edge of the village. They were both exhausted. Odilon slowed the pace as they headed down the ravine. The running water would quench his donkey's thirst before tying him to an avocado tree for a quiet night of grazing.

He sat down to rest as he wondered how different the day would have been if Anakreyon had been captured. He also wondered if he would have had the guts to use the machete packed in the donkey's saddlebag. With Anakreyon dead, his brother's death would have been avenged. Sighing, Odilon got up and plodded down the pathway to his house.

Again, his mother was not home. He went outside, walked down the pathway and looked around, surrounded by deathly silence. Not only was his mother missing, but no one at all appeared to be in the village. What was going on?

A few minutes later, he heard the faint, lilting sound of singing. He turned around to see all the villagers streaming over to the other side of the hill. Soon, he was encircled by jubilant people – celebrating the departure of Anakreyon and his worthless henchmen!

His mother ran up to him. "Here you are, my son! I was worried when people coming from the marketplace told us what went on in Saint Louis. I was afraid something bad happened to you, when you didn't come home." Wringing her handkerchief, she wiped the running sweat from her flat, broad brow.

"I'm so happy to see you!" Odilon beamed. "Where was everyone? I have a feeling you were out on a looting rampage. Some of you are completely laden down with booty and food!"

"We went to join the people at the chief's compound. I wasn't feeling well this morning, but when I heard what was going on, I was on my feet!"

There was a sparkle in his mother's eyes that Odilon had not seen since the death of his brother. It was like she was coming back to life.

"*Manman*, your doctor told you to stay out of the heat in the daytime."

"My son," Cécile laughed, "it was a risk well taken. After all we've been through under Anakreyon, how could I not be involved? This is the happiest day of my life. I feel like I'm born again. You know something, my Odilon?"

"What is it, *Manman?*"

"Freedom is something we should never take for granted. Those who live in free societies should thank their government every day for their blessings. Too many injustices were being committed in this section. I lost your brother under suspicious circumstances. No one showed up to help us find his killers.

"People have lost their lands, their animals, their crops – and no one dared to seek justice. Everyone knew it was the *soukèt lawouze*, but no one could go to the authorities to complain. Anakreyon raised taxes and set prices at will. We were zombies in the cemetery of one man. He was '*Mèt Bawon Samdi*,' guarding us and watching our every move. We were treated like dogs in a big cage. We spent many nights without food, while we watched lavish parties held every Saturday night at that evil house. How can we forget the blows we've suffered from Anakreyon and his maniacs?"

Cécile's face, etched by years of hardship and wisdom, twisted in fury, deepening the creases around her mouth and eyes. Her brow furrowed, pulling the skin tight across her forehead, while her lips pressed into a thin, unforgiving line. Her eyes burned with an intensity that defied her age, a sharp, cutting glare that could wither even the most defiant soul.

"*Manman*," Odilon said, moving closer to her mother. "You haven't told me how Anakreyon got away. I was at the head of a band of people going to his compound. But when we got there, no one was found. The house was demolished. Only the walls were left standing."

"Odilon, it was eleven o'clock this morning when I heard Patekrè from Nan Banman say he saw the chief, accompanied by two dozen policemen, heading north in the direction of Barlatier. Fosia and her children were saddled on horseback, leading them.

"My son, when I heard that, I became suspicious. I went to the neighbor and asked to turn on her radio – to see if we could find out what was going on. Every station was talking about the crisis in Saint Louis. We got everyone in the village together and marched down to the chief's house. By the time we arrived, at least a hundred people were already there, ransacking the place. They took everything they could lay their hands on – jewelry, clothing, money, and the food from Fosia's grocery store."

"Didn't you take anything, *Manman*?"

"Son, you don't know your mother, do you? I may be poor, but I have my dignity. The last thing I need is a part of Anakreyon's belongings. Here's a man who stole from the people to amass his fortune. Through the years, I was able to withstand the many punches life has thrown at me because I was able to hold onto my principles. *Pa Lisis*, your great-grandfather, always said that when one is poor and defenseless, his integrity should always be his passport in life. So, that's what I always remember."

Odilon slid his arm around his mother, gently guiding her back to their house. They were both exhausted, but for the first time, there was a glimmer of hope that tomorrow might be a better day for everyone in the village of Anwodo.

He went outside to look up at the sky for a moment before he went to bed. It was a spectacular sight, shooting stars flashing across the southern sky. He viewed them as a good sign, as if they were taking part in the celebration going on in their humble village. Anakreyon and Bèbè Le Tyran no longer weighed on the shoulders of an oppressed people. It was as if a new day, year, and era of freedom had suddenly begun. He went back into the house. By eight p.m. *Manman* was snoring in her bunk. Odilon, weary and battered, grabbed his *nat,* but could not stop thinking of the folks around the town square in Saint Louis, amidst death and destruction, now a testament to their hard-fought victory. The euphoria of triumph lingered in the air, mingling with the acrid scent of spent gunpowder and the distant hum of celebration. His body, a canvas of bruises and skinned knees, bore the marks of the fierce struggle. He recalled the harrowing moments of being tossed like a ragdoll by explosions, the frantic crawl to escape the hail of gunfire, each breath a desperate plea for survival.

The town's dwellers, exuberant in their newfound freedom, danced and sang, their faces aglow with joy. Yet, as he thought about them, a profound exhaustion seeped into his bones. The fight had drained him, not just physically but in spirit. His limbs felt leaden, every movement a reminder of the ordeal he had endured. The cuts and bruises throbbed in time with his heartbeat, a painful symphony underscoring his fatigue.

He peered through the crack of his window to take a glance at his fellow villagers also in jubilation, their eyes bright with the fire of rebellion still burning strong. He wanted to join their revelry, to bask in the glory of their hard-won liberty. The young man, though heartened by their victory, found himself yearning for the solace of sleep. The tumultuous day had taken its toll, leaving him spent and rattled. The adrenaline that had once coursed through his veins now ebbed away, leaving a void filled with aching weariness.

Choosing sleep over celebration was not a rejection of their success but a surrender to the demands of his battered body. He needed rest to heal, to reclaim some semblance of strength. Inside, while fixing his *nat*, the sounds of jubilation were becoming distant and soon faded into a soothing lullaby. He lay down, the weight of his exhaustion pressing him into the *nat* and closed his eyes. In the quiet darkness, he found peace, knowing that tomorrow he would wake to a world changed by their courage. For now, sleep was his sanctuary, a much-needed reprieve from the trials of the battle they had fought and won.

#

The heights of joy in the village of Anwodo were only one example of the festivities taking place all over the Northwest province of Haiti. From Saint Louis to Anse-à-Foleur, from Bonneau to Anwodo, people were laughing, singing, and dancing in the streets. It was comparable to the traditional News Year's bash, celebrating the anniversary of Haiti's Independence Day.

But at two o'clock in the morning, the festivities came to a screeching halt. Radio reports announced that the central government in Port-au-Price was still intact. From the southern peninsula to the Artibonite region, government security forces swiftly recaptured many of the towns that had fallen into rebel hands. What Odilon had thought were shooting stars in the southern sky was actually rocket fire.

It was the sudden silence that awakened Odilon from sleep. He got up, looking outside, hearing a radio blasting from the next-door neighbor's house. The party had moved inside, but something seemed wrong. He woke Cécile up, and together they went next door to see what was going on.

Their neighbor's house was filled with people hovering around a radio – the Haitian peasant's most effective means of communication. The announcer blared in a monotone voice that from the north to the Central Plateau, a massive slaughter was now underway. Confidence and joy were quickly replaced by fear and apprehension. At two-thirty that morning, Radio Nationale announced there was to be a live broadcast from Ti-Jean at the National Palace. Everyone vied against each other to listen.

"My brothers and sisters," he began, "no one can imagine how deeply saddened we are by the latest turn of events. A group of extremists has attempted to disrupt our peaceful nation, motivated by one goal: turning the land of Dessalines into a hotbed for terrorists. I know many of you fear that our blue-and-red flag is about to be replaced by the red communist flag. But don't worry. I remain committed to my contract with you. The vow I made the day I was sworn in as president of this great nation remains unchanged. My unconditional love and utmost dedication to lifting every child of Haiti from misery to 'poverty with dignity' are still the cornerstones of my presidency.

"As someone born into poverty, I understand your pain perfectly. I know your suffering because I've lived it! Tonight, my dear brothers and sisters, I ask for just a little more patience. Help is on the way. I have a team of experts working on a pragmatic economic plan for the next three years, designed to modernize Haiti by building new roads, schools, hospitals, and creating new jobs to alleviate your undeserved suffering.

"This plan has already received tacit endorsement by the international community. Our friends from CARICOM and the European Union have agreed to help. The USA, France, and Canada have given us their backing. But let us remind ourselves that no country can achieve economic success and prosperity without peace.

"For these reasons, I have ordered our security forces to use all means at their disposal to impose peace in our land. Although we are a democracy, no one should be allowed to challenge the authority of the State. The multinational forces currently deployed in our country have agreed to help us in this endeavor. I urge all citizens to return to their normal activities. Don't be afraid of the terrorists! Also, I have solid information that *Le Rouge* was spotted among them. If this is true, be prepared for some turbulent moments ahead. In any event, my government is up to the task. We're not afraid of *Le Rouge*."

Then, there was a quick pause in Ti-Jean's speech. Horror-struck, the listeners were in disbelief!

"On a positive note," Ti-Jean continued, "I'm pleased to announce that the Ministries of Sports and Communication have already made arrangements to broadcast the Brazil-Germany soccer match live on *Télé Nationale*. Finally, I ask everyone to play the role of a good citizen. Report any strangers or suspicious activities you may see in your neighborhood to the authorities.

"The only area still not being pacified is the northern part of the Northwest Province. Our forces in the main town of Port-de-Paix are ready to move into Saint Louis and Anse-à-Foleur to restore order. If the terrorists now holding these towns hostage refuse to surrender peacefully, our security forces will crush them. Make no mistake about it; our response will be swift, massive, and decisive. The terrorists, now headed by Olivier Zebeda, have two choices: surrender or die!"

"Am I dreaming?" Cécile asked, pounding her fists on the small table in front of where she was seated. "Did you hear what that man just said?"

"Yes, I did, Manman" Odilon nodded. "I understand why you're in shock. I am surprised, but not overmuch. Several government men were killed today, and I really expected Ti-Jean to retaliate."

Odilon turned in his chair to address everyone in the house. "You should've been in Saint Louis to hear Zebeda speak. Then, you would understand how I feel. One of the first things he said was that 'the war to liberate Haiti has just begun, and it's obviously far from over. Chasing a few assassins and their chiefs is only one small victory in a war that is going to last for a very long time.' He said many things I didn't know about, but I do know that our struggle for freedom isn't over yet."

"You heard him say that?" gasped a man standing next to Odilon. The group's eyes were aglow as they listened in shock.

"But who is this '*Le Rouge*' that Ti-Jean was talking about?" inquired an old man sitting in the far corner of the room, shaking bits of tobacco from his pipe.

"I don't know him," Odilon replied, turning around the room to see if anyone had ever heard of *Le Rouge*.

"Maybe he's some man that works with Zebeda, I'm guessing. If he's not good for Ti-Jean, he must be good for us," Cécile stated with a wry smile.

"But my son, did you hear Zebeda say all these things you just mentioned?" she continued.

"Oh yes, I did. The danger isn't over. Don't be surprised if Anakreyon and his police return to this area." The group responded with heartfelt groans.

"We'd better start packing to leave," one middle-aged woman declared, "before the wild dogs return to be unleashed upon us."

Odilon rose from his seat. He knew he was the only one who had been in Saint Louis to hear Zebeda's speech, so he felt obligated to tell everyone what the rebel leader had said.

"Look, we can choose to feel helpless; but if we don't want to fear Anakreyon, we can do something about it if he returns home. We've already destroyed his compound, and he will want justice. But so does everyone here – for the hundreds of injustices heaped upon us over the years."

All eyes and ears were fixed like glue on Odilon.

"As Zebeda said, it's up to us whether we remain slaves or not. If we don't want this evil man to rule our lives, we must stand our ground and show him that we will no longer allow him to act as our lord and master." Vivid memories of his brother's bloody body lying at Anakreyon's feet flashed behind Odilon's closed eyes, and a mournful pain struck him as he sank into the chair beside his mother.

His mind churned in turmoil, oblivious to the claps and whistles from the crowd as they cheered one of their own for speaking his words of wisdom. Despite a lack of education, Odilon had a sharp, curious mind, displaying a lot of common sense. Even in the face of all the hopeful political upheaval, he had not told anyone about what he had witnessed at the chief's compound when his brother was killed.

There was no way he could share the truth of his brother's death with the crowd. His mother's well-being had to be considered—she was just starting to move on from the loss of her youngest son. The last thing she needed was to hear the gruesome details of how he was murdered. Odilon had no tangible proof of the crime, nor did he have enough money to hire an attorney to speak on his behalf. As a sharecropper, he was considered a second-class citizen—a lowly peasant with no voice.

Not to mention, he had been trespassing on private property when he climbed over the chief's compound wall. Odilon could easily find himself in the position of being the accused, though the nearing revolution might change things, hopefully for the better. For now, silence was golden.

During these heated times, Zebeda's speech in the town square had a profound effect on Odilon. It instilled in him a sense of hope he had never experienced before. There had always been a deep, pervasive sense of dread, desperation, isolation, and fear. But the final words of Zebeda's speech were carved deep into his youthful, freedom-loving soul: "A people united will never be defeated."

However, the same words that inspired Odilon also left him confused. Many questions filled his growing mind, questions he couldn't answer. He wasn't educated enough to understand the complex historical, social, and economic problems of his country. What he did fully grasp was the suffering, injustice, and constant humiliation that he and the other peasants endured under the totalitarian rule of Ti-Jean. For many years, he had watched with dismay the passive attitude and prejudice the authorities held toward their citizens. He often wondered if they ever paused, even for a moment, to consider the contempt and hatred their countrymen felt for them.

"Well," he decided, "they're thinking about it now!"

Just then, Olivier Zebeda's voice burst from the airways as someone switched the radio to the rebels' station, jarring the dazed Odilon back to reality.

"Dear comrades, courageous people of Saint Louis and Anse-à-Foleur: the RRF high command is inviting every resolute man and woman, eighteen years or older, to a recruiting drive tomorrow at the square. This drive is designed to bolster our military forces, to create confidence within the liberated zones, and most importantly, to counteract any threats from the Creole fascists.

"We in the RRF are the natural sons of Jean Jacques Dessalines, Alexandre Pétion, Charlemagne Péralte, and Benoit Batraville. We will never yield to pressure, intimidation, and threats. We believe our struggle is just, one that is deeply rooted in the principles of social justice. It is a struggle for a better tomorrow. It is a struggle for an ever-lasting freedom against nearly two hundred years of brutal oppression and economic exploitation. It is a struggle to conquer, to gain our right to true political independence, to a decent education, a decent job and greater access to healthcare – the three fundamental rights of mankind as recognized by the United Nations Fourth Geneva Convention.

"Brave people of Haiti, you should never be afraid to organize yourselves, to defend yourselves against tyranny. Valiant people of Haiti, you should never let yourselves be manipulated by misleading words like 'democracy' and 'rule of law.' Democracy has never kept to its real meaning in the oppressed nations. Those who claim to champion this word are often the worst oppressors.

"What they will never tell you is that society is divided into different classes. And each class has its own strategic interests. Those in power will always use everything at their disposal to remain in power. Since the creation of our beloved country, it has always been one group of people that runs a monopoly. After nearly two hundred years, they've badly failed in their mission to develop, modernize, and create justice for all.

"Because they failed, and because their interests are completely at odds with ours, it is fair to say that we're right to ask them to step aside and let us guide our own destinies. Calling us 'thieves' and 'red terrorists' has unmasked Ti-Jean. His true face has finally come to light. His populist demagoguery and folklorist speeches will no longer hold our devoted attention, for everyone knows what he really is: a traitor, an opportunist, and a conformist bent on protecting foreign strategic interests and the interests of the feudal-*bourgeois* alliance.

"In the RRF, we are committed to eliminating and overthrowing this corrupt system – the root cause of our struggles and problems. We are committed to getting rid of all foreign forces from our soil, so that Haiti can be free at last. It's easy for the authorities to call us thieves, and to play the 'red' card in an attempt to bring fear foremost to our minds. Who are the real thieves, those who steal because they are hungry, or those who pillage the state treasury to fill their coffers and Swiss bank accounts? You have to decide! Don't be afraid of their empty threats. Let us not forget.

"Our rendezvous time is tomorrow at ten o'clock at the square. Anyone who believes that Haiti must be free needs to be present. *No hay un paso atras; nou pap fè yon pa kita; yon pa nago.* Not one step backward. We will defend our position at all costs. They will have to destroy us to reconquer Saint Louis, because we will resist to the last man. *Viv Haiti, Viv Libète!*"

"As long as the RRF lives," Odilon remarked after hearing Zebeda, "Anakreyon and Bèbè Le Tyran will never be able to come back to this area."

"You mean you'll be there tomorrow at the square." Cécile gazed lovingly at her son, but with dismay. "You'll be branded a criminal, jailed, maybe killed."

"Would it be such a crime if I joined the freedom fighters? These people are ready to sacrifice everything; some of them have already given up their lives."

Everyone in the small room stared at Odilon, who until this morning was considered just another peasant in their village. Out of nowhere, Odilon was considering his new role as their leader!

Cécile sensed their change of attitude and acted accordingly. "Let's go home, Odilon." She stood up, grabbing him by one elbow and pushing him toward the door. "It's getting late, and I've lost my appetite for any more celebration."

"*Manman*, don't grab me like this! I am not your little baby boy!"

The audience exchanged amused glances, enjoying the spontaneous conflict between the domineering mother and the man who, knowingly or not, was grooming himself to be their leader.

"When you're one hundred years old, you'll still be my baby. Remember, you're the only one I have left in this world."

Ever the thoughtful son, Odilon understood his mother's fears. "Where are you coming from, Manman? Are you afraid I will leave you?" He turned to face the room with a solemn expression. "Sympathizing doesn't mean I'm anywhere near ready to join them. It's a deep commitment to enter the RRF. But I can't wait to see what tomorrow brings. Come on, Manman, I'm taking you home." With a gentle yet resolute touch, he took her thin brown hand and led her out of the house, disappearing into the fading moonlight.

Chapter 5

"Please form a line, so we can quickly fill out the registrations," said a man dressed in dark khaki, with an olive-green army jacket.

He was seated behind a long metal card table. Everyone within earshot followed his orders, shuffling themselves like cards into a long line. These people were stony, patient, aggrieved, but also happy. They were ready to sacrifice their lives for their beloved country. Long lines of defiant potential revolutionaries were stretching beyond every artery leading into the square. They were young and old, men and women—ordinary people from their local villages—packed into the town square like sardines in a can.

Zebeda was nowhere to be seen, but his top lieutenants were out in full force. RRF fighters in combat gear patrolled the streets in anticipation of a foreseen and immediate government attack, as promised by Ti-Jean the night before. Wet sandbags were plopped into place on every street corner and in every strategic location, including the south entrance into town and inside and around the cemetery located across from Saint Louis River – the last water to cross going into town from the south.

Well-armed fighters carrying bazookas, grenade launchers, and shiny Kalashnikov AK-47 rifles were positioned in and around the main cemetery. The people's army was confident of victory. Meanwhile at the square, registration had reached its peak. One-by-one, the fervent fighters-to-be were being enrolled. Small farmers and merchants offered tacit support by bringing food and flowers to

Marché Mercredi in the center of town, where the RRF was being headquartered.

Odilon strolled into the town square around ten-thirty. He had left his little donkey at home. If he needed to run, he would not have to worry about the animal. It was hard enough being worried about himself.

"Wow, this is a true people's army!" he exclaimed, seeing the huge crowd signing up to join the rebels. "The people really believe in Olivier Zebeda. Without a doubt, that giant man has the charisma to mobilize things." Their enthusiasm further dogged at Odilon's heels to make him get in the registration line.

Zebeda was indeed a shrewd tactician, a great military strategist, and a heroic fighter who never retreated from battles – unless it was for tactical purposes. A noted revolutionary of both intellectual and emotional depth, a man of fetchingly puckish wit and fierce cleverness, he had all the skills necessary to run a guerilla war. Guided by his sentimentalism, his revolutionary romanticism, and his many years of fighting alongside revolutionary fighters in Latin America, Zebeda was emphatic in his belief that the people's army can never truly be defeated. To him, a military force with the support of the masses (who see it as their sole vanguard against brutal oppression) is destined to triumph over its enemies, no matter how difficult the task might be.

Born in Haiti as the son of a career diplomat, Zebeda grew up in Mexico, where his father was Haiti's ambassador in the 1970s. He attended the University of Guadalajara, rising to president of the International Student Association.

Inspired by the national liberation struggles in Sub-Saharan Africa and Latin America, he wanted to create a replica of these nationalist movements in his homeland. He was there in Managua in 1979 when the Sandinistas swept to power, after a long and steadfast struggle against the neo-fascist Somoza dynasty.

Zebeda returned to Haiti in the late 1980s with hundreds of his revolutionary comrades. He based his small army in the Haut-Piton mountains, overlooking the city of Port-de-Paix, his birthplace. Later on, his forces spread throughout the mountain chains in the Northwest Province by forging alliances with peasant leaders.

In a few short months after his arrival in the mountains, he had fighters stationed all the way from Haut-Piton to Cazalie, the last mountain tip to the north under the jurisdiction of the town of Saint Louis du Nord. A blunt man who used sophisticated terminology, Zebeda was widely known for his acute dislike of what he called "petty-*bourgeois* opportunism and folkloric populism."

His showdown with Ti-Jean would be a magnificent opportunity for his dramatic entry onto the Haitian revolutionary stage. As a romantic fighter determined to change the political landscape, Zebeda knew that surprise attacks could deliver severe psychological blows to the enemy. This strategy was the driving force behind his decision to deploy RRF fighters deep into enemy territory. In an attempt to cut off government forces' supply lines and trap them during the night, Zebeda dispatched his top commanders to lead several RRF units in a march to take over Port-de-Paix, the largest city in the Northwest Province—and the headquarters of the government troops.

Coming down from the Haut-Piton mountains, they reached the edge of town at dawn and redeployed along the main highway to Saint Louis, passing through several communities. Meanwhile, urban commandos were already in place in Port-de-Paix, preparing cobra-style to strike at any moment.

#

It was one o'clock in the afternoon when Odilon, still at the square, heard two young women talking in a loud, animated conversation.

"We're going to win this fight. Only the Americans can save Ti-Jean's criminal regime," said one of the women while shaking her pretty fist in the air.

"The Americans what?" Odilon asked, edging closer to hear their conversation.

"Who are you? Who's talking to you?" one of the young women said, sizing him up from head to toe. "*Mezanmi, n'an trave oui la a.* Roseline, do you know this guy?"

"No…" the shyer of the two girls sighed. "…this is the first time I've seen him. Maybe he's trying to get fresh with us."

"No, no, no! Don't get me wrong. I honestly thought you had some information about what's going on here. I'm as curious as you are to find out what's happening." Odilon's face blushed red as a purple beet from embarrassment.

"*Oui, nou konnen,* we're just kidding! Don't you see everyone is trying to get to a radio to hear the news? I heard Radio Nationale report that the security forces are marching toward us. The word is the government will capture Zebeda," Roseline stated with a firm but overly soft voice. Her friend was trying to pull her away, so they could find out the latest information.

"My name is Odilon. I'm not a fighter, but I totally support the cause. Your name is Roseline?" he asked of the milky-cocoa skinned girl with squinting eyes, who spoke with an unusual air of mild timidity. He would always remember her sweet, unassuming shyness. When she threw a smile, her white shining teeth sparkled in the sun's beaming hot rays.

"And what is your name?" He kept his voice casual as he inquired and moved closer to the other young woman. She was the better-looking one of the pair. She had smooth, dark-chocolate hued skin, and her seductive curves were on display. Odilon watched her bulging buttocks sway under her stretched-out, faded blue jeans.

"Why do you want to know my name?"

"I'm just curious. Your face looks familiar."

"You think you've seen me before?"

"I'm not sure; I'm from Anwodo. I think I've seen you in my village."

"Is Aunt Cécile your mother?"

"Yes!" Odilon laughed. "Do you know her?"

"You lost your brother…a short time ago?"

"Yes, how did you know that?"

"Aunt Lynia is my godmother. Your mother and my godmother are cousins. I was there with her during the funeral."

"So many people came," Odilon recalled. "It was impossible for me to see them all. But – you haven't told me your name?"

"Thérèse Petit-Frère. And I'm sure your last name is Joseph."

"You're perfectly correct, *mamselle!* Listen, it was nice to meet you ladies. But I have to find a radio. I want to get the real news, not from Radio Nationale. Everyone knows their station does nothing but propagandize for the government. I want to hear the news from the other side."

"No, wait. Don't go yet. There are rumors saying that Zebeda will address the people. I have a friend who lives nearby. We can go together to listen."

"Oh, great!" exclaimed Odilon, flattered to be seen escorting two charming young ladies as they walked to the western side of the square in search of a radio.

Both girls wore red t-shirts, blue caps, and blue jeans – symbolizing the Haitian flag. Each shirt displayed a picture of Charlemagne Péralte, the legendary resistance leader who fought the American occupation of Haiti in 1915. Péralte had become the prime symbol of the RRF fighters and their supporters. Almost everyone gathered at the square carried his picture, in one form or another.

Bustling through the crowd, still escorting both girls, Odilon was in seventh heaven. He had not been in the company of such outgoing, friendly women before. The village girls were not like them. These ladies were sophisticated.

"Although there's uncertainty about things, I'm confident we can win," Odilon shouted above the raucous crowd noises. "For the first time, I can start to think of myself as a human being. I've even made friends with two beautiful revolutionary girls. Now there's something to look forward to!"

Hearing his loud, eager words, the girls came to an abrupt halt. He flashed a broad smile. In a lusty mood, they swaggered up to him, displaying their assets to the fullest. Shaking their booties before the bedazzled peasant, they answered him in kind: "Hey man, we're happy we can be with you, too!"

Pow-pow-pow exploded like firecrackers – sounds of rapid gunfire. Odilon and the girls wheeled around to hear where the sounds were coming from.

"Listen, compatriots, the RRF is saying that the attack we were waiting for came over an hour ago," one of the top commanders cried out, standing at the podium. He finally managed to get the attention of the scattering crowd.

"The Creole fascists made good on their promise to deliver more death and destruction to our already embattled population. Our fighters are standing firm in the face of death, and they will fight to the end. That's the latest news from the front. The registration drive is over, and it was a huge success. Now we're asking everybody to go home and stay indoors. It's too dangerous to remain here. The enemy knows your sentiments, and they'll make you pay if they capture you. Go home, listen to the news, and wait for further announcements from us."

Within minutes, the square was deserted. The streets emptied as people scurried home in near silence. The only sounds left were occasional gunshots coming from RRF fighters patrolling the streets in full combat gear.

Though they were among the bravest souls in Haiti, the locals were terrified. The entire area was on edge. Odilon and his friends took refuge in a house on the outskirts of town. Inside, people sat on the dirt floors, eagerly waiting for the latest RRF broadcast. But at the moment, they were only playing revolutionary songs.

"Where is the announcer? I'm worried," Odilon said, doing his best to hide the anxiety in his voice.

"Relax man, no news is good news," Roseline insisted. She gave Odilon a sweet nudge. "Besides, I haven't heard a lot of shooting. That means the government soldiers haven't hit town yet!"

"I would be surprised if they're already in town," said an old man lying on a scrunched-up wooden cot in a corner of the living room. Curls of harsh smoke from his pipe wafted to the low ceiling, while his wife sat in a creaky rocking chair across the room, spoon-feeding a grandchild.

"Why do you say that?" the old lady asked. She sounded peeved.

"They may be on the road, coming up from Port-de-Paix. But I can tell you this, it's not going to be easy for them to come up here. My neighbor who went to Port-de-Paix this morning told me he saw pedestrians in the streets rushing to get home. Many people were saying that the RRF fighters were everywhere. He said the marketplace in Lapointe near the hospital was empty…and no one was at the hospital. Barricades were placed all along the banks of La Rivière Lakay, La Rivière Nègre, and at the edge of Morne Miguel. In LaVeaux, the religious school was taken over by the RRF.

"Women soldiers dressed as nuns but with rifles hidden under their robes were patrolling the road. As they passed Villaso, just before my neighbor's vehicle crossed La Rivière Saint Louis, fighters were everywhere. Two of them approached his vehicle to let him know he wasn't allowed to go to Port-de-Paix, because it was too dangerous. I'm thinking this is going to be a long fight before we see any government soldiers here, if they're able to make it here." The old man finished giving his version of the news, sucking another cloying drag from his pipe.

"Quiet, everyone," ordered Thérèse. "The radio announcer has asked everyone to stay tuned. There's going to be an important report from the front."

People stuck close as flies to the radio, so they would not miss one word of the news. The old man rose up, tapped his smelly pipe and put it aside on a small table. The old woman stopped feeding her grandchild, ordering the girl into her bedroom. You could hear a pin drop in the house.

Two minutes later, the announcer returned. "Courageous people of the Northwest and the entire country, we in the RRF are extremely pleased to announce that the enemy forces have not advanced a single inch beyond the positions they held yesterday.

"On the contrary," he continued, "our revolutionary forces are engaging the enemy on multiple fronts. Port-de-Paix is now a no-man's-land but will soon be in our hands. Our glorious forces control the airport, the old bridge into town at Morne-aux-Pères, and several police stations. Reports from other areas will follow shortly. Please stay tuned."

Everyone in the living room rose to their feet, both bare and shod. Was it time to take to the streets in wild, exuberant Haitian celebration? No, not yet—they decided to wait for the sounds of jubilation before venturing outside.

"I can't believe my ears!" exclaimed Odilon.

"I feel as if I'm dreaming. Am I?" Roseline inquired.

Linking arms, moving around joyfully in that tiny house, they all began to shout, "*Libète, Libète—Libète!*"

#

Pinning the government soldiers down in Port-de-Paix was crucial to the RRF leaders. It was something they believed was necessary, to give the RRF more time to consolidate its power base in Saint Louis du Nord. A city of one-hundred thousand residents,

Port-de-Paix is the provincial capital of the Northwest Province. It is also the birthplace of Capois La Mort, hero of the battle of Vertières near Cap Haitien that defeated the last bastion of the French Army headed by General Rochambeau on November 18th, 1803.

However, since the glory days of independence the city has remained stagnant and neglected by government after government. During the Duvalier dynasty, Port-de-Paix became a hotbed for Neo-Duvalierism and Creole fascism. As a result, thousands fled to big cities like Port-au-Prince, or to neighboring places like Turks and Caicos, the Bahamas, and the United States, fleeing brutal oppression and economic starvation.

Controlling Port-de-Paix would give the RRF a strategic advantage in its quest to seize power through military means. In their view, the rebels believed that a liberated Port-de-Paix could raise the hope of the Haitian population, boost the morale of their fighters, and galvanize a nationwide revolt against the Ti-Jean regime.

But storming Port-de-Paix would be a daring move, by all reasonable and strategic analyses. The Fifth Army Corps was the best-trained and best-equipped to secure a swift victory for government officials over what they believed to be a "ragtag" guerrilla army. Numbering five-thousand troops and backed by several hundred special operation forces, their size made victory seem certain, and the army generals were confident.

Nonetheless, sometimes the lack of proper intelligence combined with overconfidence can prove to be fatal in war. The military planners were severely underestimating the morale of their troops, composed almost exclusively of soldiers originating from the peasantry. These people were nowhere near prepared to die for Ti-Jean and his government.

On the other hand, the rebels, though numbering only about two thousand, had a huge political and military advantage. Armed with grenade launchers, rocket-propelled grenades, bazookas, and AK-47 assault-rifles, it was easy for them to move around in back alleys and the narrow streets. They could also blend seamlessly into the general population, for they had its full support.

Furthermore, Port-de-Paix is nestled between the sprawling Trois Rivières and mountainous upland forests, making it an ideal hideout for rebels who used its tropical jungles for cover and strike points. The city sits on a bay, backed by forested mountains to the east. To the south, the mighty Trois Rivières, the province's largest river, serves as a natural buffer for the city as it flows westward to meet the Atlantic Ocean. The southern edge of town stretches to the north bank of the river, where a mix of shantytowns and clustered villages, separated by thick stands of broad-canopy banana trees, lines the riverbed. Their sheltering leaves, often larger than a surfboard, created fertile ground for guerrilla-inspired activities.

Just north of the shantytowns lies the city's only airport, its vast unpaved airstrip surrounded by banana groves on either side. The airport buzzes with military transport planes ferrying soldiers and supplies for the government's war efforts in the region. To the north, the Port-de-Paix River serves as a natural boundary, separating the bustling city center from its sparsely populated suburbs. To the west, the Bay of Port-de-Paix offers a stunning view of turquoise waters stretching all the way to the island of La Tortue, visible in the distance. The main highway leads toward Saint Louis and Anse-à-Foleur, the province's northernmost towns, guiding travelers into the city's two major entrances.

Besides being comfortable, familiar terrain, this local topography favored the rebels. Apart from having the full backing of shantytown dwellers and the general population, they also had verdantly thick, lush green foliage around the foothills on the eastern side. This terrain provided fertile grounds and great cover for rebel fighters should they decide to retreat to the mountains.

In Saint Louis du Nord, the people were ready to take to the streets. They waited to hear the news from the RRF radio announcer, signaling the celebrations. After the RRF announcement, the independent radio reported fierce fighting in the town of Chansole, fifteen kilometers south of Port-de-Paix, deep inside government-controlled territory. Heavy fighting was also taking place in the village of Lapointe, near a missionary hospital where the RRF fighters engaged the government troops in hand-to-hand combat. Twin blazing gas stations pumped plumes of smelly, black curling smoke into the sky, obscuring the sun – transforming the whole area into an abysmal world of malfunctioning pitch darkness.

On the main road leading north to Saint Louis, rebel soldiers dressed in white carried pictures of Charlemagne Péralte. Sweatbands wrapped around their heads, they patrolled the road to cut off fuel supplies to the government soldiers, who retreated in disarray after two hours of tough resistance by the rebels. Soldiers swapped their uniforms for civilian clothes as they fled into banana fields surrounding the hospital, many of them defecting over to the rebel camp.

Three kilometers down the road to the south, government troops ran into a sea of fire coming from all directions as they attempted to rescue fellow soldiers trapped after the fighting in La Pointe. Pinned down, they were forced to retreat at full speed without retrieving any of their dead or wounded comrades. It was a complete rout!

By controlling La Pointe to the north, and by keeping government forces at bay in Chansole to the south, the RRF succeeded in cutting off all supply routes, effectively trapping the government's Fifth Army Corps in Port-de-Paix. These successes emboldened the rebel commanders, who launched a ferocious offensive to capture Port-de-Paix on that same day.

Well-coordinated, the rebels advanced from three strategic locations. From the north, they moved south, passing several villages as cheering crowds of residents lined both sides of the main road. Young women, dressed in patriotic blue and red, showered the fighters with kisses, hugs, and red roses. From the east, the fighters surged west like heavy rain, capturing the eastern suburb of La Coupe on their way to Cathedral Square, deep inside the city, where they engaged in fierce fighting with the elite presidential guards. From the south, they moved north, overrunning the military outpost at Trois Rivières—along with the airport—while exchanging heavy gunfire with government soldiers as they pushed their way toward the city center.

As the rebels reached the depths of the city, the fighting was full blown. Terrified residents cowered in their homes as tanks and helicopter gunships came from all directions, pounding the city into dust. Awful sounds of shelling mixed with crackles of automatic gunfire continued far into the afternoon. Hundreds died as entire blocks of homes were carpet-bombed from above by the army's helicopter gunships. Dozens of stalled, charred black cars full of grisly bodies cleared the way for the government troops' heavy armored vehicles to move through.

Any survivor that was caught while fleeing was stopped and arrested. All men of fighting age—even lower—were separated from their families, forced to stand in long lines with their hands above their heads. For these troubles, they were gunned down under the blazing, flooding eyes of their relatives, who begged in vain for mercy as clots of blood, bones, and brains coated everything within range. At that moment, Port-de-Paix became the City of Hell.

As the fighting reached Capois La Mort Square, located in the heart of the city and about a hundred yards from the National Bank, a stray bullet plowed into the naked back of a chubby girl clothed in a red canvas smock, making her crawl on her belly over the no-man's-land. She was desperate to reach her home, a wooden two-story house on the south side of the National Bank.

A white-haired woman peered from her balcony's window, watching the girl creeping below. She bolted downstairs, running up against a column of rebel fighters who took position behind the balustrade on her front porch, sheltering themselves from snipers on rooftops across the square. But when the breathless old woman at last tumbled downstairs, there was no need for her assistance, as an impromptu operation was already underway to save the girl.

She had been pinned down for several frightening hours behind a hibiscus edge in the middle of the square. Halfway to her house, a hail of scattering bullets had trailed her. From the porch, a dozen rebels nosedived, unthinking of their safety, retrieving the wounded girl – while an elite commando silenced the snipers. In a surprise move, precision bullets were launched. Snipers plopped from rooftops like mangoes snapping from tree branches. Spooked soldiers keeping their positions inside the Hotel De Ville adjacent to the square raced like dazed rats into the urban street canals.

For about a minute, everything was dead silent. The rebels grabbed the girl just as she lost consciousness, blood pouring in purple sheets out of her mouth. Another group of rebel fighters covered their retreat, and the girl was carried to a makeshift hospital on the east bank of the Port-de-Paix River.

The fighting kept on with feverish intensity. Driven out of the city center, disoriented infantry soldiers regrouped for a charge. Hundreds of rounds were fired helter-skelter, hitting anything that moved. An army commander was hit on his lower leg, swinging it loose as if it was boneless. Trying hard to steady himself, he stumbled over a chain-link fence. Another wave of bullets buried him there.

A daring young soldier leapt a moment too late to save his dying commander. One shot struck the soldier on his sleeveless arm, limp as he tried to steady his M-16 rifle. In his courageous run, he struck his head against the metal gate of an enclosed courtyard near the Hotel De Ville. His sight blurring, he was captured by the increasingly confident rebels – now in complete control of the high ground of the city center.

By four o'clock in the afternoon, the rebels had shot down the helicopter gunships and sealed off all but one of the entrances to the city, allowing an escape route for fleeing government soldiers. But the war only dragged on, with government gunners pounding at the rebel positions throughout the city.

Tenacious rebel fighters held firm, refusing to retreat. Divided into mobile units, they hid behind houses, striking at the armored vehicles navigating along the narrow streets. Huge clouds of smoke from an untold number of fires were plunging the entire area into virtual darkness. Meanwhile, dead soldiers along with their badly wounded comrades remained bloodied and bowed in their smoking tanks.

At the southern edge of the city near the main army barracks, the fighting was fiercest. The Rebels advanced in a final push to capture the barracks, which were sitting on a strategic hilltop overlooking the city. Dead bodies littered the road, scarecrow clothes flapping like leaves in the roaring wind. Every charge upward was answered by volleys of salvos raining down on advancing rebel fighters, exploding bodies stuffed to overflowing with flying bullets.

So, the rebels changed tactics, no longer willing to be cannon fodder for the army gunners on the hilltop. Dividing into even more mobile units, they circumvented the barracks and began charging relentlessly from multiple directions. At last, propelled by revolutionary conviction and guided by unwavering determination, the RRF fighters overran the barracks. By five o'clock, they were planting a large red-and-blue flag—with Charlemagne Péralte's picture emblazoned on it.

The government army general, along with his top commanders, fled in a speed boat across the bay, landing at the fishing village of Pointe-à-l'Ecu – leaving the foot soldiers to the mercy of the victors. By six o'clock that evening, all fighting subsided as only RRF fighters patrolled the streets. They left the government troops to be taken prisoner as the troops dropped their weapons in a universal sign of surrender.

Chapter 6

The news of the remarkable victory reached the airwaves. The entire country was rejoicing. Everyone flooded into the streets to celebrate in Saint Louis. Odilon and his new friends led a group of two hundred people to the town square where they joined thousands of other residents packed in to overflowing. Odilon was overwhelmed.

"Is it really happening?" He kept asking everyone.

"Shut up, will you? I didn't know you were Saint Thomas," laughed Thérèse, shaking her butt to the tantalizing sound of a *rara* beat. In Haiti, people who are skeptical and only believe what they see with their own eyes are given the nickname Saint Thomas.

The air was light and jubilant in the midst of the celebration in Marché Mercredi. In sharp contrast, Zebeda was flanked by his top lieutenants inside rebel headquarters in the center of town. They held a press conference before a throng of local and foreign journalists, broadcast live on Rebel Radio and transmitted to all major news organizations.

Saint Louis du Nord was now the unofficial capital of Haiti. Zebeda looked handsome, fresh, and relaxed, portraying the perfect rebel guerilla general with his bushy mustache, pepper-and-salt beard, and blue-and-red beret. The fantasy was complete with him sitting beneath the backdrop of three imposing pictures of Charlemague Péralte, Che Guevara, and Benoit Batraville, Péralte's second-in-command during the resistance struggle against the American military occupation of 1915.

Stroking his wispy beard, throwing everyone a confident smile, tapping his shining boots on the mosaic-tiled floor, he presented to the world for the first time a legendary figure with an iconic persona, a Romanesque profile outstretched by an unyielding gaze. He cast the same charismatic portrait already earning him fame throughout Central America and Mexico. Before an army of local and foreign journalists, Zebeda, at the zenith of his political career, appeared dignified and profoundly revolutionary. In pure, sweet Creole, he laid out his plans for the future of Haiti before the nation, before the journalists, and before the world.

"Today, the people of Haiti have shown their determination to be free at last. What has happened today marks a major turnaround in our history," he began with an infectious, impish smile. "Our country is living in one of the most critical moments in its history. Never before, in nearly two hundred years of our existence, has there been such suffering in the lives of our people. For the vast majority, Haiti is a virtual hell that many of us, given the opportunity, would leave in a heartbeat. In the eyes of many in the international community, Haiti is a failed state, a basket case – a country on the brink of extinction.

"While we understand these statements to be at best bias, and at worst prejudicial, we must admit that Haiti is at a crossroads. Left to survive at the mercy of foreign exploiters, Haiti has become a huge enterprise of institutionalized corruption, while its people live under direct neo-colonialist dictates. However, things haven't always been that way. Throughout its history, the people of Haiti have demonstrated great courage in fighting exploitation and oppression. Right from the start after independence in 1804, great peasant leaders like Goman, Accau, and others made enormous sacrifices in fighting exploitation against the wealthy landowners, the rich *compradò bourgeois,* and the state bureaucracy.

"In various forms, these struggles for a fair distribution of wealth marked the entire nineteenth century, continuing through the beginning of the twentieth century. During the American occupation of Haiti from 1915 to 1934, many sectors of Haitian society were driven by humiliation, oppression, and a strong sense of patriotism. This reality forced them to unite in the fight against foreign domination, demand democratic rights, and safeguard our political independence. As always, it was the peasantry that bore the bulk of both the resistance and the sacrifice. Who can forget their heroism against the occupation, under the distinguished leadership of Charlemagne Masséna Péralte and Benoit Batraville?"

"*No one!*" The crowd roared to the cry of "*Vive Haiti!*" Zebeda flashed a smile in a quick pause. Odilon had never been in such a state of elation. Amid the jubilant crowd, feeling triumphant, Thérèse and Roseline stood next to him, their arms raised high as they made the V sign, celebrating the RRF hard-earned victory. The air was filled with cheers, the shared joy of a battle well-fought and won.

"During the second half of the twentieth century," Zebeda continued, "our struggle for equality entered a new phase. Inspired and empowered by the spirit of the 1946 democratic movement, led by young revolutionaries like Jacques Stephen Alexis and Gérald Bloncourt, urban workers entered the scene, demanding their rights for better working conditions and the rights of political representation and unionism. During that period, large sectors of the middle class, independent workers, and patriotic intellectuals courageously fought and died against the unbearable feudal, semi-colonial system.

"Today, against seemingly impossible odds—including the uncertain atmosphere surrounding the international solidarity movement among oppressed nations, and the degree of aggressiveness displayed by imperialist nations in their quest for complete subordination or subjugation of the dominated countries— the people of Haiti continue to fight for better economic conditions, for the protection of their democratic rights, and to safeguard our country's national sovereignty.

"For nearly two hundred years, the Haitian elite and the religious leaders, along with some reactionary elements of the middle class, have held each other's hands firmly in a holy alliance to drive our country beyond any state of recognition. Despite the tangible evidence proving that we are a nation on the brink of disaster, the forces of evil remain solidly entrenched against any attempt to change our course. We in the Revolutionary Resistance Front, the RRF, have concluded that there can only be one solution to break the impasse: the realization of a national, popularly democratic revolution – a quintessential phase toward pulling Haiti back from the brink!

"In our struggle to ensure full participation of exploited urban workers and the oppressed masses in general, the RRF is proposing tonight to mobilize all of its forces to consolidate its political and military gains, to join hands with other progressive forces, and to forge a grand strategy that will allow us to liberate our beloved country from the hideous grip of its enemies."

Zebeda paused briefly. His eyes scanned the cheering supporters before him. As the crowd's applause surged, local and foreign journalists poised themselves, ready to unleash their barrage of questions the moment he was done. But he had more to say.

"While this dramatic coup tonight sends a chill into the hearts of the enemies of Haiti," he pressed on. "I'm confident that their unexpected defeat brings a feeling of awe to the hearts of all freedom lovers. We can only be criticized by those who, with no shame, seek to continue profiting from the misery of the Haitian people.

"While we're opting for a grand coalition with the other progressive forces, the RRF will continue to accompany the masses in their struggle for immediate economic and political reform. The RRF will assist, unite, and organize urban workers, and will rally the disenfranchised peasants, small cultivators, and patriots to fight together. We will band with all other democratic and patriotic forces in our country to overthrow the viscous and fascist regime, to earn our long overdue democratic freedom, and to work tirelessly to make life better for the population as a whole.

"The realization of this first phase, in a tactical sense, will pave the way for the creation of a genuine revolutionary alliance between all sectors of the oppressed masses to consolidate, in a strong unity, all national, patriotic, and progressive forces under the banner of a historic front that will be called the 'Péraltista Front for National Liberation' (PFNL), which will be an indispensable element for the realization of the 'National and Popularly Democratic Revolution.'" Smiling, the giant man decided it was time to wrap up his lengthy speech. "Thank you!"

Before the journalists moved in with their questions, a female commander dressed in green military fatigues approached the microphone. A pair of service revolvers swathed her waist, and the RRF flag was wrapped as a scarf around her neck. She flashed the audience her most professional smile.

"Please be brief so that everyone will have an opportunity to speak. Mr. Zebeda will answer questions for only a few minutes. Thank you!" She then moved back to take her seat at the table near Zebeda.

A French journalist jumped up from the back row. "Could you elaborate on the three aspects of the revolution you just mentioned?"

Zebeda grinned; pleased he had left them wanting more. "When we say the revolution must be 'democratic,' we mean that it will eliminate all autocratic and dictatorial forms of governments. It will guarantee equal rights for all citizens, and it will also give them the right to exercise tight control over the issues of public affairs. The revolution will be 'national,' because it will ensure that every Haitian has the right to choose, with full protection under the law, his or her own destiny. It will put an end, once and for all, to neo-colonialism, and it will achieve cultural, economic, and political independence that will then guarantee national and territorial integrity.

"It will have equal economic and industrial development for all provinces in the country, and it will develop a strong solidarity between the people of Haiti and other progressive forces around the world. Finally, the revolution will be 'popular,' because it will put an end to feudal-*bourgeois* domination, liberate the country from all foreign domination, and actively encourage the participation of the masses in the social, economic, and political life of the country. This 'popular' revolution will, without a doubt, defend the interests of the working class and work toward a social transformation for the benefit of the vast majority of the population."

"You keep referring to the idea that the State structure must be dismantled; but the Haitian people have been taught for years to respect the authority of the State. Do you think it's going be easy to change things?" asked a local journalist.

"This argument is valid when the State is crafted within the framework of democratic governance and the rule of law. But for almost two centuries, the people of Haiti have come to identify and vet the structure of the state bureaucracy and its reactionary nature that makes it the main force of oppression in the country. We in the RRF strongly believe that the burden of proof has to be placed on the State, and it must be destroyed if this burden cannot be met.

"It's obvious that the masses of Haiti are demanding change. The euphoria going on outside speaks for itself. The neo-colonialist character of the State, including its anti-national and anti-popular nature, leaves the people no other choice but to demand its removal."

"Don't you think a real national government must include all sectors of society, including the governing elite?" another man asked Zebeda.

"Listen," he responded, "In the RRF, we're not exclusivists. I said it earlier when I called for a broadly united front to rid the country of brutal oppression, and to increase the scope of human freedom. But we will never be part of any government that includes the enemies of Haiti."

"Don't you think expressions like 'the enemies of Haiti' might be too strong and overstated?" an American voice asked.

"After almost two hundred years of independence, eighty percent of our population still lives in the countryside. Eighty-five percent of the population is illiterate. There is only one doctor, one hospital bed, and one nurse for every ten thousand people. Unemployment is at the highest level it's ever been. Infant mortality is the highest in Latin America, while life expectancy is the lowest. Crime is on the rise in the inner cities; thousands of our young prostitute themselves to survive.

"This is not a pretty record for a group of people in power for almost two centuries. The international community must accept the fact that the Haitian people have known for years: the dominant classes have failed miserably in their mission to modernize the Haitian state. And it's not difficult to understand why.

"On the one hand, we have the dinosaurs, wealthy landowners possessing all the best farmlands, who essentially control all mechanisms of farming production. So backward is their thinking, they're totally absent from all forms of agro-industrial development. They rely solely on a feudal system that allows them to exploit at will the huge majority of the peasants, by forcing them to work as sharecroppers at best, and as virtual slaves at worst.

"On the other hand, we have the *bourgeoisie*, made up for the most part by a small group of businessmen, generally of foreign origin. They are mainly entrepreneurs, financiers, and managers of foreign firms in this country. As the directors of imperialist interests, they are nothing but a bunch of lumpen-*bourgeois* with no objective for economic and national development, no vision for the future, and no grand ambition for Haiti. Their money is well-stored in their foreign bank accounts, and they leave only a small portion in our country, enough to maintain their lifestyles as *bourgeois*.

"It's ludicrous to think that these people can be part of any serious process to fundamentally change the Haitian society. They don't have such a vocation! They are Haitians in name only. However, we in the RRF are committed to creating a true democratic State and to promoting economic development based on agrarian reform and the development of a national industry. Finally, we're dedicated to improving the lives of the people and to following a policy of peace, neutrality, and good relations with all nations." The revolutionary commander then glanced at the cheering crowd outside and flashed a beaming smile.

"Thank you," he stated. "The press conference is over."

RRF soldiers escorted the journalists from the room. The high command walked outside to greet an enthusiastic crowd, one ready to live the rest of their lives in freedom, democracy, and prosperity. As freedom's loud cries spread to all corners of the republic, the RRF's popularity soared to new heights. Every town and village in Haiti listened as Zebeda's press conference was relayed to major radio stations in urban and rural Haiti. This was a stunning setback for a government that, the day before, was promising quick restoration of law and order in the Northwest Province.

Throughout the province itself, especially south of Port-de-Paix, government troops were on the run. They were fleeing their military outposts in mass evacuations as rumors spread that rebels were moving in. From Bassin Bleu to Jean-Rabel, from Môle Saint Nicolas to Bombardopolis, government forces scattered like rats as the local population set up popular committees to take over their city halls – awaiting the arrival of the victorious rebels.

Chapter 7

The party in Saint Louis blazed on well into the night, lasting until sunrise. Odilon did not return until the next day. He was reluctant to leave his newfound friends, Thérèse and Roseline.

Much to his surprise, Cécile was not upset. When he unlatched the door, tiptoeing in, his mother was already up, sitting on the edge of the bed with her rosary, counting the colorful beads, immersed in her regular morning prayer. Upon seeing Odilon, she halted her ruminations and turned to him, her wrinkled face softened with relief.

"I knew you weren't going to come home right away, not with the excitement going on." She showed her son a nearly toothless smile, putting away her prayer beads with tender care.

"Manman…let me tell you…"

"There's no need to explain, my son. Here in the village, the celebration continued all night. At first, we were scared…the radio broadcast about the fighting, which was extreme. At one point, we dropped to our knees and began to pray."

"*Manman*, you mean you had the stomach to listen?" Odilon began laughing in relief. His mourning mother was now able to enjoy things.

"It was hard to listen to such horror. To me, it was like when I was in labor. The revolution was giving birth though, not me. You could hear the terrifying sounds of gunfire as the reporter was talking. Sometimes, he would stop, and you could only hear the voices of the soldiers directing operations in the background."

"Yes, you're right, Manman. But where were you?"

"I was at our friends' house, listening like you. There were times when the gunfire was so loud, I felt my heart beat with its intensity. The fighting was somehow going on right outside the door! We held each other's hands, praying. While we prayed for a fast victory, it was reported that people were dying as the government tanks crushed their homes. My son, we heard those desperate souls crying to God for help! Then I started thinking how painful it must've been for Avisène when those thieves were killing him…"

Odilon could not reply, feeling the pain echoing from his mother's voice. It clogged up his throat with tears. He paused for a moment, and then moved close, hugging her tight. "*Manman*, don't worry; justice will prevail. I'm more confident now than ever before." He patted her narrow shoulders to comfort her.

Reaching out with strong, gentle hands to an old clay pot on the floor, Odilon settled it near their small, silver chest behind the kitchen table. He began scooping up fresh drinking water from their limited store of supplies – coming from a nearby spring at the ravine.

"I'm thirsty, but the water is too warm. I'm going to let it cool in the pot."

"Yes, do that. I'm thirsty myself," said Cécile.

"*Manman*."

"What?"

"I notice that one of our plants is dying." Odilon said this as a distraction to take her mind off the violence of the revolution.

"When did you see that?"

"Just now."

"I'd better go water it," his mom sighed, rising from her seat.

Pushed to the brink of absolute exhaustion, Odilon rolled over to his stretched-out *nat,* leaned back, and within seconds was blissfully asleep. Though it was morning, he needed to rest his body after a sleepless night of celebration.

Cécile strolled outside, clutching a watering pot, and began to water the plants in their tiny garden. Her clean blue cotton dress fluttered in the cool tropical morning breeze. As she stooped, her large, greying straw hat cast long shadows over the freshly watered ground.

#

In Port-de-Paix, rebel commanders were establishing a revolutionary tribunal to try government soldiers for their crimes against the people. Government informants like M. Jean-Baptiste were also being put on trial. Though M. Jean-Baptiste was nowhere to be found, he was tried in absentia. In all the liberated areas of the countryside, peasants seized and held onto any land previously owned by the "dinosaurs."

Although the atmosphere was triumphant, the people's feelings were bittersweet. It was sweet because the informants were finally off their backs. But it was bitter, as they found it cruel and heartbreaking to witness so much death and destruction in such a short period of time.

Houses were destroyed, cars smashed, brothers lost sisters, wives lost husbands, and children were butchered. Those alive wandered the streets, homeless. And those streets were piling ever higher with trash, rubble, garbage, and animal feces, mixing with the mutilated bodies of dogs, goats, and people. Homes were also half-destroyed, unsafe for their owners to return. Bloodstains were everywhere – on housing walls, sidewalks, and in the public squares.

It was a hellish scene, straight out of Dante's Inferno. The rebels were overwhelmed. It was clear they were unprepared to handle this gruesome aftermath. The RRF fighters were taking on the slow task of collecting unclaimed bodies and burying them in large, open pits as mass graves. Under the RRF's guidance, neighborhood vigilantes were appointed to safeguard the new freedom, keeping looting in check and ensuring that goods were distributed to those in need. Little by little, the city regained a sense of normalcy. Haitian conventional wisdom held that, despite adverse conditions, life must go on—clean, peaceful, and dignified.

But if Port-de-Paix was going back to normal and developing a new sense of freedom and hope, in Port-au-Prince that optimism was replaced by a mood of all-enveloping despair. Misery reigned supreme; every diplomatic circle was in a state of shock. How could a ragtag guerilla "army" defeat the well-armed, well-trained elite Haitian government forces in just one long day?

When news of the government's defeat broke, the President of Haiti was meeting with foreign dignitaries in Villa d'Accueil, the lavish, official headquarters of the country's prime minister. Apart from the diplomats, prominent members of the one-percent upper class were also present, for the president was celebrating his birthday in his classic, beyond-*bourgeois* aristocratic style.

Born as a petty *bourgeois*, whose becoming president of the republic had made him extremely wealthy, he always threw lavish, extravagant parties. These were organized as a way for him to gain acceptance as a mainstream member of the *bourgeoisie*.

President Ti-Jean was a soft-talking man of slim stature, with brownish-red, roving eyes set in a beardless, boyish face exposed by angular, scraggy, rawboned cheeks – and a large forehead, shaped like a coyote. To compensate for these deficiencies, he used sharp, faultless, pointed words with impeccable meanings to sway his friends.

In formal gatherings, he typically dressed in a white suit and bowtie, resting his hands on his hips to give weight to every word that came out of his mouth. To his foes, the "words of love" he preached, liking to prophesize like a messianic leader on a mission to rescue his people from misery to "poverty with dignity," were nothing but words of deception. Overwhelmingly elected with a mandate to salvage the country from its deplorable state, he had yet to back any of these words with deeds. But his diehard followers saw in his character something very different: a slight, supple, svelte, and sylphlike gentleman of medium height, one who spoke in low-pitched vocal tones to show the sense of humility dwelling in his heart.

Like most petty *bourgeois* politicians, Ti-Jean had humble beginnings. To be precise, he came from the disenfranchised branch of the petite *bourgeoisie*, a thin layer between the two major classes constituting the Haitian society. Historically, politicians from this faction were the greatest traitors, betraying their own class of origin, motivated by a "holy" sacrament to fill their lots at a quickening speed – even if it meant to deceive, on the sly, the same people who had ushered them into power.

Ti-Jean was no different. He had built his political career by becoming a community organizer under the brutal regime of the Duvalier dynasty. He was only in his early thirties when he first gained fame among the marginalized masses and the grassroots communities within the Catholic Church, for his daring moves at challenging the "Baby Doc" regime. After the Duvaliers fled and the presidency became a free-for-all, the masses saw in Ti-Jean a Divine Providence sent from Heaven to free them from their hellish world. During the next election season, recalcitrant politicians, opportunists from the left and other dubious figures from the political class jumped on Ti-Jean's bandwagon, literally hand-picking him to be their candidate. On Election Day, they threw their entire political muscle behind him, a sleazy maneuver to impose their own hidden agendas.

A master manipulator like a deadly coral snake masquerading as a harmless king snake, Ti-Jean said nothing, putting forth a dovish demeanor, acting like a saint from the local parish. Beneath his political *soutane*, however, he engineered his first political blow, a colossal coup against his allies of convenience. He systematically eliminated them one-by-one while creating his own niche, which was submissive to his dictates. Now, standing in the way of his quest to have it all was the military, for which he had already developed his own game plan. Those ideas, though, would have to be put on hold for now. He must first deal with a growing insurgency in the

Northwest, for which he needed the military. Otherwise, his political future was doomed.

Like most *arriviste* politicians, Ti-Jean had unscrupulous ambitions, but could not attain his upstart, dramatic *parvenu* status if he could not gain social acceptance amongst the same class of people he had sworn to defend the masses against. Despite his new fashionable appearance – coiffing under Louis Vuitton blue-blacker sunglasses, which had become his trademark – his social climb would not reach its highest plateau until his total assurance as *bourgeois* was achieved. Money, power, and fame alone would not suffice; a beautiful, desirable *haute-couture* woman from the upper class must become his soulmate.

He married Sandrine Duvivier, an olive-skinned *mulâtresse* Creole with lustrous green eyes and golden, wavy hair molded into the straight texture fit for a First Lady. Strolling with the most refined feline gestures, she looked dignified, tall, and slender as she stood next to her husband at their public and private gatherings. Sandrine was obsessed about her looks, hiring a twenty-four-seven stylist to ensure her appearance was flawless wherever she went. However much she wanted to be closer to her Caucasian bloodline, her repressed nose and bluntly thick lower lip – coated lavishly in scarlet-rouge lipstick – proved that her African lineage outweighed what she would have preferred. Nonetheless, she was pretty, voluptuous like a stem of wild red roses springing from the source of an isolated, refreshing brook. She even spoke flawless British English, for she went to school in Scotland soon after high school. She also spoke in the most unusual, domestic French – like that of her friends in the uptown suburbs. "*Je suis là, oui, chéri…*" ("I'm here, honey") she answered Ti-Jean when he would inquire about her whereabouts over the telephone from his presidential office.

Sandrine liked to smile; but her grin was false, broad, and disengaged that at first glance what anyone noticed was an unhappy soul, dovishly gloomy, soul-deadened, wallowing in bitter chagrin.

She was nostalgic for the frenetic world she had been accustomed to before her marriage. Wedding Ti-Jean was a bitter pill to swallow. But however tough it might have been for Sandrine romantically, there was one course she could never have deviated from. She understood the unspoken consensus among *bourgeois* in Port-au-Prince, for which she was ready to sacrifice any romance or sentimentalist orgies. Beauty and wealth must always be backed up by the powers that be, and the president's birthday was Sandrine's first opportunity to flex that power.

That night in Villa d'Accueil, the feast was sumptuous. To gratify her voluptuousness, Sandrine wore a low-cut neckline, *décolleté* in pure coquettish fashion. Her diamond necklace glittered under the florescent lights. She sat next to her husband, casting subtle sideways grins at each guest as they entered the room. One by one, her elegant friends arrived. First was Élodie Malbranche, whose reddish-brown skin complemented her thin, trimmed eyebrows. She wore Chanel glasses, accentuating her high-class demeanor even on a tropical night. Her parrot-like hooked nose added a certain sharpness that contrasted with her otherwise diffident, kittenish, and prudish mannerisms.

Next, along came Catherine Desgranges, a chubby girl with a tangerine-like tan whose humble smile, the arc of her lips, her glaring makeup, her sleepy blue eyes, and her overmodest and skittish attitudes could force any man to succumb to her coquettishness at first glance. She sat down next to her fiancé, a flamboyant bachelor with a strong, muscular frame who was dressed in a white suit. He was from the Casimir clan, powerful coffee exporters in town.

One-by-one, sometimes in pairs, the guests were coming — gleeful, haughty, and bashful. As each guest arrived, the hostess checked them off her list of "friendly enemies," saving that lengthy sheet in her mind for her husband's use as well.

Traditional Haitian cuisine was pushed aside, as French *cuisiniers* were brought in to prepare multiple dinner courses. The dress code was rigorously enforced. Each *cavalier* strutted by, accompanied by his dame dressed in seventeenth century fashion, *classic à la européenne*. Security was tight. The entire block was cordoned off to keep unwanted guests away, to protect the prominent invitees and their fancy cars – and most importantly, to keep the lavish party out of the public view, out of sight and reach of the oppressed and exploited masses. Extravagance like this could enrage the hungry population, whose daily struggle to make ends meet was a constant nightmare.

The sky was crystal-clear that night over Port-au- Prince. A cool tropical breeze was blowing through the royal palms, caressing the beautiful faces of those in attendance. These fancy guests sat at tables made from Brazilian cherry, covered with bottles filled with the most expensive European rums. This show of wealth was organized on an over-decorated marble terrace just outside the mansion. A cordial atmosphere among *bourgeois* reigned, as they gossiped, joked, and drank French Bordeaux, all against the backdrop of a beautiful, well-kept tropical garden displayed under the natural brilliance of a full moon.

At eleven p.m., the president, dressed in a blue suit rather than his traditional white, stepped up to the microphone to welcome his distinguished guests. A special tent with expensive light fixtures and a makeshift podium had been set up for the occasion. This was designed to ensure that the president could address his guests with an air of total dominance. Under his blue blazer, a double-knotted tie hung neatly over his Yves Saint Laurent light-blue button-down shirt. His Pierre Cardin brown belt cinched his navy-blue pants with sharp precision. Everything gold glittered under the bright crystal chandeliers. The night itself was golden—luxurious beyond measure.

"*Bonsoir,*" he began, "it's a great honor for me to welcome all of you to 'the people's' house. I feel flattered by the presence of so many of my personal friends. Haiti looks beautiful tonight. Doesn't it?"

"Oh yes, it does," oohed and ahhed the fancy guests, raising their crystal glasses in a toast to the "birthday boy".

"I have to say that I feel blessed to be the leader of this great country, and to be able to preside over all these beautiful people. None of you can imagine how humbled and lucky I feel to be the one at the receiving end of so many beautiful gifts. As we celebrate in our paradise, I'd like to take this opportunity to announce that the European Union has just released a fifty-million-dollar aid package to Haiti, and my government is negotiating, right at this moment, with other donor nations for more economic aid of this kind.

"But the most interesting thing of all," the president continued, "was the unexpected news that I received, just before I came here, from my chief diplomat in Washington, Ambassador François Duchatelier. In our telephone conversation, I was informed that Haiti might soon become part of the North American Free Trade Agreement. If this happens, it will be a glorious first, a major breakthrough for Haitian diplomacy!

"I must say that our friends in Washington, Paris, and Ottawa have not forgotten us. That is why I cannot conclude this toast without extending my special thanks to Ambassador Paul de la Fournier of France, Ambassador François Pignon of Canada, and Ambassador Mark Stephen Reardon of the United States. And to all of you..."

"Wait, Mr. President, wait!" cried an officer dressed in a navy-blue uniform, bursting into the room.

Everyone turned to see what was going on. The man was hustled out of the room, for he was seen only as an intruder. Glaring at each other in bewilderment, the guests began to smirk and laugh, thinking it was a party joke.

The man tried to explain as he was dragged away: "Demonstrations are going on right now, all over the city. From Carrefour to Pétionville, from Delmas to Laplaine, everyone is crying *'viv Zebeda, viv RRF!'* The demonstrators have surrounded the National Palace!" Twisting in the grip of a guard, the man was horrified.

"What the hell are you talking about?" the guard asked, slamming the alarmed man against the giant concrete wall that surrounded the compound.

"Please, don't hurt me!" the man pleaded through bleeding lips. "Listen to the noise coming from the street – tell me what you hear!" he cried, begging for his life.

"*Viv Zebeda, Viv RRF, Viv Saint Louis du Nord, Viv Port-de-Paix!*" echoed loud, troublesome voices from a distance.

The security agents became frantic. Outside, the chief security attaché leapt over an enclosure, rushed back inside, and approached the president just as he was about to take his seat at the banquet table.

"I think we need to get you out of here, sir."

"What's wrong?" the president asked, confused. He flashed a smile at the audience, all while hissing through his teeth at the embarrassment the commotion was causing.

"The whole city is up in arms. It's not safe for you to remain here. We may not be able to guarantee your safety." In mere seconds, the attaché whisked the president out the back door, leaving the roomful of bewildered guests in the hands of his spokesperson.

"*Mesdames et Messieurs*, the president had to leave for an urgent meeting. Something unexpected has come up, beyond his control. However, he asked me to assure you that his unconditional respect for you, and the gratitude he holds in his heart, will remain forever intact." The spokesman, a short man in a tuxedo with a black bowtie pressed tightly against the collar of his white shirt, struggled to find the right words. "Dinner will now be served," he concluded, resembling an alcohol-addled impresario.

Outside the Villa, the president flapped his arms in devout rage as he was placed in his presidential limousine. The radio was on, so he tried to digest the latest news.

"That twerp Zebeda is on the move again," he told his aides.

"Mr. President, he's in total control of the Northwest Province."

"He…is *what?*"

"News reports have confirmed his fighters are in charge of Port-de-Paix. Our forces are on the run, and all other security personnel have vacated their posts. The wire service stated that the town of Môle Saint Nicolas in the Far West has also fallen."

The president's flesh crawled up and down his silk-suited arms. He had been dealt a major blow, one that stuck into the deepest fibers of his soul. "This…is…my birthday!" He screamed in a high-pitched, anguished voice.

Once seated in the back of his luxurious limousine, the president, sipping on a glass of champagne from the in-car bar, began to regain his composure. Leaning forward, he jabbed his right index finger into the stomach of his personal security advisor, who was shifting uncomfortably in the seat adjacent to him.

"Look here, I'm going to fire the entire chain of command!"

"Why, Mr. President?"

"Hell, this is insane! Are you telling me the Army of the Republic can't defeat a band of ragtag terrorists? It's humiliating! I sent our best troops to prevent exactly this kind of catastrophe! Just when I thought I was only dealing with Saint Louis du Nord, now I'm facing a national crisis!" He took a hefty swig of wine, smacking his lips.

"Mr. President, I know you've always been a man of great wisdom. I'm confident you'll find a way out of this crisis," the aid whispered, trying to avoid another jab in his aching solar plexus.

Using several ploys, the security entourage safely brought the president into the National Palace. It was two o' clock in the morning by the time a meeting was called to handle the impending crisis. It was held inside a sumptuous room decorated with priceless seventeenth-century ornaments. Pictures of Haitian independence heroes loomed tall, as the military planners sat at a fifteen-by-ten over-polished, dark mahogany table.

Three crystal chandeliers illuminated the room, casting shadows across the walls and the thick velvet curtains floating against the window – their pleasant wavelike motions being generated by the air conditioner. Sitting next to the president at one corner of the table was the army's chief of staff, surrounded by top officers. General Louis Lacroix, a tall man with a scarred face, always walked with a pair of sidearms about his waist – even during meetings with the president. He was a fearsome personality in the Haitian military, a "prince of a guy" who had made his fortune through bribery, intimidation, and manipulation.

"General Lacroix, explain how we came to this point!" the president's voice boomed, his red, unflinching eyes fixed on the general.

"I don't know, Mr. President. My best guess is that our intelligence service did a poor job in assessing the situation in the Northwest. Now that we have a crisis in our hands, we need to face it head on," answered the wary general.

"With all due respect, General Lacroix, I find it hard to comprehend how the best and brightest in our army could perform so poorly. In our planning the other day, there was never a reference to Port-de-Paix being a hot bed for terrorists! Our mission was to cleanse Saint Louis of those bandits, and to capture Zebeda. Now, I'm living a nightmare. They beat us in our own territory, leaving Saint Louis du Nord as the official capital of terrorism in the country."

"Mr. President, do you seriously believe what's going on in the Northwest right now, spreading all over the country soon, are the actions of a few terrorists?"

"What do you mean, General Lacroix?"

"No sir, I believe we're dealing with much more serious forces. These people are well-disciplined, well-trained, and use sophisticated weaponry. We're facing our greatest challenge since the Duvaliers left the country."

"Are you sure of this?"

"I hope I'm wrong. But all indications show that my assessment is proving to be right."

"How can you explain…what makes you so certain?"

"Let's face it. We sent in half a dozen tanks, the best and most modern in our arsenal. Not one of them returned to base. They all were destroyed, with many of our soldiers killed inside. The only helicopter gunships we have in our arsenal was shot down. Now, we're defenseless in the air. We may be able to repair one or two of them, but so many were destroyed.

"We sent in five thousand soldiers and military officers, supported by seven hundred elite presidential guards. Only one thousand managed to escape. The rest are either dead or captured. Now, tell me if you still think a ragtag group of bandits could accomplish these military coups. I have every reason to believe the enemy is well-equipped and well-organized. I never really thought you believed they were just a small band of thieves. I always assumed you said that for political propaganda."

"General," sighed the president, trying to calm down, "to be honest with you, I never had any suspicion that I could be facing such a serious threat to my presidency from the Northwest. It's such a backward province."

"But Mr. President, you know as well as I do that popular revolts are grown out of people's frustration and their desire for change. You just mentioned the area as being a backward place. But the people there are citizens, like Haitians everywhere in the country. If they feel abandoned and neglected, they will follow anyone who promises them salvation. Look at the rest of the country. Look at Port-au-Prince. Demonstrations and celebrations of the revolution are everywhere. Yes, it is a revolution!

"All eyes are on Zebeda and Saint Louis du Nord. It's a clear example that this is going far beyond the Northwest boundaries. If we don't take necessary steps to put an end, a quick end, to this, we might not be able to control it."

"General, do we have the means…after suffering so many losses?"

"I'm afraid not, Mr. President."

"Damn – so what do we do?"

"As a military man, I can suggest possible military solutions. But as far as creating a long-lasting political solution, I think this will have to rest with you and your political advisors."

"What possible military solutions do you foresee?"

"My solutions may not be easy to swallow," the general cautioned. "First, we should seek help from the Americans. They are anti-communist."

"What kind of help are you suggesting?"

"Military advisors and ammo," General Lacroix stated.

"But you know what the implications are. It will further delegitimize our sovereignty and political independence. But without the Americans, I don't see how we can win this one. Lose-lose situation…it's a bitter pill to take."

"But what can we do? We can choose not to ask the Americans for help and be slaughtered by the commies. Or we accept their help and lose our pride. Besides, we may not have that much of a choice. If the Americans perceive this movement to be a communist threat to their region, a solution will be imposed on us. That might be worse than what we're already dealing with. Honestly, I think we should take the initiative and make these requests right now."

"What can we ask in military terms? Be specific."

"Permission to use their global positioning satellite to monitor Zebeda's troop movements. Night-vision goggles to attack them in the dark where we can see them, and they won't be able to see us. A jamming device used to silence their radio signals. An emergency loan package to buy modern weapons to resupply our military, to modernize our arsenal, and to make our readiness more effective to deal not only with this current challenge, but also with any future internal threats. Finally, we can ask for military advisors that will train our troops to be better skilled in urban warfare."

"Can we do all this without turning Haiti into a protectorate?"

"I'm sure we can. And it won't be the first time the Americans have given us this kind of help. In 1969, when the communists landed in Casale, the American black berets rescued the Papa Doc regime. Besides, we won't be the only ones receiving this aid. In Latin America, the Colombians are getting it, the Peruvians got it to put down the Shining Path rebellion, and El Salvador got it too during their bloody conflict with the Communist Party of the FMLN in the seventies and eighties."

"Alright, we'll do that! Hopefully, we'll get some aid right away, so we can deal with Zebeda and his brigands."

The brief meeting adjourned with no concrete solutions, but the president had gained the grim resignation to swallow his pride – with a glimmer of hope that he might be able to squelch the insurgency.

Meanwhile in the north, Zebeda did not remain idle. Peasants all over the country gave their support and their lives to the cause. Young, old, men, women, boys, and girls traveled from all corners of Haiti – swelling the ranks of the growing RRF.

In short order, they had more volunteers than they could arm. Zebeda was fast becoming the foremost new player in Haiti, occupying front and center of the political stage while exposing the true nature of class struggles. In an overnight twist of fate, he was now the major topic of the conversation in editorial boardrooms, diplomatic circles, and the Haitian Parliament. Newspapers and radio stations made his speeches their main breaking news. The public could not get enough of him.

The unexpected turn of events also triggered a dramatic surge of shuttle diplomacy between the U.S. embassy, the National Palace, and the French and Canadian embassies. Traditional politicians, the so-called credible opposition, and all sectors of the Haitian elite, of course, rallied behind "their" government. These *bourgeois* bureaucrats went as far as accusing Zebeda of treason for betraying his class of origin in favor of shantytown dwellers and ignoble, ignorant peasants.

Chapter 8

At the RRF headquarters in Saint Louis, the war room was packed with strategic planners studying the war's next phase, while Zebeda exhibited great confidence in their victory. In an emergency meeting designed to counter government propaganda, the giant revolutionary was optimistic about the future.

"There is nothing they can do to stop our movement," he told his top commanders, who were listening with the utmost respect and admiration.

"Our intelligence service has informed me that many *bourgeois*, bureaucrats, and *konpradò* have already sent their wives overseas. While some of these lumpen-*bourgeois* are publicly supporting the fascist regime, they are getting ready on the sly to leave the country, crossing the border into the Dominican Republic. As I've always stated, these people are nothing but nomadic exploiters who believe Haiti is not worth dying for. They have no nationalistic convictions, being Haitians in name only."

"But we should be wary of our approach to this sensitive issue," cautioned one of his eager lieutenants.

"Of course we should! Not all *bourgeois* are unpatriotic. In our 'declaration,' we referred to that small, insignificant sector of the *bourgeoisie*. They're too afraid and weak to change the course of history. Just because someone is a *bourgeois* doesn't mean he's a reactionary. Many who began this long and torturous march toward Haitian socialism were once children of the rich. But this isn't a sensitive issue—it's shameful, as the bourgeoisie as a whole never hides its gross disdain for the disenfranchised masses," Zebeda answered.

"We know they're preparing to attack again. What would be the most effective way to maintain our strategy?" another lieutenant strongly implored.

"Without a doubt, they're working on something," Zebeda responded, quick to continue. "If I want to follow the path of history, this time Ti-Jean won't be alone. I'm sure the entire class he represents, and its imperialist allies will be with him. Even though we don't have sophisticated weaponry, the minds, hearts, and souls of the people will forever remain our greatest military asset."

"What if they massacre the population?" asked a breathless sub-commander. But few of them doubted their leader at this point.

"They will surely try," Zebeda replied, his voice firm.

"How can we be certain? I think Ti-Jean's watchful about his reputation. He can kill a lot of civilians and soldiers, but hasn't the stomach to kill…thousands," suggested another lieutenant.

"No, I disagree – judging from their past record, they wouldn't hesitate for a second to commit genocide, just to hold onto their status and stay in power. As you well know, we are not sitting ducks. We have fighters deployed near the edge of Gros-Morne and all the way to Môle Saint Nicolas, creating a shield for the province. Before they reach Saint Louis, they will have a hell of a fight ahead of them. Every main road is booby-trapped, and bridges will be blown up to deny access for their vehicles. So, I think we're ready to contest every inch of our territory."

Zebeda knew his entrenched enemies, confident that their best strategies would work against them. Wheeling around, he strutted from the room, whistling *"La Dessalinienne-Ladesalinyèn"*—Haiti's national anthem.

#

In Anwodo, Odilon went back to his regular routine. After the big celebration in town, great feelings of hope lingered in his heart. The villagers felt the same way, as the RRF victory was all anyone talked about. Odilon understood that Zebeda was not promising a miracle, nor offering an immediate economic recovery in their province. But total confidence that tomorrow would be a different story was uppermost in the minds of everyone in the village.

Though happy now, Odilon still had to assume two duties after the death of his brother: taking care of their small herd and proffering his services for a tiny handful of Haitian *goud* to anyone interested. And yet, he viewed his peasant future in a brighter light. Still confused by many things Zebeda said, he nonetheless kept resolute in his determination to be a part of the revolution coming to his beloved homeland.

At six o'clock most mornings, under Odilon's watchful eye, the hens outside clucked and pecked into their morning breakfast of dried cracked maize, mixed with grit. It was fatty but sufficed for their small group of birds.

"*Manman*, I found one lonely, large brown egg in a hidden nest behind the cacao trees," he cheerfully called out early one morning.

"Didn't I tell you to leave the coop latch locked? And to leave the latch unlocked at the kitchen door?" Cécile replied, wagging her finger to chide them.

"Yes, you did. You know, what's been going on, I get carried away and forget my responsibilities. I'm sorry, I won't do it again—I promise!"

"You shouldn't be forgetful, my son. Those hens, and only two of those scrawny goats, are our main possessions. The other animals don't really belong to us."

"I know, *Manman*."

"Well, I'm reminding you…in case you forgot."

"You don't have to, *Manman*," her son bowed his head in embarrassment.

"Your father was a man of great responsibility. Many times, when we quarreled, it was only due to his strict discipline. Back then, I didn't see his point of view about responsibility. But now that he's gone and I'm alone, I think about what he was trying to tell me, and I really miss him."

Frowning, Odilon drew closer to his mom. "I really miss Papa, too. I was young, but I remember him taking me to the river, bathing me, and showing me how to catch fish and shrimp in the ravine. Avisène was little, and we used to take him with us and have him sit under the *kowosol* tree by the bank while we fished. Sometimes, he cried to be put into the water. He would complain that the ants chewed on his behind. Papa told me to cut a banana leaf for him to sit on, to protect his little butt from bugs."

"Odilon, stop this talk about the past…it's too much for me to bear," cried his mother, putting a hand to her sweating forehead. "First it was your father, and now my Avisène has been taken away. How unfair can life be?" Cécile moaned, voice and hands shaking as she reached for a faded pink hankie to dab at a flood of tears.

"*Manman*, I know it's hard to think about. But how can we stop remembering the good times? They're an unforgettable part of our lives that's gone forever. If we don't remember them, who will?" Drawing forward, her doting son put his arm around her thin waistline. "*Manman*, you tell me all the time that the living have an obligation to keep the memory of their dead alive. Otherwise, you always say, they will face a second death harsher than the first one, forgotten forever." With bony fingers, Odilon massaged his mother's shoulders, consoling her dog-tired soul.

While acknowledging the reality of Odilon's words, Cécile felt guilty for not following her own advice. She walked out of the house, went into their small kitchen – which was separated from the main house – taking up an armful of dry wood and a book of safety matches to light a fire.

"What are you doing, *Manman*?"

"I'm going to make some coffee and *boukousou*," answered Cécile.

"*Manman, boukousou* takes forever to cook! Although I'd love some, we're going to miss an opportunity to lure that hen inside to lay her eggs. I made a nest and put her egg in it. But if you're busy inside, she won't come!"

"You're right, my son. Why don't I bring the fire outside? We need fertile eggs—more chickens to sell to the open market. Do you think we can afford to keep our own rooster?" Cécile asked, not wanting to pester Odilon for a large sum of money. Humming the kids' song "*Ti Zwazo*" (Little Bird), a favorite of Avisène's, she smeared a little bit of butter in a pan to cook the *boukousou*. "We're depending on the neighbor's roosters right now, but they sometimes want our eggs over that!"

"If we don't protect the eggs, the rats and snakes will feast!" Odilon laughed.

"This is no laughing matter! The eggs aren't safe unless we put them in the big green glass jar and leave only one in the nest for the hen to come back to. If we don't, we'll lose all the eggs—rats are everywhere. In the morning, droppings are all over; at night I hear them moving across the roof."

"Papa used to say that taking the eggs from the hen and leaving only one in the nest will earn you more eggs in the long run," Odilon said. "The hen lays as many as twenty eggs before sitting on them to hatch her chicks." Odilon picked his way through the sticking bushes to gather dry wood for their fire. "We can afford to give some to the neighbors."

Cécile pulled a chair from inside the house, placing it next to the fire to wait for the coffee to be ready. Ten minutes later, Odilon returned.

"*Manman*, I can smell the coffee all the way from the bushes. Maybe it's too strong for your heart. Remember, the doctor said you can't drink coffee – it's going to raise your blood pressure." Odilon gave his mother a stern glare, his narrowed black eyes reminding her of the danger to her health.

Laughing now, she pooh-poohed him, "One cup every now and then won't kill me!" She was grateful and happy her son cared so much about her.

"We have to go to the clinic, and soon—no check-up in six months! We missed your last appointment because of the political situation. Let's hope things eventually get more normal. I heard on Rebel Radio that government soldiers are massing around Gros-Morne to attack again."

Chapter 9

Two weeks later in Ti-Riviyè, Odilon accompanied his mother to the doctor's office. Dr. Charles Duchaud and Rosana, the receptionist—a middle-aged woman with a robust posture—ran the clinic. Dr. Duchaud worked tirelessly, attending to a stream of multigenerational patients. The clinic was modest, with peeling walls and a few worn-out chairs in the waiting area, where elderly men, women with children, and young adults sat patiently. The doctor moved from one patient to the next, offering care to the elderly suffering from chronic ailments, children with malnutrition, and mothers seeking advice for their newborns. Supplies were limited, but the doctor relied on resourcefulness, treating each patient with compassion and dedication despite the clinic's lack of modern equipment and medicine.

"I'm very pleased, Cécile. Everything looks fine," Doctor Charles Duchaud said with a sigh of relief. "Your blood pressure, sugar levels, and weight are perfectly normal. You don't even have high cholesterol. For a woman your age, that's amazing! It must be your low-calorie peasant diet. I'm not prescribing any new medication, nor am I increasing your current dose. Keep up the good work!"

They were in a small consultation room. Odilon always went to the clinic with his mother and was quite pleased to hear the results of her examination.

Dr. Duchaud was a short man, standing less than five feet tall, and in his late thirties. Dressed in clean, well-pressed khaki, he wore prescription glasses, half-combed his hair, and was always smoking a smelly corncob pipe. Despite his somewhat disheveled appearance, he had deep compassion and a strong sense of professionalism, treating each of his patients with the utmost care. Friendly not only with close associates but with nearly everyone he met. He had become an important member of the RRF medical team. Cécile and Odilon were grateful for his service to their poor village.

"Thank you, doctor. But why did you say you're pleased to find my blood pressure stable? Is it normally very high?" Cécile asked. She sat against the backdrop of a large eleven-by-twenty poster full of pictures of healthy food and Creole medical advice, telling his patients how to care for themselves at home.

"No, no…this wasn't the first time I found your blood pressure stable. I was actually thinking of other patients I've been seeing throughout the week. Most of them have alarmed me greatly…you're just great!"

"Why do you say that?" Odilon asked.

"You should see how high the blood pressure is for most folks."

"Why do you think that's so?" Odilon inquired.

"I think it's the political tension. Everyone is on edge. I'm worried about many of my patients." The doctor wiped his spectacles with a clean white piece of soft cloth. "I don't think it's their diets."

"If that's the case, their blood pressures should be lower! Everyone seems happier now that the government is defeated," stated Cécile, a wide grin crossing her face.

"Yes, they were happy yesterday. But rumors all over town last night claimed we could be attacked at any moment. Didn't you see all the activity going on when you came into town?" The doctor's voice dropped with concern.

"Yes, we saw a lot of it this morning coming to the clinic," answered Odilon. "*Manman* and I thought it was just more celebrating. The marketplace was overcrowded, and the streets were filled with people. At one point, we thought it was Saturday."

"Didn't you see the RRF fighters all over?" the doctor asked.

"I didn't see any," piped Cécile, shrugging her thin shoulders.

"Yes, *Manman*, we did see a few by the square. Don't you remember?"

"Oh, now, I do. I guess everyone is buying goods to store up in case there is another attack on the town." Cécile's cheerful, happy frame of mind vanished as she realized what was happening.

"Is there anything you want us to do, Doc? We can go to the marketplace and buy the things you need to safeguard your home," asked Odilon.

"That's nice of you to ask, young man. My wife has us squared away. You need to go get yourselves ready." The doctor's face soured with concern as he watched Odilon open the door for his mother and lead her outside. He cast an odd glance at them as Cécile kept one pace behind her son.

"Goodbye, Doc," they chimed almost in unison.

"G'bye, remember to stay safe," advised Dr. Duchaud.

Odilon was well on his way to the marketplace when he heard the doctor calling after him. "Hey, wait, Odilon…stop please, now!"

Odilon swiftly turned around. "What's going on, Doc?"

"Where's your mother?"

"She went across the street to buy some *piskèt*."

"*Piskèt*, are you sure that's what she's buying?"

"A woman from La Rivière des Barres sells them. Do you want some?"

"I've have always loved *piskèt* since I was a child," the doctor replied. "My wife will definitely buy some."

"What is it, Doc? Is something wrong with the *piskèt*?"

"No, no-no-no…! That's not why I called you. Come back into the clinic, I want to talk to you. This is about something totally different."

"What is *it*, Doc?" Odilon reiterated.

"I didn't want to alarm your mother."

"What's wrong with her? I knew there was something."

"Don't get upset now. There's nothing wrong. I just wanted to say that you should go to school. You always speak your mind with such fervent emotion, love, and patriotism whenever you talk about the problems facing our country today. You're like most everybody out there – hating the current regime with a passion. But unlike everyone else, you seem to understand the root causes of the problems. I've heard you express yourself about what you feel; you deserve a chance at an education."

"Me, go to school? I'm just a poor peasant!" Odilon protested.

"I can help you begin your education. Listen to me. While everyone condemns and despises Ti-Jean, he only represents the symptoms of a disease that's ravaging the internal organs of an otherwise healthy country."

"What kind of disease is that, Doc? You've got me scared."

"No, it's not a human or physical disease. I only use medical terms because I'm a simple country doctor. Haiti's problems are much more complicated than that. However, I'm sure you understand the differences between the rich and the poor, the city and country people – those who go to school, and those who don't."

"Yes, Doc…I do…I've always longed to go to school. But really, I don't want to think about it much, because I have to look for any job I can find to support my small family, what's left of it! I've done everything from gardening to construction. When I come home at night, I'm beaten down – so tired I don't have the strength to eat. I sincerely want to go to school, but I feel trapped. I've already given up trying to make my life better. I know it will just never happen."

"Stop, Odilon! That's not what I want to hear! There's hope for a better tomorrow now, so don't give up to poverty. I'm sure you've been listening to Zebeda, haven't you? Hope hasn't run this high in decades, maybe longer."

"Yes, I have. And I was enthusiastic about many things he said. I felt as if he were my voluntary lawyer, defending me in a court of law.

I've even been thinking of joining the fighters." Odilon drew up to his full height, which was not much.

"You can go to school and still be a member of the RRF. Beginning next week in the back room of this clinic, there will be night classes for people who are busy working during the day. My colleagues and I will be the teachers. I'm expecting you there."

"Okay, Doc! That sounds like a great plan to me!"

"Go back to your mother, I'll see you soon."

Odilon passed through the waiting room on his way outside. There were many people waiting to be seen – babies crying on their mothers' laps, infants crawling aimlessly under the watchful eyes of their parents, and older folks from as far away as Fond Philippe, near Cazalie behind the steepest mountains of the province. That little waiting room was stretched beyond its capacity.

Jézula, an old woman, paced back and forth with ever-mounting impatience. Her cow-skin sandals, hidden beneath her ragged karako, clapped against the wooden floor with each step. Her dark, purple-crimson-rimmed eyes widened and turned moist each time the consultation room door cracked open, and the doctor's assistant stepped out to call the next patient. Her wrinkled cheeks drooped in distress, her haggard face expressing disappointment whenever she was not called.

Newly arrived toddlers sprinted into their mothers' loving arms, hiding deep within them at the sight of Jézula—they thought she was a sorceress! No, she was merely lost in deep pain, comforted only by her teenage granddaughter, Egrenia, a barefoot, pretty girl with a wide gap between her two front teeth, dressed in a loose, shapeless, faded button-down garment. Egrenia flapped a shredded straw hat in front of her grandmother, using it as a floppy fan, but it failed to ease the suffocating heat that rippled through her grandmother's pain like waves of stone.

Marveling at this scene, Odilon stepped onto the terrace to watch a horde of peasants pouring in like a cavalcade of sweet black syrup from all the rural sections of Saint Louis. As he crossed the street, Cécile waited for him, a bowl of *piskèt* folded inside her plastic bag. Overjoyed, Odilon poked at the tiny, living fish—minnows and silvery others—zigzagging inside the clear wet bag.

As the rumors of oncoming conflict spread to the villages, anxious villagers were rushing into town to buy whatever they could carry before the fighting broke out again. This sudden onslaught of peasants on a weekday turned into a panicked, tremendous confusion that Saint Louis had never experienced before. Pedestrians bumped against mules and horse riders, bicycles and motorcycles competed with automobiles – raising clouds of dust over the unpaved, narrow dirt streets.

Panhandlers stationed on street corners wiped sweat, blood, and dust from their tear-filled eyes. Domestic servants marched through the marketplace, scrambling to grab whatever the peasants had left behind. Homeless, bony children were chased by skinny, snarling dogs snapping at their heels. People trotted past, their ribcages visible beneath their flapping clothes. The bloodshed and violence had transformed Saint Louis into a city on the brink of disaster.

The entire town was alive, but just barely; thieves were on high alert, preparing to strike their next victims. Everyone jogged up and down, bouncing like flies in a rushing free-for-all of hardship and pain, displaying overjoyed celebration one minute, sadness and unlimited terror the next.

In the community of Vertus, northernmost suburb of uptown Saint Louis, desperate residents were mesmerized by the latest turn of events. Most of its inhabitants were jobless individuals relying on relatives living overseas, mostly in the Bahamas and in South Florida, to send much-needed cash to stay alive. The fortunate few who survived on their own were also feeling the pinch. They could only watch as their savings drained dry, and there was nothing they could do about it.

The central government in Port-au-Prince blockaded the province, and basic necessities became scarce while prices soared. Even the coffee speculators, normally staying way above any hardship, were forced to shut down on their allies of convenience – seaside *bourgeois konpradò* near the Port-au-Prince harbor, who were being prevented from entering the province to buy the lucrative coffee beans.

In this chain of exploitation, local coffee speculators were the middlemen, paying coffee growers from the peasantry next to nothing. They stole the crops from these poor subsistent farmers, who at the break of day braved the morning dew, the snake-infested forests, their hunger, the ill-fated haze, and all other forms of human misery to bring those coffee crops to harvest. The middlemen then turned around and sold it for a modest price to greedy coffee exporters—Arabs and mixed-race businessmen alike from the downtown district in Port-au-Prince—with no shame, no sense of patriotism, and worst of all, no sense of industrial development. These furtive *bourgeois konpradò* were motivated by greed, by raw exploitation of the disenfranchised masses. But these "coffee growers" remained unnerved, consumed by deep-seated prejudices, focusing only on an underhanded inheritance, an unexplained short-sightedness, and a complete lack of vision for the "motherland" – even as their country crumbled into blood-soaked road dust around them.

Popo Laurentin, richest *grandon* and most powerful speculator in Vertus, was forced to close down his great storage hall filled with humungous one-hundred-pound sacks of coffee. The future looked bleak for people like him. Uncertainty kept them wide awake at night. He, and those like him, whose interests were completely at odds with the wretched masses, felt paralyzed by the arrival of the RRF at their front doors. It had become a constant nightmare. These people were praying, desperate for government soldiers to fight their way into town and bring a hasty return to the shameful status quo and its ante.

But on this day, Popo could only dream of such distant realities. Whatever was burning inside of him must be concealed, deep beneath the most remote fibers of his broken soul.

As Odilon and Cécile were rushing around outside, they could not keep themselves from casting a glance at Popo, who sat in his rocking chair on his front porch across the street, gazing upward and biting his nails. His face dull, his skin withered, he appeared drawn by the weight of uncertainty. His mouth tightened as strange, shadowy circles began to form around his eyes. This became more apparent as he cast down a forced smile at any pedestrian seeking accountancies from him. He rocked his chair, trying to appear nonchalant, while the gray poodle sitting on his lap wagged its tail. The poor nervous animal kept squeezing its head between its front paws. The little dog was voracious, but Popo was unaware of this as he cradled his half-starved poodle.

Like every coastal town, Saint Louis could not escape the harsh reality of class antagonisms. Every time internal conflicts break out in a country, conflicting interests from the different layers of society always collide. The masses applauded the revolution, and they embraced their hardships with stride. The privileged few, however, opposed it with uncontrolled hatred. The stakes were too high for both sides.

Odilon shook his head in disbelief. "*Manman!*" he screamed over the crowd noises, "I can't believe this is Popo! He looks so different than when I saw him last month, not the happy man I've known. What's going on here?"

"People are scared…I'm not going to pretend, my son: I'm frightened, don't know how much longer I can take this confusion. Popo must be afraid of losing it all."

"I'm not afraid, *Manman*. I really believe the rumors are false."

"I hope I'm wrong, but I sense something terrible is going to happen. We've been lucky so far. The war hasn't come down to us."

"*Manman*, if government soldiers were marching into town, the RRF would've told everyone to be on the alert and ready to evacuate."

They stepped down the terrace, making their way into the crowd as the scalding temperatures from the merciless tropical sun beat down on them. Beyond the shelter of the modest buildings, the sun rose to its peak, stabbing at the people with knife-like rays as the desperate pedestrians rushed through the marketplace.

The humidity was unbearable, bathing everyone in bitter, salty sweat. As people walked down the dusty main street, the heat became more intense. Dust rose in clouds from dozens of passing vehicles, painting people's faces and hair in the broad strokes of a muddy ash-grey. Their torn, billowing clothes soaked up drops of sweat, running in rivulets down their bodies, creating a rising steam that made it difficult to breathe. Nonetheless, they all had to hurry—before supplies ran out at the marketplace.

There was nowhere to hide. There were no sidewalks, no public fountains to get water to quench their thirst.

"*Manman*," Odilon gasped, his chest heaved as he panted, "The heat is worse than usual…I can't take it any longer. It's too hot. I'm thirsty…hungry."

"I'm hungry too. But what's bothering me most is the humidity, the dust…"

"Are you feeling all right, *Manman*?"

"No, I'm not…I'm going to pass out, 'less I find something to drink."

"Is your blood pressure high? Are you feeling dizzy?"

"I'm not sure…" Cécile whispered. Odilon could barely hear her over the mutual roaring of the crowd and the bloated sun. "…not feeling well."

They finally reached Nan Gwo Twou, a volatile section sheltering a densely populated shantytown. Here, Odilon and Cécile came across Capricine Adèle, a middle-aged woman with a nut-brown tan. This *bourgeois*, high-class woman was hastening in the opposite direction of

Odilon and his mother, like many others. She used to be the "Princess Charming" of this tightly-packed tin-plated community, its most heavenly prize for hundreds of local suitors. She had been a red-hot knockout, gut-wrenching beauty queen. But with time, her youthful glow had receded. Any natural beauty left required subtle craftsmanship from makeup to keep it alive.

Adèle was shielding her face with a parasol. Seeing Odilon and his mother, she turned her almost lovely head sideways to avoid making eye contact. Odilon got the message, hardening his face and quickening his march. Empowered by revolutionary fervor, wilted by the sun's fever, he would not be pushed around by those standing arrogantly in the top echelons of society.

Further south, they met Melanie, rushing like the others. Her face was flaky, mud-colored and dry, blushed with clots of grey dust. Her hands were rough and callused, hardened like concrete from years of labor under the unforgiving sun. She was a laundry lady, scrubbing clothes with her bare hands down along the riverbed. Hopelessness chiseled into her gaunt fac. Her ragged blue dress was turning grey, sun-bleached by time. It did not hide what was obvious. Ravaged by corns, her feet displayed bloody lacerations, worst around her dull, split-open toenails.

Melanie was once the prettiest girl in Nan Gwo Twou, with lustrous, green, playful kitten eyes that stood out against her coffee-colored complexion. She had beautiful, button-hole cheeks that enhanced her exuberant smiling features. Not being flamboyant like Adèle, who liked to brag about her self-confidence, Melanie's faultless composure had been enough to make her coy smile attract many flirtatious men. These days, however, her youthful glow gave way to a careworn, resigned old-looking woman, one overwhelmed by blatant poverty and outright despair.

"*Bounjou, Konmè Melanie,*" Odilon grinned – grimacing really upon meeting Melanie. Cécile gave her a somewhat repressed smile.

"How are you guys?" Melanie drawled, showing quiet uneasiness.

"I'm doing fine, but *Manman* is not. We've been rushing to find what we can get from the marketplace."

"You need to hurry up," Melanie's breath was hot as she gasped, "because I just came from there, and what I saw was indescribable: people shoving people into the dirt to grab whatever they could lay their hands on. Prices were exorbitant, only going up, so I returned empty-handed. I'm going to die from hunger. It's been two days since I put something in my mouth. Unless a miracle takes place, a lot of people are going to die." Melanie's eyes turned teary. She moved away, walking northward. Odilon and his mother decided to continue south toward the marketplace.

They walked into the Lòtbò Pon neighborhood, where they met a group of teenagers, boys and girls, all in their bathing suits and appearing lighthearted and unaware of the harsh reality of their surroundings.

A jealous Odilon stared at the teenagers, envious of their happiness. He had to admit that he wished to be one of them. These carefree youngsters were laughing, joking, and gossiping about "you know what?". Teenagers talk about something, anything, and nothing when they congregate. One of the girls told a story about an albino man named Joe Lidi, who lived at the edge of the bridge, and Cécile overheard her.

She was not pleased. "Children aren't supposed to make fun of adults. God will surely punish you," she called, her voice stern.

"Look," her son interposed. "We're already in Marché Mercredi. Why don't we go to the RRF office and ask for fresh water? They have doctors inside. Maybe someone might be able to help you," Odilon suggested.

Exhausted, thirsty, and hungry, Odilon and Cécile crossed the street, pushing their way through a crowd of people milling around in front of RRF headquarters. Since the revolutionary victory, there were always large groups of people inside that building, seeking retribution for past abuses they had suffered at the hands of the former police.

Unfortunately, they were mainly filing complaints against people who had already fled, which made their complaints impossible to enforce.

The building was a three-story mansion, made of bricks with huge metal doors. It was surrounded by a six-foot concrete wall and fortified by heavy sandbags, a clear sign that the war was not over. Painted in beige, the building emitted a fine quality of freshness – thanks to its distance from the dust-filled main street. A lush garden of exotic hibiscus shrubs and tropical flora reinforced the beauty of the mansion. It contained twenty rooms, including a sizeable eleven-by-seventeen living room that Zebeda had converted into a reception room that he used to receive the media and other important guests.

A breezeway lined with almond trees connected the double front doors to the main road. The house was the former home of a prior government commissioner in the 1940s, who sold the property to an Arab merchant in 1948. This was two years after President Elie Lescot was forced from power in 1946, under pressure from angry, politically charged university students. The RRF seized the estate after they overran the town, making the mansion their main operational urban base.

"I've never been in here before," said Odilon, walking toward a receptionist standing at her desk.

"What can I do for you, young man?" the slight young woman smiled, likely in her early twenties. She was tall, dressed in a neatly pressed and starched olive-green military uniform – revolver at her hip, and an AK-47 lay on the desk.

"My mother's not feeling well. Her mouth feels dry; she's thirsty and dizzy. Is there any way she can see a nurse?" Odilon asked. His mother was sitting bowed-over in a chair at the opposite corner of the room.

"Sure, she can," replied the ever-smiling young woman. "Where is your mother?" she asked, looking around the packed room.

"There she is," replied Odilon, pointing to Cécile.

The young lady walked around her desk to greet the old lady, who by that time appeared to be passing out, about to pitch forward from her chair.

"Ma'am are you all right?" the young woman asked, her tone shifting from welcoming to concerned.

"I don't know. I'm…dizzy," Cécile answered, catching her breath.

A female nurse rushed to her aid from a back room, carrying alcohol, water, a long blue towel, and a high-blood-pressure kit. The nurse took her pulse and blood pressure. Surprisingly, everything was fine – including her blood sugar.

"Your pulse is a bit fast, but that's okay, considering the heat and humidity. I think your mother is just anxious about the confusion in town," said the nurse, facing Odilon – who was visibly relieved by the news. He gave Cécile the glass of water he had gotten from the receptionist.

"*Manman*, you scared the hell out of me!"

"Where do you live, ma'am?" the nurse asked.

"I live…in Anwodo, near Bwa Chandèl." Cécile was still somewhat out of breath and felt like she was dying of thirst. She knew she was not, though. She was more worried about Odilon than herself, as usual.

"Do you regularly go to clinics?"

"Yes."

"Which one do you go to?"

"Odilon takes me…to the one in Ti-Riviyè."

"Who is your doctor, there?"

"Dr. Duchaud…he's short, but he's a wonderful doctor."

"You have a good doctor there. I know him very well."

Odilon listened at rapt attention, knowing the connection between Dr. Duchaud and the RRF. But he did not dare show it in front of his mother. Nor did he want her to have the slightest suspicion about his conversation with Dr. Duchaud, regarding going to night classes at the clinic.

Remembering the crowd at the marketplace, Odilon grasped his mother's trembling hand. "*Manman*, if you feel better now, we have to do our shopping. Remember, we have no gas, no salt, no sugar, and no soap. We need to hurry…before everything is gone."

"You're right…we have to get back on the road again," replied Cécile. She tried to get up, in an attempt to leave.

"No, no…not yet, don't!" the nurse clucked, pushing her back into the chair. "Don't leave now. It's not safe or wise! You can't go back out into the same heat that exhausted you. You need to wait until the sun goes down. Besides, Dr. Duchaud will be here in about an hour. It would be best to wait here for him."

Throwing back her shaggy head, Cécile rose from the chair. "I told you I just came from his clinic. I was going down to the marketplace when I got sick. He already checked me and told me everything was fine. I feel fine now – we have to leave. We need to get to the marketplace. Thank you so much…may God bless you," said Cécile, walking with determination to the front door. Odilon soon followed.

The nurse smiled but blocked the two people from leaving. "Don't worry about the marketplace. We'll get you everything you need," she said, signaling the receptionist, who was busy writing medical info down on a legal yellow notepad.

"My girl, why show such sympathy for me?" Cécile asked, offering no resistance. She was escorted back to her chair. "Me? I'm just an old peasant woman!"

"Ma'am, the RRF always does what it can to help people like you. But we're not yet in a position to provide for everyone. I'm not sure if we ever will be."

"Why do you say that?" Odilon said, eyes wide with suspicion. He trusted the RRF but was unsure about this type of handling of his beloved mother.

"Our mission is to provide security and guidance as we accompany our brothers and sisters on their final journey to freedom.

We don't have the means to provide financial support to everyone. However, in this heroic struggle, we strongly believe that freedom is in sight. And when all the guns are silenced, each Haitian citizen will become master of his own destiny," answered the young nurse, her face lined with care beyond her years and a grim determination.

Harrumphing to get their attention, the receptionist spoke her piece. "I'll have everything ready for you, ma'am. We have lots of supplies here, right behind the counter, and when you're actually ready to leave, let me know." Her response was curt, but kind.

"What is it you have in there for us?" Odilon grinned.

"Don't worry, we have whatever you need," replied the smiling young lady.

"Don't listen to my son! He often asks silly questions. God bless you and the RRF," crowed a happy and calmer Cécile, bursting with pride at being treated like old-time royalty there at RRF headquarters. "You are all such dears!"

Five minutes later, a jeep camouflaged in dark olive-green and black jungle colors pulled up to the building. The entire security personnel, cradling their weapons, were on guard. Four large men dressed in military khaki, each wearing a bulletproof vest, jumped out from the jeep. Three of them moved in quick concert to protect a tall gentleman seated in the rear of the vehicle. They held their AK-47 assault rifles in combat-ready positions, effectively forming a human shield. Each guard planted him or herself firmly at every door, as the important man in the jeep got out and walked into the building.

"*Manman*, that's Zebeda!" Odilon screeched, astonished.

"Oh, are you sure?" Cécile replied. Pushing herself up from her chair, as she felt somewhat weak, she edged closer to the front door to witness his entrance.

"Of course I am! I've seen him before."

El comandante made his grand entrance through the front door, sending a jaunty salute to his devoted comrades. His hair bounced under his blue-black sunglasses and olive-green cap, and his black leather boots cracked like a whip with each step as he strode across the tiled entryway.

Once inside, the six-foot-tall man beamed his famous, impishly impudent grin as everyone advanced to greet him. He noticed Odilon and Cécile and strode up to them.

"Oh, Olivier, how are you?" Cécile cried out, happy to see him.

"I'm fine," replied Zebeda with a smile. "Do I know you?"

"You don't remember me, do you, Olivier?"

"No, I'm sorry…but your face looks familiar."

"It's me, Cécile Joseph from Anwodo, near Amazile's house."

"Ah, I remember now…we used to eat the delicious mangoes at Grandma Amazile's house. My mother would take me there while she went to check on the family land in Nan Banman. I'm so happy to see you, Aunt Cécile! You bring back memories of, oh, more than thirty years ago."

"Olivier, we're all scared. As you can see outside, everybody is rushing to the marketplace to buy whatever they can in preparation for another attack." Cécile peered into the giant man's beaming face. "Do you think this is true?"

Zebeda paused for a moment, pushing his beret-style cap a little backward, and took a deep breath. "You see, dear auntie, what's going on outside is the same exact thing going on in every town in the Northwest. I have just visited Port-de-Paix. People. There are…well, they're clearly losing their minds.

"As we all know, Port-de-Paix suffered the worst during the last fighting. They're still recovering; they've barely finished burying their dead. Many residents there who didn't receive any physical damage, and many who did, are now also suffering from major mental problems. Electricity is scarce, and water distribution is at a minimum. People lost their homes, children lost their parents, and elderly people have no place to go – they are now all being relocated to the covenant village in Laveaux.

"I ordered this as a temporary measure to help ease their suffering. I've just received reports of major panics in Bassin Bleu, Jean-Rabel, Môle Saint Nicolas, and most of the other towns bordering the Artibonite region. I also consult daily with my representatives in the southern region. So far, they've detected no troop redeployment from the enemy side. What's going on now is called psychological warfare. What I mean is the fascist regime is now using fear tactics – through both radio and word of mouth – to spread false rumors in order to make us afraid." Zebeda smiled through bared teeth at his carefully chosen words, as everyone listened with bated breath.

"That's what I thought! Those thugs will never come back!" Cried Odilon, Zebeda's words filled him with deep reassurance. He stuck out his scrawny chest and gave a loud crow as he thumped it three times to show his power and determination—a Haitian tradition. Everyone hooted in total agreement with the young peasant from Anwodo.

"Well, my son," Zebeda quieted the mood, "We can't be naïve, thinking that they're not preparing to attack again. I'm sure they're cooking up something. Do I know when they'll make good on their promise to 'smash' us, as Ti-Jean says? I really don't know. Our cells in Port-au-Prince have informed us of a major counter-offensive that the government is preparing. Since we broke their backbone last week, and since the Haitian Army is in no shape to launch an offensive on the scale they've been bragging about, foreign troops would have to be called in – probably American ones."

"What should we do in a situation like this?" inquired a bespectacled elderly woman, piping up from the crowd of people gathered inside the building.

"Do what the RRF has been preaching on the radio: remain vigilant, always ready, but calm. We'll never abandon our people. From the beginning, we've made it clear that our mission is to provide all forms of security to the population as it embarks on this historic struggle to rid our people from tyranny, humiliation, and exploitation. In the RRF, we know they'll return.

"We also know that we're ready to repel any attack, wherever and whenever it occurs. Every day we have people joining our ranks, and we've never been stronger in spirit, numbers, and logistics. Each passing hour, victory comes closer…I can smell it. So, I'm asking everybody to go home and listen. Please, listen to the RRF radio. It's your best source of information for any new developments. I love you all!"

Zebeda gave a jubilant shout, throwing kisses with both hands to the hero-worshipping crowd. Wheeling about in true military fashion, as befits a proper people's soldier, he entered the conference room to confer with his security personnel. The crowd dispersed, leaving Odilon and Cécile with a bag full of the needed supplies they had received from the smiling receptionist.

Chapter 10

Saint Louis had emerged as the nerve center of the revolution, not by pure providence, but rather for what it once was in many aspects. For years, the town was the social-looking-glass through which a sharp divide between the arrogant rich and the disenfranchised masses could be seen. But if there was a section of town where such arrogance was the rawest, it was in Lòtbò Pon. Young men from this neighborhood were flamboyant, and the ladies were so proud of themselves that it was almost impossible to win their hearts – unless one was of a certain social standing.

Youngsters from the other parts of town called them clannish, shunning them with contemptuous irreverence. But there were exceptions, however scanty they may have been. For example, there was Angeline Dominier: a tall, slim girl with the hue of milk chocolate candy, unique features and a distinct assertiveness beyond compare. She freely succumbed to Adrian, an unobtrusive young man from Vertus, to the outright shock of her family. Adrian was Odilon's cousin.

Most boys were intimidated by Angeline's decisive, feisty, domineering, and sometimes overbearing attitudes. Appearances can be deceiving. Angeline's love was not skin-deep, as Adrian boasted to his friends. She was romantically real, soulful, and softer than a dove's outstretched wings, with a deep-seated sentimentalism that young men in Lòtbò Pon yearned for.

Another local girl, Rosaline Justin, a reddish-brown cinnamon roll with droopy bedroom eyes, firm straight breasts and bulging taut buttocks – who spoke flawless Parisian French – claimed she wanted nothing to do with boys from Vertus, as well as those from the Downtown District. Shaped like a Coca-Cola bottle when stationary, Rosaline made the boys crazy as she stood draped over her front porch, showing off her *décolleté* while manicuring her long red fingernails. But she was pretentious, egotistical, snobbish, and inexplicably scornful. And like the rest of her peers, she was also cocoonish – living her life in her own little world.

A handsome, short, and clever young man named Eddy Eustache from Latiroli in the southern fringes of town was madly in love with her. However, she rebuffed his overtures at every turn, claiming the boy was the son of a goat herder, despite the fact that the young man was in college in Port-au-Prince, living in a boarding school. Everyone else in Lòtbò Pon saw in Eddy a quick-witted, fastidious and rational character that any parent would hope to acquire for their daughter.

Few youngsters outside Rosaline's box mingled with her. She was the daughter of Altéon Justin, renowned country folk musician – he even owned the only music store in town. Altéon also owned one of the biggest folk bands, competing only with Fasio Joseph, master of square-dancing from Desrouvrays, a hillside village near the southeastern part of town.

Lòtbò Pon got its name from a rickety bridge that carved a jagged swath through the rest of the town. People there felt a sense of exclusiveness that they did not want to lose, even as time wore on and their "exclusivity" grew more and more precarious – and morally repugnant.

Many people in Saint Louis were furious about this. For the sake of the nation, Haiti must come first, St. Louis' youngsters cried out when referring to the inhabitants of Lòtbò Pon. Unless national unity crafted under an utmost patriotism was achieved, every Haitian was doomed to suffer a similar fate, others would say, stating that petty prejudice has no place in a country on the brink of disaster.

But folks in Saint Louis were no different from those in other parts of the country. When life is tough and opportunities are scarce, the privileged classes usually adopt a cloistered attitude of self-defense, imposing an imaginary caste system through psychological, and sometimes physical torture. They are the lone wolves the lower-class people would love to emulate but are terribly afraid of. Saint Louis was a mirror reflection of the complex nuances existing in society at large.

Before the revolution's fever, Saint Louis was an ordinary town inhabited by ordinary people: humble, full of good humor, and resourceful. It was a town filled with happy children, yet unaware of the intricacies of life. Most importantly, like children everywhere, they were oblivious, unenlightened about the daily injustices their parents faced. These parents understood that children never ask to be born. They must be happy and should never be asked to share any unspoken parental ordeals.

Summer was the best of times. It was when the kids were out of school. French ditties blared through the cacophonous airwaves, and the girls felt an awesome pride in singing the latest from Mireille Mathieu, Sylvie Vartan, and Isabelle Aubret. The boys were busy bragging about the latest movies, starring either Alain Delon or Jean Paul Belmundo. Field trips on weekdays, picnics on Saturdays, "*bal des enfants*" on Sundays, it was a time of *joie-de-vivre*, and the rosy days seemed endless.

Sunday afternoon, the main destinations were the nightclubs in town: *Beau Rivage*, or Beautiful Shore, and *Coquillage*, or Seashell. Their names were due to their geographic locations —facing the turquoise waters near the seashore. Shame was heaped liberally upon any boy who could not be in one of the two places on Sunday. Music has no boundaries, and so children from all parts of town rendezvoused there – including the withdrawn group from Lòtbò Pon.

Handsome young men dressed in the latest fashions waited patiently to win the heart of at least one pretty young lady, each displaying the rich, attractive hues that characterize the magnificence of black women. You name it, they were there! The golden honeys, the nut-browns, the jet-black straight coffees, the reddish-brown cinnamons, the milk chocolates, or the *café-au-laits* – all were there for male beauty hunters to admire, and to catch if they could.

For the highschoolers on vacation, romance was the topic of the day, and everything else deemed of strategic importance must be forsaken for the furtherance of love. A boy named Chico with a nut-brown complexion and ridiculously handsome black eyes, outmaneuvered more than a dozen competitors in one Sunday's hunt to catch the heart of Martine, the most charming girl in Sou Fò, an upscale part of town. Martine was tall and slender, graceful in a sleek way – with adamantine eyes and coffee-colored skin, carefully moisturized with fancy creams. As she walked downhill to the town's main square, her strolls commanded a lot of attention. She looked voluptuous, fancifully and eternally beautiful.

The news of Chico's win over Martine mesmerized his male peers, especially the boys from Marché Mercredi, where he lived. Adding to this dark-chocolate love was Chico's upbringing. The son of a preacher, brought up behind the pulpit of his father, Chico was the last boy one would suspect of becoming an exotic player. But he was a sweet talker who promised everything; and Martine, following her heart, fell into his seductive, loving arms in a kind of bittersweet bewilderment.

Gaining fame for winning Martine, Chico soon found the girls rushing to get a piece of him. Even a mixed-raced girl like Yamilay, with long golden hair and slanted eyes, was going crazy for him. The product of a Haitian-Chinese gentleman and a woman from Saint Louis, she was the town's ultimate prize to win. She was not crafty like some of her peers. She was downright foxy, playfully mischievous, often throwing her sly smile at anyone for pleasure. Breasts shaped like a pair of plum puddings were wrapped below her reddish-brown cinnamon tan.

Yet at sundown, when the tropical breeze began to filter through, Yamilay could be found sitting atop a huge boulder near the Saint Louis River basin, naked from the waist up – combing her long yellow hair into twin pigtails. Awestruck, the boys whiled away their time contemplating this most gratifying splendor. That beautiful girl, with an edible drupaceous-fruit profile and her own pristine character – she was widely thought to be a virgin – fell into Chico's arms one Saturday afternoon. It happened in a sandy cove near the river delta on the edge of town. In an instant, he was crowned the town's number one *romancero*.

It was truly the best of times back then, but soon lost in the perplexity of life, giving way to incertitude with its accompanying, dallying bitchiness. Oh well – those "happy times" were never happy for all. Only a few could enjoy those unforgettable moments. To the vast majority in Saint Louis, life had always been hellish. Few work opportunities existed. For those lucky enough to secure petty jobs, life was difficult. It was impossible to live a decent lifestyle on those meager salaries. However, while the revolution had only worsened economic stagnation, those who were dirt-poor before the war claimed they had nothing to lose, as they had nothing to begin with.

Chapter 11

By ten a.m., the bustling capital city of Port-au-Prince was locked into a state of high anxiety. Even "low" eighty-five-degree temperatures, laced by Haiti's moist tropical winds, made the heat index land within the hundred-degree range. This failed to dampen the uprising spirits of thousands of nearby villagers descending upon the town, demanding social change and the immediate removal of Ti-Jean's hated government.

The desert-hued outlines of the barren mountain chain surrounding the eastern side of the city backdropped a surging sea of dark-skinned angry profiles, as demonstrators streamed in from the mountain communities to join the thousands already stationed on the Champs-De-Mars, the city's main public square – just a few hundred feet from the national palace.

"*Aba Ti-Jean, viv RRF, viv Zebeda!*" the riotous crowd screamed. With tensions running high, the government officials ordered their security forces to take up positions at strategic locations around the city, ensuring the demonstrators were kept at bay. Key installations were secured, lines of demarcation drawn, and armed police barricades lodged into place. A looming bloody showdown was inevitable.

By midday, Ti-Jean summoned his entire cabinet for a crisis meeting as an escalation of shuttle diplomacy began between the national palace and the US embassy, supported by both France and Canada. Other representatives of the *bourgeoisie*, foreign investors and marginalized traditional politicians (commonly labeled "the political class") assumed their roles, dying to take part in these important matters.

Once again in the war room, top advisors, cabinet ministers, and the military high command were soon apprised of the situation as Ti-Jean ordered his topmost officials to take immediate action to avert the forthcoming holocaust of public violence.

"We must find a solution. We must find it now!" bellowed Ti-Jean, slamming his fist on the vibrating mahogany conference table. His ministers and other political advisors trembled in fear – for their jobs and their lives.

"I totally agree with you, Mr. President. But there seems to be no clear solution to the problem…that we can see," said his prime minister.

"You're in charge of the government! You shouldn't have let the situation deteriorate!" Ti-Jean asserted, shaking a finger at his entire cabinet.

"But…Mr. President," the upper-crust man argued, "I don't think it's wise to start putting the blame on me. You can blame or even fire me, but I'm afraid our current measures are not strong enough to reverse the situation. They will only expose our weaknesses, showing the world that we're in total chaos."

"Don't be silly. Dismissing the government and creating a standby coalition will put us in a much stronger position to deal with Zebeda."

"There's no need to do that, Mr. President. The entire opposition is already on our side. The big-business establishment, the Planters Association, and the foreign embassies are all united behind our goal to crush Zebeda."

"You're right," Ti-Jean said, "but before coming to this meeting, my office received a fax confirming America's approval of our requests for military assistance."

The entire cabinet applauded, some of them cheering. Shaking their manicured hands all around, they swiftly raised their wine glasses to toast the good news. But following the toast, there was an eerie moment of complete silence. Everyone looked at one another, wondering what their next move would be.

"Politics is Hell," coughed one cabinet minister into his handkerchief. "…it's simply, truly Hell."

Finally, Justic Minister André Malveaux raised his hand to speak. Malveaux, a forty-five-year-old, tall, mixed-race gentleman with a golden tan and black-bushy eyebrows, sat adjacent to the president. A social democrat flirting with Marxism in his early years, Malveaux was a soft-worded individual who rarely spoke in meetings, but he was considered the most astute among Ti-Jean's wolf-pack. He was no button-down technocrat, though his trademark sports jacket suited over a flannel shirt with no necktie gave people that impression at first glance.

His straight black hair, neatly combed back, and the silverfish pipe clenched between his teeth at the corner of his mouth only accentuated his intellectual demeanor. A strange uneasiness among his peers, particularly during war decision-making meetings, positioned Malveaux as the quintessential petty bourgeois. He expressed sympathy for the masses' social disenfranchisement, demonstrating an acute understanding of the materialist dialectic in the context of Haitian history. However, he was not yet ready to abandon his social aspirations of becoming a cabinet minister and make the final journey to freedom alongside the very people he professed to love.

"We must have a clear understanding of what we are about to do," Malveaux stated, with his typical cool presumptuousness.

"Where are you coming from?" asked the irked president.

"I mean, we should prepare for the consequences."

"What consequences are you talking about?"

"I smell blood…lots of it…genocide."

"I know people will die; that's what war is! So be it. I won't be the first Haitian president who used force to restore order. This won't even make a big splash – it's in a very small pond. The Northwest is…isolated. We can impose a blackout on the news coming out of there, allowing only our government-dedicated journalists to cheer and speak for us. Besides, the foreign press is sympathetic – just read their editorials, why don't you?"

"I understand, Mr. President…I just don't think we can act like our predecessors. We've received a mandate to put an end to that. We promised the people that we would steer the country in a new direction. We can't go on the offensive against them, for the same reason they voted us into office. We'd be regarded as traitors.

"I believe we need to act rationally. We need to take criticism, and admit we've made mistakes. Understanding the people's grievances is legitimate. We must have the courage to do that…killing people in revolutionary crowds is considered to be a form of modern genocide. It's clearly out of the question." Malveaux was firm in his carefully-chosen words.

"Do you mean I must capitulate, resign my office, invite Zebeda to march triumphantly into my capital – à la Fidel Castro – to take over my kingdom?" Breathing hard, the president thrust out his head, eyes bulging from their sockets.

"No, sir…that's not what I mean."

Complete stillness filled the room. Stern men froze in absolute terror, wrinkled mummies in a mass sarcophagus, as Malveaux and Ti-Jean continued their bitter, differing dialogue.

"Mr. Malveaux, you are surely dreaming. I've always looked upon you as an important statesman. I'm having second thoughts! You really don't believe in the authority of the State. We cannot let Marxists take over our country. I wouldn't be a responsible president if that was to happen, would I?" Ti-Jean growled, looking straight at the Malveaux.

"I strongly believe that it would be a mistake to be on the opposite side of the people. I'm always careful in analyzing a situation. I don't see things in black-and-white, unlike some people." Malveaux deliberately looked away from the president. "There are shades of grey…there's still time for peaceful solutions." The man was hiding angry shivering – emotionally spent. He tilted sideways, glancing at the immense patriotic portrait of Jean-Jacques Dessalines on the wall. Then, as if he was trying to swallow a gasping breath, he continued.

"Going against the masses to please those who see them as barbarous, thieves, lazy, half-human – as beasts to be placated and zombified – will only inflame their anger, radicalizing them even more, and pushing them deeper into Zebeda's camp.

"The insensitive people believe only in keeping the masses ignorant, illiterate, and in abject poverty. To them, this is necessary to maintain their own daily safety and privilege forever. I cannot be part of that. I'm resigning from my post."

The Justice Minister, without giving Ti-Jean a chance to reply, stormed out of the room – to the shocked astonishment of his colleagues. He didn't make it far, though; Ti-Jean quickly ordered the palace guards to stop him.

As he reached the palace lawn, he was apprehended by two guards dragging him back inside, where he was taken to meet Ti-Jean face-to-face in the war room. Malveaux's sports jacket was wrinkled up and unsightly, and his right sleeve torn wide open in his mighty struggles with the palace guards. A major blow to his mouth sent his silver pipe flying across the palace lobby – like a rocket launched on a deadly mission. It bounced against the ceiling, falling onto one of the plush velvet window draperies, gushing dark tobacco traces all over it. This irritated the sergeant guard leading the apprehension operation.

A short and stocky man, bulky brown fingers laden with gold-chunky rings, the sergeant swiftly closed his rough, outstretched hands. He tightened his golden fingers, closing his meaty palms and balling them into deadly fists. With brutal force, he unleashed an avalanche of blows on Malveaux's face, the gold nuggets perforating his forehead and swelling his left eyebrow. Blood spurted from the wounds in gushing trails, like a river in a scarlet blur, springing out of the ground and watering everything nearby.

Stoically, Malveaux resisted, never losing consciousness; but he was no match for these well-armed savage hawks, men who worshiped torture only to gain in military promotion. Like a stubborn child rebelling against the natural order, he was dragged by the legs, kicking strongly as he could. He was then carried upstairs to the war room – in the midst of rapid footsteps, slamming doors, and high-pitched screeches and sounds.

Stunned officers with blazing eyes muttered their curiosity, standing at attention in long lines along the corridors. Some of them, lost in total disbelief, raised their entwined fingers above their heads, while others, in complete shock, leaned with their backs against the walls. They watched in mounting terror as Malveaux was led inside by his captors. Completely baffled, paralyzed, and spooked, they wondered at this, for Malveaux was a man of pristine character, considered one of the most respected politicians within the Ti-Jean government.

As they reached the main entrance to the war room, which was wide open, one of the guards used the butt of his rifle to push Malveaux toward the president, who refused to look his former justice minister in the eye.

"Shoot me if you can!" shouted Malveaux, facing Ti-Jean as the other cabinet ministers gazed at this incredible scene, mumbling in utmost astonishment.

Malveaux stood erect but dazed, weaving back and forth under the weight of a myriad of heavy kicks and blows. Sweat mixed with blood poured from his gashed-open cheeks, streaming through his moisture-stained flannel shirt. Bloody and bowed, he knew his fate was sealed, but he strongly desired to take a courageous stand against what he believed was a doomed regime. Ironically, he must have inwardly thanked the guards for giving him this last opportunity.

Almost everyone else in the room froze in fear, trying clumsily to suppress their emotions.

Ti-Jean did not reply to Malveaux's brave statement. Instead, he raised his right hand – twisting his thumb down, signaling his butchers that they were free to do away with the former justice minister. Another guard attempted to drag Malveaux back out of the room, but he refused, forcing himself down to the floor.

"You're a shameless coward. Go face the people, if you have the guts!" Malveaux screamed.

The guards lined up, their fingers dancing on the triggers, while the prisoner was pushed against the wall adjacent to Ti-Jean's seat.

"Shoot him," Ti-Jean growled at the guards, who instantly unleashed a hail of bullets into Malveaux's chest.

Eyes unyielding as he collapsed on the floor, he kept looking straight at Ti-Jean. "Haiti will not perish…you will…" he wheezed, rendering his last breath.

The situation outside the presidential palace remained chaotic. In the Bicentenaire section by the Port-au-Prince harbor, thousands attempted to storm the Parliament building. They were repelled by riot police throwing tear gas into the mob. The crowd dispersed after a two-hour standoff, but not before an enraged police officer ran amok and was struck hard by a hail of stones thrown by a group of teens hiding behind the Parliament building. Infuriated, the officer raced after them.

As the other children fled the snarling officer, one of them bumped his feet against a giant boulder on the pavement, sprawling in a heap on the torn-up ground. He was now at the mercy of the enraged *gendarme*, who grabbed him by the throat like a starving *malfini* on his first catch. The boy screamed, but quickly subdued under the tight grip of the officer, who dashed him to the ground. With the heel of one black leather boot, he stomped him on the neck and head until his tongue turned blue, sticking out of his mouth as blood gushed from his nose and ears.

The major arteries around downtown Port-au-Prince streamed furious, swollen rivers after a violent rainstorm. Trails of politically-charged Haitians swelled the streets for miles, waving olive branches in the air to cries of *"Aba Ti-Jean!"* Thousands of their compatriots stood on balconies lining both sides of every street. In response, they banged empty aluminum casserole dishes loud and clear, showing total defiance to the regime. Meanwhile, hundreds of tap-tap drivers blatantly blew their horns in solidarity with the demonstrators' demands.

Further east, three-hundred-thousand demonstrators invaded the palace square, soon approaching the front gates. Special units from the elite presidential guards moved in, shooting the crowd at close range, killing hundreds and wounding thousands. Shrieking, the people pulled back as heaps of bodies littered the streets. A lifeless child lying on the roadside was smashed open like a rotting pumpkin by the government's armored vehicles. Security forces now patrolled the perimeter around the palace – keeping the enraged demonstrators at bay.

By four o'clock in the afternoon, news-breaking headlines hit the airwaves: Radio Nationale announced the assassination of Justice Minister Malveaux. A *communiqué* claimed that he was killed by an angry mob as he drove into a gas station in Lalue, near the main road leading east to the suburban town of Pétionville. Knowing better than this, few people believed this assertion. Malveaux had been somewhat beloved by the people for his occasional caring views.

To the south of the city, in the suburban section of Carrefour, demonstrators burned a government-controlled police station to the ground. They effectively blocked the main road leading south to the rest of the country to the cry of *"Viv Zebeda!"*

By six o'clock in the evening, Zebeda's Rebel Radio was on the air – starring the giant man, who had a desperate speech to make.

"We're asking the heroic people of Haiti to stand firm in the face of death, destruction, fear, and humiliation. The regime is now at its twilight. We won't be intimidated by false accusations, lies, and threats. Our sources in Port-au-Prince have informed us that Justice Minister André Malveaux, a popular man of the people, was assassinated inside the National Palace by the Creole fascists. This was done under the direct supervision of Ti-Jean – for opposing their genocidal plans to eliminate everyone in the Northwest.

"In the RRF, we stand ready to face any attack by Ti-Jean and his international plotters, goons, and *bourgeois* cronies. We're reaching the revolution's final phase; but it will only grow bloodier, uglier, and more deadly as the recalcitrant *bourgeoisie* and its lackeys feel increasingly threatened. As we always say in the RRF, the day the dominant classes in Haiti feel cornered will be the day they unleash the biggest weapons from their arsenal. What we're witnessing now is a classic replay of the gruesome oppression that took place during the grisly days of the Papa Doc regime in the 1960s. I know how badly they want to lace me with bullets – as they did our beloved justice minister. But what they fail to understand is that while Olivier Zebeda is the leader of this whole movement, he is by no means the embodiment of this revolution.

"What's going on right now has its roots in the people's determination to be free at last, after almost two hundred years of unbearable oppression. In the RRF, we know things will get darker before they get brighter; but we smell freedom. We see it rising behind the heavy grey clouds, billowing on the horizon. Soon, it will be a brand-new day!

"Under the direct guidance of the spirit of Charlemagme Masséna Peralte, Benoit Batraville, Jacques Stephen Alexis, Jean-Jacques Dessalines Ambroise, and still more of our predecessors – who gave their lives to make this country better – freedom will once again shine. Let freedom ring throughout the land! It will ring and shine anew over our mountains, over our plateaus, over our valleys, and over our plains.

"Every Haitian will soon be master of his or her own destiny. Let's not be disturbed by our quest to rid *Haiti Chérie* of its enemies. Remember, the people united will never be defeated. *Viv Haiti, viv* the courageous Haitian people, *viv* sweet liberty...*viv* the revolution!"

Zebeda's heartening message, relayed by every station except the government's own in the capital, poured gasoline on an already inflamed population. History has shown that the oppressed masses always play a pivotal role in shaping its course, and the people of Haiti were no different. The RRF revolutionaries were simply seizing the opportunity to accompany the people on their extraordinary journey to freedom. Though devoted to their cause, they couldn't fully grasp that they were making history. Yet, every revolution is, forever and always, a historic event.

The Ti-Jean regime, pliant to international dictates and totally beholden to the venal economic and political establishments, was at a crossroads. The slightest concession to the people's demands could be just enough to cause the beleaguered regime's downfall. Moving ahead with sustained repression could earn Ti-Jean the distinction of being the "number one butcher of the Caribbean." However, the latter option was easy for him to choose.

As a conformist politician and an affluent member of the *nouveaux riches*, Ti-Jean well understood the classic definition of class struggle – from which he had already chosen his camp. Ensconced in the driver's seat of his oppression machine, he would not hesitate to use every means at his disposal to protect the corrupt state bureaucracy, his personal interests, and those of his close associates at the upper echelon of his regime.

Meanwhile, the traditional elite—*konpradò* and dinosaurs alike— lived above the fray. Despite major past quarrels with the government, they were all desperately praying for a Ti-Jean's rapid and crushing defeat of the masses, so that the "fat cats" could resume their affluent lifestyles.

The execution of Justice Minister André Malveaux, a mixed-race individual and a prominent member of the *bourgeoisie* who joined the government because of his liberal views, was a prime example of the fragile coexistence that has always simmered between the different factions of Haiti's ruling elite. However, conventional wisdom dictated that when facing a "red" revolution, national interests must be placed high above personal ones. Among them, there was a tacit understanding that a united front was quintessential to putting one's best foot forward against a mortal enemy. The murder of Malveaux was just a minor distraction on the road to crushing Zebeda and the RRF in order to deal a major blow, once again, to the people's dream of a "brighter" tomorrow.

Ti-Jean was given a free hand to put down the rebellion. Aided by foreign interests, the government received the logistical support it needed to move against the people. By seven o'clock that night, the massive protest was crushed. Hundreds were killed; the wounded were left to die on the debris-filled, deserted streets. Hospital morgues overflowed, and emergency rooms were crammed beyond capacity.

An uneasy peace reigned. On both sides of the conflict, everyone knew the war was far from over. But the RRF remained entrenched in the Northwest, readying for their final showdown with the oppressive government.

Chapter 12

Three weeks later in the valley of Ti-Riviyè, near Saint Louis:

"Knock, knock…"

"Who's there?" asked a voice from behind the door.

"It' s me, Odilon, Aunt Cécile's son."

"Oh, yes." The door swung ajar, a slit in the darkness. "Odilon, I remember you. How's your mother doing?"

He was an old man, maybe seventy. His grizzled grey hair and scruffy beard revealed his sorrows, but the bulging muscles beneath his shirt, visible as he raised the latch, spoke of the great power within him. As he spoke through tight lips, tiny clouds of steam blew from his mouth, a tropical oddity – whenever he released his words.

"*Manman* is doing fine. Thank God, with all these things going on these days, I'm blessed that my mother is still alive…and me, too!"

"I'd be lying if I said I'm not scared," said the old man with a laugh. He didn't look like the type to be scared by anything, though. "So, what can I do you for?"

Odilon laughed right back at the old joke. "Mr. Dorgelus told me last week to come here for this job he wanted me to do."

"Did he tell you what kind of job?"

"He wants me to weed his barley field, on the other side of the hill."

"He's not here…but I'm sure you don't need him to begin the job."

"I really…need to talk with him," Odilon muttered.

"Why?"

"It's because we haven't agreed on a price."

"I see. But you can always come back this afternoon."

"Thank you. I'll do that."

Odilon slumped down the front porch, disappointed for not getting to make a little cash. He made his way south, heading in a casual trot down the walkway leading to his home. He wanted to get there as fast as his skinny legs could carry him to get out of the screaming midday heat. But the sun rose to its full roaring strength, a Brahma bull in the China shop of Haiti. It scored grooves down Odilon's back, piercing through his ragged clothes, triggering gallons of sweat to pour in blinding waves from every pore in his body. To save time, he traveled within a large cornfield that stretched all the way to the embankment of Ti-Riviyè. With each step, he pushed the old, barren, dead cornstalks aside as he maneuvered through the pathways.

The sun scorched the bushy cornfield. It whipped his exposed face, arms, and legs worse than a field overseer. He rushed along, grabbing whatever little shade he could find. Odilon stayed as close as he could to the main trail until the path began to fade. He faced the blinding, lime-green under-growths near the edges of the cornfield. His wandering led him to a chain-link fence against a ditch, several feet away from the riverbank.

"How do I get out?" he mumbled in mounting horror, fainting to distraction from the ever-increasing heat.

Clapping footsteps echoed from the main trail outside the fence. Picking his way with caution, he sneaked through the wire – seeing a line of young women carrying wooden jugs filled with river water, balancing them on their heads. They were humming old country songs to distract themselves from the unbearable, suffocating heat. As they chatted and gossiped, they loped along with energetic strides over the brown pebbles, heading east toward the mountain. Odilon recognized one short girl, golden-hued with large, appealing, almond-shaped eyes.

She sat gracefully atop her mule, seemingly unaffected by the piercing tropical sun. With her back straight and shoulders squared, she rode proudly and tall down the rocky, dusty trail. She was the only one not carrying a water jug on her head, and she was the last one in the procession, perched atop a dark-red mule with an odd greyish-white bushy tail. Instead of the traditional wide straw hat of Haiti, she wore a veil – its hood portion made from rich silk velvet, completely covering the back of her head. Most of her peers in their neighborhood shunned her for her aloof, out-of-the-norm demeanor. Her pretty, bright, floral calico garment sprawled, straggling upward each time a rolling breeze swept through from the mountain.

Her name was simple: Ilène. Her mother was Ivenante, and she was her youngest daughter. Ivenante was a well-known merchant in Fond Boulé, a small settlement along the foothills of Mòn Méris. Ilène had wanted to be a nun, ever since her parents took her to a congregational school in downtown Saint Louis. Having the distinction of being Odilon's first true love, her soft, tender voice awoke an aura of memories in his breathless mind. That had been some five years ago, when life was not so scary, the sky seemed endless, and the quest to find an infinite love was his lone, secret and sheltered unequivocal desire.

Odilon sighed as memories bubbled up; how they spent hours on the banks of a small, hidden brook. It trickled within the thick walls of a banana plantation, just east of this same cornfield. He remembered when he and his lady made love on a thick carpet of emerald, green grasses, feet gently wrestling against the rolling, splashing brook stones. Désinor Laurore, Ilène's father, owned the property. Whenever they heard footsteps coming from an unknown direction, they were quick to crawl out of the grass. They crept their way toward the thickness of the banana trees which bent forward under the immense weight of their heavy bunches.

For a while, Odilon found Paradise – without making the giant leap from Purgatory. But when Ilène rendezvoused him at the same place on a windy Saturday afternoon, amid lightning and thunder rumbling from the sky, to tell him their relationship was over and that she had made a vow to become a nun, Odilon was devastated. He spent weeks without eating, dazed like wounded rooster after a fierce cock fight. Months ran through him like water. He withdrew from his daily routine, wandering aimlessly around the rural section. Odilon would talk to himself as a loathsome ball of misery, repeating Ilène's name at every crossroads. Finally recovering from his trance-like state, he never set foot in that area again – until now. What should he do?

Ilène's bursting appearance, even as she faded away into the green foliage at the foot of the hill, lingering for a mere split-second, had brought back those hated but bittersweet memories. In an instant, sexually-charged ideas invaded his mind like a thief in the night. Ilène's gorgeous, filled-out warm body with firm, straight breasts and bulging buttocks vibrated under the harsh pressure of her close-fitting undergarment. Lasting memories of her long, loose-fitting button-down flowery gown, which made it easier for him to penetrate her in their delirious, innermost moments of sexual intercourse – all came back in a fleeting blur – haunting him with a vengeance. Groaning, he cursed the skies that he had ever come this way. What could he do now about this endless torment from their catastrophic breakup?

"Girls are necessary evils…can't live with them…can't live without them," he would arduously repeat to anyone who paid the tiniest attention to his ordeals. His everlasting hallucinations had become the talk of the day. But it also had created a window of opportunity for most other local girls, especially those living in unexplained solitude.

One of them was Odile, a jet-black coffee Manx of a girl, her feline eyes like those of a panther stalking its prey. With pinkish, well-manicured fingernails, fat, sexy lips smeared with rouge, and careful felicitous phrases when expressing her feelings in a francophiled-Creole, she intimidated all the boys.

Odile yearned for Odilon for years, ever since she returned from Cap-Haitien, where she had been the maid of a rich German-Haitian family. Her city-girl demeanor tended to keep the country boys at bay, and so she suffered. Upon hearing about the sentimental coup Ilène had dealt to Odilon, Odile was happy to fill the gap, offering her sexual urges to the man in mourning, using their almost identical names to sway him over to her desires. Dazed, Odilon rebuffed every coy advance, because he was too heartbroken to notice her.

She lived along the foothills of Morne Lecturne in the settlement of Legros Pierre Jean, with her father, a well-off peasant owning several pigs and goats. On market days, whether Wednesday or Saturday, she would make Anwodo her main transit village, finding every excuse to stop by Odilon's house in a desperate attempt to square her love with his. When all that failed, she accused Odilon of being feeble-minded – an eccentric punk who was not ready for love at its zenith.

There were those other girls. Louisinette, a reedy slim trotter with a *café-au-lait* complexion, her long determined strides were elegant as she walked. She wore gigantic hoop earrings to enhance her exuberant features. Boys mesmerized by her seductive charms wondered at her longing for Odilon. Deeply affected by what had happened to him, she offered him her unexplored heart.

Louisinette lived on the ridge of Morne Cabrit, running a small fashion-design school for stay-at-home girls who would otherwise be in the field with their parents during the day. She learned that trade after spending two years at a vocational school in Port-au-Prince. The girl all boys craved; her chemistry was geared to only one man: Odilon Joseph. He was unaware, lost in his nightmarish state of infinite melancholy. But as yet he was too stony to notice, despite countless sentimental overtures orchestrated by Louisinette.

What was it about Odilon, that she craved? The other boys in the valley found it hard to understand why he was the most cherished, courted man available, the subject matter of most pretty girls in their section. Only a slim young man with big, agate-like eyes, a flat, handsome nose and bushy black eyebrows to match, his beardless, boyish face somehow made him look like the most attractive songbird of the valley. He was slender without any firm muscular strain, walking stiff with a clear lack of normal elasticity, the results of working too much in the fields. Being really neither tall nor short, his gaunt body framed a tangerine's facial complexion – gradually turning leathery, tanned by years of spending torturous hours clearing weeds out of fields and gardens.

Somehow, his looks did not betray the truest soul of Odilon Joseph. Despite the entrenched poverty in which he dwelled, and despite the hellish conditions of his existential realities, Odilon was a man who strove high above the *milieu* in which he was forced to live. He was, if you will, a singularly dignified individual, always speaking with meticulousness and an acute awareness of his surroundings. He was ambitious but never pugnacious, and he rarely used foul language to sway his peers to succumb to his wants – unlike many of the swearing, fight-hardened other boys. One could often see the shadow of greatness he cast, being a promising young man who was pinned down by more than his share of uncertainties and everyday realities.

Odilon was also a clean man, notwithstanding the unbearable work he performed daily under the full display of the tropical sun. He wore wrinkled trousers, a shredded t-shirt, and his cow-skin sandals. Odilon typically kept a double-edged machete hidden well inside his palm-frond sack as he took long, lean, lanky steps on his way to some appointed tasks in the mountains at the predawn hours. At work, he would become something of a mess, caked with filth and sweat. At sunset, however, he was a different fellow in style and appearance. His dusty, dirt-smeared face in the field during the day and the strong smell of sweat soaking his ragged shirt under the midday sun's merciless rays were difficulties long past.

Every afternoon at sundown, he greeted his anxious mother, dropping his tools in the corner by the silver chest. Then he raced down at demon-speed to the narrow ravine where it streamed along the downslope gorges beneath a tiny coffee field to cleanse his fragile body. Village children were accustomed to his soulful humming as he strolled past, displaying a cheerful, clean face on his way back home. On the approaching evening, the sunlight beamed its crepuscular rays on his refreshing, clean boyish face. His neat, trimmed hairstyle, perfumed with basil, the stiffness of his fine, starchy outfits – each worked well to camouflage his crestfallen attitude, ahead of the arrival of the crescent darkness. After stuffing himself with whatever he could find in the manner of dinner, he would stand, hands folded inside his pockets, leaning against the balustrade near his simple front porch – every inch a tropical Prince who had gone astray somewhere.

Shoppers returning from Saint Louis – especially the valley girls – could not resist his formal demeanor, his subtle smile that catapulted into full outbursts of laughter when someone told a great joke that he could not ignore. But these days, Odilon looked more like a tormented literary character. He was lost in the complexity of raw injustices faced by his fellow countrymen, the dehumanizing conditions endured by those living in the shadows of death, and the degrading, existential state of shantytown dwellers. He also grappled with the hopelessness of defenseless peasants like himself, condemned to wallow in poverty forever.

What the girls were seeing, however, was none other than Odilon's phantom, not his potential true self. They could waltz through him, without touching him. And though the misery of his lost love had finally worn off, he was a changed young man now, after hearing Zebeda's heroic and meaningful speech at the square in Saint Louis.

Therefore, Ilène was the very last person he wanted to see during the most troubling hours of his existence.

#

In the midday stillness of the cornfield, he lay low – afraid of being mistaken for a thief. He had no business inside a stranger's crops. He leapt over the hard-to-reach top of the fence, continuing his course on the dirt path until the road ended, branching off in two directions, east and west. A humongous mango *monben* tree buffered the tail of the path, its over-hanging branches, bushy leaves, and shade offering him brief relief from the excruciating hot haze. Odilon stood panting by the roadside, spent from his exertions, leaning against the great brown trunk of a mango tree, enjoying the relative coolness. A thin breath of wind swept through the leaves in a long, rustling whisper. Hands folded in his pockets, he was lost in thought.

A flock of wood pigeons fluttered past, bending one of the mango's branches and causing the leaves to crackle like crumpled paper in an office cubicle. The sound jolted him from his deep thoughts, and he began to hear the clacking of hooves coming from the east. Stunned, Odilon thought it was Ilène on her mule, returning. Panicking, he jumped behind the tree and lay motionless on a bed of white-and-pink vincas mixed with wild, multicolored crotons.

Heart racing, his eyes turned glassy – he was like a hunted prey, betrayed by an empty, hollow gaze crafted in outright despair. He was but a ponderous, defeated warrior of time, one who forsook his right to fight to the finish.

Luckily, he was wrong. The sounds instead came from a group of ambulant merchants of Bwa Chandèl, returning from the Basen Tounen marketplace across the hill from the village of Barlatier. Tired beyond measure, they leaned forward as they rode their donkeys down the pebbled pathway. The road ahead seemed to weigh heavily on them. They had a long way to go before reaching the hilltop of Bwa Chandèl.

Odilon waited for more than five minutes after the merchants disappeared behind the banana leaves to make his way back onto the main pathway. He staggered sideways, staring behind his back several times before regaining his march out of the east, toward the riverbank.

From a distance, Odilon could hear the rushing currents of Ti-Riviyè, seeing its purplish silhouette as he strolled down the slope. Nearby was the settlement of Nan Fòn, where groups of peasants played dominoes under the shade of the towering royal palms at Madame Délivrance's courtyard. Odilon could see children playing hide-and-seek around the small slaughterhouse adjacent to their outside kitchen. He could hear the rustic music, splendid sounds of the banjo and acoustic guitar echoing over the valley floor. That warmed his heart. He wanted to get there fast as he could, but the fear of meeting Ilène again crippled his legs.

Madame Délivrance's home, infamously known as the 'house of the valley whores,' was a place where prostitutes roamed freely in the courtyard, even in broad daylight. It was also a refuge for awkward lovers seeking to strengthen their relationships, as they came in search of magic charms to find true love and cast love spells over their prospective wives. Délivrance was a tall woman with a peculiar birthmark on her pudgy dark nose. She walked in an unsteady profile and chewed tobacco powder, spitting it all over, regardless of who or what was there. People did not dare to bother her, for she was the richest butcher in the valley, competing only against Amélia Bilzon, the most powerful *manbo* in Ti-Riviyè.

As Odilon advanced, he spotted Inacio Louicius, dressed in a white tunic and blue trousers, smoking a pipe while watching a group of children perched on a rock by the riverside, casting their nets to catch freshwater crawfish. Inacio was Odilon's father's most bitter enemy and lived in the hollow of Morne Lecturne near the village of Grassette. Odilon shrugged off the idea of visiting his courtyard. In Haiti, it is customary to point fingers when a relative dies, even if it's from natural causes. After Odilon's father passed, rumors spread that Inacio was behind it, having cast evil spells on him. The last person Odilon wanted to meet after his father's untimely death was this "werewolf" that every parent in the valley was trying to avoid.

However, a few feet away from the courtyard by the river pass, behind her grocery table and under a small tangerine tree, Lovinia Deshommes sat – selling the most popular commodities in the section. Lovinia Deshommes waved her blue hand fan with a gentle flicking of her wrist, high above in the air to fight off the tropical heat. She had it all, sitting erect behind two big Dame Jeanne coffee containers filled with *kleren* for *tafyatè* at the last hour. She also carried soap, candies, peanut butter, biscuits, pastries, dinner rolls – and the most popular item of all: "My Dream," a twenty-five-cents-an-ounce cologne that every male and female in the valley could not go without.

Odilon waved to Lovinia when he emerged from the bushes, reaching the east bank of Ti-Riviyè. She waved back, inviting him to come and taste her latest peanut butter sandwiches.

"I'll give you two for seventy-five cents. Come and taste. I have free tries!" she urged Odilon.

But he resisted, for he only had fifty cents, needing twenty-five of it to buy detergent for his dirty linen. "I'll be back…later," he promised Lovinia with his infamous grin.

Wavering in the heat, he did not cross the river. Instead, he swung eastward along its bank, where he sought refuge on a giant boulder under a large fig tree to catch his breath. The crystal-clear water and glittering bodies of small fish swimming in the light currents attracted his attention. He was starving and his throat was dry from thirst.

Sliding down the slippery rock, he slid off his sandals, rolled up his pants, and began to enjoy the cool, exhilarating sensation of squishing his toes through the soft silica sand lining the riverbed. It was so refreshing. He had to cross the creek to get home. The canopy of evergreen trees guarding the banks and a cool tropical breeze coming down from the mountains into the shade, however, tranquilized him. In an atmosphere of unbelievable peace amid breathtaking scenery, far different from any chaotic city madness, he leaned against the rock, soon asleep with his feet dangling in the water. An occasional minnow nipping at his toes failed to disturb him.

At that moment for Odilon, life was at a standstill. Nothing was heard but the occasional whirring of hummingbird wings. The tiny creatures sipped nectar from the overhead garlands of colorful flowers. In the shadow of fear, as the threat of war loomed, Odilon appeared to have found paradise again – at least for the time being.

Some thirty minutes later, a female voice came from the other side of the stream, out of nowhere. "Odilon, is that you? What are you doing out here by yourself this time of day?" The voice sounded lonely, as if desiring company.

Odilon failed to awaken, so the voice called out again. Her "Yoo hoo, Odilon!" carried such power that the sound rustled fig leaves above the sleeping man. At last, the voice woke him. Gasping, he yanked his feet out of the water, jumping up from the rock.

Startled and shocked, he shouted out, "*Oui!*" Thinking he was still in a dream, he raised his right hand across his forehead to shade his eyes as he peered across the stream, to better see who was calling his name.

"It's me, Thérèse," answered a young lady in a bathing suit, grasping her brightly colored shirt and wielding a parasol.

"Oh…you're only Thérèse," Odilon stammered, trying to stand up. "I mean, what brought you here? I didn't know you could come all the way out here."

"What do you mean?"

"City girls like you don't come this way."

Thérèse threw her head back in a loud guffaw. "That's what you think! I always come here to bathe. I call this place my secret paradise. I saw you, but you scared me. I thought something was wrong when you didn't move the first time I called out."

"I was sound asleep. Then I heard your voice, coming from far away. I thought it was part of the dream. You scared me, too."

"How was that?" she cooed, coyly rotating her parasol.

"I was having such a nice dream. I had found paradise one more time…while floating in a purple haze. I wish I could return to my dream."

"Are you saying I invaded your privacy? If that's the case, I'll leave. I'm sorry. But you really scared me. When I called and you didn't reply, I thought evil spirits had bewitched you." She shuddered and turned to leave.

"Please don't go! Seriously, it was a nice dream because it involved you."

"Well, what was your dream about that involved me?"

"It's too complicated to explain." Odilon cast his eyes down, seated well enough on the riverbank to twiddle the water with his bare toes.

"At least, you could give me a hint."

"I guess because I was destined to meet you…I had that dream."

The girl frowned at this idea. "Where are you coming from?"

"Why, I…nowhere in particular."

"Please, clarify that statement," she begged.

"I dreamed of such a beautiful creature…" Odilon crooned, showing he could be coy in his own way as well as any woman.

"Maybe, it was an angel?"

"Yes," he agreed, "an angel like you."

"Oh, Odilon, you stop teasing me."

"No! It's real. Let me cross the stream, and I'll show you something."

Odilon waded across the shallow water as Thérèse simpered and watched from the other side. She stood by the southern bank, twirling her parasol. Giggling, she anxiously awaited Odilon's explanation. Sticking out her chest, her small breasts stretched high under the bathing suit – like fallen star apples. Her brown, slender legs complemented her well-formed rear end. She showed Odilon a fetching smile; her white teeth glittered in the blend of sunlight with rushing water. No defects could be detected in this Creole beauty. She was every bit what a youthful young woman ought to be.

"I'm waiting to see what you have to show me," she declared, planting a kiss on Odilon's grateful forehead.

"Come with me," he murmured, taking Thérèse's hand as they moved closer to the water's edge.

"What are you trying to show me?"

"Look into the crystal-clear water. Just look for a moment."

Thérèse stared down. "I only see my image," she said, chuckling.

"This is no laughing matter. You really are a beautiful angel. Did you ever take a moment to look at yourself in a mirror?"

"Of course, I'm a young woman. For ladies my age, having a nice appearance is always an obsession. But I'm not obsessed with myself, although I always try to make sure that I look the best I can. So, why are you telling me this, M. Joseph?"

"Well, you really impressed me…from the moment I first saw you."

"If this is true, how come I never saw you since the last time at the square?"

"You know how things have been over the past couple of weeks. With the threat of war every day, there's little time to think of things other than your own survival. But you're always on my mind. Not a night goes by that I don't think of you."

"Why should I believe you, Odilon?"

"Well, you see Thérèse…it's…difficult to express my feelings for you, and make you believe me. They say poor people are unable to express feelings of love."

"I don't know what you're talking about. I'm not rich, like most people in this region. Yet I think that love is important in anyone's life. The big question is-?"

"Yes, what's the big question?" Odilon tried to put his hands into his pockets, but his pants, soaked with water, stuck to his trembling legs.

"Well, the biggest problem nowadays is how to find out if a person is really in love with you."

"I see what you mean," he sighed. "It's not easy, even in the best of circumstances. But this dilemma is not only a woman's problem. The problem goes both ways."

"But I think it's tougher for the woman. Some men are only interested in…pleasure. If I allow myself to be exploited, not only will I lose my virginity, but also my dignity. You know how people in this section are when it comes to gossiping."

It was now midday. The sun peaked skyward at its full height. It was sweltering; so hot, their bare toes dwindled in the sand as they stood together, holding hands.

"Let's cool off in the water," suggested Odilon.

"Yes, you're right. It's too hot to stand here," replied Thérèse. Her voice was submissive, soft as the sweet sounds of a turtledove.

Thérèse folded her parasol, taking off her hat and sandals, and laid them with her colorful shirt on the ground near a big, mossy boulder. Odilon shed his pants and shirt, leaving him in his cotton underwear. They waded into the cool, crystal-clear water: two innocent birds, two doves, two *kolibri*. In spite of their harsh poverty, they were able to smile, hope, enjoy, and preserve their full sense of humanity. And as Odilon would soon learn, they were able to do far more than simply love.

They jumped and played, frolicking, splashing like children as the clear water shimmered and sparkled in the sun. Suddenly, the young man pulled Thérèse against his naked chest, softly caressing her back.

"Stop, Odilon! Your massage makes me want to go to sleep," laughed Thérèse, trying not too hard to push Odilon away.

"Why are you pushing me?" murmured Odilon, a sly smile playing across his face, as he held Thérèse tightly.

"I know where you want to go…I can't do it."

"That's not what you think. You know."

"What?" The young girl gasped, taking a sharp inhale.

"My heart thumped with joy when I awoke from my dream. I saw you standing there on the other side. I knew then that my dreams would be coming true…"

"Stop teasing me, Odilon!"

But he was too deep in ecstasy to stop. When Thérèse continued to offer no real resistance, he put his arms around her back, drawing her close to his waist. Overcome with the heat of the moment, she locked into Odilon's arms. It was irresistible. She succumbed to the warmth of his embrace, and when their lips finally met, an avalanche of French kisses tumbled into their willing mouths.

Lust and passion, whether you're rich or poor, run deeper than the Earth.

Chapter 13

Waking from a long, intoxicating kiss, the young lovers, happy and excited like kids in a candy store, playfully splashed in the water. The sweetness of their kisses and the accompanying bliss brought them a taste of infinity. It was sweet—sweet like biting into a custard apple in a tropical rain, like the juicy yellow flesh of a mango eaten in the summer heat, like nighttime serenades shared over a glass of lemonade, and sweet like an old-fashioned peanut butter sandwich on cassava bread.

Thirty minutes later, their idyllic interlude was shattered by cracks of gunfire rolling in from a distance. The pop, pop, pop, increasing over time.

"Did you hear that?" Odilon gasped.

"Yeah," replied Thérèse, "it's the guys in training over the hill."

"How do you know that?"

"I saw some of them crossing the ravine as I came up here. A few men were sitting on a ditch at the bottom of the hill…cleaning their rifles."

"I heard people saying that *Le Rouge* is in Haiti."

"I heard that too, but I'm not sure, Odilon."

"They say he's the mastermind behind the movement. But no one has ever seen him."

"That's what I heard, too. Shhhh, listen."

"Yeah…I hear the sounds getting louder," Odilon whispered.

"That's part of their training. They have to shoot, yell, move forward, and do lots of other practices to be ready to fight."

"Do you really think the government soldiers can make it all the way here?"

"I sure do," Thérèse said, flashing a firm, self-assured grin.

"What makes you think so?"

"Odilon, that's the only conversation in town," she stated.

"Everybody talks about it," Odilon explained, with a drawn-out sigh. "It's also all they report on the radio. Remember the false rumor last week that sent everyone into a panic? I nearly lost *Manman* because of it."

"How was that?"

"Well, we'd just walked out of Dr. Duchaud's office. I took her there for a checkup. As we stepped out onto the street, we ran into a swarm of people – going to the marketplace to buy stuff to be prepared. So, we joined them."

"But how was your mom nearly killed?

"Hold on! I'm not finished."

"Then…what happened?"

Pausing for dramatic effect, he continued, "Well, in the rush to get to the marketplace, my mother almost passed out from the heat. She has a weak heart."

"Oh, I'm sorry to hear that. How was she rescued?"

"Thank God, in Marché Mercredi, near the RRF office. I pulled her into the building, and the nurse there helped us."

"She was lucky, Odilon. She could've died on the street."

"I think she's always been fortunate. The nurse and a receptionist gave us what we needed. We didn't even have to go to the marketplace anymore."

"Wow…what a stroke of luck!"

"On top of that, I had the chance to meet Zebeda…" he continued, pausing again to make his wonderful story more elaborate and awesome to his ladylove.

"Are you sure it was him?"

"Of course, better yet, he remembered my mom."

"What do you mean, Zebeda remembered her?"

"Exactly that…when he was a kid, he used to go with his friends to play in Anwodo. My mom used to make them delicious *dokounou*, giving them juicy *mangfransik* mangoes that Zebeda remembers to this day. You should've seen how happy he was when he saw his 'Aunt Cécile'. He really knew her quite well."

"Wow, I wish I could've been there! I'd really love to meet Zebeda. He's fighting hard, ready to die for people like us."

"Every night I go to sleep with guilt, because I'm not one of his soldiers yet."

"But why don't you join them? They're always recruiting."

"Thérèse, if my brother was alive, it would be easy for me. But I'm the only son…the only child my mother has now. If I join the RRF in the mountains, I know she won't live long. She has a serious heart condition. She can't handle traumatic incidents anymore. Just listening to the war the other day on the radio made her terribly upset. Can you image what would happen if I was among the fighters?"

Odilon's explanation of his dilemma as a loyal son touched the deepest strings of Thérèse's heart. She could tell he was in pain. He was torn between his unconditional love for his mother and his unquestionable patriotism and love for his country. His voice quivered as he twisted his tongue several times, to pull out the right words to express his thoughtfulness. Trying to hide his emotion, he paused to catch his breath, the words coming out in a blur of loving concern and tears.

Thérèse clasped Odilon's thin body to her open bosom – a mother comforting her young child, or at least a great substitute. Holding him tight, she started kissing his face in an effort to calm him down.

"That's okay, *chéri*," she whispered. "I was only joking about you joining Zebeda. You're not the only one not joining the RRF. Go downtown, and you'll see so many young people like us who're not in training. Just because I'm a woman, it doesn't mean I'm less obligated to take part in what's going on. You saw with your own eyes, the many female fighters at the square last week. People saw them fight, endure chaos, and die bravely. So don't make me feel guilty too…*mon amour.*"

"I think you're right," mumbled Odilon, peeling himself away from Thérèse's arms. Then he froze, listening carefully. "Wait! I hear something crying out behind the mangoes. Can't you hear it?"

"I can," replied Thérèse. "But it's not coming from the men on the hill."

They strained to figure out where the strange noise originated. Beginning as the meowing sounds of a wild cat, the noises turned into the agonizing cries of a desperate person. Each new cry carried a savage foreboding, sending terror through the amorous twosome.

"Odilon, let's go see what's going on. Someone's in trouble."

"But where are they? I can't pinpoint the sounds," answered Odilon, attempting to be composed, keeping his cool as he struggled to pull on his pants.

"Let's go downriver and find out what's going on." Concealing her deep fright, she nonetheless clung to her lover once again.

"I think you're right, *chérie,*" he admitted. "I've lived here all my life, and I have never heard a sound like this. Someone is in big trouble."

Without picking up any of their belongings, hand-in-hand they hurried downriver as fast as they could – running along the riverbank in the direction they believed the sounds were coming from. As they walked further, they grew more certain they were heading in the right direction.

They rounded a bend in the river where the water deepened, discovering a small boy partly submersed – desperately clinging to a tree branch. The undertow was sucking him under, and he was in danger of being swept away by the current.

Thérèse cried out, "Odilon, for God's sake! Get something for him to grab and pull him to shore before he drowns!" Full of motherly instinct, her entire body rattled and shook with profound fear for the young boy's life.

Within a second, Odilon dove into the water like a river otter, swimming out to the boy, grabbing him by the arm just before the tree branch snapped. The boy loosened his grip on the broken branch, with Odilon pushing him toward the water's edge.

Thérèse waded in, down from the bank, to grab the boy and drag him out to safety. She was happy and proud of her Odilon for saving the boy's life.

"I got him…as he was about to go…under," Odilon gasped. "But we need to get…the water out…of his lungs."

"Yes, we have to move quickly," replied Thérèse. The rescued boy went unconscious, so she flipped him onto his stomach, turning his face to the side.

Coughing up water himself, Odilon began pressing on the sprawled-out boy's aching chest. After several attempts, river water gushed from the boy's mouth, and he started to cough, gag, and breathe on his own—looking pale and helpless as rainbow-colored droplets, refracted by the sun, cascaded down his face.

As soon as he stopped coughing, Odilon questioned him. "What's your name, boy? What were you doing in the water?"

"Dieudonné…" gagged the boy, barely opening his eyes as he turned over to look up at the pair of strangers who had saved him from certain death.

"What do we do now?" Thérèse begged Odilon.

"I don't know…but one thing: we can't keep him here," he muttered and gently patted the boy's face on each side to revive him.

"I live in…Nan Banman," answered the boy as soon as he was alert.

"How old are you?" Odilon asked, helping the boy sit upright.

"I'm…eight…years…old." Coughing up more water, he gagged as streams spurted from his flat, button nose. His scarlet-rimmed eyes, scorched by the merciless sun, sank deep into his haggard face.

Ill-shaped and disfigured beneath his raised cheekbones, the poor boy looked dazed—like he was under the weight of a bitter curse. His soaked khaki shirt, buttonless and heavy with river water, clung to his body. The right leg of his bluish trousers was rolled up to his knee, and his left tennis shoe, missing its laces, made it difficult for him to walk.

"How did you get here, all by yourself? Nan Banman is too far, isn't it?" Thérèse's voice was stern as she questioned him.

When the little boy was able to catch his breath, he answered, "I was at the demonstration…with my mother in downtown Saint Louis this morning. There were so many people…I lost track of her. I thought she'd already left. So, I decided to go back home alone."

"You said you were where?" Odilon asked, astonished.

"I was…at the demonstration."

"What demonstration?" Thérèse spat, her suspicion growing by the minute.

"Yes, the demonstration. People came from all over…"

"I live in town, and I heard no such thing this morning!" she interrupted, looking perplexed. "I would've been there if I'd known about it." She couldn't tell if the boy was lying, but he clearly had no motivation to lie.

"My mother said she heard on the radio that the government was going to kill everybody in town. So…everyone came to the streets…to stop it."

To reassure his ladylove, Odilon laid a moist hand on her shoulder. "As soon as the boy is well enough to walk, Thérèse, let's hurry into town. We certainly don't want to miss this."

"Yeah, let's go! But we need to help Dieudonné get home."

"No, no, I'm okay now," the boy bravely asserted. "You guys can go. All I was trying to do was cross the river." Sounding stronger, the small boy was much more in control of his faculties.

"We can't walk away and leave you here. You're coming with us. Let's go. We'll walk you to the bottom of the hill," said a relieved Odilon.

They went back up around the bend, picking up their clothes before they crossed the river at a shallower spot, making their way east in the direction of Nan Banman. They headed down the path, strolling into the sun toward another hill.

A voice shouted from behind the trio, "Dieudonné, whatever happened to you?"

"*Manman!*" cried the boy, running up to his mother in tears. "I lost track of you in the crowd. I was looking for you everywhere. Finally, I left, thinking you might've gone home."

Odilon and Thérèse heaved sighs of relief, knowing the boy was not going to be left alone at the bottom of the hill while they continued into town.

"Dieudonné, you scared the hell out of me! You know I wouldn't leave you alone in the city. I went looking everywhere for you." His mother, a short woman wearing a khaki dress and plastic sandals, had a kerchief tied around her small waist. She scooped up her son and clutched him in her waiting arms, kissing him on top of his little head.

"Long after the crowd broke up, I waited there for you. I gave your description to everyone passing by – in the hopes that people might tell me where and when they saw you. I finally went to the RRF soldiers. They took your name and description, promising me they would investigate. Then they told me to go home, and someone would get in touch with me. Thank God, I have found you!" She was exhausted, her untamed hair strewn over her neck, but she was overjoyed to have her son back.

"What happened at the demonstration?" Odilon asked. He frowned at the boy, who was afraid to tell his mom he had nearly drowned while trying to cross the river by himself.

"The demonstration is over. When everyone learned that the rumors about the government coming were not true, they all went home," she answered.

"How did they know it was a false alarm?" Thérèse asked.

"The RRF commanders came and spoke to the crowd. There was a lot of tension amongst the people. Many were scared out of their minds, after they heard about what the soldiers did to the demonstrators in Port-au-Prince," the woman said, her voice shaking with emotion.

"This is crazy," said Thérèse, "Just this morning before I left town, everything was so peaceful."

"But Dieudonné, you need to tell me where you went." Taking his head into her cupped hands, she probed his wan, care-worn face. "Your eyes look red," said the woman. "Have you been crying?"

"*Manman*, I was under the bamboo tree, waiting for you by the roadside. Yes, I was crying," answered the boy. His sad eyes appealed to Odilon in an attempt to prevent his mother from knowing the truth about what had happened.

Odilon got the message. There was no reason to further upset anyone. The boy had surely learned his lesson about not going into the river all by himself.

"You see, we found him walking along the road. He said he was looking for his mother," Odilon fibbed. He gave Thérèse a look, telling her not to divulge that the boy had almost drowned.

"Yeah," Thérèse gave a blithe smile. "He's such a handsome little guy. We're glad we were able to help you find your son. We must go now…we need to hurry to town, to find out what happened today."

Odilon did not say anything further as Dieudonné hugged him and Thérèse goodbye. The boy whispered, "Thank you for saving my life, and thanks for not telling my mother what happened. I promise I will never go into the water by myself again."

The boy rejoined his mother, leaning against her waist. As the pair of young lovers wended their way home, they heard behind them,

"Never leave me like this again! If you do, I'll paddle you 'til your bottom is sore!"

Odilon and Thérèse laughed hard as they heard her departing words.

"Well, my love," said Odilon, "we lied, but I guess it was for a good cause. I think the young man has learned his lesson." With that fortunate mission completed, their brief love affair had proved to be exciting.

A few minutes later, they disappeared beneath the trees and loose foliage of a lush green coffee plantation.

Thérèse broke the silence between them. "Odilon…"

"What?"

"Instead of going straight into town, why don't I go home with you? I haven't seen your mother since the day of your brother's funeral."

"Are you sure you'll have time?"

"Of course, today is my day off. I have until six o'clock to go home."

"You know what, my love?"

"What?"

"I look forward to the day when you won't have to work as a domestic servant anymore," Odilon said in an almost fatherly manner. "Many of the things Zebeda is saying give me encouragement that one day this will come to pass."

"Odilon, let's pray that the RRF can win their struggle."

"Look at me, Thérèse."

Frowning, she turned her pretty head to him. Her hair earlier had been beautifully coiffed, now hung in mussed strings from their river adventure.

"What's wrong with you?" Her voice was high with worry.

"There's nothing wrong with me physically. But there are lots of things that are wrong to me…in my head."

"And…what are they?"

"First of all, I don't have an education. I don't have a decent job. I don't have much to live for, but my mom, and now you, have priority in my life."

"Oh, Odilon, don't be so negative. Remember, we may be poor, but we're young. We just saved a young boy's life. That should count for something."

"You're right. But I'm tired of my life as a sharecropper, working for people who never pay me what I'm worth. I'm tired of cleaning other people's plantations and gardens for a few *goud*. It's too degrading."

"Don't say that, Odilon! Your job may not be the best in the world, but I don't think it's degrading. Stealing is degrading."

"Thérèse, maybe 'degrading' is too strong of a word. However, there's nothing pleasant in what I do almost every day. There are times I wish I was dead. Then I think of *Manman*, and I change my mind. I'm now enrolled in a night school, but some nights, I can barely make it. Sometimes I feel so tired, hungry, and rotten that I'm unable to go to class. I feel embarrassed. But there's nothing else I can do."

"Which one of the night schools?"

"I'm going to the one at Dr. Duchaud's clinic," Odilon explained.

"I started to go to school last week, too…the one near the Catholic church by the square. Ms. Glaude is my teacher."

"Is that right?"

"Yes."

The two of them stopped, looking as if to size each other up.

"Two years ago, I enrolled in that school." Odilon said. "After three weeks, I dropped out."

"Why?"

"Because all they ever did was preach about God and Jesus."

"Odilon, you don't like God?"

"That's a silly question. Of course I do. But just because I believe in God, it doesn't mean I have to believe in everything someone might say."

"Give me an example."

"For instance, Ms. Glaude always said that we were supposed to respect the authority of the State – when it has committed so many injustices. Ms. Glaude said it was all right to be poor, and that the poor will be rewarded in heaven. After three weeks, I decided not to go any longer. I had enough! All of it was a lie. If being rich is a bad thing, why are the rich people ready to do everything in their power, including killing, to protect their privileges?"

"I think you're right, Odilon. Every night before we leave, Ms. Glaude gives us a lesson like that. And she doesn't like it when the students talk about politics. She doesn't say not to support Zebeda, but she tells us to always be nice to the people who allow us to stay in their homes – so we can clean for them. I'm really nothing but a 'house slave.' Many of us in the class are questioning why her last piece of advice every night is a reminder to be obedient to these people."

Odilon listened to her words with keen attention.

"But the other night," Thérèse continued, "a young lady named Lucette who has just recently enrolled told us why."

Odilon moved closer. "What did she say?"

"Well, she said that many of these *bourgeois* are active, strong supporters of the Church. They give a lot of money to the Church. They want everyone to think the way they do. They're brainwashing us to respect both the Church and the State."

Odilon was relieved, for at last he was able to confirm in his mind the same questions that had been haunting him for so long. Now he was going to a different school, one where the students were taught legitimate subject matter and not government propaganda.

However, due to his inconsistent attendance, he had missed vital lessons and information necessary to understand the social contradictions in his life. Now, he regretted skipping those classes. Yet, the few times he had managed to attend had helped him immensely and made his efforts to go to school worthwhile. He was now able to read a simple letter, write his name, and begin to learn about the great divide between the rich and the poor. He was able to learn where their interests lie in Haitian society, which people are their natural allies, and which ones are their enemies.

Odilon was truly beginning to comprehend the root causes behind the class struggles in Haiti. He was starting to understand why his forefathers, though utterly devoted to the principle of independence, could not agree on a common formula to move the country forward. He took great pains in trying to comprehend why André Rigaud, head of the Republican Army in the south, who had openly declared anti-slavery and anti-feudalism practices, was ready to strike a deal with Hédouville, the French commissioner in Le Cap, to deliver the head of Toussaint Louverture. This was when only a few days earlier, Toussaint's army swept the south to stop a British advance on Rigaud's stronghold of Les Cayes, eventually saving him from a British onslaught. Odilon thought to himself, "Politics certainly do make strange bedfellows."

Plunged deep in their frantic conversation, they were unaware of leaving the entire banana grove that edged the south bank of Ti-Riviyè, while the valley floor was yawning open right before their eyes. Small houses with green vegetable gardens festooned their courtyards, and every single one of them had huge, bushy mango trees of many delectable varieties clustering around their yards. It was December, blooming season, the lime green décor of Nan Fòn now overshadowed, taken over by the colorful blossoming of mango trees.

From yellow to orange, each variety carried a distinctive trait – readily apparent when the flower was shed, and small bunches began to sprout. Later in the season, their uniqueness could not be ignored, with their bulging fruit ranging in hue from dull green to yellow, or even red, as they started to ripen. The juicy, succulent fruit also varied in shape and size, from ovoid to long, and from plum-sized to melon-sized.

The new lovers walked hand in hand down the trail, blissfully waving to everyone they passed at each house along the way. They looked for all the world like two newlyweds walking down a dirt aisle after a long wedding ceremony. Their white teeth gleamed in the sun as they waved to the bewildered onlookers, who stood dumbfounded. This was the first time they had seen Odilon in a romantic interlude since his crazy days with Ilène. Thérèse exhibited no signs of shyness, intertwining her hand with that of Odilon's. His other hand held her wide-spanning parasol aloft, guarding his princess against the powerful rays of the relentless sun.

Thérèse knew many of the inhabitants, for she was born right up the hill in Nan Banman – where roosters crowed at midday, owls ventured out in broad daylight, and *malfini* were relentless in the hunt for hens and chicks, even on rainy days.

To their left, they waved to Aunt Philomène, who leaned forward, raising her greyish-white eyebrows to get a clear glimpse of the young lovers. She was standing on her front porch, talking to two boys who were taking coffee beans from inside the house to dry them in the sunlight. But Aunt Philomène's jaw dropped upon realizing it was Odilon Joseph, the only surviving son of her best friend Cécile.

A thousand wrinkles emerged from her open, careworn face. Struck dumb, her thin lips puckered – as if she tasted a sour grapefruit from her vegetable garden. Gnarled hand clutching her rosary, she made the sign of the cross three times over her chest; and yet she still could not believe it. Her rabbit-like ears pricked up at attention, and her voice quivered when she called out to Odilon,

"Pitit an mwen, koman-w ye?" Grinning broader than a banana leaf, she leaned against a wooden pole to support her aging knees. She used two pieces of old towels to tight-wrap those knees, ravaged by rheumatism.

A group of young, malnourished children with swollen bellies, thin legs, and auburn-red kinky hair were running butt-naked around the yard. They were quick to surround Aunt Philomène, gripping her dress tight. They too waved to the passing lovebirds. Thérèse threw a timid grin, while Odilon reciprocated with a puckish twinkling in his eye. He was in seventh heaven, as they say in Haiti. There was no time to stop and chit-chat with any gossipers.

Aunt Philomène was an old maid, living in this valley for as long as anyone could remember. No one knew for sure how old she was, and other elders claim to have always known her to be the same: dull dark face, reddish-brown eyes, salt-and-pepper hair, always tossing off laughter at the first sign of meeting someone. But few souls in this community could believe Aunt Philomène's apparent joy. With no husband or kids, she relied on the children of others to bring a semblance of normalcy to her beautiful, well-maintained tropical garden. It was easy to think that her life was anything but normal or joyous. Many believed the smile that brightened her face at first sight was none other than a sneaky farce to camouflage her everlasting solitude.

Leaving the trail, Odilon and Thérèse took a narrow path that led them west to Anwodo. They maintained their stroll under the gleeful eyes of old friends and bystanders. This unheralded romance was ushering in new signs of hope in the hearts of the people of Ti-Riviyè, who were quite worried about Odilon's seemingly endless ordeals and difficulties as he coped with the death of his younger brother. After twenty minutes of walking and talking, plus stopping for an occasional embrace, the two lovers reached the edge of Anwodo.

The afternoon sun slanted, stretching their shadows into long, skinny ghosts that seemed to disappear into the nearby forest. The suffocating midday heat was beginning to fade, drifting off into the atmosphere. A timid afternoon breeze swept through, coaxing the mango leaves to sway under the gentle caress of the wind.

"Look, isn't that your mom over there?"

Thérèse pointed, rubbing her clothed bosom firmly against Odilon's chest. She wanted to spend these final minutes savoring the new man in her life, adoring his tender touches and sensuous French kisses. They nearly made her climax along with Odilon, who could feel beneath the folds of her blousy skirt the smooth motion of her warm, thrilling legs and the lusciousness of her attractive body. Their quest for pleasure peaked, reaching a new plateau as they edged near a bushy avocado tree, shedding their clothes. But nearby, voices and footsteps grew louder, disturbing them. Afraid and thwarted, they redonned their simple clothes, maneuvering south back onto the main pathway.

"Did you see my mother?" Odilon's voice was timid as he looked about for Cécile.

"Yes, she's right over there."

"Over where?" he asked, peering all around them.

"She's behind the cacaos, by that huge *mangfransik* mango tree."

"Yeah, I see. She's in the garden. She always has something to do there. That's her only pastime, working with our plants."

Placing a bowl of tomato seeds on the ground, Cécile prepared to plant in her vegetable garden before the rainy season ended, so she wouldn't have to water as much. As she carefully planted the seeds in a mound, her bright blue dress fluttered in the cooling tropical afternoon breeze. A wide straw hat, secured by a chin strap, cast a shadow over the freshly tilled soil. On the east side of the road, a group of young men sang a cappella over a fresh, clean field as they hoed and plowed the soil in preparation for planting maize.

"Hey, Odilon, where were you? We've been here all morning," cried the group's leader, a stocky young man who paused with both hands on his hips, heavy drops of sweat streaming down his sun-bronzed dark face.

"I knew the maize was supposed to be planted. But no one told me when. If I'd known, I would've been working with you," Odilon replied, smiling at his buddies.

"How come you didn't know? I left a message with Aunt Cécile yesterday afternoon," called out another young man.

Turning, the entire group stopped, now that they knew Odilon was there. Frowning, they saw him as a straying *romancero* who had traded his professional obligations, turning his back on his colleagues, for a romantic jaunt in the valley.

But Thérèse wrapped both arms around his waist. This unexpected show of affection stunned Cécile, who knew nothing about Odilon's new love affair.

"Oh dear…yes, Odilon, he did tell me. I forgot, and you came in so late last night," said Cécile, eyeing Thérèse up, down, and sideways.

"You came home late? Where did you go?" Thérèse whispered from her commanding position behind him.

"I was at school last night."

She left Odilon, going over to hug his mother. "How are you, Aunt Cécile?" she cooed, planting a kiss on the old lady's forehead.

"I'm fine, my girl. Look at you! You are…sharp!" she replied, her face aglow with delight.

Odilon grinned, a tired smile playing across his thin but handsome features.

"Aunt Cécile, I'm so glad to see you. Since the funeral, I haven't had a chance to visit. My friend Roseline and I planned to visit you last week. But we had household problems. You know; when you're working as a maid, people think they're kings and queens, and that you're supposed to be their slave," said Thérèse.

"And worst of all, they believe they're above the law," said Cécile — a statement laced with more than a distinct trace of bitterness.

"You're right, Aunt Cécile. Those with money rarely go to jail."

"If they ever go at all. In Haiti, there's no justice for those who are poor. Tell me, how is Roseline doing?"

"She's fine. But she's not here right now."

"Where is she?" Odilon and Cécile chimed in perfect unison.

"A friend of hers found her a job in Port-a-Prince. She left the other day. I can only wish her well."

"Me too," sighed Odilon, relieved at this news.

They talked, joked, and laughed with one another until it was time for Thérèse to leave and get back to work. An obliging Odilon happy to walk her down the pathway leading into town. As they reached the town's edge, they paused under the outspread shelter of a giant breadfruit tree. Odilon pulled her close to him.

"You look so beautiful. I wish one day you and I could have a home of our own," he said. No one from the street saw them as they kissed under the tree branches, saying goodbye to one another as if before a long voyage.

Although they became good friends on the day of the huge demonstration at the square, it was hard to imagine their relationship could grow so quickly, blossoming strong and pure like the spreading mango trees. True love was beginning to sprout in their hearts. But after fifteen minutes of heated smooching, they realized it was getting late—it was time to say goodbye for now.

Reluctantly, Thérèse hurried downhill, heading through a back alley leading to the main road. Heaving heartfelt sighs, Odilon leaned against the breadfruit tree – watching his princess strut under a canopy of banana leaves – until she disappeared behind the palisades. He was lost in his thoughts as he ambled back home, a happy man who had finally found the one true love of his life.

Chapter 14

Everyone agrees that war is an ugly, cruel, and barbaric practice, an enterprise without logic – going beyond any rationale for acceptable behavior. Yet at times in history, resorting to this dreadful enterprise may prove to be inevitable, as the antagonists on both sides become convinced that the only way to reach the height of their "golden means" is through war. This reasoning played on, lingering in the hearts and minds of the leaders on both sides of the Haitian conflict.

Since the day of the massacre in the capital, Saint Louis and Port-au-Prince had been hard at work, preparing for total war. In Port-au-Prince, the hawks were rapidly gaining the upper hand. Since the assassination of Justice Minister Malveaux, those within the government who nourished dovish views were silent. Leading the hawks' position was Defense Minister Lacroix – backed by the president of the republic.

In Saint Louis, the voices of moderation could have prevailed, but the constant barrage of threats from Port-au-Prince never stopped, forcing the entire population to be on alert. The RRF high command had no other option but to prepare for what they believed was already a "given factor." War was inevitable. For the first time, they began distributing flyers with safety tips outlining everything the population needed to do to protect itself in the event of an invasion.

In every town and village in the province, people were cautioned that once the bombing began, they were to stay indoors and turn on their radios for up-to-the-minute information. Batteries were distributed to ensure that each household could power its radio. There were no bomb shelters in the region, so the most vulnerable, especially those who lived in shantytowns and in the villages, were ordered to evacuate to more bombproof structures, such as the centuries-old churches.

The army had begun sending reconnaissance aircraft into the area, to monitor rebel positions. In response, the RRF moved to fortify every strategic building in the province. In Saint Louis, the entire town was transformed into a huge fortress. Thousands of volunteers mobilized to sandbag the entrances at every street, and in both the north and south entrances leading into town.

One afternoon, about two weeks after the massacre in Port-au-Prince, Zebeda called a meeting inside RRF headquarters. Flanked by his top lieutenants and dressed in his traditional olive-green khaki uniform, he calmly addressed his group.

"I have just received a fax from Port-au-Prince," he began, pulling the paper out of a brown folder carried with him into the meeting room.

"Who sent it?" asked those seated around him.

"It's from the 'Office of the President,' requesting that we set up negotiations to diffuse the crisis." Zebeda smiled.

"Should we pay attention to it?" one of his top lieutenants asked.

"Of course, we should," he answered, holding up the paper in his large hand. "Not only must we pay attention to what they say, we must also respond to them. I know Ti-Jean and his cronies are not interested in peace. They want to use every means at their disposal to win, including intimidation, manipulation, lies, and deception." His voice was firm as he shook the paper for emphasis.

"You're right, Olivier," said one of the RRF officers. "As I was coming here, Radio Nationale reported the news. The announcer said it was an overture in good faith by the government to avoid a bloodbath in the Northwest."

"We will respond by letting them know that we're ready to negotiate – with one condition," said Zebeda.

"What condition is that?" asked one of his top aides.

"That he agrees, in principle, to step down and let a transitional government that includes civic leaders and revolutionary elements to take control of the government."

"We already know what his answer will be," said another aide.

"Let's face it. If they want to play a game of 'masters of manipulation,' let them do it. I know all they really want to do is hoodwink the population through their propaganda machine. But let's be realistic. Any delaying tactics would play well enough in our favor. It would give us more time to prepare for war. We must be honest with ourselves."

He paused, his eyes searching over the assembled group, as if hunting for any weaknesses. But all eyes were locked onto their leader.

"We don't have the military might to hold the entire province," he continued, "should they decide to invade. Our biggest weapon is the will of the people, and their determination to rid themselves of this fascist regime. We have many volunteers ready to give up their lives, but we sorely lack the military supplies to sustain any protracted, fixed battles. We cannot send people to be butchered by these criminals. Ti-Jean will never agree to our terms. It would be suicidal for him if he was to accept."

The meeting adjourned with an overall understanding that the RRF would enter negotiations only if the government wanted to play the game. All the RRF supporters wholeheartedly agreed that Zebeda was correct in his assumption that playing a waiting game at the negotiating table was the only way to deal with their adversaries, even though that tactic might not be enough to ensure any military victories on the battlefield.

The RRF army was well-disciplined, but only its core troops could be depended on to lead a military offensive. Numbering about five thousand and backed by another three thousand volunteers, the military wing of the RRF was inadequately armed, spread too thin to hold its ground against a major government assault. The best hope for Zebeda and his planners lay in the mass protests around the country – acts of civil disobedience to facilitate the regime's downfall. This also proved uncertain, as the government had already flexed its muscles in all the major cities and intensified its systematic repression, unleashing its death squads to kill, on a moment's notice, those who took to the streets on behalf of the RRF. Nonetheless, against all odds the RRF was standing firm and ready to fight.

In addition, since its victory in Port-de-Paix, the RRF has enjoyed a significant psychological advantage. Few were aware of its internal weaknesses, and the government soldiers were ill-prepared to achieve their ultimate goal of annihilating the RRF. Being village people themselves, the government troops were reluctant to die for Ti-Jean and his associates. Except for the fat-bellied generals in Port-au-Prince, most regional officers lacked the readiness or zeal to execute their mission with the same fervor as the RRF high command at their headquarters near downtown Saint Louis du Nord. Since mid-October, the revolutionary forces had expelled all government soldiers from the Northwest, now renamed "the liberated zone and free territory of Haiti."

#

It was mid-December, and the important Christmas holidays in Haiti were fast approaching. Exclusive nightclubs in the suburbs bloomed with festivity; lavish parties in elegant living rooms and around pool decks became nightly events. However, as Christmas Eve drew near, an uneasy peace settled over the country. In the war room at government military headquarters, there was no time for celebration. The hardliners, led by General Lacroix, were growing impatient. They could not understand why Ti-Jean had yet to order an assault on Saint Louis.

Angry beyond passion, Lacroix felt rejected for not having been consulted during Ti-Jean's decision to draw the RRF into negotiations. He had only heard the news like the rest of the population, after it was leaked through the media. He then fitfully concluded that a coup must take place to overthrow Ti-Jean. The coup was not to be carried out until the last week of December – in order to establish an obvious reason to stage it.

Lacroix sent his personal friend and second-in-command, General Roger Ardouin, known for his ruthlessness in the pursuit of his enemies. His mission was to initiate the reasons for the coup and to share their plans with influential interests outside the country. There was soon a meeting held in *Manoir Des Lauriers*, an imposing mansion in an upscale section in the northern part of town, which served as the official residence of the French ambassador in Port-au-Prince.

The sun had faded, capitulating to the invading nightfall when Ardouin and his entourage left their headquarters in Carsernes Dessalines, a huge army barracks right behind the presidential palace near downtown Port-au-Prince. He had traded his usual olive-drab military uniform for a perfumed navy-blue business suit and bowtie.

With his face buried under his traditional blue-blacker sunglasses, he was shielded from anyone viewing inside the bulletproof, tinted windows of his black Mercedes. Even the deep scar on his left cheek was not enough to unveil his identity. He relaxed in the back seat, cross-legged, stroking what was left of his disappearing kinky hair. Ardouin had an incredibly hairy body, kept in shape by jogging at the break of dawn along the trimmed bushes in the courtyard of army headquarters.

School children on their way to the Champs-de-Mars in the early morning hours dreaded that compound with immeasurable fear. They called the general "the caveman," for he resembled a werewolf. At least, that was how the children saw him, leaping in giant steps to get away as fast as they could to avoid an unwanted encounter with this extremely feared individual.

His gleaming bald head was always hidden under a special green cap, for he had been the chief Leopard in the infamous "Baby Doc" paramilitary corps, of which he was commander-in-chief. Long after the Leopards Corps was disbanded, shortly after the Duvaliers fled the country in the predawn hours of February 6th, 1986, Ardouin would continue to wear his leopard uniform. This was a vivid reminder to his friends and colleagues of how much he missed his "glory" days as the number one butcher in the country.

Sitting in the backseat with him were four of his bodyguards, all in combat-ready uniforms, their M-16s lying across their laps. Ardouin looked tense, despite his serious efforts to suppress his mounting anxiety. He fit the profile of a clumsy bachelor out on a blind date, not an opportunist politician on a Machiavellian mission to deceive his innocent constituency. However, to show off his chauvinistic nature, and most importantly, to camouflage his embarrassing uneasiness, he would beam a broad, toothy smile every few minutes, or order his chauffeur to veer in a certain direction – to demonstrate his complete command and doubt-free authority.

A few stray, corpse-fed dogs barked on the deserted streets when they pushed through the main gate and headed east, passing through the Champs-de-Mars and then Rue Capois on their way to Avenue Charles Summer. The Champs-de-Mars was nearly empty. All ambulant merchants were gone, the *balladeers* were gone, the college students were also gone, except for some diehard, authentically engaged ones who were willing to brave the bogeymen. The gossipers, concubines, sneaky *bouzen* in search of a one-nightstand, lonely love-seekers, haggard-faced teenagers hungry for romance, and any predator tourists preying on the vulnerable were nowhere to be seen that night.

But on the corner of Rue Capois and Rue Saint-Honoré, a middle-aged couple could be seen promenading on the sidewalk. Their romantic interlude was interrupted by roaring sounds cascading from the Mercedes' muffler. They glanced at this a bit, quickly turning their faces when they saw the car – strolling in gigantic strides as soon as they realized who might be cruising inside. Crossing the street, they reached the old Rex Theâtre – breathlessly waiting for the departure of the Mercedes, then returning to their romantic stroll as if nothing had happened. Nighttime in Port-au-Prince can be dangerous for any naïve souls trying to navigate their way through the city.

The black Mercedes rolled through the upscale suburb of Bois Verna, running into an unexpected power outage. The entire neighborhood was thrust into virtual darkness. The blackout somehow followed them, for the outage was a slithering snake, moving through the streets in the silent tropical night. Ahead of each block, here it came. Ardouin's veneer of a cool demeanor was shattered. His spooked bodyguards were speechless watching the rolling blackout. He screeched for his chauffeur to veer westward to the main boulevard of Lalue, where the sidewalks on both sides of the grand boulevard were thronged with pedestrians.

Their ragged clothes and nonchalant, flat demeanors marked them as the most wretched poor, with no real aim, refuge, home, or destination. They vacillated between the imaginary and the real until the purple glow of dawn consumed them. Exhausted, they collapsed shamelessly on the benches of nearby public parks, their eyes twinkling under the starry skies of Port-au-Prince.

On Lalue, the Mercedes roared down the road, picking up speed. Florescent lights glittered in the tropical night, while passing vehicles navigating down the hectic road enhanced the relaxing natural atmosphere. The further they pushed north, the fewer vehicles there were out on the street. And as soon as they drove into Bourdon, the atmosphere became even more serene. They advanced with steady caution as they reached the front gate of the ambassador's residence. It was an imposing mansion reminiscent of the traditional, colonial mansions of the American South in grandeur and architectural sophistication.

Manoir des Lauriers was strategically perched atop a low hill in full view of the Port-au-Prince harbor. It was indeed a historic landmark, owing its name to the magnificent and abundant wild pink *lauriers* and *Nerium* oleander that freckled its exotic tropical garden. Majestic towering palm trees stood erect above the lime-green, well-kept, lawn. The picturesque garden was filled with more than fifteen acres of walled, gated and gorgeously landscaped designs. The space offered a grand sunset view of turquoise waters glowing in the distance.

A flagstone veranda, running along the back exterior of the house, offered one of the most stunning views of the blue-ridged mountain of the Massif de la Selle. Well-trimmed lilies and shrubs edged the veranda. It crafted a fantasy come to life, with a dreamy tropical ambiance. The estate contained great outdoor amenities for aristocratic social gatherings, and *les grandes dames de Port-au-Prince*, fat-bellied politicians, and members of the *Alliance Française* made the most of it to strengthen their brotherly kinship under the direct guidance of *La France: La mère patrie*. It was a white three-story estate, considered one of the most beautiful mansions in the Americas. The house featured enclosed and elegant terraces, along with a vast reception area that could accommodate more than one hundred guests. Crystal chandeliers sparkled like twinkling stars on a clear night, casting a brilliant prismatic display across the mosaic floors.

The rolling field provided a perfect backdrop for heated political discussions or romantic gossiping, while the fancy guests would wine and dine over French Bordeaux and Haitian Barbancourt. Everything was right at their fingertips, all possible amenities from a wine cellar to an outdoor dining *loggia*.

This spectacular mansion with its exceptional craftsmanship had changed hands over the years, from American millionaire businessman Edgar Elliot, a founding member of the Haitian-American Sugar Company (HASCO), to former Haitian President

Elie Lescot, to the French top diplomat in Haiti. Built by skilled artisans in 1927 during the United States' occupation of Haiti, its local and international architects had flexed their ingenuity to create this replica of southern grandiosity. The floors were hand-set in intricate patterns, and the ceilings were sculpted by master plasterers. Fancy light fixtures and all sorts of hardware were custom-made, giving birth to a sumptuous collection of rooms that spanned three levels and over fifteen thousand square feet of living space. And all was safeguarded by a state-of-the-art security system to maintain the peace of mind necessary for the jolly, fancy people in attendance against the dangerous and maniacally hectic life of Port-au-Prince.

Manoir Des Lauriers had become the nerve center of France's diplomatic maneuverings in Haiti, housing former Haitian government functionaries allied to France, hiding them from persecution by the newly emerged coup leaders. Traditional politicians wanting to play "the French card" had to first seek their blessings inside the estate. It was no surprise that General La Croix had sent his protégé General Ardouin there to seek some endorsement for his prospective military coup.

It was close to 8 p.m. when the Mercedes pulled into the circular driveway. The guards, in haste, pushed the door open – and Ardouin waltzed out. Motion-sensor floodlights flicked on in a blur to light their path as he took quick strides to the main mahogany door. A cool breeze caressed the giant palm leaves when the men passed by a cluster of hibiscus blooms. In seconds, a trail of wild jasmine shot its fragrance into the general's hairy face. As they reached the main front porch, Ardouin ordered his guards to take their places on some rocking chairs lined up along the terraces. He then walked in, at once being taken to the diplomatic corner, where the foreign diplomats were waiting for him.

All three of the most important foreign diplomats in Haiti were in attendance that night, De la Fournier of France, Pignon of Canada, and Stephen Reardon of the United States. Sitting next to Reardon in the diplomatic salon where they gathered, General Ardouin prepared to lay out his mission.

"My friends, I can assure you that Ti-Jean has no intention of getting the job done. Here we are three weeks before the New Year, and the brigands in Saint Louis are firmly in control. I don't see how the military parade of January first can be held, when a large portion of our country still lies under the control of communists.

"General Lacroix needs to get your assurance and approval of a plan to get rid of Ti-Jean. He also promises that he will not act immediately. He will wait for the next few days to see how things develop," Ardouin growled, his blazing eyes fixed on a giant portrait of Napoleon Bonaparte displayed on the wall. He was avoiding any eye contact with the diplomats, who watched the deceptive general with outright astonishment. Ardouin had turned into the master of manipulation in a stage play, designed to forestall Ti-Jean's diplomatic overtures in order to pave the way for an all-out war on the Northwest.

"General," replied the Canadian ambassador, "don't be overly concerned! Ti-Jean wants to get the job done even more than you do. But remember, he's a politician. Like all politicians, he must watch out for his political career, something that you, as a military man, don't have to worry about."

"If you overthrow the government now, it will send the wrong signal to the enemy. It'll tell anyone watching the coup that your camp is in disarray," added the French ambassador, De la Fournier. "Remember, General, it should be okay to wage war when your ultimate aim is peace. That way, you'll never be called a warmonger."

Ardouin listened, displaying vast displeasure at being rebuffed by the diplomats. "We have nothing to negotiate with these…bandits!" he growled.

"Don't be naïve, General. Zebeda and his troops may seem like 'bandits' to you, but they're heroes in the eyes of the people. If you can't see that, I don't think you're ready to win right now, either militarily or politically. To defeat them, it will take a combination of many things besides taking military action," asserted De la Fournier.

"And what are these things you refer to?" Ardouin snarled once more. He was displeased that his plans for a coup were being rejected.

"Deceptions, lies, disinformation…these are designed to create panic and confusion in Zebeda's camp, especially in the minds of the people supporting him," replied the French ambassador.

Reardon, the American ambassador, put in his two cents. "Besides, the questions Ti-Jean will put on the table will never be acceptable to Zebeda."

The meeting ended with Ardouin unable to convince the diplomats of the need to overthrow Ti-Jean. But that is precisely what Zebeda had in mind. With both sides not interested in making any genuine concessions at the negotiating table, the time was ripe for full-blown warfare. For different reasons, each side desired negotiations, not to win the peace, but to achieve their own strategic and political aims. In fact, they were both heavily arming themselves, making ample preparations for war. The Haitian military invested everything it had at its disposal for the campaign, including its prestige – or what was left of it. The hawks from the high command had dreamed of the day when Haiti would possess short-range missiles, when commanders would be given free rein to decimate any enemy target at will.

Fiercely committed to restoring the shattered prestige of the Haitian military, the high command was devoted solely to a decisive win. Anything short of a swift victory would not only be demoralizing but would also constitute a crushing blow to their historic dream of recapturing the days of their geo-strategic advantage on the island – something they had enjoyed before, for more than a century.

The military's glory days were long gone. From 1915 to 1934, the nineteen years of American military occupation had reduced the Haitian Army to little more than a ragtag militia. Its only role being to safeguard the interests of the multinational corporations, the *bourgeoisie compradò,* and its estranged ally, the dinosaurs, against their natural enemy, the masses. Morale among the rank-and-file ebbed low, so low that field commanders received *carte blanche* to shoot anyone suspected of deserting his post on the battlefield. Nevertheless, the hardliners ardently determined not to be cowed by Zebeda's popularity and shrewd guerilla tactics, which had already earned him the entire Northwest Province.

Two days after the meeting at the French ambassador's residence, the high command converged with Ti-Jean in the east wing of the National Palace. This meeting was even more inflamed with the tropical passions of those present. Flanked by his top generals, Lacroix was curt in expressing his growing impatience with Ti-Jean.

"I'm convinced, Mr. President, you're not ready for war!" he declared, shaking down to his boots with anger. His colleagues blanched at this outburst.

"And what makes you think so, General?" Ti-Jean was irritated with the General's audacity to challenge his authority.

"It's now two weeks before Christmas, three weeks before the Independence Day parade. I was shocked to learn you're ready to enter negotiations with the terrorists in Saint Louis…we in the military weren't even consulted!" Lacroix bellowed.

"You forget your role as a military man, General. I am the president of this country, and I don't have to ask permission from any military personal before making political decisions. The army is subordinated to the executive. I thought you were the one who reminded me last week that this Zebeda is no terrorist; he's a skilled man we need to deal with in a professional manner. As much as you may want to kill him, I will only order an attack when I think the time is appropriate. For now, there is still time to outmaneuver Zebeda."

"And how do you intend to outmaneuver him?" Lacroix questioned – his defensive attitude was apparent to everyone present.

"By blocking his propaganda offensive…"

"And how do you plan to achieve that, Mr. President?"

"By going to the negotiating table with him knowing we will never agree to his demands."

"I still don't see how you can stop Zebeda with negotiations." General Lacroix looked irritated.

"Negotiations may not stop him," Ti-Jean grimaced with tight lips, "but they might diminish his popularity. That's the goal we seek, just for right now."

"Do you really believe that the people will side with you if Zebeda walks away from the negotiating table?"

"No…I don't believe they will, but the record will show I was not the one rejecting peace. In time, I think, I'll be able to win the people over."

"Are you saying, Mr. President, we will fall into protracted warfare?"

"I really cannot answer that. I haven't received the war plan, or the review of the thorough situational assessment I requested two weeks ago. I need them to draw valid, tangible conclusions. Until then, I must be prepared for any possible scenario."

"Mr. President, the commission is working on it, another three days are needed to complete the report."

"Assuming the report is not yet ready, where's the war plan?"

"The plan has been ready for a long time. But it's a bit too complicated to explain. I can tell you that everything is ready to move against Zebeda. All military armaments have been moved into position. General Ardouin will lead the attack from his base of operation in Gonaives. Lieutenant Colonel Prosper Emile will be stationed in Gros-Morne, ready to strike at the enemy positions two miles north of Rivière Pendu. In Terre-Neuve, Captain Yvon Jouanis is already in place to retake the Far West. And from the north in Le Borgne, Lieutenant-Colonel Elysé Baltazar, one of our best, will lead the army's Third Corps, sweeping down from Tibouc Au Borgne to Anse-à-Foleur. From there, the noose will tighten around Zebeda's throat."

"This sounds well-coordinated, but I'm concerned about that only one corps will be leading the drive to retake the Far West."

"Don't worry, Mr. President, The Far West is the softest target."

"General, why is that?" Leaning forward, Ti-Jean seemed unconvinced. And a convinced Ti-Jean was even more dangerous, if he got too angry.

"Our intelligence confirmed that it's the least defended."

"How can you be so sure? Do you recall what happened in Port-de-Paix?"

"Of course we remember, Mr. President. That was a wake-up call. We're going in this time with full knowledge of the enemy. Zebeda doesn't have enough troops in Môle Saint Nicolas, Bombardopolis, or Jean-Rabel to drag us into prolonged warfare. After the heavy artillery bombardments, our forces will simply walk into town. My biggest fear is that we might be drawn into guerilla warfare in the nearby hills. Other than that, the Far West will come back to our hands rather quickly."

"What about Saint Louis and Port-de-Paix, the heart of Zebeda's movement?"

"It's not as easy to predict the outcome. Our sources inform us that the RRF is well dug-in around those two cities. They're heavily fortified and reinforced by hundreds of armed civilians. I'm thinking that even if we overrun these towns, it's going to take a lot of time to appease them. But in any event, we should prevail."

While it was easy for the General to speak about the Far West and Anse-à-Foleur as sure-win victories, he used carefully chosen words to explain his predicted victories over Saint Louis and Port-de-Paix — having sure-fire reasons to be careful about those two places. Also being careful about dealing with the president, by now he knew, as well as Ti-Jean, that rumors of a coup had been leaked to the media. The President of Haiti was furious, but there was little he could do.

Playing a cat-and-mouse game secretly terrified the General, who was now walking a thin, blue line. He thought that Ti-Jean's agents could have him assassinated. But as ordered by the triumvirate diplomats—the ambassadors to Haiti—any internal quarrels must take a backseat, so that they could all create a united front to defeat their *Enemy Number One*, Olivier Zebeda.

Chapter 15

The public square in Saint Louis teemed with milling throngs of concerned people, overflowing once again. Thousands from all over the country poured into town in support of the revolution, coming to listen to Zebeda's message of defiance and determination. Some of them brought seasonal flowers; others offered themselves as human shields. In the nearby villages of Barlatier, Anwodo, Berger, Desrouvrays, etc., committees swiftly convened, ready to defend their territories against the feared and hated government invaders.

Now a well-known "heir apparent" leader, Odilon led an imposing delegation from Anwodo. Seventy-five strong supporters marched into the square. Odilon held a bright rouge-colored banner with the RRF's slogan in black lettering: 'We will not take one single step in retreat!'

Thérèse joined him with her own delegation of domestic servants from their neighborhood. These young men and women were determined to face the street-dusty haze of their coastal town in the defense of their leader.

"*Chérie,* do you know if Zebeda is here?" Odilon asked. He peered lovingly at her, one hand shielding his crinkled eyes from the intense sunlight.

"I don't know," Thérèse replied with a sigh. Kicking off her blue sandals, she wiggled her toes as she planted a kiss on Odilon's eager lips.

"Let me find out!" a happy Odilon yelled with a pronounced grin, starting to push his way through the crowd to find Zebeda.

"No-no-no, Odilon…!" Reaching wildly, she grabbed at his arm, almost missing it. "There's no need to leave."

"Why?"

"I heard someone say he'll show up any minute. He's not here yet."

"Let's stop here, *chérie*. It's rough today. There's no breeze, which is unusual for December, and it's hot and humid as hell in town," complained Odilon.

"Wow," Thérèse mewled like a newborn kitten.

"What's so funny?"

"You are! Didn't you feel that gust of wind?" Thérèse responded, squinting at him with crinkled eyes in the sunlight.

"No, I did not."

"How come…why…ahh, I know why?"

"Why?"

"Because you're getting all uptight, trying to find Zebeda."

"That's not true, *chérie*."

"What do you mean it's not true? Is this our first lover's quarrel?" Laughing, the girl stuck one long, brown index finger into Odilon's t-shirt, twisting it slightly, drawing his open mouth closer to her outthrust lips.

"I mean, I only want to hear what he has to say. It's not just me waiting for reassurance from this man. Look all around you."

"I know, baby. I'm waiting for it, too. If I tell you I'm not scared, I'm lying. I can feel the war coming our way."

"I can feel it, too, Thérèse. I'm ready for it. I'm not afraid."

"Are you ready to join the fighters?"

"I already told you about my situation," he said as he heaved a heavy sigh, his voice dark as the thought weighed on his conscience. "It's hard to leave my mom alone. But if push comes to shove, I'll do what I have to do."

"I'll be the first one behind you, *mon chéri*," Thérèse chuckled, sweetly stroking his thin, shoulder blades.

A few minutes later, a second gust of wind drifted through the crowd, stirring up a giant wall of smoky street dust. The sun vanished beneath a darkening sky. Then, without warning, gigantic raindrops peppered the people in the square, pinging off the thin corrugated metal roofs of nearby houses. The drops hissed as they hit the hot rostrum where Zebeda was scheduled to speak.

Acting as a prism, the droplets clouded, bending and splitting into the atmosphere to form a distant rainbow. Was it a sign? If so, no one saw it. Instead, everyone gaped open-mouthed in dismay as the revolutionary slogans, carefully hung on huge poster boards around the square, began to tear apart, sliding off the boards into the saturated streets. The rain poured down. No one ran for cover, not during this important moment. Nothing could stop the people from waiting for Zebeda, certainly not a typical tropical downpour.

"Odilon!" Thérèse cried, surveying the rain-drenched crowd. She clung to her man, unsuccessfully attempting to hide as raindrops smacked her in the face.

"What is it, my love?" Odilon asked as he wrapped his loving arms around his-and-only in response to the unexpected downpour. He used his hands to try to shield her from the pelting raindrops while he himself was soaked.

"Oh…if I could only walk between the drops…"

"That's funny, *cherie*," he laughed. "I wish we both could do it!"

After a lingering half hour of sheet after sheet of downpour, the rain stopped as suddenly as it had begun. Within minutes, water drained off the streets, leaving clumps of mud in the chunky rubble and debris. Seconds later, a raucous of loud cheers arose from the north entrance of the square.

"*Viv Zebeda, Viv RRF…*" the jubilant crowd cried out as they spotted their hero.

"Oh, Odilon!" Thérèse squealed with delight. "Here he comes!"

"Are you sure it's him?"

"What's the matter with you? Of course it's him!"

"Yes, I see him in his olive-green uniform. He looks…strong and sure of himself…like nothing the government throws at him will ever stop him."

"*Viv RRF, Viv RRF*," Odilon and Thérèse shouted themselves hoarse.

"*Viv RRF, Viv RRF!*" The crowd roared, stamping their feet in the mud, raising their fists skyward in support of their beloved revolutionary leader.

Emotions ran high; determined people, hungry for freedom, were ready to face their ultimate fate of civil war with undaunted courage. "*Viv Ayiti, Viv RRF, Viv libète!*" rang in Zebeda's pleased ears as he reached the stage.

Despite the sudden downpour, the square was filled to capacity. The rain had merely cleared the air. The heat wave also subsided somewhat, but the ground shook as if Saint Louis experienced tremors from the hundreds of feet stomping the earth while the people chanted their revolutionary slogans.

Calm, yet passionate as ever, Zebeda stepped up to the microphone. He raised his hands, leaning forward to display the unity sign, crisscrossing his fingers as a symbol of peace and democracy.

The crowd fell silent as Zebeda clutched the microphone, ready to deliver another inflammatory sermon. Security was tight. RRF personnel had cordoned off the entire town square, from the old church building to the colonial-style houses surrounding it. Security guards took their positions on nearby rooftops and balconies. They essentially shielded the crowd and the RRF high command in the square below from any government intruders.

"*Bonswa*, comrades," Zebeda began his speech. "Today the courageous masses of our country are working with us. Not since the Revolution of 1804 has freedom been so close. There is no need to ask you to choose between revolution and reaction, because you've already demonstrated your hatred for the Creole fascists, the *bourgeoisie* and their cronies.

"Who would have thought three months ago that we could've organized the unified group that's here today? This is a clear indication that no one else holds the outcome of the revolution—only the valiant people like us. No one can force us to live like zombies anymore. We will defend our freedom at all costs. We would rather die a free people than to live like slaves or be treated like dogs in the dictator's backyards."

Hearing those words, the valiant crowd rose in jubilation. Thérèse held Odilon tighter and then let go of him as they jumped along with the rest of the people. Zebeda flashed a smile and then he continued.

"Not only will we hold our position in the Northwest, but we will move beyond the boundaries of this great province to rid our country of its enemies, local or international. But let's make no mistakes about it. The enemy is not twiddling his thumbs in frustration. As we speak, major plots are being drawn up to destroy us, once and for all. The Creole fascists are working right now to eradicate our desire for justice, for the right to a decent education, a decent job, affordable housing and healthcare. With foreign backing, they're ready to put to rest our righteous dreams of freedom for good.

"But we Haitians want to tell the world that we as a people have an unquenchable thirst for human rights – and that we cannot be judged by the criminal acts of the mercenaries who rule our lives. In the RRF, we're not afraid to fight and die for what we believe in. And what we're fighting for is the total liberation of all our people, for Haiti to be free at last, and for the application of the three fundamental human rights ratified at the United Nations' Fourth Geneva Convention."

Zebeda held his breath in a brief pause, gazing upward as if looking for the right words before he continued.

"Despite the many obstacles that lie ahead, and the bumps we must overcome on the road to freedom, we as a people will reach the light at the end of the tunnel. Then, it will be a brand-new day. We know that many of us will not make it to the other side, but that's okay! We've never believed that the price of freedom would be easy, fast, or cheap. The Creole fascists and their cronies are trembling in fear because they finally understand that things will never be the same again.

"We will either triumph together or perish together. Either way, we cannot lose, and we will never go back to the old days. There is nothing they can do to stop us. We will no longer be slaves in their sweatshops, maids, or restavèk in their wealthy suburban homes. We want them to know on this December afternoon that we're ready to win. Anything short of total victory is unacceptable. Now, you must listen carefully to what I'm going to say."

Everyone in the crowd looked at each other for a moment, turning back to face their leader with the utmost respect and their full attention.

"It's almost certain that war is heading our way. I'm not sure there's anything we can do to avoid it. The criminals in Port-au-Prince have their war machine in place, and they've made it very clear that they will transform Saint Louis into a killing field. Their bombs may start raining down on us at any time. But our struggle is a *just* and honorable one. No bomb will ever be able to force us into submission. Are you going to let Ti-Jean overtake you with his bombs?"

"No, no, no!" The crowd's voices rose in a heated wave of anger.

"Over my dead body will Ti-Jean take over my town!" Odilon shouted. Thérèse guffawed as she hugged him, planting sloppy wet kisses on his cheeks. Odilon's face reddened more than from the sun, from her moist lipstick kisses.

"Are we going to let ourselves be humiliated again?" Zebeda cried out in courageous defiance. The crowd knew that, as their leader, his life was the one most at risk. If the government captured him, they could subject him to unimaginable torment. But for Zebeda, the act of losing itself would be the worst fate.

"No way in Hell!" responded the revolutionaries.

"Listen brothers and sisters, since we have no bomb shelters, we're asking those of you who live in sturdier, better constructed homes to take in those who don't have that luxury during this time of civil war. Try to do the best you can to stock up on food supplies. The homeless will be under the direct control of the RRF for shelter and supplies.

"However, there's no need to panic. These are only precautionary measures that we must take in case the Creole fascists make good on their promises to stop our course of action. We will find a way to defend ourselves, fighting them in our territory. Let's not forget that this war is the people's war, so we all are potential targets. *Viv Ayiti! Viv Ayiti! Libète ou lanmò!"*

Following that sodden cloudburst of a storm, a cool breeze appeared to place a blessing on the crowd – finalizing an unforgettable afternoon. Zebeda was led away from the square by his lieutenants. Meanwhile, the revolutionary faithful trudged their way through the mud-clogged streets, chanting *La Dessalinienne*:

Pour le pays, pour les ancêtres
Marchons unis, marchons unis
Dans nos rangs, point de traîtres
Du sol, soyons seul maîtres
Marchons unis...
For the sake of our country and our forefathers,
Let's walk united, let's walk united.
Within our ranks, there should be no traitors;
To this land, we are its sole masters.
Let's walk united...
Odilon herded his defiant group back to Anwodo—under their soggy but proud red banner, honor of their beloved leader.

"We'll not take one single step in retreat!"

Chapter 16

Six o'clock in the morning, there was a knock on the door. Odilon sprawled snoring on his *nat* on the floor. Struggling to awaken, he didn't want to get up; he'd been complaining about his bad knee before he went to bed the night before.

"Who's there?" grumbled Cécile.

"I don't know, *Manman*," he replied, stretching out full length in every direction possible on the floor to ease out the kinks in his body.

The banging on the door grew louder, *Knock! Knock! Knock!*

"I'm coming," growled Odilon, rising slowly from his *nat*. Cécile, still in bed, waited apprehensively, frightened at the prospect of opening her door to soldiers. Odilon peeked through the holes in the wooden door, seeing who was waking them up so early on a winter morning.

"Odilon, it's me, Thérèse. Please, open up."

"Thérèse, why're you here so early?" He scratched his aching head, rubbing his eyes with his other hand, trying to fully awaken.

"Odilon, you don't know what happened last night?"

"No, I don't," he replied, cursing to himself. How could he know what happened over in her city, after lying asleep all night in his mother's house?

"For one thing, nobody slept in my neighborhood."

"What…why?"

"Around ten o'clock, news broke out that the government soldiers had entered Port-de-Paix."

"No…! Was it true?"

"No, it was just a rumor."

"So…why did everybody in your neighborhood stay up all night?"

"Well, because there were persistent rumors about a possible government attack during the night." She dropped her head, and Odilon could see her red-rimmed eyes, shadowed by dark circles like demons lurking beneath them.

"The RRF radio was on the air last night when I was at the neighbor's," Odilon recalled. "It stayed on up to the time we came home, but I heard no mention of a possible attack."

"That was the problem, everyone was waiting for news from the RRF that was never announced. The radio only played patriotic songs. And by three o'clock this morning, RRF radio announced that the revolutionary forces are in full control of Gros-Morne."

"Are you kidding?"

"Why would I kid you? Celebrations are going on in town, right now!"

"Baby…this is the greatest news I've heard…in several days." Wrenching his scruffy head awake, Odilon dragged Thérèse closer to him.

"What's going on?" Cécile begged, staying in her bed after she realized it was not government soldiers at their front door.

"Great news!" chimed the young lovebirds.

"What news?" Cécile croaked, barely audible while she slowly left bed to get a better sense of the important events.

Thérèse filled Cécile in on the latest war news. Giggling, she then pulled Odilon over. "I brought you something," she whispered, gripping tight to her lover.

"Well, what is it? I don't see anything in your hands."

"Wait a minute, silly!" she chided. "Let me go back outside. It's a surprise."

Plunging out the door, she drew an anxious Odilon close behind, stepping past a bed of flowers. She leaned down to pick up his gift: a small short-wave radio.

"Here, I bought you this yesterday at the flea market."

"*Chérie*, you bought this for me?" Delighted, he closely examined the gift, searching out its various features. "I'm ashamed. I haven't given you a thing since we've been together," he added.

"Odilon, what's that supposed to mean? We're not even married yet. Please, don't worry about giving me anything. My love for you has no strings attached – it's pure and natural, and I can feel it growing stronger every day."

"But *chérie*, buying that radio for me must've been hard for you. The money you make as a maid is not enough for you to buy me something like this…"

"Don't worry, Odilon. It wasn't a big sacrifice; it was only fifty *goud*."

"*Chérie*, fifty *goud*, that's a lot of money for poor people like us."

"My cousin Rosnel from Miami sent me twenty dollars for the Christmas holidays." Smiling, she wondered why Odilon no longer smiled at her.

"Why are you looking at me like this?" Perplexed, she continued, "Wouldn't you do the same thing for me?"

"Of course I would. I'm surprised. I didn't know you loved me this much. I grew up in this house, and I can't remember the last time we had a radio, *chérie*. This is wonderful for *Manman* and me! Now we can get the news at home."

"Oh Odilon, I love you so much."

"I love you too, Thérèse…you make me so happy. Come on, let's go back inside and show *Manman* your gift. But wait a minute, *chérie*."

"Why? What's wrong?"

"You need to get the batteries. They aren't in it yet."

Thérèse bent over the flowerbed, grabbing up a plastic bag. Opening it, she took out two AA batteries, following Odilon back into the house.

"*Manman!*" cried Odilon. "Look what Thérèse bought us!" Grinning broadly, he held the radio out in front of his mother.

"What is it?" Cécile squealed. "Did you say a radio? How nice…" Finally rising from the edge of her bed, she moved closer to her son.

"Yes, it's a radio, *Manman*."

"Wow, my son; this is really great!" the old lady trumpeted, scraping the ceiling in her joy. Thérèse took in Cécile's reaction with utmost delight, wide grins spanning their faces as the young lady received hugs and a kiss on the cheek.

Odilon placed the new radio on their tiny table. "Thérèse, will you stay with *Manman* for a few minutes?"

"Where are you going?"

"I have to feed the animals. It won't take long. I'll be back shortly…I have to bring us fresh water from the ravine."

"Can I go with you?"

"I don't think it's a good idea."

"Why?" Still smiling, his ladylove cupped his face in one hand.

"The morning dew provokes stomach cramps if you walk through it."

"Well! What about you?"

"I'm used to it, *chérie*."

Turning away, Odilon headed off to a nearby coffee field to feed the animals. Grabbing a worn-out housecoat to cover up her old pajamas, Cécile stepped outside to feed the hens and roosters eagerly awaiting their traditional morning breakfast of ground-up maize.

Thérèse stayed inside to put the batteries into the radio. A few minutes later, she stepped outside to get Cécile's attention. "Listen!" she shouted.

"What, girl?" The old lady began to wonder about all this excitement, but she was secretly very glad that Odilon had found someone new to love.

"Zebeda is on the air."

Cécile dropped the chicken feed, moving next to Thérèse. They bent their ears to listen close to the broadcast.

"Dear compatriots," the RRF leader's voice boomed over the airwaves. "In the face of the great dangers we are facing, and the determination of the enemy to annihilate everyone in the Northwest, the RRF has decided to take the initiative – pushing the war into enemy territory.

"We refuse to die like sitting ducks unable to defend ourselves. For some time now, our intelligence people have been monitoring government troop movements. Our sources tell us their plan is simple: to destroy the whole province, so it will never again be a threat to their power. Two days ago, they moved all their troops into offensive positions, ready to strike at any moment.

"Publicly, Ti-Jean has been talking peace. But privately, he's been aggressively preparing for an assault against us. In the RRF we say over and over again, 'war is the tool of last resort in a liberation struggle.' We try to avoid it at any cost. But as the vanguard of the people's struggle, it would go against our cause for us to remain stationary, defenseless and allow Ti-Jean to destroy us all. As our forces now in Gros-Morne have demonstrated, we're not only ready to defend ourselves. We're also ready to fight for the people's long-awaited thirst for justice.

"While we are committed to an equitable restructuring of Haitian society, we want to make it abundantly clear that anything short of total victory, guaranteeing full rights to the masses through their representatives, will be unacceptable to us. That is why we must continue to fight until our victory is fully achieved.

"Our forces marched into Gros-Morne early this morning, for the people had asked us to provide security after the government officials were chased out of the city. We will continue to push forward until we reach the heart of Port-au-Prince. We're asking everyone to stay alert and listen to future announcements. This can only mean 'Liberty or Death,' for we will surely succeed."

Zebeda's message uplifted the hearts of Thérèse and Cécile. His strong, thoughtful voice filled their souls with enough patience and fortitude to face another oncoming traumatic day. This held true for the other people listening in the province, who were left wondering when they would come face-to-face with the reality of war. Odilon came trudging up the path just as Zebeda finished his speech – to hear the news from the women in his life.

As the sun pushed and shoved itself from behind the purple mountains, the morning dew disappeared. Most villagers continued with their daily routines. Young boys accompanied their fathers into the fields, tending to the animals. Barely clothed, the boys appeared half-starved under the weight of sacks filled with maize for the hungry chickens. Meanwhile, the girls were busy with household chores, helping their mothers fetching water from nearby streams, sweeping the dirt floors of their huts, sprinkling water to keep down the dust, and chasing away the hungry crows competing with the chickens for their maize. The busy morning engulfed everyone in the village.

This local activity provided the perfect backdrop to the natural beauty of rural life in the area. Everything seemed routine and normal that day. No one in the village of Anwodo, or anywhere else in the province, knew that their fate was being decided a hundred miles away in Port-au-Prince.

In every corner of the province people waited, praying for their deliverance to arrive. Displayed on poster boards in front of almost every household, the RRF symbols and slogans gaily festooned most doorways and yards. For that reason alone, the RRF revolutionaries felt a genuine responsibility not to fail the people, knowing that their faith in the RRF put them at risk of extermination by the war machine in Port-au-Prince.

War was imminent. The RRF takeover of Gros-Morne emboldened the revolutionary spirit of its leaders, convinced that with the people at their side they were invincible. For weeks, they had stationed an elite unit on the north bank of Pendu River, four miles outside of town – while sending urban commandos to test the strength of the government security forces there.

A brief skirmish one afternoon forced the town mayor, the police chief, and all other officials to vacate the town, vanishing without a trace. At the request of its citizens, the RRF soldiers were invited into town, marching victoriously into the community without firing a single shot. This shrewd maneuver energized the RRF base, but also played well in the hands of the hawks in Port-au-Prince, who believed that from then on, total war was unavoidable. The hardliners sat, already at war. Military plans drawn up a few weeks before were ready to be activated. Given the green light, army commanders prepared their all-out assaults against Zebeda.

If in Port-au-Prince the war of dialectic seemed replaced by the dialectic of war, in Saint Louis the RRF high command equally prepared for an inevitable showdown. Two days after it seized the strategic town of Gros-Morne, deep inside government territory in the Artibonite region, the RRF high command converged in Saint Louis du Nord for an urgent meeting ordered by Zebeda.

Under a torrential rain that broke in waves over the town, amid bolts of thunder and lightning, the commanders marched one by one into headquarters at Marché Mercredi to finalize their plans. Dressed in traditional olive-green fatigues with their caps turned backward, they took their seats at a large eight-by-ten mahogany table, flanked by two large portraits of Charlemagne Péralte. Each waited with bated breath for their leader to speak.

Olivier Zebeda, at the height of his career, sat at the head of the table. At his right hand was the thirty-two-year-old, flamboyant, well-articulated Arthur Auguste, Zebeda's most trusted comrade. Short and stocky, he perched his prescription glasses on the farthest edge of his pointy nose. He was entrusted with the northern district of Anse-à-Foleur. But he was not the only intriguing soul at the meeting.

Isabelle Dominique, a golden beauty who walked with distinguished, confident strides that revealed her exuberance and voluptuousness, breezed through life despite clumsy efforts to camouflage her naturally seductive charms. A well-educated romantic revolutionary, she was promoted from community activist in charge of education to the head of a military command post after her legendary husband was killed in an ambush during the first battle in Port-de-Paix.

At twenty-nine years of age, six feet tall, and reedy thin, she captivated the entire doting population. Her timid smile carried a unique finesse, hinting at a quiet, moral heroism befitting a revolutionary princess. Around her lovely neck, she always wore a red-and-blue handkerchief, and a pair of revolvers was strapped around her waist. Like many others, she remained steadfast in her determination to free her country from its seemingly dark, helpless, and pitiable state of distress.

Jean-Michel Desquiron was a mixed-race, thirty-year-old gentleman with an imposing seven-foot-tall frame. His modest, fair complexion often led people to mistake him for a white man. Tall and flamboyant like his leader, he served as Zebeda's second-in-command. His lengthy, straight hair blended into his bushy beard, making it hard to tell where his sideburns ended and his beard began. Not only did his looming height make him conspicuous, but he also topped it off with a red-and-blue beret, à la Che Guevara. Desquiron was a patriot *"bon teint"* and a revolutionary to the bone. Daring and uncompromising, he gained fame after leading his unit from Lapointe to Port-de-Paix, contributing to the decimation of the Fifth Army Corps in Port-de-Paix.

To the left of Zebeda sat Joséphine Lacroix, a twenty-eight-year-old mixed-race young woman with vibrant liquid emerald eyes and the stone face of a menacing tiger. But for all that, she was sweet, tender as a dove – with a heart as warm as the Virgin Mary's. Golden, wavy hair stylishly piled into a trim *coiffure*, she held her many fans and followers spellbound, for her astonishing gift of using descriptive, revolutionary scriptures to fire up her audience. She was one of the most esteemed cadre members of the RRF.

Like Desquiron, Joséphine was from a wealthy family from the Central Plateau area – joining Zebeda to found the movement in Mexico while she was still a young student at the University of Guadalajara. Chubby and short with a muscular frame, she buried her mop of hair under an olive-drab cap. Joséphine was an RRF hardliner. She believed that nothing short of total victory was acceptable, carrying only one slogan to the battlefield: Victory or Death! In charge of the far southern edge of the province, she led the bold move to capture Gros-Morne without a single round being fired.

Finally, there was Ricardo Alcindor, a fearless young man born in Santiago de los Caballeros, Dominican Republic, to a Dominican mother and a Haitian businessman from Saint Louis du Nord. Better known by his nickname "Dodo," Ricardo was only twenty-five, with a medium height and build, and large, straight ears reminiscent of a rabbit. His big, bushy black eyebrows suited his shiny, wavy black hair, giving a youthful charm to his boyish face. The youngest of the commanders, Ricardo's charisma made him an exceptional revolutionary leader, fluent in French, Spanish, and Creole. He was in charge of the entire southwestern seaboard of the province, including the key towns of Môle Saint Nicolas, Bombardopolis, and Jean-Rabel.

Zebeda, bravest of the brave, was in charge of Saint Louis and its outlying villages. As he prepared again to speak, it was a tense moment. The only sounds to be heard were raindrops, drumming like tambourines on drooping almond leaves, and the buzz of crickets, chirping outside – wafting in through the open windows. Everyone was silent, accepting that the moment of truth was upon them.

The tall, defiant revolutionary leader glanced across the room, gazing at the wall, seeking comfort from the portrait of a smiling Charlemagne Péralte hanging adjacent to his seat. His eyebrows contracted, arms resting on the table with fingers intertwined while stroking his thumbs, struggling feebly to suppress his emotions. As his colleagues stirred, looking on with great anxiety, he finally spoke.

"Comrades, there are moments in history, in times of war, when only great men possess the integrity and conviction to lead the way to victory. The history of our country is filled with these great men, who because of their bravery and unshakable patriotism have defied insurmountable odds to make impossible dreams come true."

Pausing a moment to catch his breath, he could not see clearly. His comrades watched in awe as his eyes began to fill with tears. He brushed them away before continuing. "Let's not forget that our country's liberty springs from the heroic leadership of its forefathers, who didn't hesitate for a moment to sacrifice themselves so that freedom could reign for millions of our ancestors. They were demonized, demoralized, and reduced to nothing but slaves to serve the men who were the masters of the criminal enterprise called colonialism.

"As free men bound by a shared commitment to liberating Saint-Domingue from the poison of slavery, they faced tremendous challenges. Despite lacking the advantages of formal education, receiving little to no assistance from the outside world, and confronting overwhelming opposition, their heroism and unshakable bravery pushed them forward. They rose to recognize their inherent dignity and ultimately claimed their place among the most advanced civilizations of their time.

"However, we must remind ourselves that in 1804, while oppressed people everywhere gleefully applauded our independence, there were people here at home who weren't dancing to the same tune. They never supported the liberation project. I'm referring to the enfranchised population, the old free blacks and mixed-race people alike. Although many of them could be found in the ranks of the rebel armies, as a social class, they hated the revolutionary leaders with a passion. They pledged allegiance only to their own selfish interests, vacillating between the colonial forces, depending on who could guarantee their own interests, for they themselves owned slaves. They were French one day, British the next, and Spaniards the following day.

"In 1804, they became a 'de facto' dominant class, with no patriotic or nationalistic agenda. They totally disregarded their mission as the dominant class, which would've been to contribute to the industrial development of their nation. They plotted with corrupt officials and international mercenaries to pillage our country's resources. That's the price we're still paying, almost two hundred years later.

"As leaders of this prodigious moment in time, we must recognize that our task in this movement is monumental. But it's one we can't walk away from. We'll either make the final journey with the people, or we'll perish with them. However, my question to you now is simply this: who is afraid to confront the Creole fascists?"

No one said a word. There was a moment of silence.

Before too long, Desquiron looked at those seated around the table, speaking in a strong, firm voice. "Olivier, your question needs no answer. If we were afraid, we wouldn't be here. We could've done what the average citizen would do: stay away. We would have simply played by the laws of the jungle, enjoying our lives shamelessly in utter luxury. By being here at this meeting, we have made our choice. We've already chosen our path, taking on the consequences coming with that choice. I am under no illusion that the challenge we're about to face will be easy. But from the bottom of my soul, I believe that the benefits of a free Haiti will far outweigh any risks we must face as a result of our choice.

Now Joséphine spoke. "Not only do I agree with what comrade Jean-Michel said, but I believe we should make the fascists pay a heavy price for their crimes. We will turn captured soldiers over to the people, to burn them alive!" she declared in an inflexible, angry voice.

"Be careful," warned Isabelle, "Let's not forget our revolutionary principles. Let's remember that we've chosen war as a means to an end. We shouldn't kill captured soldiers; nor should we turn them over to an angry population. In revolutionary politics, there's no place for revenge. Although the people's anger is justified, we must understand that most soldiers who commit crimes do it out of fear, following orders from their commanders. We stand to lose our moral high ground by doing what our enemies would do. Captured soldiers must be re-educated, not killed." As Isabelle finished, Zebeda gazed at her with great admiration.

"My territory is the least fortified for war, and poorly defended. That puts me in a very weak and untenable situation," piped up Ricardo, the lilt of his brave young voice not revealing any real emotion on his part.

"I recognize that, Ricardo. That's why I'm ordering you not to stage any fixed battles. You'll only do it when you realize the enemy is defeated," said Zebeda.

"Does that mean we have to give up Bombardopolis, Môle Saint Nicolas, and Jean-Rabel?" gasped an astonished Joséphine.

"No," answered Zebeda. "What I mean is that it's not a good military strategy to oppose them head on. We must deny General Lacroix the opportunity to showcase his militarism in the Northwest. In terrain like this, you run the risk of being destroyed – since you don't have the manpower or military power to beat back the enemy. You don't want to fight on the enemy's home turf.

"Joséphine, you will remain visible and invisible at the same time. By that, I mean you should always force the enemy to keep on guessing where your strengths lie, until their soldiers are caught and demoralized in the midst of a hostile population. Your front is well-defended. You've got Gros-Morne as a buffer. It should always be defended, at all potential costs."

"Yes, sir!" Joséphine chirped.

"Isabelle, don't forget you need to send reinforcements to the front in Gros-Morne, if Joséphine gets in trouble. Jean-Michel, you're in charge of coordinating both the Far West and the southern front.

Arthur, the northern front, although it's not too heavily fortified, it should be handled equally well. You know the terrain, and I count on you to make it difficult for them to get to Anse-à-Foleur," Zebeda continued.

Arthur, brimming with confidence, responded with glee. "What I did yesterday was move my troops to the edge of Tibourg Au Borgne. The enemy is currently stationed inside the town of Au Borgne, and my intelligence unit has already signaled that their morale is extremely low. Spooked soldiers there will shoot at the first sound of a battle cry. I positioned fighters in and around Tibourg, and all along the treacherous, narrow road leading downhill into Anse-à-Foleur. They might get to me, but it isn't going to be an easy ride."

"Listen, you see how empty this building is? We shouldn't anticipate another meeting here," Zebeda warned. "I have reason to believe that it will be a prime target. My instinct tells me it will be bombed shortly. But don't you worry. As I told you before many times, all precautionary measures have been taken to ensure that none of our sensitive documents will be lost or fall into the hands of the enemy."

After a few more minutes of discussion, the commanders stood up and began singing "La Dessalinienne" as they exited one by one through the front door. They quietly disappeared into the safety of the leaden downpour that continued to pound the town.

Chapter 17

"Odilon!" Cécile cried out that morning, shaken from deep sleep by an apparent resounding thunderclap.

"What, *Manman*?" Odilon shook on his *nat,* barely awake.

"Didn't you hear that?"

"What?"

"That huge explosion. At first, I thought it was a thunderbolt. But now, I don't think so. Wait! There's another one. Didn't you hear it?"

"Yes, *Manman*…it sounds more like mortar fire."

"Do you suppose the war has finally come to us?"

"I don't know, *Manman!*" Odilon tried hard to keep his voice soft and winsome, so as not to disturb his mother. "Why don't we turn on the radio, and find out if we're at war?"

"Yes, my son. That's a good idea."

He got up from his *nat,* striding toward the table to turn the small radio on. The voice of Jean-Michel Desquiron wafted through the air, responding to the questions of a journalist from Rebel Radio about the onset of war in the province.

"Early this morning, at around three a.m., the regime in Port-au-Prince made good on its promise to destroy all citizens of this great province. Their army of death and destruction has begun a relentless assault on all major cities and towns in the region.

"The attack appears well-coordinated. While we're pounded nonstop from the air, a ground offensive was also launched, to capture our frontline towns. As we speak, heavy fighting is in progress outside of Gros-Morne on the southern edge of town. In

Bombardopolis, to the west, the enemy has entered the town, shooting indiscriminately at anything that moves. To our north, they broke our defense lines, passing through Tibourg au Borgne and moving down toward Anse-à-Foleur," Jean-Michel explained, his voice overflowing with raw anguish yet filled with revolutionary resolve.

When the journalist asked about the fate of people in those areas, Jean-Michel replied, "It's difficult to get an exact figure. But we won't be forced into submission. We're not afraid of their bombs. We will resist to the last!"

What he described was just the tip of an impending iceberg. When the bombing began, residents panicked, straining desperately to find safe refuge. By six o'clock in the morning, a five-hundred-pound bomb wiped out the RRF headquarters in Marché Mercredi. The bomb was so powerful that it decimated homes, leaving a huge crater where the RRF building once stood. Shrapnel attacked everyone in the blast zone. Emergency crewmen were overwhelmed trying to retrieve the injured and the dead beneath the rubble.

In Bombardopolis, resistance fighters met the heartless tactics and enormous firepower of the Haitian Army. Infantry divisions waited patiently on the outskirts, while tanks and other armored vehicles reinforced by helicopter gunships pounded the RRF positions at the heart of the small town, attempting to wipe out all rebel positions.

Barrages of shells, rockets, heavy-caliber machine guns—hell itself—boomed down from overhead. The barrage forced terror-stricken residents to barricade themselves behind closed doors and to find refuge under their beds. Hundreds perished beneath mounting piles of jagged rubble, their homes struck by artillery bombardments and pipe bombs with phosphorous rounds exploding into fireballs that couldn't be extinguished. The firepower unleashed on a small town such as Bombardopolis underscored the purpose behind the military planners in Port-au-Prince. They wanted to destroy the insurgency, once and for all.

But Ricardo Alcindor, shrewd tactician and ardent revolutionary, was not about to give in. Soon after the bombings began, Alcindor realized that there was no match between sustained bombardments from the enemy and the meager AK-47s, artillery shells and bazookas the RRF was using. He ordered his troops to abandon their fixed positions behind the sandbags and trenches. They staged a well-disciplined withdrawal to the nearby hills, waiting for the government soldiers to begin their advance into a ghost town. Most of the population, who had also braved the attack, fled with the rebels. Shortly thereafter, the government soldiers moved in – quickly initiating a massive search designed to flush out any remaining rebels hiding in the vacated homes.

In Gros-Morne, things were no different than in Bombardopolis. Relentless aerial bombardments left part of the city in ruins, with hundreds of citizens buried alive under heaps of demolished buildings. This town saw the worst carnage in its history: a scene of mass devastation, with bodies of dead people and animals strewn everywhere.

The situation at ground level was far different, from a military standpoint. By three o' clock in the afternoon, in spite of the bombing and shelling, not one government soldier could be seen patrolling the center of town. At the south entrance of the city, rebel fighters, taking advantage of thick cover from a mango grove, engaged the government soldiers in a tempestuous firefight, keeping them firmly at bay. Houses along the main highway leading north were raked yawningly open by tank fire. Many of these brave residents held their ground and refused to flee.

Isabelle had launched a call for the people to resist – they responded in droves. Old men and boys as young as ten took up arms to defend their town against the invading government soldiers. Isabelle had been preparing her defense for days. Her rebel army had managed to refurbish an old fort built during colonial times, using it to fortify their positions. With the help of a local militia, she built a redoubt about three hundred yards from the south entrance of the town – an extra layer of fortification.

In and around the fortress, she placed small detachments of rebels, who would resist at all costs. At the first sign of approaching army soldiers, Isabelle ordered a battalion of intrepid fighters, made up exclusively with new recruits from Gros-Morne and its hinterlands, to man the redoubt. Then she led two columns of rebel fighters, one on each side of the main highway, to go down to meet Lieutenant Colonel Prosper Emile, who was advancing to crush the rebel front. She set up snipers at strategic locations along the highway to cover her flank. She was confident of this stratagem, taken directly from the book of war for Haitian independence in the late 1700s.

About three hundred meters from the army's infantry division, a sniper struck at the advancing government troops, causing vivid confusion in the army's ranks. Isabelle and her columns of fighters made a hasty retreat into the redoubt, leaving government soldiers exposed to the rebel fire raining down on them like fatal sheets of hail from all directions.

Within minutes, more than fifty government troops lay dead; several hundreds were left wounded, including Lieutenant Colonel Prosper Emile. He owed his life to some daring soldiers carrying him to safety as they withdrew in shambles back to their original position – ten kilometers away. From Bassin Bleu to the north of Gros-Morne, rebel commanders pushed down three columns of fighters. They stayed off the main highway, creating a trail under the sugarcane and coffee plantations, reaching the north edge of Gros-Morne in order to beef up the southern front.

The Haitian army, however, was determined to break the rebel line and push north. To the war planners in Port-au-Prince, retreat was not an option. Two hours after the disastrous advance from their southern position, a coordinated effort by the Haitian Army and Air

Force bore down on the rebel forces, launching a new charge to the north. Leading the charge this time was Captain Élizé Dubuisson, a fearless officer who would stop at nothing to achieve his objective

Dubuisson was a fervent reactionary, widely known for his conservative rhetoric, vehemently despised by the masses. Jet-black, his angry, pudgy face moistened with sweat glistened in the shadows of the afternoon sunlight – swollen belly bulging upward over his belt at each huge military step he took. His sidearm's pearl-inlaid handle glittered like a rare gemstone. As he boot-stepped past dead government soldiers lying on the ground, his reactionary anger turned into total witless fury. He never realized he could have fallen into the same trap as those bodies.

Rebel fighters hunkered down along a deep-wooded gorge, about two hundred yards from the redoubt, waiting for the last government soldier to move north – and then struck them from the rear. As they retreated again, a withering, deadly fire greeted those forlorn soldiers from the front. About one hundred and sixty of them lay dead; among this shattered army, chaos and confusion reigned supreme. Trapped on all sides, they could only whine and whimper as their leader refused to surrender under Isabelle's demands.

His fate turned, and a bullet struck Dubuisson in the leg. His heavy frame thudded to the ground, hard. He crawled face-down in the dirt like captured prey. Facing extermination, the remaining soldiers laid down their arms at once, scraping cloth together to wave a white flag. All of them were taken prisoner, including "Godfather" Dubuisson, whose glaring, hate-ridden eyes now shivered in cowardice, fawning at the RRF troops. They executed him on the spot. This tactical victory greatly boosted the morale of the southern front. Righteously, Isabelle and her rebel fighters remained masters of Gros-Morne.

In Anse-à-Foleur, the northern front was still surprisingly quiet, apart from sporadic bombing and occasional gunfire in and around the town. The attempt by government forces to maneuver downhill to capture Anse-à-Foleur was consistently blocked by rebel positions along the treacherous country road. Pinned down, the army was dragged into firefights around the town of Tibourg Au Borgne and was paralyzed. But by late afternoon, the bombings intensified. Cluster bombs dislodged well dug-in rebels after army commanders radioed their positions to the air force. Still, the battle raged well into the night – with rebel fighters denying the army any access to the main road leading south into Anse-à-Foleur.

Throughout the day, fighting had been fierce along the three fronts. But in Saint Louis and Port-de-Paix, enemy bombardments were most intense. Since the first opening salvo at dawn, the maelstrom continued – unabated, interminable chaos.

Every intact home, and everything that moved was a target. It was as if the government forces were determined to wipe these two cities off the face of the earth to send their deadly message to the insurgents. Schools flattened, church buildings crumbled in heaps, and hospitals were set ablaze. Entire residential blocks – gone! And beneath the rubble lay hundreds of dead and injured, while emergency workers fled their jobs to find refuge anywhere away from the city. Those witless enough to venture out into the open would face certain death from the helicopter gunship hovering directly overhead. Search and destroy was the order of the day. In less than twelve hours, Saint Louis and Port-de-Paix were no longer cities – they were monstrosities on the road to Hell.

Zebeda stood valiant and defiant despite what was happening to his cause. By nine o'clock that evening, Rebel Radio was still able to broadcast the war news. He sent a straightforward message to his people.

"The savagery taking place in our province represents the true face of Ti-Jean and those who claim to be the friends of Haiti. The whole Northwest is being destroyed. More than a thousand people are dead from indiscriminate bombardments. Men, women, and children are slaughtered, while the whole world looks the other way.

"Valiant people of Haiti, where are you? Are you going to let the fascists prevail? Where are you, sons and daughters of Dessalines, Capois, Pétion, and Christophe? This homicidal rampage rages – not only to tear away the Northwest from the rest of the country, but also to show that Ti-Jean and his blood-thirsty-warmongers stand ready to commit genocide. Their aim is to destroy every voice of opposition to their fascist regime. These acts of genocide taking place against our people constitute crimes of immense proportion. They will neither be forgotten nor forgiven. And when our country is ultimately liberated, justice will prevail.

"Wherever they are found, these criminals will be prosecuted. We're asking everyone to defy the authority of this illegitimate regime, to stand up right now before it's too late. They may bomb us from above, but we'll meet them on the ground.

"We're proud to announce that while their bombs continue to pummel our towns and villages, our RRF forces remain strong in the face of tyranny. Contrary to their propaganda machine, apart from a strategic withdrawal from the town of Bombardopolis on the western front, our forces are holding firm. We have effectively blocked their offensive on the ground.

"They will continue to bomb and kill us, but in the end, Haiti will prevail…it was never destined to perish. This war is not about me or the RRF. It's about freedom, the freedom we all dream of for our beloved country. I may not live to see the sweet freedom that's our goal. That's okay…I'm already at peace about that. War is an ugly reality, but dying for freedom is far more precious than living like a pack of zombies. We will not be forced out of our motherland! Nor will we allow ourselves to be slaughtered by the forces of evil. A free and democratic society for Haiti is engrained in the deepest fibers of our souls. For that, we're prepared to sacrifice ourselves.

"I am here now to say: *Viv Ayiti…Viv libète…Viv Dessalines…Viv Charlemagne Péralte! Libète ou lanmò*, we will triumph."

Zebeda's message trumpeted throughout the country, despite the regime having imposed strict restrictions on the press, forbidding news organizations to report on the war from the RRF's side. The government strained for a total freeze on information, to deny the population the real story – the truth. Merchants from the Northwest were not permitted to enter other areas in the country. Radio Nationale, the official government voice, supposedly the only source of realistic information, sent out nothing but propaganda for the regime. In order to prevent massive demonstrations, martial law was declared. A dusk-to-dawn curfew was imposed on the big cities.

Chapter 18

Chilling night spread through Saint Louis, as fear, despair, and hopelessness tightened vise-iron grips around the hearts of those surviving that abysmal day. Despite the fact that no bombs had been dropped since six p.m., every buzz emanating from low-flying jet fighters and the remaining helicopter gunship blew shockwaves through the terrified residents desperately seeking a way out of this vicious, horrible nightmare.

The friendly chalk-pale moon was nowhere to be seen. It was covered by voluminous death clouds of smoke. The darkness annihilated any light that would have shone on the valleys of obliteration lying below. As the bombing decreased, only one sound prevailed – that of the crickets resuming their nighttime symphonic recital – which had become a funeral dirge.

The mad rush to find safe refuge left no time to bury the dead. Masses of families abandoned their homes, using the unlimited darkness to flee into the nearby hills, in perfect accordance with an unspoken consensus of silence. Dogs didn't bark, cats didn't meow, and babies slept angelically in the protective arms of their mothers.

Long lines of people covering their noses trudged in silence past the exploded buildings and bloated bodies. The overwhelming stench of decaying blood and human flesh was everywhere. As they reached the edge of Anwodo, their trail disappeared, fading away under the bombed-out breadfruit trees.

To push forward, these night-voyagers placed clusters of volunteers carrying flashlights in disproportionate positions along the trail, guiding them along. From a distance, these unsteady stars winked and waved in lit-up spots to one side of the dark, menacing, cloudy horizon.

As night progressed in Anwodo, a few actual twinkling stars could be seen in the firmament. Peace and quiet reigned here, for the time being. Midnight rapidly approached as Odilon, anxious and frightened, stood outside in front of his home, astonished to see the long line of silent people moving along the pathway heading into the bushlands.

"*Manman*," he whispered.

"What…" answered Cécile from inside, "What is it?" Gulping, she lowered her soothing voice to quiet the fear overtaking her fragile, aging body.

"This is amazing!"

"What is so amazing…the bombs?"

"No, no, *Manman*. It's the never-ending line of people going toward the mountains…some of them waving lights like stars…"

"What kind of line are you talking about?"

"I'm standing out here, watching the people pass by. I bet Saint Louis is empty…only the dead remain in the city."

"Odilon, where are they going?"

"I wish I knew, *Manman*."

"Where is Thérèse?"

Kicking himself for not having helped her, he stammered, "I don't know, *Manman*. I'm very worried…I heard thousands of people died today."

"Son, please stop talking about the dead."

"How can I stop thinking about them?"

"I understand how you feel, my son. But-"

"But what, *Manman*…whatever did they do to deserve it? I haven't seen or heard from Thérèse…she might be one of them."

"Odilon, don't talk that way. I'm sure Thérèse is fine. God is great."

"*Manman*, don't talk to me about God. I'm beginning to think there's no such thing as God. What has He ever done for us?"

"Be careful, Odilon."

"Why do you think I should be?"

"You shouldn't talk like that about God. He's our Great Protector."

"*Manman*, don't be so naïve. If God was our Great Protector, why does he allow these criminals to kill us? All those stories about God are designed to turn us into mindless zombies…religion is the opiate of the people. *Manman*, we may not be dead, but many people are. And they did nothing wrong."

"Odilon."

"*Manman*, I have to go find out what happened to Thérèse."

"And where do you think you're going, my son?"

"To find Thérèse, the girl I love."

"Do you know where to find her?"

"I don't know. But I can't stay here, not knowing where she is, or if she's dead or alive. With each passing minute I don't see her, I grow more scared and angrier. I can no longer picture myself living without Thérèse. Last night before she left here, I made her a solemn promise."

"What promise?" Cécile grew frightened for her son. Was he planning to marry this woman? Delightful as she was, surely not during these times.

"I promised never to abandon her, should war break out."

"Odilon, are there people still passing by?"

"Yes, *Manman*…but it's not the same massive amount."

"Do you see anyone going the opposite direction?"

"What do you mean?"

"Do you see people going toward Saint Louis?"

"No, there's not a single person going that way. *Manman*, why don't you get up to see for yourself?"

"Odilon, you know I'm not feeling well."

"Thérèse," he suddenly spurted, "I'm coming!" Sylphlike, the young man launched his small, shadowy body out and away from his mother.

"Odilon? Where are you going? Odilon!"

Jumping up in a rush, Cécile pulled the window curtain open, sticking her head out in a desperate attempt to call Odilon back. "Odilon!" she screamed. But it was too late. She watched his silhouette fading in the darkness.

"Oh God, what have I done to deserve this? I've always thought life was a living hell. But now, I don't know how to describe it," she murmured, eyes flooding more than a monsoon as she fell back onto her bed.

#

Desperate to learn the fate of his soulmate, Odilon headed west toward Saint Louis—one lone *romancero* of the night, in search of his princess—moving against the tide of people pushing toward the mountains. He said nothing to anyone, trying to get a grip on his emotions. Staying close to the refugees as he passed by, he peered into their faces, searching for Thérèse. But the further he walked toward town, the more terrified he became. Though several of the women's faces made him pause, Thérèse was nowhere to be seen. His heart pumped, blood pressure soaring – spells of dizziness – he shook his head, pressing on.

"What will I do without Thérèse?" he muttered to himself.

Near Saint Louis, fewer people traveled on the road. The closer he got to town, the more he saw the place was deserted, everyone had gone except for RRF fighters patrolling the dusty, vacant streets. Some were on foot; others rode in jeeps.

Odilon almost reached Thérèse's house, when an RRF foot soldier stopped him. "Where are you going this time of night?" the fighter asked. He was dressed in green camouflage, a fierce, dark green; so dark that it was difficult to pinpoint where his clothing stopped, and his features began. He was tall and lean, cradling his AK-47 in one hand, and a bazooka in the other, in a combat-ready position.

"I'm looking for my fiancée."

"Where does she live?"

"She lives…if she lives…in the third house on the corner."

"You can't go down there."

"Why?"

"It's too dangerous."

"Too dangerous…she might be buried in there somewhere!"

"Yes. Two bombs hit the next-door house earlier, completely demolishing it. The area is covered with debris, and the street isn't passable."

"What?" Stunned, Odilon tore at his hair in disbelief.

"Yes, that's what happened." The soldier dropped his voice to try to soothe him, "It's too dark to go any further. You won't be able to see your way through the rubble."

"What happened to the people?"

"They're…all presumed dead."

"Even everybody in houses next door?"

"No, some of them survived, but I don't think the survivors are there. Like the rest of the city, everyone is gone, except for the dead. Hurry up, go back home before the bombing begins anew!" A young man like Odilon, the trooper tried a fatherly pat on his back. But this failed to assuage Odilon's worries.

Odilon said goodbye, disappearing into the dank odors of death and destruction permeating the midnight air. Gagging from the putrefying stench, he pulled a bandana from his back pocket and covered his face. As he entered the back alley leading to Thérèse's home, he tromped heavily through the ruins. Dilapidated houses lined the path, most of them on fire and burning bright.

Hopping like a kangaroo to protect his feet, Odilon needed to avoid making any noise that would attract further attention from the RRF, in order to reach the back gate of Thérèse's house. The great concrete wall surrounding it was still intact. Layers of barbed wire and jagged bits of broken bottles lay on top of the walls to keep intruders out. Inside, two large, vicious dogs were on post, ready to jump on the first thing that moved inside the enclosure.

Holding his breath, praying for any signs of life, Odilon knocked on the metal gate, bang! Bang! Bang! The dogs leapt up at the intrusion, barking to keep their furious mission. A dim light was visible on the second floor beyond the balcony, from an oil lamp or a candle. Greatly relieved, Odilon knew someone was inside.

"Thérèse!" he shouted with all his might.

"*Oui*," Thérèse called back at the voice of her lover. Racing at lightning speed down the stairs, she calmed the dogs, staying inside the gate. "Odilon, is it you? I have to be sure before I open the gate."

"*Oui*, baby…it's me. You scared the hell out of me." He hopped up and down, lost in cascades of utmost joy. "They said you were probably dead!"

Thérèse ordered the dogs into their cages, locking them in before she ran to the gate, removing the latch. Delirious with joy, Odilon swept her into his arms, no longer tired and hungry – planting kisses everywhere he could reach.

Oblivious to the aroma of war, they began hugging with extreme emotion and loving passion. "I thought…you were dead…*chérie*," moaned Odilon.

"I thought I was going to die, too. But I was resigned to it," she sobbed, grabbing at his t-shirt, holding tight to her lover.

"Why didn't you get out and run with the rest of the people?"

"Mon *chéri*, it was impossible for me."

"Why?"

"Around eleven o' clock this morning, a hideous bomb fell on the blue house on the corner."

"Isn't that Jean-René's house?"

"Yes!"

"And where were Jean-René and his family?"

"They were inside. Shortly after, many people came to try to save the children who were still alive."

"Then what happened?"

"What happened next, you'll never believe."

"What? *Chérie*…what happened?"

"Another bomb came down in the exact same spot, killing almost everyone inside and around the outside the house. Those who were still alive were seriously injured. People got blown apart…losing legs, arms, and their heads…smashed, bloody…body parts flying…I saw these things, I'll never forget…so horrible." Sobbing, she continued, "I…watched an old woman from this balcony…crying with her hands over her head…screaming that everyone was killed. Then another bomb dropped and flattened all the mud houses near the shorelines."

She stopped for a moment to catch her breath. "I thought about running but didn't know where to go. I saw people killed because they fled their homes. It was safer to stay here, rather than try to escape. I was losing my mind! I thought I was one of the undead, the zombies. I thought of you, our future, my parents; I thought of the future of the province, our country, and the plight of all oppressed people of this world. I wished I'd never been born…facing a country filled with so much hatred."

Thérèse cried like a baby for five minutes. Odilon, broken with emotion, massaged her shoulders in a caring but lifeless manner. "There, there, baby. It's okay now. You can cry. You're safe with me."

Suddenly, Odilon sensed an urgent need to get away, out of the danger zone. Gently, he pushed her in front of the gate. "Are there people inside?" he asked.

"What people? Who're you talking about?"

"You were alone in there?" Odilon questioned.

"Of course," snuffled Thérèse, rubbing salt from her eyes. "You thought the people were here? Didn't I tell you they all left last week? They told me to take charge, and that they won't be back until the war is over."

"*Chérie*, no, you never told me they were gone! Every time we meet, we're too busy making love to talk." Shaking his shoulders, he pulled her closer. "Silly girl, how could you be so naïve? Would you sacrifice yourself to protect these people's property? They've been humiliating you for years! Yet in the shadow of death, you remain docile, totally obedient to your exploiters."

Thérèse began to cry again, as Odilon continued. "If they really cared about you or your service, if they had the slightest sympathy for you, they wouldn't have left you behind with the dogs, and to care for their property. The truth is that they could easily find someone to take your place!" By the time he finished, his whole body quivered with raw rage and hatred.

"Oh, Odilon, what you say is the truth. Since those people went away, leaving this house has been on my mind. But…leave it for where? I'm the only one who can help out when my folks need something. If I leave here, there's no hope for me to get another job. You wouldn't like to see me going back to Nan Banman, to live in that tiny house with the rest of my family – all crowded into one room."

"Yes, I would," Odilon sternly replied. "Before Zebeda explained our situation in this society, I probably wouldn't have wanted to see you go back to your parents. Now I know better. Come on, you're coming home with me."

"I'm what?"

"Yes, you're going to live at my house. I would love to see this happen. It's my favorite dream – how someday we could live together. But even if you don't want to live with me, you won't sleep in this house tonight. It's too dangerous…I love you too much to walk away alone. Come on, let's go."

Drifting into his outstretched arms, Thérèse caved in. But then, she pulled away – pointing to the house as Odilon frowned.

"Wait, I have some things to pack up. Come inside with me, while I get ready. Then we'll go to your house."

Relieved, Odilon went inside the gate behind the concrete walls. They picked their way slowly across the backyard, going between the outspread palms and drooping mango trees to reach the metal back door. Thérèse hiked up the creaking stairs to her room, as Odilon followed one pace behind. Grabbing her nightgown and a few clothes, she swiftly shoveled them into a large plastic bag, slinging it over one wanly bare shoulder and heading downstairs.

"I'm ready to go…but what about the animals?" she asked Odilon. "We can't leave them to fend for themselves, locked up in their cages like…dogs."

The simple joke had them both laugh for several minutes. "I'll wait outside the gate, and you turn them loose, we'll come back tomorrow to take care of them," Odilon declared, secretly wishing that he had not promised to do this.

Chapter 19

Shutting the gate behind her, Thérèse was grateful to leave behind what had been her home for several years. The young couple plodded down the alleyway, disappearing into the darkness along the debris-filled corridors leading to the main street. Their faces were covered with Odilon's bandanas, blocking out the noxious odors of smoke and decaying flesh permeating the air.

Nothing broke the night's silence but an occasional stray dog howling its lungs out in search of its owners. At first, Thérèse gripped Odilon's hand tightly, but it couldn't last. He had to raise one hand to carry her belongings on his head, while the other held a wet bandana across his face. Walking as fast as possible, they soon crossed the deserted main street, passing through the empty square and heading east behind the old neighborhood Catholic church.

All of a sudden, flashing lights and the whirring of a helicopter's blades shattered the night, buzzing directly overhead. Within moments a huge explosion followed, only a few meters away. Its target was the Catholic school behind a former army barracks, overlooking the town's square and its familiar shopping district.

"Odilon!" Thérèse screamed, in a blur of sound and motion.

"Yes, *chérie!*" he screamed back, grabbing her shoulders as her belongings hit the ground. Odilon scooped them up, rearranging the bag on his head.

"Do you think we'll make it to your house?"

"Yes, I do…we will…because you're with me."

"I'm afraid…my heart is beating so fast!"

"*Chérie...*" he gasped, pausing for breath in the muck.

"What?"

"Let's stop for a few minutes. There's an abandoned house near here, a bit further on in the woods. Let's go find it...I know where it is."

Feeling spent already, she had to trust him. "Okay."

To avoid detection from an aircraft bombing the street, they followed a thin, winding dirt trail several feet away from the main road. The trail curved downward to a wooded gorge swamped by thousands of flying bats. A small creek streamed through the middle of this blessed hidden gorge. In the midnight stillness, its rushing current splashed noisily over boulders that guarded a waterfall, before it cascaded into a river basin a few meters below.

The lovers paused briefly to pinpoint their direction, then resumed their march to find the abandoned house. Swarming bats scattered off ahead of their advance, rustling cracked tree branches in the night breeze. Their hearts pounded at every crackle, as the fading sounds of exploding bombs in the distance served as a vivid reminder that they needed to press on. Going back to help the dogs was no longer an option, Odilon mused. In silence, they tiptoed down to where the creek narrowed over a shallow passageway, crossing without looking back.

Upon reaching the south bank, they lowered their unneeded bandanas, trailing off an overgrown pathway that led to a small garden of freshly planted maize, which rose up toward a dense mango grove. At the entrance of the grove, the pathway vanished, blending with the tall and bushy tropical undergrowth. In the eerie remains of that brutal atmosphere, they found themselves puzzled: the abandoned house was nowhere in sight.

"What do we do now?" Thérèse gasped, confused and panting as she held onto her man, who still balanced her belongings on his head.

"*Chérie,* we can't be too far off. I know this area...I've done work here in the past. It's the darkness that's confusing me...let's continue," Odilon stated, punctuating his speech with a firm kiss on Thérèse's pouting lips to calm her down.

Edging along cautiously, they entered the hollow world of the mango grove. To get to their destination, if they even had one, they had to cut through the grove, unless they went back to the main road. In their rush, Odilon bounced against an old tree trunk, sending him stumbling several feet. Thérèse dove down to rescue him, with sweat welling on her dripping cheeks, soaking her dress — it plastered her body, revealing the outline of her firm breasts. Seeing this, Odilon regained his self-control just as he was about to trip over a big chunk of log resting across a ditch.

Gasping for breath, they sat on the moist ground for a few minutes. When they got up again, there were only a few more long steps before the grove was behind them. A little walkway led them to a pebbled hillside road branching out into two pathways: one leading east toward the hilltop, the other threading down to a sugar-sand road, where a visible cottage hid in the foliage.

"I think I know where we are," Thérèse whispered with relief, lowering her voice to conceal how reassured she was.

"Me too!" His determination renewed, Odilon surged with vigor to reach the old cottage.

Two lines of pigeon pea trees guided their path all the way down to the front porch of the cottage, while a cool breeze wafting downhill greeted them. Approaching the front door, they found it rusty, but open. They entered without a sound. The windows were gone, paving the way for lofty night-time perfumes, soft fragrances of wild jasmine entwining with the glassy, silken caresses of the breeze. Dew from sprouting weeds poked out of the cracked dirt floor — resembling holy water sprinkled on Sunday mass parishioners. Glancing through a window to be safe, the lovers breathed alone in the nightmarish night, away from the bogeymen, beyond any werewolves.

The moon boldly emerged from behind the dark blue sky, casting ghostly rays of light over the rolling hills and beating down on them.

Odilon stuck his head further out the window but could only see the marvels of the fields across the trail. In the near-silent night, a rooster's crow broke. For a moment, the natural order of tropical night returned. That rooster, however, alerted the lovers, who remained interlaced in each other's arms to weather this latest wave of fear.

In the still of the night, a lone songbird chirped a sharp piercing squeak, soon followed by a mounting sequence of warbles and trills like that of a nightingale. The continuous stream of sharp, high-pitched shrieks shooting through the dilapidated house was enough to send chills into the hearts of the lovers. Odilon released himself from Thérèse, clapping his hands twice out of the open window. The echoes scared the noisy bird away. The flapping of wings and the rustling on a mango tree's branches right outside the house convinced him that it was none other than a stray mockingbird in search of its lost nest.

"Come here and lie with me, *cherie*," urged Odilon, softening his voice to cool off his terrified, sweat-soaked lover.

"You see…" sighed Thérèse.

"What do I see, my love?" he queried, pulling a clean handkerchief from his back pocket to wipe the tears, sweat, and filth with care from her face.

"If I die in your arms, I will be fine…when I'm with you, I always feel a sense of great comfort. Come, let me taste your mouth again, before I die."

"Don't worry. It's not going to happen tonight," Odilon replied, pulling her close as they exchanged ardent kisses. Soon, they slid down onto the mossy carpet beneath their feet.

As they made love inside a crumbled house in the woods, explosion after explosion could be heard from far away. Sex is a delirious release of pent-up emotions. Often, it's the only legitimate happiness that poverty-stricken people can attain throughout their entire lives. Each rousing explosion was followed by a sparkling array of fireworks bursting in the sky, amplifying the ecstasy of their exquisite lovemaking. These "fireworks" originated from RRF ground fighters, responding to the bombings as they tried to shoot down that one pesky low-flying helicopter.

A sated and relaxed Odilon asked, "Can we continue our journey to my house now, my love?" Just then, a bomb engulfed the nearby main road. That sound which seemed far away during their lovemaking loomed too close for comfort.

"You bet I can," she gulped. "Let's get the hell out of here!"

Scrambling to their feet, they brushed off their clothes. Odilon tossed Thérèse's bag of clothing across his back with one hand, held her tight with the other, and tried hard to alleviate her anxiety. They wove their way through a sugarcane field. It was odd; that night, they traveled completely without fear of werewolves. Their real enemy was the bombs from the helicopter gunship. Needing to reach Anwodo as soon as possible, after some twenty minutes of pushing their way under long, scratchy sugarcane leaves, they reached the banks of Bassin Joseph River. They then crossed to climb toward a rocky hilltop just above Anwodo's valley. The farther away they got from the city, the bombs grew less intense, with the sounds of gunfire also decreasing. For now, they were out of danger.

"Odilon," said Thérèse.

"What, *chérie?*"

"Why did we take this long way to get to Anwodo?"

"It was too dangerous to travel on Main Street."

"If we took Main Street via Uptown and Vertus, we could've made it to your mother's house much faster."

"I couldn't take you through what I handled to find you in town."

"What do you mean by that, exactly?"

"I didn't want to upset you before, but I encountered many horrible things on the way to your house." Odilon dropped the clothes bag on the ground, turning Thérèse around to face him — speaking in a solemn voice. "From the hill to the main street, when I entered the city to find you, every single home I walked by was either destroyed or seriously damaged. When I got to the bridge in Vertus, I saw a young boy, alone in his tears. I stayed away at first; I thought he was a *lougarou*, a werewolf."

"After I watched him for a moment, I realized he was a real boy. I went to him and asked about his parents. Unable to speak, he directed me to a little mud house behind a grove of almond trees near the shoreline. When we got there, the house was empty…all the surrounding homes destroyed…many dead bodies sprawled outside. Blood and body parts were…strewn everywhere. The smell of burnt flesh was gut-wrenching…no one alive, except for me and the little boy."

"Odilon!" Shocked, she mouthed, "You mean you just left him there?"

"No, no. Of course not."

"Where's the boy now?"

"I tried to get him to leave with me, but he refused. A group of RRF fighters came along and took him to safety."

"*Mèsi bondye!*" She thanked her God.

"I followed the main path down to Marché Mercredi. Every house near the RRF office was destroyed. The debris blocked all access to the other side. So, I had to detour. I found my way through some back alleys to reach the seaside. I kept stepping on soft things…didn't know what they were. That's when I covered my face…couldn't see in the dark…must've been dead bodies," he mumbled, feeling miserable. Is this what true freedom leads to? "I was relieved when I finally got to the sea. From there, I went south to your house."

"You mean Vertus and Lòt Bò Pon were…wiped out?"

"No, many houses were standing there; but in the darkness, I couldn't see how badly damaged they were. Most of them looked abandoned. Their doors were wide open, but I couldn't see or hear any movement inside. I'm certain those who survived fled to the mountains."

"Odilon, what have we done to deserve this?"

"I don't know, *chérie*. But if we survive, I'll never forget this night."

"Let's go quickly, *chéri*. I'm afraid to see your mother's face. She must be losing her mind right now, with you gone."

"Please, don't mention it to her! You should've seen her reaction early this evening – when I told her I was going to look for you."

"What did she say?"

"Nothing bad about you…she was afraid I might die looking for you. She tried to stop me, but I came for you anyway. I was losing my mind, looking through every group of people that passed by me on the road. When I didn't see you, my anxiety kept growing. I finally reached a point where I couldn't hold back. I broke down and cried. I wanted to be with you, dead or alive."

"Oh, Odilon!" Tears flooded her eyes.

"Yes, *chérie?*"

"I didn't know you loved me this much…"

"I always knew that I loved you, from the first moment we met. But I was unable to measure the depth of my love until tonight, when I thought I lost you."

Thérèse was speechless – amazed by her lover's candid remarks. She leaned forward, grabbing Odilon by his waist. Holding each other, they began to cry – the gut-wrenching sobs of innocents witnessing profound evil. They cried over their uncertain future, the fate of their friends and relatives whom they feared might have perished in the bombings. They cried over the fate of their beloved town, their beloved province, and their beloved country. They could not understand, as they cried with the sobs of the forlorn, why there was so much intense hatred in life, especially between the inhabitants of their own country.

The jerking sound of a non-stop, normally crowing rooster from the valley below forced them back to reality. "It must be almost daylight," whispered Odilon. "Roosters don't begin to crow until four in the morning."

"We'd…best get going," urged Thérèse, sweeping up her plastic bag.

"Here, let me take it."

Thérèse gave him the bag, holding onto his arm as they crept down the sides of the rocky hill. Approaching the valley, they began to hear filtered voices, seeing the flashing flames from distant torchlight dancing around like fireflies. They couldn't see too far ahead as it was still dark, but the closer they moved downhill, the louder the voices became.

Upon reaching the valley floor, they ran into a sea of people camping on a large banana plantation. Children were inconsolable as they cried in the arms of their exhausted mothers. Meanwhile, irritated fathers searched for a place for the family to settle down. Hundreds of people surged like wiggling earthworms in a fishing tin within an area the size of a football field. RRF soldiers had set up tents in the middle of the night, to accommodate the children, the sick, and the elderly.

Passing through the crowd, Odilon could not believe his eyes. "It looks like the whole town of Saint Louis moved here!"

"It sure does," answered Thérèse, nodding to people she recognized.

"Thérèse, I see a lot of people from Nan Gwo Twou. Look!"

"Where?"

"Over there," he pointed. "See that man in the jacket?"

"*Oui.*"

"His name is Dorgelus – he's the chief werewolf in Nan Gwo Twou."

"Odilon, what's he doing in here? Is he after the children?"

"Shhh…lower your voice. Let's go. We must get home before sunrise."

"You're right." The young girl, weary as she was, couldn't wait to finish their journey – telling herself she should be taking care of Odilon's mother.

They made their way down the path leading to his house, taking a U-turn in the direction of town. Faint sounds of gunfire and bombs could still be heard, echoing far off in the distance.

A few minutes later, they got to the front door of Odilon's house. The gas lamp merrily twinkled and threw off fitful sparks, low on fuel. This was the first time the light had stayed on all night, awaiting Odilon's return. He was quick to extinguish it.

"*Manman! Manman!*" he called out.

"Odilon, are you okay?" Cécile sprang from bed, pushing the door open.

"I told you where I was going, *Manman*," he replied.

"Is Thérèse with you?"

"Right here, *Manman*."

"Listen, my children. This has been the longest night of my entire life on Earth. I don't think I'm going to make it through the war. I've been so very worried about the bombs…and you." Tears splashed down her sagging cheeks, spreading across her tear-streaked face.

"Yes, we're all going to make it, Aunt Cécile," reaffirmed Thérèse – moving forward to hug her and gently wipe away her tears.

"*Manman*, if the attacks continue, we have to evacuate," Odilon ordered.

"What do you have in mind? Where do you think we should go?"

"Perhaps over the mountains, in Nan Banman."

The sound of exploding bombs could no longer be heard; eerie silence overtook their village. No barking dogs, meowing cats, or crowing roosters could be heard – and certainly no "early birds" moved along the trail on their way to work. The refugees had moved on, either to the mountains or the campground.

Their village was almost deserted. Many villagers had fled to the mountains during the night. Still quite black, that tropical night carried the fear of darkness and the uncertainty that came with it – enough to keep Odilon, his mother and Thérèse on edge. Unpredictable times create uncertain futures, and those who live through them tend to feel nothing but fear and apprehension until they are over.

In this stressful and scary existential reality, they were unable to sleep. Cécile opted to relax as best she could on her bunk bed, while Odilon and Thérèse stretched out on the *nat* – wrapped in each other's arms.

"Thérèse," whispered Odilon.

"Yes, my love."

"Why don't we turn on the radio?"

"Sure!" Thérèse answered. "You never know. There might be important information coming through this morning."

"Maybe you're right," responded Cécile, overhearing their conversation.

Odilon got up and turned on the radio, switching between Radio Nationale and Rebel Radio to catch the latest news. However, nothing but classical music on Radio Nationale or patriotic songs from the RRF station played from the device.

Tired of not finding any news, they fell asleep at last, leaving it on Radio Nationale. It was unusually quiet. Only the breathing sounds of sleeping people could be heard in harmony with the soothing music from the tiny radio.

Some three hours later, a haze-filled day found the sun trapped in a bitter struggle with smoke-filled darkness from the preceding night. A soft drizzle spread in trickles across the village. Heavy, steel-grey clouds approached from the horizon, effectively blocking every attempt from the sun to reach its zenith. Inside the little house it was pitch dark, as if night had just fallen. Exhausted, the inhabitants wrapped their poverty-stricken, careworn selves deep in the arms of Morpheus.

Suddenly *La Dessalinienne* – Haiti's national anthem – blasted over the airwaves, shooing away the classical music. An announcer reported that an important press conference by the President of Haiti and his topmost generals was about to begin, airing live from the presidential palace.

"Odilon, wake up, wake up!" Thérèse cried, "It's not music anymore, there's a big news announcement on the radio! Wake up!"

"Yes, dear. What's…your problem?" Odilon begged, weary and confused. As it hit him, he bolted up like lightning from the *nat*.

"The president is about to speak," announced Thérèse.

Cécile struggled out of bed, joining them on the *nat* to hear the latest news from Port-au-Prince. All three were wide awake, ready to do anything needed. Wartime stress tends to heighten the senses — making one ready for whatever happens.

Chapter 20

At the press conference, Ti-Jean looked fresh, smiling beneath his olive-green uniform. For the first time, he looked like a generalissimo, poised for an attack against his archenemy, rather than a buttoned-up technocrat waging a deceptive campaign. A lime-green cap sat tilted backward over his triangular bald head, which he tapped every few seconds—a gesture of his unchallenged authority in an era of dwindling credibility. Seated at a cherry conference table in the east room, he was surrounded by tiny microphones placed in front of the seats around the table. Flanked by his top generals, all clad in combat fatigues, he prepared to address a legion of journalists, poised to launch their barrage of questions.

"I'm happy to announce that the criminals in the Northwest have been dealt a major blow. Yesterday, in the early morning hours, our courageous army launched an offensive to restore order in the Northwest – and to put Olivier Zebeda and the *attachés* of his criminal enterprise behind bars. Our great army is pushing north in several directions, capturing the town of Bombardopolis to the west, breaking the enemy line in Gros-Morne, and pushing south from Tibourg Au Borgne on the way to capturing Anse-à-Foleur.

"Meanwhile, our courageous air force is pursuing them from the air. They have no place to hide. They will soon be either dead or prisoners. I'm here this morning to send a message to the silent majority in the Northwest: you will shortly be free from those assassins. Do not hide them in your homes. Be patient. Deliverance is on the way."

A journalist broke in on this self-congratulatory diatribe. "Sir, I want to believe what you just said. But unconfirmed reports from the Northwest portray a different picture of the situation on the ground. It appears that it doesn't look good. Could you please shed some light into that?"

"I don't know where these so-called 'reports' are coming from. I have checked with our army commanders on the ground. There are no such things going on. I have just received reports that the population is receiving our disciplined soldiers with flowers," replied the president, sounding a bit disturbed and irritated.

"It would be nice to give us privileges to see the video. That would put to rest the shocking rumors circulating all over the country," another journalist piped up.

"What shocking rumors?" The president was incredulous. "What nonsense is this?"

"Mr. President, we've heard reports of bodies blown apart, blocks of houses flattened with people in them, and men, women, and children summarily executed. Could you please, sir, let us see that video?" another journalist asked.

"First of all, I can't release it – for security reasons. Secondly, there's no need to question the president's statements," Ti-Jean answered emphatically. "Those spreading the false rumors are the ones who would love to see the country plunged once again into chaos. My government is committed to eliminating all bandits in the Northwest, and not to killing innocent people," he added.

"Mr. President, coming into this press conference, did you receive the latest reports from the northern front?" a journalist asked, eager to drop a bombshell.

"What do you mean? We have only a modern army here in Haiti. As I sit here, I have instant contact with all corners of the battlefield. Believe me, everything is fine. If you will now excuse me, I have to leave. I have important work to do…I have to work for my people."

"Mr. President, Rebel Radio's broadcasting Lieutenant Colonel Baltazar from the northern front!" cried the journalist, raising the volume as everyone gasped in disbelief. The President and his entourage, trapped in their golden chairs, were unable to move as they listened with great surprise and embarrassment.

"I'm never going to allow myself to be part of genocide," affirmed Colonel Baltazar with a stern, staunch voice. "We came here to help unite our country under one central authority, as we were told. But the rates and levels of destruction, the indiscriminate killing of innocent people, the use of cluster bombs mixed with sustained artillery barrage to level entire blocks of houses…all of this leaves me no doubt about the government's main aim…in Port-au-Prince," he continued. His voice broke, quivering with emotion.

Ti-Jean gazed upward, avoiding any eye-contact with the journalists, remaining speechless while glued to his chair.

"Colonel, is there a specific message you want to send to the people of Haiti?" The RRF reporter on the radio asked as he interviewed Colonel Baltazar.

"I'm asking the population and those with good faith in the international community to rise up and demand the immediate removal of this regime. I hope they set up an international tribunal to try them for crimes against humanity.

"I'm a military man. I joined the army because I wanted to serve my country against any outside invaders. I'm prepared to die if necessary. But I'm not going to be part of genocide. I walked through town, coming down here this morning. I couldn't believe my eyes. Never in my life have I witnessed such a horrible crime. Saint Louis du Nord is practically destroyed. Half of its residents are dead or fled to safety. It's heartbreaking to view hundreds of bodies, soaking in blood, lying in pieces – while the smell of human flesh becomes more and more impossible to tolerate.

"This is another sad chapter in our history. I witnessed the same tragedy in Port-de-Paix, in Jean-Rabel, in Bassin Bleu, in Gros-Morne, and in Môle Saint Nicolas. Besides the horrible destruction taking place in these main towns, many villages were wiped out in an ugly attempt to suppress guerilla resistance. So, I'm asking every Haitian, every son of Dessalines to stand up in the face of tyranny. Don't be afraid! We can't wait one minute longer. Speak to your conscience. If you don't believe in genocide, you must stand up now to bring down this criminal regime!"

The president, his entourage, the press corps – each remained obtusely dumb. After all, this press was sympathetic to the president's cause. All eyes turned now onto Ti-Jean, who remained trapped in his seat, pondering what to say. The shocking words did not come from Olivier Zebeda; nor did they come from one of his lieutenants. Those words came from a familiar voice, an unmistakable one that most of the journalists and most people of Haiti recognized. In fact, the colonel was for a long time the army's chief spokesperson.

After a long, tense silence, the president finally spoke. "I'm asking everyone to be patient. My government will formulate a response to this new situation. I'm hoping that what I just heard was a hoax. Remember, the bandits in the Northwest are masters of deception. Now, if you'll excuse me, this press conference…is over." Rising swiftly from his seat, the president headed to the war room, with General Lacroix and the rest of his entourage in tow.

"Mr. President! Mr. President, could you please tell us?" several journalists begged, but they were unsuccessful in following him. The president was already gone, disappearing into the many rooms of the palace.

News of the interview spread rapidly over the airwaves. Haiti was again in a state of shock. From Port-au-Prince to Cap-Haitien, from Gonaives to Les Cayes, from Jérémie to Jacmel, people were enraged. Everyone took to the streets, refusing to return home until the government was brought to its knees.

Thousands of young men and women poured into the Northwest to fight. The crisis was full blown. Their rage reached an unbelievable pitch, spilling beyond the borders of Haiti to join with the thousands of Haitians across the globe, who were as furious as the ones back home. From Paris to Washington, from Montreal to New York, from Miami to Cayenne, thousands of Haitians and their sympathizers descended on the streets. They were demanding justice for their brothers back home while denouncing, with all their might, all foreign governments supporting the Haitian regime.

Inside the presidential palace, however, the hawkish position stood firm. A crisis meeting was held to form a coalition government, initiated by Ti-Jean in a desperate attempt to reassure the world that he could lead. The big business establishment, through its cronies, the opportunist traditional politicians, quickly rejected the idea, saying that it would send a wrong signal to Zebeda. This was something that almost the entire diplomatic corps wholeheartedly endorsed.

So, the war dragged on, unabated. But during the last twenty-four hours, the situation on the ground had shifted in the RRF's favor. The army's northern front had collapsed. The government's air supremacy virtually vanished, for the one helicopter gunship left had been put out of commission by the RRF's newly acquired weaponry. The playing field was level. The RRF fighters made the most of it to recover lost ground.

In Port-de-Paix, Jean-Michel Desquiron, guerilla commander of the city, and his fighters stood firm. He led a long procession, proceeding from Trois Rivières near the southern fringe to the Cathedral Square near the center of town, where thousands lay flowers down in memory of the dead. Enraged residents swore to defend their city to the death. The square was filled beyond capacity, and every artery leading up to it swarmed with citizens. Lines of children in green military uniforms, holding pictures of Charlemagne Péralte, paraded in their own long procession. The parade stretched from the eastern fringe of town along the foothills of the Haut Piton Mountains to the main square.

Their cries for revenge were heartbreaking and boisterous. They unleashed an unruliness that struck deep into the hearts of the RRF officials at the square, igniting a patriotic and revolutionary resolve—not only to resist, but to carry the fight all the way to Port-au-Prince and overthrow the unpopular government. Amidst this fury, Jean-Michel, flanked by other top commanders on a makeshift stage, stepped up to the microphone.

"Compatriots, I can feel your anger. I have to tell you that I'm as angry as you are. The fascists, in the twilight of their power and privilege, are unleashing the most lethal weapons from their arsenal in a last-ditch attempt to drive every voice of opposition underground. Tonight, brothers and sisters, I can safely tell you they have failed. You've already heard the news about the northern front.

"Colonel Baltazar is a man of good heart, and we salute his patriotism. Ti-Jean and his government have failed because they are nothing but mercenaries serving imperialist dictates. Their diabolical plan has always been a recipe for disaster. They have failed because the entire nation and the world stood firm, declaring that Haiti will not perish. Despite the fact that many residential homes and public buildings have been destroyed, they'd be mistaken to think they can enter this city unopposed. We know they may have more secret weapons yet to be unleashed on us. But…we're not afraid!" he declared defiantly.

"Are we afraid?" he cried out.

"No, we're not!" replied the revolutionary crowd.

"Let Port-de-Paix be their graveyard if they try to enter it! Here, our secret weapon is our unshakable desire to be free at last. Over the wreckage and under the rubble, we will fight them head-on. They're committing a grave mistake if they think that their hideous acts will eventually zombify us. If anything, this has shown their true faces, exposed their Machiavellian plans, broadened our resistance and deepened our revulsion and opposition to their sadistic regime. *Vive Haiti! Vive Liberté!*"

The demonstration dragged on through the night. Many people refused to go home, or to what was left of their destroyed houses. The crowd did not disperse until three o'clock in the morning. Ending only when Jean-Michel launched a plea for patience, reiterating that they would be protected at all costs.

But if Port-de-Paix felt a sense of relief now that the bombing had stopped, in the far western front, Ricardo Alcindor faced his biggest challenge ever. Retreating to safety under relentless bombings, he had not been able to launch any counterattack. The government army had used a tactic that seemed to work well.

While advancing cautiously, the army reinforced its supply lines, leaving no chances for rebel fighters who might have wanted to attack from behind. Meanwhile, inside the town of Bombardopolis, a gruesome oppression was underway. Soldiers, going door to door in what they called a "mop-up" operation. They hurled grenades and poured bullets into each house before barging in. Everyone over the age of fifteen found alive was dragged away, bound and hooded, to torture chambers or concentration camps near Gonaives, some fifty miles away. Fortuitously, the majority of the town residents had already fled, following retreating rebel fighters to the nearby hills.

In Saint Louis du Nord as well as the rest of the country, rumors spread that Ricardo had been executed. RRF radio, still able to broadcast, could not comment on this issue. Ever since the war started, the high command had not been able to establish contact with the western front. Since the news of Ricardo's disappearance reached Saint Louis, well-wishers never stopped praying for his safe return. The day after the huge demonstration in Port-de-Paix, the boiling tension in town spilled over, sending thousands to the town's main square. These people refused to leave until they knew the fate of their beloved "Dodo," as they liked to call him.

Consternation reigned supreme around the square in Saint Louis du Nord. Ricardo, the town's favorite son, was nowhere to be found.

Throngs of people gathered in front of his parents' house, their voices rising in patriotic songs.

As before, Odilon led a major delegation from Anwodo. Amidst the horrible destruction and death, most people who had fled the day before returned to bury their dead and pick up the pieces. Taking advantage of a pause in the bombing, many residents did their best to restore a sense of normalcy to the town. But with rumors swirling about Ricardo's possible death, despair had given way to a far greater thirst for revenge.

For the first time, Cécile was right in the middle of it. Dressed in a long Cinderella-style outfit—fancy clothes saved for a day like this—she wore her traditional straw hat, a red scarf around her neck, and her best pair of low-heeled cow-skin shoes. She cut a dignified figure; her face loaded with anger.

Framed by Odilon and Thérèse in front of the crowd, she could not contain herself. "I have hope that Ricardo's alive. God is great," she intoned, raising her hands in devotion and prayer. "Papa Danbala is great. *Kote lwa nan Lafrik Ginen yo?* Come, come, to protect *tout zanfan peyi d'Ayiti yo*," she proudly growled with astonishing power, commanding the rapt attention of the demonstrators from Anwodo.

"Odilon," whispered Thérèse.

"What?" he replied, adding, "I'm listening to *Manman?*"

"I think your mother is being possessed."

"What makes you think so?"

"Look at her eyes. They're soaring! Look how she shakes her head, jumping and stamping her feet against the ground."

"Maybe she is. I haven't seen her that way in a long time; not since we held that ceremony for the dead in the village. That was, oh, five years ago."

"Look, Odilon…look over there."

"What's going on?" He peered around in the crowd.

"Don't you see those people on the other side of the square, dancing, hopping and clapping?"

"Listen, *chérie*. I can hear the loudspeaker. Can't you?"

"Yes!"

They raced to the other side of the square to get a better grasp of things, and it became clear that Ricardo's voice boomed over the airwaves. The enraged people in an instant turned into a crowd of hushed, mute parishioners – in a desperate search to find their lost parish priest. Only the occasional whirl of the wind and flying debris from the wreckage of bombed-out houses nearby intruded on their silence.

"No, compatriots. I'm not dead yet! And there is no collapse of the western front. Not a single fighter under my command has died or been taken prisoner. But we had to evacuate three-quarters of the residents. The enemy controls the town. The residents who couldn't leave with us now face an uncertain future. The criminals are killing everyone they can get their hands on, no matter who they are. But in the face of this tyranny, we're standing firm. Courageous people of Haiti, do not let Ti-Jean and his reactionary army intimidate you. Haiti will not perish. Resist, resist, resist..."

Pushing his way through the devoted crowd, Odilon finally made it to the center of the square. "*Rezistans, rezistans rezistans!*" he screamed, lifting the red-and-blue Haitian flag, floating it in the air as everyone responded in unison, "*Rezistans, rezistans rezistans!*" The demonstration lasted until late in the afternoon. Only an unexpected heavy downpour forced the revolutionary crowd to disperse.

While Saint Louis du Nord and the rest of Haiti breathed sighs of relief after hearing Ricardo's voice, the western front was by no means out of danger. Ricardo knew that; so, did the rest of the RRF high command. But they would not dare reveal it to the enraged population. Instead, now that the army had beefed up its supply lines and reinforced its positions in and around Bombardopolis, Ricardo made a bold move.

Needing to comprehend the army's strategy, he ordered his fighters – along with the evacuees camping two kilometers outside of town – on a long march to the village of Mare Rouge. It was located on a strategic plateau, some thirty kilometers down a rocky trail linking his current position to the village, where he positioned his forces adjacent to Môle Saint Nicolas, Bombardopolis and Jean-Rabel, the three main towns in the Far West.

It was a torturous walk along the hot, lone, dusty trail, exposing his fighters to possible unexpected bombings from the air. This was a high risk. But Ricardo felt it was worthwhile, because doing otherwise would have been suicidal. To minimize the risk, the move had to be made under the cover of darkness. In the middle of such precariousness and insurmountable fear, he summoned his fighters and all evacuees for some last-minute instructions.

Camping around a tidy coffee field curtailed by lines of royal palm trees, the people stood at willing attention. Heavy lines of cacti on the edge of town shielded them from the town proper. In their arms, mothers held their children tight, offering them sincere assurances that the upcoming nightfall would not be scary, and that all werewolves would be kept at bay. Rebel fighters formed a long, tight cordon around the crowd to beef up security. It was a somber moment when Ricardo moved forward to instruct the fleeing residents.

"When the sun goes down, we move to higher ground. We're going north, in the direction of Jean-Rabel," he said, holding firm to his AK-47, wearing his traditional military fatigues, looking pale as his beard was starting to grow.

"Do we need to bring everything with us?" asked an older woman from the crowd, raising her wrinkled face – ruined by fatigue and fear.

"Yes, don't leave anything behind. I know it's going to be difficult, but we must do the best we can to reach the plateau of Mare Rouge before sunrise. There, we're going to set up a temporary camp near the old flea market. Hurry up and pack – it must be everything. We're leaving no traces behind. We leave in two hours."

"When will be going back home…to Bombardopolis?" a ten-year-old boy wailed, standing right next to Ricardo.

"We don't know, son. But I can assure you that we'll return you to your home, someday soon," the big, brave revolutionary replied, gently massaging the boy's back to energize him for the long march.

Moaning and groaning, joking quietly to keep the mood convivial, the entire crowd fitfully packed their belongings – ready to go by the end of the day. At eight p.m., they tramped down the path as a trailing line of Haitian citizens and revolutionaries. Newborn babies and children under five were placed atop the horses and donkeys. Anyone seventy or older rode on the mules.

After winding about ten kilometers down the path, they reached the sandy banks of the Bancou River in the valley of Savanna Môle. This windy flatland, covered with light tropical undergrowth, was split by countless sweet potato fields and thick, fleshy stem cacti bristling with needles. The terrain made it difficult for the older, barefoot children to walk down the trail in the frightening darkness of nightfall.

They crossed the river and continued their march along a rocky mountain road, where wild citronella and cashew nuts freckled the vast landscape. A few flashlights guided them, minimizing their exposure. Suddenly, an unexpected blast from the Windward Passage disrupted their quietude. Turning their faces leeward, they pressed on, passing several cacao and banana plantations while thousands of crickets chirped in accompaniment.

The on-foot civilians, the revolutionaries led by Ricardo, and the plodding animals stretched out along their difficult trail for more than five kilometers, numbering well over a thousand. Using sticks to prod the animals trudging beside them, they occasionally mooed to calm the creatures as they sang old revolutionary songs, ambling slowly through the dark banana fields. By midnight, they reached the gate of the village of Lavaltière, about halfway down the trail. As they entered the sleeping village, a ghostly silence greeted them. Not a single light twinkled inside the little mud houses.

"*En avant!*" called out one young woman in combat fatigues.

"*Avanse, nou pap domi isi ya, n'ap kontinye!*" another RRF fighter answered. The wind grew stronger, carrying dust that coated the people's faces, parched their throats, and clogged their nostrils. It smeared the faces of the little children, who desperately tried to swat the giant mosquitoes buzzing around them.

For a distressing hour, the night voyagers felt as though they were approaching the gates of Hell. Then, without warning, the wind died down, giving way to a violent storm that drove sheets of rain through the heavy blankets under which children and elderly folks were sleeping. Thunder rumbled as lightning flashed across the unfathomable sky. Yet, they pushed on. Against all odds, they were determined to reach their longed-for destination before sunrise.

"Papa, when will we get to Mare Rouge?" a sad little girl whined, drenched to the roots of her hair in her own sweat and the rain.

"When the first rooster crows, we'll be there," her bewildered father pled, as hardship and fatigue splayed across his darkening face.

By five a.m., they arrived, soaked, at the foothill of Mare Rouge. There, they paused for an hour of well-earned rest, preparing to climb onward to their ultimate destination. Many parents took the opportunity to drift away from the main group, forming small clusters of families as they discussed their individual ordeals. As night gave way to morning and the dew made its presence felt, the people reloaded their loved ones onto the donkeys, horses, and mules.

Stumbling over large stones along the rocky trail, the animals were frantic to give up. However, they were cursed at, lashed, and shouted at, which forced them to stay the course. After forty-five grueling minutes of treacherous climbing, the last exhausted civilian finally reached the plateau of Mare Rouge, where the ancient trail branched into two directions. One path led westward to Môle Saint Nicolas, the historic town where Columbus had first landed on the island in 1492. The other path veered northward to Port-de-Paix, passing through

Jean-Rabel in Lower Moustique, a windy coastal plain stretching westward to the fishing village of Point à l'Ecu on the Atlantic Ocean.

This latter trail was of great strategic importance to the hawks in Port-au-Prince. They were convinced that crushing the western front was not only a matter of principle but also of survival. The Haitian Army was denied total access to the south from Gros-Morne. Joséphine and Isabelle, working in tandem, remained firmly entrenched along the banks of the Pendu River, mining and booby-trapping the main highway leading northward through the town of Bassin Bleu all the way to Port-de-Paix. With the northern front lost due to Colonel Baltazar's capitulation, dismantling Ricardo and his army in the west was vital to the war planners in Port-au-Prince. Overrunning the western front would bring Port-de-Paix and Saint-Louis du Nord—nerve centers of operations against Port-au-Prince—into view.

But there on the plateau of Mare Rouge, knowing exactly what it meant, Ricardo drew his own line in the sand. After all, he had a sympathetic audience in front of him.

"Here, we will resist to the last fighter. We'll show the fascists that in this region, we will always be the sole masters of our destinies."

These brave words were spoken before a cheering crowd of more than two thousand people, as folks were trickling in now from the towns and villages nearby to listen to the RRF's message. They welcomed the refugees from Bombardopolis. Many of these new people offered to join the fighters. So, the RRF had to face another recruitment "field day".

"It's okay to join, but it must be done in an orderly fashion," Ricardo ordered. "You don't have to take up arms to be part of this struggle. We have many children and older folks who are sick and need immediate medical care. Sharing meals and providing shelter are also vital forms of participation in this war. This way, we'll show our enemies and the world that we Haitians are well-disciplined and organized." He finished by giving the victory sign to the cheering crowd. Everyone responded with their own version of the sign, from small fingers to large ones.

Ricardo then ordered his fighters to descend the other side of the mountain—the Jean-Rabel side—on a historic pilgrimage to the site where it is said that Jacques Stephen Alexis, the late legendary figure of the Haitian revolutionary movement, was taken into custody by the *Tonton Macoutes* and later killed in 1961. The precise location of Alexis's disappearance remains unknown, and his body was never recovered. However, his ideas have forever served as a guiding light and cornerstone for all patriotic Haitians in their long and treacherous climb toward human equality and social justice—this latest march being a vivid example.

Many people now followed Ricardo and his fighters. An older, seemingly invincible woman, dressed in blue-and-red clothes, bore a long machete aloft as everyone faced east, toward the rising sun. She took the lead, singing the "Envokasyon Soley," calling on the African gods to bring Jacques "Soleil" Alexis back to the mountains.

"*Soley. Oh! Oh! Kote ou ye.*" She sang, whirled, jumped, and eagle-spread her arms and legs as she spun skyward.

"*Soley, kote ou ye? N'ap chèche w,*" the revolutionary crowd responded, lighthearted despite their woes.

Ricardo stood erect in his olive-green military uniform, weighed down by fatigue as he tried to hide his emotions. Gazing upward, he trembled, struggling to hold back tears that were a mix of joy and sorrow. No one saw his struggle as he prepared to address the growing crowd.

"Jacques Stephen Alexis will always linger in my soul. He is the sun rising over the mountains, guiding us through our most difficult times. The Creole fascists attempted to silence his voice, but their criminal act was a total failure. They couldn't understand that Jacques Soleil lives beyond the boundaries of his physical state. We all carry a piece of Soleil within us. Soleil is the energy that drives us forward—our shooting star that will forever shine in the firmament. Long live the ideas of Soleil!" (Soleil was the adopted revolutionary name of Jacques Stephen Alexis.)

The joyful ceremony lasted two hours, with many speakers addressing the crowd, teaching them about Alexis's legacy and the importance of following his ideas. Only the harsh, excruciating heat from the rising sun, bearing down on the barren landscape of the mountain ridge forced the politically charged crowd to disperse, amid the valiant cry of "Long live Jacques Soleil!"

Chapter 21

An ill wind blew through the mango trees in Anwodo when Odilon had arrived with Thérèse. They were war-weary, exhausted, and unable to energize themselves, having moved from the *nat* over to the bunkbeds. They looked like rare twin *mangfransik* mangos, wrinkled and sullen, sold at the village center. That morning, after listening to the president's broadcast, Cécile went to the small kitchen outside to make tea – complaining about a migraine headache. That hectic day at the demonstration near downtown Saint Louis had taken its toll.

It was noon—high noon for the resilient people of the Northwest. Night's persistent haze clung to their fear and despair, as the sun, in defiance, refused to follow its natural course, hiding behind the thick foam of clouds over the rugged mountains. Though it was noon, darkness prevailed, giving the eerie impression that midnight had somehow arrived at midday.

In the nearby forest, where darkness at midday was merely part of the daily routine, it was even more desolate when the sunlight – usually permeating the foliage, breaking up the patterns of green shade into blotches of light – was nowhere to be found.

Inside their little house, Thérèse and Odilon slept like angels floating in the sky. After the broadcast ended, they fell into a deep sleep, only to be rudely awakened hours later by the raucous crowing of roosters in the yard, demanding their afternoon meal. Thérèse, a city-bred girl, was startled by the noise and stumbled out of bed.

"Odilon, where's your mother?" she snapped. "Why hasn't she fed those birds?"

"I think she went to Ti-Riviyè. I don't know…I'm not sure." Stretching and yawning, he rubbed his eyes, full of sleepiness. "Oh! I need to get up," he groused.

"Why now? Why can't we go back to sleep?"

"I have to feed those chickens. Besides, I haven't taken my donkey to the ravine for fresh water."

"Oh, can I go with you? It's daylight…a little dark outside."

"Of course you can. But I'm going to make a detour through the forest."

"What for?"

"Purple avocados…I need to get some before the rats eat them."

"I never like to go into the forest."

"Why do you say that, my love?" Wincing from back twinges, he smoothly eased himself out of the little bunkbed.

"Odilon, you know it's too dangerous."

"Because of the ghosts?"

"Yes. And the ravine is not safe, either. You know there's a *simbi* there. Don't you?"

"I've heard about her, but I'm beginning to believe it's only a rumor. I go there almost every day. I have never seen her, and she has never called out to me. Anyway, let's get ready and go."

They went outside to feed a flock of angry hens and roosters, ready to launch an attack on the old canister filled with dry maize. Odilon scattered the meal, it was snapped up as soon as it fell to the ground.

"I'll bet *Manman* didn't feed them before she left. See the brown hen at my feet?"

"Yes. What about it?"

"She's already a mother. Those chicks over there are newly hatched," said Odilon.

"Well, our own chick may be on the way," Thérèse murmured slyly.

"You'd better be teasing me. A baby is no small business," Odilon replied, placing a light kiss on her outstretched lips.

With the chickens fed, they headed toward the forest, walking through the cornfields on the eastern edge of the village to enter a dark and eerie place, the exclusive, dangerous world of the tropical rainforest. As they passed by the great fig trees, grey fungi from Spanish mosses trailed down from their branches – the long, drooping beards of an old wizard who once lived in the jungle. Like crystal-clear water from the river, the air felt cool, flowing with the sweet perfume of the anise and the soft, fragrant scents of jasmine, eglantine, and wild lilies.

This exotic atmosphere brought the two young lovers a taste of infinity. An instant bliss, an immediate obsessive desire for life, *a joie-de-vivre* came back in full force to rejuvenate their minds, bodies, and souls, leaping into their inner selves to solidify their unconditional love for one another, elevating their beings to a level higher than the one empowering them the morning they met along the sandy banks of Ti-Riviyè.

They strolled atop the brown mulch and giant, dry breadfruit leaves covering the forest floor. For a moment, human suffering was replaced by a sense of paradise—an escape from the depths of a hellish world. Hand in hand, they passed between tree vines hanging in clusters like stringy green ropes. Amidst the chorus of thousands of chirping crickets, they reached the weedy banks of a small, winding forest stream.

Odilon opened his makeshift corral and led the donkey to the stream, with Thérèse following a step behind. They stood almost motionless, watching a colony of bushy-tailed mongooses chase one another in and out of the dense underbrush. The sun had finally risen above the mountains; its reflection penetrated the foliage, illuminating the young lovers' faces as they observed the playful creatures. Those restless little animals, along with hundreds of other species thriving in the jungle, were a special bonus—enhancing the breathtaking beauty of the hinterlands near Saint Louis du Nord.

The little donkey nudged Odilon's arm. He led it back to the corral near the forest, replenished its food supply and latched the gate. Surveying beneath a huge avocado tree, he searched for ripe fruits that had fallen on the ground.

He shook his head in disgust. "The rats beat me to it again!"

"Oh," Thérèse sighed. "I wish the entire country was as peaceful as it is here."

"We share the same wish, and it feels good. But Haiti needs more than good wishes to return to the way of life our parents told us about," Odilon replied, pulling Thérèse close as they hungrily exchanged moist, lingering kisses.

"But Odilon," Thérèse whispered, almost out of breath, "wishes bring hope, and hope empowers life." Breaking free from his loving grasp, she stood with her arms akimbo, emphasizing her words. "If there weren't any hope, we would've died. Without hope, life is meaningless. The wish for a better tomorrow is what gives us the courage to go on. Now that I have you in my life, my hopes have never been so high."

"Oh *chérie*, I don't know what I'd do without you in my life. You're right... Haiti must change for the better. We might not live long enough to see it, but from the bottom of my heart, I truly believe change will happen. There are two reasons for that."

"What are they, my love?"

"First, they will never be able to kill us all. Second, the people are no longer afraid to fight. That's why I think in the end we'll win this struggle."

Strengthened by the natural beauty of the forest and bolstered by the hope that their country would someday be hospitable for all its citizens, they left the forest. With renewed resolve, they headed back toward the village.

"Do you still think the forest is a dangerous place, my love? We didn't see the *simbi*, did we?"

"No, I don't think so anymore. But do you always come this way?" Thérèse eyed her steps with care, leaning on Odilon to avoid falling on the rocky pathway as they sauntered down the hill.

"Sometimes, not as much as when I used to come this way to pick up the fruit. My brother was still alive. We'd fight over the cashew apples. He only liked the red ones, but I liked yellow and red. If there were very few reds, he grabbed them up. So, I struggled with him. One morning when we were fighting, he almost stepped on a snake...scaring him badly...he never fought with me again."

"What do you mean, 'never fought again'? Was it a poisonous snake?"

"No, there's no such snakes here. But my brother believed that if he hadn't been stupid enough to fight me in the first place, he wouldn't have risked the snake." Odilon set his face into a firm scowl, his eyes dark and misted like the storm clouds hanging above the indigo mountains.

"Thérèse, I feel that I will never rid myself of the deep anger in my heart for those who killed my brother and the other innocent people in town. My heart surges with so much hatred that I'm afraid I may never be able to control it. I only find comfort when I'm with you," he admitted, his voice trailing off with emotion.

"Odilon, no matter how painful it is, life must go on... even if we don't know what the next hour has in store for us," Thérèse said, her voice heavy with empathy as she cupped his face in her hands to console him.

"I know you're right. But it's just too hard to forget. It brings me horrible chills each time I remember seeing my brother lying dead in a pool of blood at the chief's compound, and those innocent bodies, including dead children, rotting in the streets for crimes they did not commit." Tears stung Odilon's eyes.

"Well, that must...wait, did you hear that?"

"What is it, Thérèse?"

"Rifle shots."

"Wait a minute. I hear them too. Thérèse, let's hurry home!"

Sounds of gunfire crackled from a distance. The sounds increased as they crept toward Odilon's village.

"Odilon, do you think we're under attack again?"

"I don't know. But it sure sounds like it."

Upon reaching the village center, they encountered a large column of RRF fighters, marching and singing as they fired their rifles into the air—on their way as reinforcements to the western front. They had taken the back route to avoid a government attack. The villagers were overjoyed, greeting them with revolutionary salutes and slogans. Women gaily handed yellow hibiscus stems and red roses to the marching troops, while people lined up on either side, cheering like jubilant spectators at the *18 Mai* military parade.

"I want to join them right now!" Odilon cheered.

"Be quiet, will you? We've had this conversation before," Thérèse chastised him, sliding her body closer to his while brightly waving at the passing rebels.

#

Back in Mare Rouge, Ricardo was busy preparing for a counterattack. Reinforcements from Saint Louis and upper Moustique had beefed up the western front defense lines. He divided his army into several mobile units, dispatching them deep behind government lines, effectively forcing the government army to halt its advance. Jean-Michel Desquiron came down from Port-de-Paix to help coordinate the counterattack. Government soldiers were besieged from several directions. What seemed to be an easy march to Port-de-Paix, just three days earlier, now appeared to be a no-man's-land that was rapidly shifting into rebel hands. Advancing government troops retreated at full speed, rushing to provide support to army units that were being attacked from the rear.

Insurgents, their faces dabbed with green paint to blend in with the dense foliage around the rugged mountains, waited for the government soldiers to pass along the treacherous, rocky trail at the foothills. They swooped down with such brute force that the spooked soldiers retreated in droves, randomly shooting and killing several of their own fighters. By the time the soldiers could pinpoint the direction of rebel fire, the revolutionaries had already disappeared into the mountainsides.

Throughout the valleys of the Far West, a sense of calm returned. The rebel army had pushed the government soldiers all the way back to Bombardopolis, cutting off their main supply route. This maneuver trapped the army, throwing the war planners in Port-au-Prince into total disarray. Saint Louis had never been so far from their control.

The regime in Port-au-Prince felt pressure on all fronts. Despite continued tacit support from its original backers, mounting pressure from the streets, the liberal media, the same nations that once supported it, and the battlefield had taken its toll. Trembling with fear, barely able to mask it with rage, Ti-Jean struggled to think straight as he began to run out of options. The defection of Colonel Baltazar in Le Borgne and the effective collapse of the government's northern front dealt a colossal blow to the war planners. This exposed their fascist nature and weakened their fervent supporters in their arrogant quest to publicly amass logistical support, weaponry, and military personnel—all under the pretext of fighting communism.

The question remained: What to do with an insurgency that showed no signs of backing down? If anything, it was gaining strength by the minute. Within the rebel movement, confidence grew. For the first time, they began to believe they could seize power, even though the Péraltista front Zebeda suggested during the Marché Mercredi press conference—shortly after the RRF victory in Port-de-Paix— had not yet materialized.

Now that they had effectively stalled the government offensive, the RRF launched their own propaganda campaign. Two weeks after the aerial bombardment that left thousands dead in the province, they released a video of the massacre to foreign news organizations. Gruesome photos of the desecrated bodies made the front pages of nearly every major newspaper worldwide. Millions of posters and flyers depicting the massacred victims were distributed by the RRF's underground networks throughout the country.

The base communities within the Church and their leaders, university students, Voodoo worshipers, trade unions, peasants, servants, and housemaids—all were united behind one goal: bringing down the regime. They saw this as an urgent necessity to end the genocide in the Northwest. The vast majority of Haiti was outraged after seeing the gruesome photos. In an instant, the last vestige of hot, sweaty fear that had kept the people from confronting the Ti-Jean regime evaporated. A consensus emerged across Haiti: dying for freedom was far more important than living like zombies.

A *communiqué* signed by forty-five peasant organizations from the southern peninsula added more fuel to the blazing fire – broadcast loud and clear on Rebel Radio – while leaflets were distributed throughout the country.

In a few courageous words, these leaflets read:

"We stand with you, courageous brothers and sisters of Saint Louis du Nord, Port-de-Paix, Bassin Bleu, Jean-Rabel, Bombardopolis, and Môle Saint Nicolas. We stand with you, valiant citizens of La Saline, Delmas, Carrefour, Bizoton, Poste-Marchand, Carrefour Feuilles, and Fontamara. All of lower Port-au-Prince, we are with you. You have led the way for the rest of the country to follow. Zebeda and the RRF have demonstrated that Haiti can and will survive if we all refuse to be cowed by the threat of death and destruction. The blood of those who died in the Northwest and Port-au-Prince will have been shed in vain if we sit idle and do nothing.

"They would face a second death if we allow Ti-Jean to run free like Bawon Samdi in his cemetery filled with submissive ghosts and zombies. *Fòk nou leve kanpe.* Haiti is not their private property, and our forefathers did not die so that slavery could be reimposed on us by a group of thieves, villains, and traitors. Despite the thousands of bombs that continue to rain down on their villages and towns, the heroic people of the Northwest continue to resist. Shame on us if we let them fail! Let their bravery and unconditional love for the land of Dessalines be recorded in history as the driving force that uprooted fascism from our homeland.

"We must not allow them to fail because the destiny of our country always rests in our daily struggle for freedom and democracy. What is happening in the Northwest right now holds the key to that destiny. Even if the courageous people of Saint Louis du Nord were to be wiped out, as the threat of genocide continues to loom, we must preserve their fame, their bravery, for they will forever be our guiding lights along the difficult path ahead, leading us in our quest to be free at last."

"Let us stand together to deliver the final blow to this doomed regime."

"*Viv Haiti liberé!*"

"*Viv* democracy!"

"*Viv* the RRF!"

"Down with fascism!"

The message could not be clearer, and the people responded in droves. Ti-Jean, back against the wall, faced an unforeseen dilemma – failing to win in the battlefield. The RRF effectively neutralized his military offensive. Despised by his own population, he knew that his political future looked bleak to the point of desolation.

In an effort to control things, a curfew was imposed on the major cities. A *communiqué* read on Radio Nationale warned that anyone found violating the curfew would be shot on the spot. This latest move failed as the population rapidly lost its fear. The curfew was greeted by general disobedience and violated at every turn. On the first night, everyone took to the streets at midnight, each soul carrying a pan they banged on loud and clear in open defiance to the Ti-Jean regime. Soldiers simply looked the other way. They just did not have the stomach to kill so many people.

Besides, all of them were children of the poor. Had they decided to shoot, they would have been killing their own. Even if they followed orders, they would be quickly overpowered and disarmed by an angry population that would not have hesitated to oppose and kill them. Clearly, the politics of *main de fer* did not work. If anything, it deepened the crisis further as the population stood firm.

Wincing and searching for any viable solutions, Ti-Jean decided it was time to placate the masses. In his most conciliatory message to date, he appeared before the cameras in a televised broadcast, which was also relayed live by Radio Nationale. Ti-Jean, ever the embodiment of oily self-confidence, was dressed in white with a red-and-blue tie neatly double-knotted over a white-and-blue pin-striped shirt. Against the backdrop of an imposing Haitian flag and a portrait of Toussaint Louverture, he delivered his propaganda message with a cordial tone in his voice.

"Bonsoir," he began. "My fellow citizens, tonight, as I address you from the people's house, I offer a new social contract to every honest citizen who is committed to seeing Haiti rise above its economic and political crisis. Over the past few weeks, our nation has been plunged into a deep political crisis that threatens our very existence as a free and independent country. The root of this crisis is deeply embedded in the economic difficulties that have plagued Haiti for decades.

"I acknowledge that I have been blamed for the worsening of this crisis, and I accept that responsibility. However, it's important to remember that this problem is one I inherited from my predecessors when I assumed the presidency. Despite my efforts to reverse the situation, things have not been working well for us. My fellow citizens, remember we are part of a global economy currently in its third year of recession.

"As someone who grew up as the child of a divorced mother, surviving on one meal a day, I understand the hardship of going to bed hungry because there is nothing to eat. I hear your cries, and they resonate deeply within me. But believe me, Haiti cannot remain in this state forever. There will come a day when every child in this country will have access to education, three meals a day, and free healthcare. However, to achieve this, we must first establish peace. Economic prosperity cannot come to a nation ravaged by war. Some might argue that when I took office, the country was relatively peaceful and question why I didn't alleviate the suffering sooner.

"It is easy to criticize from the sidelines. Yet, I am just one individual working within a framework fraught with challenges. Change will come, but it requires time and patience. War destroys; it does not build. Therefore, I propose we sign a new social contract. Let us be patient and work together for the benefit of all. Starting tonight, the curfew is lifted. I have ordered all soldiers to return to their barracks and all police units to return to their stations. I am also initiating a voucher program to assist the most economically disadvantaged citizens and offering amnesty to the rebels in the Northwest, including Mr. Zebeda, provided they lay down their arms. We invite them to participate in a representative democracy, where every Haitian can voice their grievances through their elected representatives. In the name of peace and in honor of our forefathers, let us give Haiti another chance."

Oddly enough, there was a great deal of truth in his message, but most people shrugged it off, calling it just another ploy in the president's maneuvering to regain control of the situation. Others said that his admission was nothing more than a half-hearted move of self-contrition that came across as too little, too late. The population took ample notice of the fact that he made no reference to the bloodbath that had been taking place in the Northwest; nor did he acknowledge the massacre of hundreds of Port-au-Prince demonstrators a few weeks earlier. In any event, no token admission would have sufficed to pacify a population whose hatred for fascism and passion for freedom was at an all-time high.

To the oppressed masses, no admission or self-contrition could mitigate their bloodshed and humiliation. Thousands of survivors had lost relatives, friends, and lovers in the carnage. To them, the struggle was "now or never" to eradicate greed, oppression, brutality, and cruelty let loose upon them by a brutal regime – supposedly in a battle against communism. The disenfranchised masses concluded that fighting alongside the RRF was their only salvation, their best opportunity to relieve Haiti from the grip of its enemies, so that freedom could prevail. They fully realized that only a true and genuine political independence would guarantee the everlasting freedom they desperately sought. To the folks ready to die so that true independence could blossom in the land of Dessalines, economic and political freedom was far more important than the elusive, representative "someday" democracy that Ti-Jean was promoting.

Once again, the president had underestimated the depth of the people's anger, failing in his latest manipulations to zombify a population whose determination to fight for liberty had already reached a fever pitch. Playing the poverty card to remind the masses that he used to be one of them did little to appease the people's anger.

On the contrary, it helped enflame their rage – opening their eyes even wider on petty-*bourgeois* like Ti-Jean. Such politicians are always quick to betray their roots as they become conformists, bent on serving in total submission to those whose sole vocation was and may forever be nothing but a raw exploitation of the land of *Toussaint Louverture*. Nonetheless, Ti-Jean was not ready to give in, certainly not when he had the political establishment behind him.

Chapter 22

It was New Year's Eve. But the traditional yearly bash, celebrating Haitian Independence Day with live music, firecrackers, and delicious soup *joumou*, was nowhere to be seen or heard. The soup, an authentic symbol of the liberated slaves in 1804, had marked the day for almost two hundred years. There is no Haitian New Year celebration without that juicy, tasty, yellow squash soup. But for the first time in almost two centuries, the masses in Haiti showed no interest in having the soup, or any other form of celebration. This was a sophisticated, organized maneuver, designed to send a message to Ti-Jean and his government that Haiti was officially in mourning, and only his departure could restore their shattered hope.

In Saint Louis, the marketplace was nearly deserted. Only a few peasants sold their meager supplies of breadfruit and coyote squash. About a block away at the square, street vendors were selling *piskèt* – at prices so exorbitant that the sellers outnumbered buyers by a ratio of five to one.

In the center of the square, two *troubadour* musicians dressed in overalls did their best to pump some amusement into the somber atmosphere. Each man leaned against an electric light pole, strumming a banjo and singing newly composed revolutionary songs to attract stray shoppers from the marketplace. Their romantic ballads, mixed with revolutionary fervor, turned out to be more lucrative than all the activities in the marketplace combined. Curious bystanders dropped whatever change they had left from their shopping money into a colorful ceramic hat the folk musicians placed on the ground before them, filling it with *goud*.

Further north, local children played competitive soccer, pitting uptown against downtown right in the middle of the main street in Marché Mercredi, near the bombed-out RRF headquarters. Passions soared when the uptown team scored a dramatic goal, solidifying an upset victory against downtown, which was heavily favored to win.

For twenty years, no uptown team had won a single game against the downtown team, traditionally well-funded by businessmen from the shopping district. But those Haitian-Arab businessmen were long gone, the *konpradò* merchants having fled to safety in Port-au-Prince, and the playing field was thus leveled.

On that dusty, stony field, it was difficult for non-local visitors to determine who was on which team – as the young players wore no uniforms. Their bare legs bruised in purple blushes as they ran, dribbled, and kicked in the bitterly contested match. Innocent but fierce, their faces were those of children anywhere else, happy and sincere even under the most horrible war-torn circumstances. Each of these children represented an extraordinary asset for Haiti, but only if the corrupt bureaucrats in Port-au-Prince came to understand that human intelligence is the most effective and important natural resource for poverty-ridden countries.

Odilon and Thérèse attended the match, sitting in a cluster of people from Anwodo. But Cécile stayed home, one of the few people getting *Calabasas* soup ready for New Year's. Saddened, she felt embittered at the injustices she endured every day. It was ruining her usually festive mood. Too much tragedy had occurred in such a short period: the loss of a young son and other people in town that she loved dearly, happening within just a few weeks. Life could be so miserable.

Since that last day of carnage, the sun never rose to its zenith in Saint Louis. Perhaps Mother Nature sympathized with the embattled residents as survivors returned to bury their dead and assess the bombing damage. A third of Saint Louis lay in ruin, and there was no guarantee the war was over. An uneasy calm prevailed throughout the country. All eyes were on the Northwest, especially Saint Louis du Nord, the heart of the resistance. To the Ti-Jean regime, defeating the rebels would require regaining control of the town.

#

Strolling in the twilight, Odilon and Thérèse returned from Saint Louis. There was no activity in the village, as its inhabitants kept to their state of mourning. Cécile was still in the kitchen when the young lovers entered the courtyard.

"*Manman*, how come you never made it to Saint Louis? We met Tant Lunia near the marketplace. She asked me to tell you she'll be here later."

"She did?" queried Cécile as she took a wooden bowl from the small kitchen table and plopped large, stringy chunks of yellow squash into it, chopped in preparation for the soup.

"Yes, *Manman*. I forgot to ask if she meant tonight."

"I don't think so," Thérèse mused, with just a dab of I know something you don't know. "She wouldn't come tonight."

"Why'd you say that?" asked Odilon.

"I know Tant Lunia. She wouldn't come up here tonight. She always hosts a party at her house, every New Year's Eve."

"Thérèse," replied Odilon, "You must be dreaming. We were just in town. All we could see were people mourning their dead. Most of them even talked about leaving, because the memories of their dead were too fresh in their minds."

Coming out of the kitchen, Cécile looked the young lovers in the eye. "Tonight, we're going to Nan Jean-Louis. We'll hold a ceremony to honor the dead."

"What about the soup, *Manman*?" Odilon asked.

"All I need to do is put everything together. The soup will keep. Tonight, Aunt Lunia and I are hosting a ceremony to remember your father, Avisène, and all the ones who perished in the bombing. We're also going to ask the *lwa* to protect our troops in the battlefield, so that this war will be over soon."

They went inside to get dressed and prepare for the long walk to the village of Nan Jean-Louis near Dédé Sapotille, a tiny village on the eastern bank of the Acajou River, nestled in the foothills of Morne Grassette, the last mountain tip in the Haut Piton chain. This place, shrouded in mystery and located ten kilometers outside of town, was known for legends that claimed no one could traverse the trail at night without being devoured by werewolves unless they were shielded by supernatural forces.

To reach Nan Jean-Louis from the northern entrance of town, one had to trek three kilometers down an open, rocky riverbed that stretched all the way to the mouth of a narrow trail. This trail led to a colossal fig tree, soon followed by a sugar-sand road, flanked by rows of star apple trees. The journey continued inland, crossing several shallow ravines before arriving at a mysterious one-thousand-pound boulder, oddly positioned next to the eastern bank of Acajou. This was where children, often naked, liked to perch after long hours of swimming in the river basin. Just a few meters to the east, on a mountain ridge amidst neatly kept coffee fields and scattered mango and breadfruit trees, lay the village of Nan Jean-Louis.

Frowning, Odilon was anxious about the upcoming journey.

"*Manman*, can we go through Barlatier instead?" he insisted.

"Why go the long way?" inquired Thérèse.

"I'm afraid to walk under the *Mapou* at night. I've heard too many bad stories about…that place," answered Odilon.

"Don't worry, my son," Cécile broke in, "Nothing will happen. We're protected by the power of Gran Bwa. Besides, you should remember why we're going. Tonight is New Year's Eve. There's no better time to be in perfect harmony with the *lwa*," the wise old lady affirmed. "Are you ready to go? It's getting late."

"Yes, we are," chimed the young lovers in unison. But Odilon, still nervous, was plagued with doubt.

"Wait, *Manman*…we have to wait for Tant Lunia!" he blurted out.

"I never meant she was coming here to meet us. I said we have to meet her tonight. She'll join us in Nan Jean-Louis."

Shrugging off his doubts, Odilon joined the other two as they stepped outside into the eerie atmosphere of the hazy tropical night. With no firecrackers to dazzle the sky, no twinkling stars in the firmament, and no moonlight glistening over the cornfields and banana plantations, pitch darkness enveloped the village of Anwodo.

"This is a real *dekou*. It's so dark!" Odilon exclaimed, putting the latch on the small wooden door, double-checking to make sure it was properly locked.

They headed north, passing through a large yucca field where the longhorn beetles had transformed the landscape into a breathtaking display of phosphorescent lights. These tiny insects, with their flashing yellow tails, made the countryside of Anwodo resemble a miniature New Year's celebration.

In complete silence, the trio made their way down a rugged hill, purplish in hue, following an old trail flanked by banana plantations and clusters of sugarcane fields. It wasn't long before they reached a gigantic bamboo tree, rooted at the edge of the main highway leading north toward Nan Jean-Louis. This bamboo tree was well-known for its mystical significance—it was believed to empower those seeking to serve Gran Bwa, the god of the forest. According to local legend, aspiring houngan would enter the tree's trunk, remaining there without food or water for days until their initiation was complete. They would emerge as powerful Voodoo priests, tasked with maintaining cosmic order through their communion with the spirits.

Despite the natural festivities and legends, that holiday night in Saint Louis du Nord was unlike any other New Year's Eve on record.

The streets were deserted, save for the aforementioned trio on their mystical quest. Odilon walked between Cécile and Thérèse, the latter clinging to his arm, trembling with fear. Each gust of the ocean breeze that whispered through the roadside trees sent a shiver down her spine, her heart leaping into her throat.

Upon reaching the south bank of Ti-Riviyè, they opted not to cross but instead followed the rocky riverbed winding toward the river delta. As they walked along the wave-lashed shoreline, Odilon turned to Thérèse and pulled her close, sealing their moment with a kiss on her lovely lips.

He leaned against his mother, asking, "*Manman*, why do we need to come here?"

"To seek protection coming from Agwe, the god of the sea. He's going to guide us along this long walk to the mountains. We also need Agwe to protect the troops against the assassins in Port-au-Prince."

Wading into the river where it merged with the sea, Cécile pulled a bottle of traditional Haitian rum from her dress pocket. With careful tenderness, she poured it into the ocean facing north, offering her highest form of respect to the spirits.

"Oh Agwe, the country needs your protection more than ever. Shield us tonight from all invisible beings that seek to distract us from our pilgrimage to the mountains," she sang with such force that Odilon and Thérèse stood agape, frozen in complete astonishment. Her voice, resonant and powerful, cut through the stillness of the night, as if reaching out to summon the sea-god's power, desiring the Divine Essence to infuse her being.

Dressed as a true *manbo* in a long, button-down dress adorned with a blue-and-red handkerchief around her neck, she embodied the quintessential female priest, endowed with profound voodoo mysteries, including the power to heal and communicate with invisible spirits. Odilon and Thérèse remained silent, careful not to distract Cécile during her intense spiritual possession. In Haiti, voodoo rituals are deeply respected, even by those who do not follow the faith.

Having completed this initial ritual, they slipped back into the jungle, making their way to their ultimate destination, Nan Jean-Louis—where the houngan would conduct the main ceremony in his *badji*. They crossed several streams cutting through rugged mountain passes, moving in virtual silence. They were solemn voyagers of the night, reluctant to speak to one another for fear of drawing unwanted attention.

After some time, they began to hear the murmurs of many voices. Entering a large courtyard, they found it filled with voodoo worshipers dressed in white, many huddled together, chatting and gossiping. Their ceremony had not yet commenced.

The houngan eagerly awaited the arrival of Cécile, his *wounsi*. Tall and stocky, his ebony-black skin bore the pure lineage of Africa. Standing about six feet tall, he was dressed in a clean red undershirt paired with blue polyester pants, and a new red bandana wrapped around his long neck. His face was partially obscured by an arching straw hat. Seated proudly on a lush divan at his altar, he exuded dignity as the man of the moment, though he occasionally glanced at his watch.

Cécile, Odilon, and Thérèse were greeted with great jubilation upon entering the yard shortly after midnight. Coleman lamps hung from six wooden poles strategically placed around the area provided light. The open yard featured three distinct buildings. The main one, a large, humdrum four-room structure painted white, was situated in a remote corner of the courtyard; this was where the houngan lived with his family. A few feet away, a wall-less hut roofed with thick palm fronds served as the kitchen. It was supported by four gigantic logs at each corner and enclosed by palisades.

Inside, three cheerful women prepared ginger tea. One of them was a striking, busty Amazon with a saffron complexion and glittering hair, uncorseted and barefoot. She carried a golden kettle that matched the metallic hue of her large hoop earrings, which floated in the cool breeze with each strident step she took to serve the hot tea. Just outside the kitchen, a slim girl with haughty eyes served *kleren* and roasted peanuts. A line of eager, dark-faced lads formed a submissive queue, each waiting for a chance to purchase their favorite alcoholic beverage.

Between the kitchen and the main house stood a two-room cottage, about half the size of the large white house. This was where the *badji*, similar to the altar in a Catholic Church and designed for performing voodoo ceremonies, was located. A light-blue wall adorned with images of the Virgin Mary divided the *badji* from the reception area, where worshipers gathered impatiently to see the houngan. Pictures of baby angels on the walls seemed to fly across the sky.

Inside the *badji*, emblematic images of significant *lwa* adorned the walls. Prominently featured was Lasirèn, the mermaid and queen of the sea, depicted rising from the underwater world to join Met Agwe, the god of the ocean. Together, they symbolize the balance between the sky and the sea. Nearby, an image of Papa Legba, traditionally invoked first in all voodoo ceremonies, completed this sacred ensemble.

Behind the altar, where the houngan presided, a poster of Metrès Ezili, the *lwa* of initiation, was displayed. Surprisingly, this evening blended faith with politics more than usual. Voodoo initiation played a secondary role, as the primary purpose of the gathering was to call upon the *lwa* for mystical protection of the rebel fighters, affectionately known as "the kids." Inside the *badji*, a large RRF flag stood in the eastern corner of the room. Outside, in the courtyard, murals and posters bearing RRF slogans created a dazzling display, reminiscent of the historic 1791 ceremony in Bois Caiman where Bookman, the legendary houngan and leader of the revolting slaves, officially signaled the start of the war for independence against France.

Upon her arrival, Cécile was led to the *badji*. Tant Lunia, dressed in a vibrant red ballerina suit, rose from her seat to greet Cécile with a hug. Her gray hair was tightly bound under a white kerchief, giving her the appearance of Ezili Freda during times of initiation. With evident joy, she escorted Cécile to a seat near the houngan. However, at the entrance, a young lady also dressed in red and offering charms and *kleren* intercepted Odilon and Thérèse. Odilon cast a shy glance at Thérèse, silently seeking her permission to accept the rum. Thérèse, taken aback, stepped back to appraise the young woman from head to toe before nodding.

"Let's take it," Thérèse decided.

Odilon took a long swig from the bottle of *kleren* and then offered it to Thérèse, who sniffed it cautiously. Upon realizing the contents, she declined.

"I've never had *kleren* before—it has a strong alcoholic scent that makes me nauseous," she explained, grimacing.

"You're right, my love, this *kleren* is particularly strong!" Odilon agreed.

After a brief pause, the young couple proceeded into the room, now ready to partake in the voodoo ceremonies. Inside the *badji*, Cécile (the *wounsi*) and three assistants were diligently preparing the *vèvè,* a sacred mixture of corn meal and soil, reminiscent of the ingredients used in Navajo sand paintings. The drumming would not begin until the *vèvè* was properly laid out.

"Odilon, why does your mother have to sit on the dirt floor against that pole in the middle of the room?" Thérèse asked.

"*Chérie,* you act as if you've never been in a *badji* before."

"No, I haven't, I swear to God! This is my first time. Remember, I was raised a Catholic."

"Listen, *chérie,*" said Odilon, lowering his voice. "It's important that the *vèvè* is prepared around the pole."

"Why?"

"Because it represents the entrance between our Earth and the world of invisible beings. This is where they invoke the *lwa*."

A few minutes later, the *vèvè* mixture was ready. Cécile and her assistants turned to the houngan, exchanging a look that signaled their readiness to bridge the two worlds.

As the conch shell horn and the *tanbou* drums began to sound, the invocation process commenced. Cécile rose from the floor and took her seat next to the houngan, while her assistants jumped, sang, clapped, and whirled around the center-pole.

"Odilon, look!" Thérèse shouted, pointing at a chubby, bow-legged girl in the crowd who had just been possessed. She collapsed to the floor, her body convulsing like a fish out of water in a net. Her long white garment billowed around her like clouds as she rolled her eyes in ecstasy. The crowd responded with cheers, their joy exploding around her.

"*Li gen lwa,*" uttered Odilon, holding tight to Thérèse.

The girl's wild gyrations gradually slowed, her slender body pressed face down against the center-pole. No longer singing, she hummed tunes that were unintelligible to the onlookers. The atmosphere quieted as the small group of worshippers respectfully followed the sacred rituals ordained by the *lwa*. At that moment, Cécile transformed. She abruptly jerked the red bandana from the houngan's neck, rose from her chair, and began dancing in erratic steps. Her arms flung out and upward as she whirled, bending and extending her red madras to the enthralled crowd, making it flutter in the air. She then began to scream, her voice starting low and swelling to a crescendo before abruptly ceasing. She was possessed: Metrès Ezili had entered her body.

It soon became clear that someone else was needed to manage this newfound power. It was now the houngan's turn to take the stage. Rising from his divan, he grasped a rebel commander's right hand and presented him to the goddess, seeking her blessings for the revolution.

Arthur Auguste was a revolutionary to the core. Although he did not subscribe to voodoo beliefs, he fully grasped how the ceremonies could further his cause. With a swift leap, he positioned himself at the center-pole. Cécile, embodying Metrès Ezili, drew Arthur close, performing ritualistic gestures that symbolized spiritual connection and protection, as per the traditions of Voodoo. She draped her red madras around his neck, symbolizing the *lwa's* implicit endorsement of the revolution.

The crowd erupted in ecstatic joy, reaching a fever pitch. Suddenly, one of the assistants—a striking beauty with starry eyes and slender limbs—danced toward the center-pole, performing the Zarada, an ancient African dance. She threw herself onto Arthur, her energy unbridled. As she danced, her movements became wild and erratic, her body shaking as if electrified. Her intensity electrified the crowd further, her energy seemingly transferring to them in a defiant display of ecstasy.

Finally, the spirit of Gran Bwa seized the houngan. Known as the god of the forest and a natural healer, Gran Bwa was revered for bestowing his followers with the energy and wisdom to amend humanity's errors. The crowd awaited his pronouncement with bated breath. Tonight, his presence had a singular purpose: to empower the revolutionary fighters, affectionately known as "the kids." Roaring mightily, using the houngan's body as his vessel, Gran Bwa made a dramatic entrance. His powerful manifestation was so intense that the houngan struggled to remain upright.

Instead of speaking, he burst into motion, spreading his arms and spinning around the center-pole. He moved rhythmically around the room, his dance steps matching the beat of a Haitian Samba in a folkloric rhythm, until he came to a halt in front of Cécile, his *wounsi.*

A hush fell over the room as a cold muteness gripped everyone's lips. Cécile took a red scarf and solemnly wrapped it around the houngan's neck as he stood motionless, his hands resting on his waist, exuding an aura of complete control and authority. In a spontaneous moment, a jolly woman from the crowd handed him a small bottle of *kleren*, which he downed in two swift gulps. Then, retrieving a shiny new machete from behind the altar, he strode toward Arthur, handed him the weapon, and retreated back to his seat, where he collapsed into a state of profound exhaustion.

Now, the celebration had truly begun. With the tacit endorsement from *Lafrik Ginen*, the drumbeat surged anew, echoing into the courtyard where the fervent worshippers danced, sang, and drank *kleren* into the night. The divine spirit had indeed suffused their bodies.

Chapter 23

Odilon and Thérèse went outside the *badji,* startled to see an elderly man in his early seventies standing nearby in the shadow of a huge mango tree. He stuck out like a sore thumb from the group of revelers.

Standing tall and smoking a pipe, he wore a white, long-sleeved shirt and khaki pants. Two pens in his shirt pocket gave him the air of an engineer. His salt-and-pepper wavy hair was combed back, and grandpa-style prescription glasses perched on the tip of his nose, accentuated by a Spanish mustache with Daliesque twisted ends. Every so often, he pushed his glasses up the bridge of his nose with his thumb to get a better look at the crowd, all while leaning against a tree at the edge of the open courtyard.

Watching the enthusiastic group, he smiled with amusement as they danced and sang to the beat of the Haitian Samba. His demeanor didn't fit that of a traditional peasant. He wasn't singing or dancing. As Odilon observed him, he couldn't shake the impression that this strange man was a retired professor on a wild quest to recapture his lost youth.

Odilon and Thérèse were experiencing an important moment in their lives, although they were totally unaware of it. They stood in the presence of a living legend – the vague, shadowy, revolutionary figure the security forces had been searching for since the beginning of the war – the mastermind behind the RRF movement. Yes, that older man was indeed *Le Rouge!*

Every revolutionary movement has its own ideologue, and the RRF had found its prime thinker in Daniel Achille, whom most people knew by his nickname. *Le Rouge* was the son of an Arab merchant and a peasant woman from the Valley of Forge, not far from Nan Jean-Louis. He was conceived as the result of an unwanted encounter.

Young Daniel grew up without ever meeting the man who had violated his mother's dignity. As he got older, he came to understand his heritage and the reasons he looked different from his mother, his schoolmates, and most of those around him. This realization filled him with a deep frustration, fueling a fervor that would shape his character and life. At first, he harbored a burning hatred for Haitian-Arab businessmen. Over time, this hatred spread to encompass the entire Haitian elite, whom he regarded with profound contempt. Yet, the light skin he despised after learning the truth of his birth eventually granted him access to spaces denied to the average Black child in Haiti.

His mother enrolled him in Saint Louis De Gonzague, the most prestigious Catholic school in Port-au-Prince, while making a living as a laundry woman, washing clothes for the wealthy in the Pétionville's fashion district. Using forged documents, she claimed to be his servant, not his mother. Daniel remained unaware of her secret until years later, when, during a visit home from Europe, she revealed the shocking truth to him.

After graduating high school, he earned a scholarship to the Sorbonne in France to study neurology. It was there, in 1956, during the Congress of Black Artists and Writers (*Le congrès des écrivains et artistes noirs*) in Paris, that he first encountered the tools necessary for a structured and organized revolution. This experience had a profound impact on him. His rage against political oppression and racial prejudice, coupled with his passion for social justice, fueled his revolutionary romanticism. His unwavering conviction in the need for a proletarian revolution in Haiti led him to embrace Marxism, though not Leninism, pledging allegiance to the ideals of the Communist Manifesto. However, he soon stumbled, unable to find peers willing to adhere to such a rigid, dogmatic code.

Efforts to establish a proletarian party quickly collapsed. His comrades, rejecting his insistence on revolutionary perfectionism, distanced themselves, accusing him of getting lost in theoretical labyrinths. Both in Paris and Port-au-Prince, many labeled his vision a surrealist form of Marxism, long dismissed by orthodox revolutionaries. They claimed he was 'full of hot air' and out of touch with reality.

Feeling abandoned, very much aware of the fact that a revolution can never be a one-man-show, he went into self-imposed solitary confinement on a desperate search to recover his inner self. He emerged a few months later, not only as a reborn Marxist but also as a newly converted Leninist. By then, he had come to believe that the peasantry and the urban exploited masses, organized under the direct guidance of a revolutionary party with a strong nationalistic flavor, must be the driving force behind any real movement that could succeed in Haiti.

Lenin's political pamphlet, "What Is To Be Done?" became his Holy Bible. In several leftist newspapers, he published numerous articles offering a candid self-criticism, paving the way for reconciliation with his former comrades. Among them was Olivier Zebeda, a younger man who recognized Daniel Achille's brilliance as an invaluable asset not to be wasted. And indeed, he was. From Alaska to Patagonia, Scandinavia to the Cape of Good Hope, and the Black Sea to the South China Sea, he traveled the world, rallying support for his cause. Tall, handsome, and articulate like his estranged father, Achille possessed the charm, charisma, vision, and education to command respect in any forum.

During a conference in Crimea, he met and fell in love with his soulmate, a young and energetic Russian-speaking Ukrainian woman named Ludmila Lutimov. She was a devoted revolutionary, eager to travel the world on a crusade to liberate oppressed nations from their exploiters. However, after three years, the marriage fell apart. Achille realized that there was only one woman he could truly be married to: Haiti, the country of his deepest and truest love.

In the late sixties, he returned home to help unify Haitian communists and founded the new *Parti Unifié des Communistes Haïtiens* (PUCH), or Unified Haitian Communist Party. However, when Papa Doc's secret police brutally crushed the party, he fled to Santiago de Cuba, where he continued working clandestinely with the survivors. Despite the severe setback the internationalist movement had faced, Achille remained steadfast in his belief that Haiti's fate would be different.

In spite of his unwavering conviction and determination, he couldn't escape his deepest pain—the quiet suffering he endured with stoic resolve as he struggled to understand why so many of his surviving comrades had abandoned the movement. Some had become traditional politicians at best, and at worst, reactionaries serving the very bourgeoisie against which they once fought. This betrayal not only brought tears to his eyes as he recalled his romantic revolutionary past, but it also left a raw melancholy that forever shrouded his soul. Even after losing so many comrades and seeing the movement falter, he remained convinced that Haiti could still defy the odds, just as it had in the early 1800s.

Late in life, Achille found himself fueled by the same revolutionary zeal that had defined him on that chilly day in 1956 at the Paris Congress. Yet, weary from the uncertainty and the hollow triumphs of international reactionaries, he became more reflective. He began to examine his own life—missed opportunities, the separation from his beloved mother as he ventured off to fight for a cause most of his comrades had long forsaken, his failed marriage with Ludmila, whom he had loved deeply but sacrificed for the demands of his revolution, and his neglected career as a neurologist. Surrendering completely to his natural impulses, all he had once hoped to achieve had been cast aside for an elusive dream—one that now seemed ever more distant, if not impossible, to realize.

Trapped in a bleak and desolate world, powerless against the growing emptiness of his existence, he withdrew once again into isolation—this time in a desperate attempt to stave off total physical and mental collapse. Yet, within this nightmarish microcosm, his new solitude only deepened his despair, as he sank further into a chronic state of profound depression.

During this hermit-like existence, his mind would occasionally shift from dark pessimism to fleeting euphoria as he reminisced about the beautiful, unforgettable moments with Ludmila, his estranged wife—their walks along the Danube in Budapest, romantic strolls through Leningrad, revolutionary gatherings at beach resorts on the Black Sea in Crimea, and their explorations through Central Asia.

Facing the looming threat of madness, terrified of losing his grip on reality, Achille once again set out in search of himself. Quietly leaving Santiago de Cuba, he returned to Europe, where he had lived before, as he tried to reclaim his lost past and rediscover his inner self. By then, the Duvalier regime had fallen, and Haiti was caught in a frenzy of wild, carefree celebration, as the people reveled in the collapse of twenty-nine years of Creole fascism.

Zebeda and his group, campaigning in Mexico, waited anxiously for Achille's final signal to begin their entry into Haiti. News of his disappearance was met with deep concern. For weeks, the RRF high command remained in Mexico, hoping for any indication of his whereabouts. Unable to act without him, they feared internal dissent and possible desertions within their ranks.

Many of the soldiers had joined solely because of the unwavering trust they placed in Achille; moving forward without him seemed unthinkable. He was revered as their messianic leader, a bold, charismatic figure in whom they wholeheartedly believed. To them, no revolutionary struggle in Haiti could succeed without his guidance.

The underground network in Haiti was on the verge of collapse. Then, one day, the high command in Mexico received a note from Achille, folded inside a wrinkled, faded brown envelope postmarked from Almaty, Kazakhstan, in Soviet Central Asia. The note confirmed he was alive and well and promised he would return to the troops soon. Though the note raised more questions than it answered, it offered a crucial chance to reinvigorate the RRF base. Seizing the moment, Zebeda activated their long-awaited plan. Three weeks later, the group landed on the sandy beaches of Méyans, a fishing village just south of Anse-à-Foleur.

Three months later, Achille resurfaced in the mountains near Port-de-Paix, where the revolutionaries had been stationed since their arrival. In a tense meeting with the RRF high command, doubts about his leadership surfaced, and his abilities were openly questioned.

He struggled to face his comrades, who had once revered him as their *maître à penser*, their indispensable guide, their revolutionary saint. They had looked to him to instill the fearlessness needed to win on the battlefield. But now, bronzed by age, with his face dark-brown, leathery, and deeply wrinkled, he appeared diminished. His cheeks sagged under his chin, revealing decaying teeth and wavy, grey-white hair. His wearied appearance wasn't the result of tropical heat or years spent in the arctic cold of Northern Europe. Rather, it was the direct consequence of a life marked by spoiled hope and crushed by despair.

Entering an olive-green army tent to meet his comrades around a rustic table set in the middle of a tropical forest, Achille, heart heavy, was bewildered by their lukewarm greeting. The cold reception tormented him deeply. As the war dragged on, and the weaknesses and flaws he had predicted became all too evident, his fear and sadness only intensified. The anxiety of defeat drained him of his revolutionary charisma, even robbing him of the ferocious laugh he had once used to energize his stance. The war's outcome left him more solitary, pensive, and taciturn than ever, retreating to a hermitic existence in a modest two-room house furnished only with two lamp tables, a small wooden bed, and a table where he wrote his memoirs—though they would never be published.

Known to his friends as Daniel, Achille divided his time between coordinating the war with Zebeda, writing or reading at night, and tending to his beautiful garden of exotic tropical plants, which he spent hours contemplating as he sought a possible symbiosis between Marxism and the supernatural. Few people had seen him until that holiday evening when Odilon and Thérèse discovered him hiding behind a mango tree, silently watching the Voodoo dancers in the midst of their festivities.

Chapter 24

Upon seeing Odilon observing him, Daniel went over. "Young man, I recall meeting you before." he grinned, as Odilon looked on in total bewilderment.

"Where?" Odilon gasped.

Thérèse was worried as she watched the man with her eyes wide in astonishment. She did not have a clue who this strange man claiming to know her lover was.

"At the square near the marketplace," the old man said, flashing a smile at the youngsters to reassure them that he wasn't as strange as they might think.

"I still don't remember," insisted Odilon. "When I go there, I always meet a lot of people. But it could be true that I've seen you before."

"It's true," answered the man. "I met you behind the great wall, inside that Catholic church's courtyard while the bullets flew. You had your little donkey with you, and you were terrified about its safety. It was the day the RRF defeated the government forces in town. If my recollection holds, your name is Odilon Joseph. You're from Anwodo, near Saint Louis. Right?"

"Yes, I remember now. You tried to stop me from joining the crowd. You were afraid I might get hurt," Odilon laughed. "But why were you so scared?"

"I wasn't afraid…simply trying to keep us from getting killed. I knew well what was going on, and I totally supported the cause."

"But why did you remain far away from the action?"

"I'm not in my twenties like you young folks. I didn't want to end up a prisoner of Ti-Jean's henchmen. Since I was twenty, I've been married to the revolution. Even now, I remain true to myself, loyal to the cause and my comrades. Every night, I go to bed dreaming of only one thing."

"What's that?" Thérèse asked, eager not to be left out. The conversation had begun to fascinate her, capturing her once-wandering attention.

"To see Haiti regain its old glory and become a free, prosperous country. But for over fifty years, that's all it's been—a dream. I'm afraid I'll die without seeing it come true. Throughout my life, I've seen these moments, though not like the warfare we're witnessing today. There were times I thought victory was within our grasp, only to watch it slip away right under our noses. It's always been painful."

"What's your name?" Odilon asked.

"Daniel Achille, also known as *Le Rouge*. I was born here but grew up in Europe—France, to be precise. That's where I met many of my comrades. Together, we founded a revolutionary party and managed to recruit patriotic Haitians from all over the world, including right here. I traveled far and wide, spreading the message that Haiti must be free. I visited remote places where Haitians lived in terrible conditions, like the *bateyes* in the Dominican Republic and in the migrant camps in the Bahamas.

In 1983, I was in Panama City for a major conference aimed at reorganizing the Haitian revolutionary movement. Zebeda was there, along with the legendary Haitian folk singer and actress Martha Jean-Claude, who came straight from Havana, Cuba, for the event. Afterward, I was arrested by the Dominican secret police at the Santo Domingo airport and sent to Port-au-Prince, meant to die in prison. I spent two years behind bars but was eventually released... thanks to some good Samaritans," Daniel said, sharing his revolutionary adventures with the entranced young lovers.

"Wow! You've really done it all!" Thérèse said, clearly spellbound. "But I don't understand why you think you might die without seeing Haiti liberated—especially now, when it seems the whole country is behind our movement."

"You see," Daniel said, pushing his glasses up his nose for a better look at his admirers, "a revolution doesn't succeed overnight. It has to go through stages, like a baby who crawls before learning to walk. In this radical and painful process, there are always many pitfalls. The history of the Haitian revolutionary movement is filled with setbacks."

"And what are they?" Thérèse asked, eager for him to expand on his so-far brief political statements.

"My dear, it's hard to give you a simple answer," Daniel replied. "First, it's getting late. Second, it would take days for me to explain everything in the detail you're hoping for. But I can tell you one thing."

"What's that?" Odilon asked, just as curious as Thérèse.

"A revolution has many enemies, and they'll work together to ensure it doesn't succeed. These enemies aren't all Haitians. Some are foreign governments or bourgeois from other countries, with a vested interest in keeping Haiti the way it is. We have to fight against all these factions. And while it's difficult to defeat them, it's not impossible. But for that to happen, we need to mature in terms of strategy, experience, and logistics. However," he paused, locking eyes with them, "you might find this intriguing—the biggest threat to the revolution comes from within."

"What do you mean by that?" Odilon asked.

"There are plenty of people inside the revolution who are potentially dangerous. Many join not out of deep conviction, but from personal ambition and greed. They never truly believed in the cause. They join only for what they can gain. These people are easily recruited by the enemy because they believe only in themselves and their own selfish interests. And since they're working from within, it's hard to identify them."

Removing his dirty glasses, Daniel carefully wiped them with a cloth from his pocket. "They are as deadly as the worst weapons you can imagine. Sooner or later, they will become traitors. And because of them, many of our good-hearted, brave, and loyal comrades will perish.

"I've seen close comrades die because of these chameleons. Some may not become outright traitors, but they'll remain the opportunists they've always been. They won't make the final journey to freedom with us... those last steps are too dangerous. Don't count on them. I've watched many who started the movement in 1946 turn into reactionaries, enemies of the very people they once vowed to fight for, even to the death," the old man said, his voice trembling with emotion. His eyes, red and moist, reflected the weight of the tragic tale he shared with the young lovers.

"So, what happens this time? Do you think we have a chance?" Odilon asked breathlessly, his heart pounding in his ears.

"Oh, absolutely! I can't remember the last time we were this close. But be careful—not too much optimism. There are still many obstacles ahead. That said, I truly believe that even if it isn't this time, Haiti will be free. I may not live to see that day, but I'm confident freedom and real democracy will come. There's nothing they can do to stop us now. It's too late!"

Just as Odilon was about to throw another question at the captivating stranger standing at the crossroads of his life, a voice from the crowd interrupted.

"Listen, folks, it's late... time to get going!" Cécile called out joyfully, free from the trance of gods and spirits. She looked normal again as she watched Odilon and Thérèse talking to the man.

"Oh! Sorry, we have to go... hope to see you in Saint Louis!" Odilon shouted, jogging over to join Cécile. He was eager to leave, feeling the old man hadn't been as forthcoming as he had hoped.

They waved goodbye to *Le Rouge*, unaware they had just been speaking with the true architect of their Haitian dream—the driving force behind the revolution.

"Be safe, my children!" the old man yelled over the noise of the crowd.

As they passed through the jubilant crowd of dancers to catch up with Cécile, Odilon couldn't contain himself. The samba beat pulsed through his soul, lifting him to seventh heaven. He grabbed Thérèse by the waist, and they began singing, dancing, and leaping to the exotic rhythm. Cécile burst out laughing.

"Crazy kids! You wanna dance 'til daylight!" she teased the delirious lovers.

"Yes, Manman! Let's do that!" Odilon cried.

"Shut up, will you?" Thérèse retorted with a smile, knowing their situation all too well. "Home is a long way from here."

"Yes, we'd better get going before the sun rises. That would be a bad sign for us, and a bad way to start the New Year," Cécile affirmed. "Besides, the soup loses its meaning if it isn't cooked before sunrise."

Winding like a river through the jungle, they made their way behind the big house, disappearing beneath the trees of the coffee plantation as a glittering moon emerged spectacularly from behind bunching, lead-grey clouds. It arrived just in time to illuminate the treacherous path for these nighttime travelers. This time, they followed an old trail downhill, avoiding the rugged mountains, to reach the banks of La Rivière Des Barres, which runs along the foothills—a shortcut home. The area blossomed with the unique beauty of Haitian flora, its natural splendor impossible to ignore, especially under the soft glow of the moonlight.

The rugged landscape, cleaved by dense tropical forests, created a world all its own—a place frozen in time, where the inhabitants lived freely under the full protection of the RRF, far from government oversight. The mountain range formed a two-pronged cordillera, with steep plateaus crowned by sandstone peaks that soared up to a thousand feet above the surrounding mountains. To the west, these windy highlands sloped down to the fertile coastal plain of the Rivière Des Barres Basin, resting in majestic silence against the vibrant turquoise backdrop of the hills on the horizon.

Strutting down the moonlit path, no longer afraid of werewolves or *simbi*, the revelers heard the distant drumbeats fade, replaced by the soft chirping of crickets. Walking in silence, each absorbed in reflection on one of the most exhilarating nights of their lives, none of them knew the night was far from over—nor what awaited them ahead.

Chapter 25

It was barely four a.m. when Cécile and her group crossed La Rivière Des Barres, just a few hundred meters from the river delta. As the largest river in the greater Saint Louis area, it flowed westward along the rolling foothills of Mòn Méris, emptying into the Atlantic Ocean near the northern outskirts of town.

Rivière Des Barres held strategic importance for Saint Louis du Nord, both economically and militarily. Locals referred to it as the "Northern Gate," as its crossing from the north served as the main entrance into the town. On the south bank, near the crossing point, stood a bustling marketplace, second only to the main market in the old downtown district.

The Rivière Des Barres marketplace rivaled flea markets in the United States, including the renowned Swap Shop near Fort Lauderdale, Florida. Everything could be found there—fresh produce, seafood, second-hand clothes, household items, and more. Activity thrived at all hours of the day. It was also one of the few places in Haiti where visitors could still enjoy classic troubadour music, played on the banjo, the favorite instrument of most rural bands in the Northwest. At night, especially on New Year's Eve, the party often continued past sunrise. *Kleren, fritay*, music, and prostitutes could be found right along the riverbed, catering to any adventurer in search of life's wildest pleasures.

But that New Year's Eve was entirely different—no music, no *kleren*, and certainly no prostitutes. Not a single soul could be found around the marketplace as Odilon, Thérèse, and Cécile walked through. They were met by the darkness of the night, brightened only by scattered twinkling lights from the houses on the hill. The sound of ocean waves crashing against the river current filled the air as the river emptied into the sea.

As they passed through the community of Des Granges, the main neighborhood at the northern entrance, a huge meteor—or something like it—flashed across the sky, lighting up the entire area, followed quickly by a massive explosion. It was nothing like the usual New Year's fireworks.

"Manman, what was that?" cried a startled Odilon, clutching Thérèse as they walked toward Ti-Riviyè.

Before Cécile could respond, another explosion erupted, even more powerful than the first. It tore the old bamboo tree to pieces and set nearby houses on fire. The trio watched in horror, their screams filling the night. Their journey abruptly ended as they realized it was too dangerous to cross to the other side of Ti-Riviyè, now under heavy aerial bombardment.

What began as sporadic explosions every few minutes quickly turned into a relentless barrage of bombs on the river's southern bank, transforming the area into a raging inferno. The target was Dr. Duchaud's clinic and his small community school. Then came the all-too-familiar whirring of a helicopter gunship. Despite the devastation, no one rushed into the streets to witness the burning neighborhood. For weeks, the RRF had warned the people to stay indoors if war broke out. But for those stranded and paralyzed by fear on the northern bank, it was a living nightmare.

"This is Ti-Jean's New Year's present to us!" Cécile bellowed, straining to be heard over the violent noise. Odilon and Thérèse struggled to pull her away from the main road, trying to avoid detection by the helicopter gunship.

"Children… can we make it home safely?" Cécile shouted, her voice thick with rage, pain, sorrow, and fear. Her head was lolled between her sagging breasts.

"Oh, yes we can, Manman!"

"I don't think we should go back to Anwodo," Thérèse said.

"Why?" Odilon asked.

"It's… too close to town," she stammered, grabbing his hand.

"I'm not going anywhere but Anwodo!" Cécile declared. "If I'm to die, I want to be at home. I will not be a slave again. Ti-Jean may kill us all if he wants—Haiti is his private property."

"What're you talking about, Manman?" Odilon gasped, defiant. "How can Ti-Jean kill us all? He'll kill many, but in the end, Haiti will stand firm. The survivors will emerge victorious."

"I believe that too," Thérèse added, her usual bravado shining through as she tried to recharge her energy, ready to face the danger and stumble on toward Anwodo.

"This is Ti-Jean's New Year's present to us!" Cécile bellowed, straining to be heard over the violent noise. Odilon and Thérèse struggled to pull her away from the main road, trying to avoid detection by the helicopter gunship.

"Children… can we make it home safely?" Cécile shouted, her voice thick with rage, pain, sorrow, and fear. Her head was lolled between her sagging breasts.

"Oh, yes we can, Manman!"

"I don't think we should go back to Anwodo," Thérèse said.

"Why?" Odilon asked.

"It's… too close to town," she stammered, grabbing his hand.

"I'm not going anywhere but Anwodo!" Cécile declared. "If I'm to die, I want to be at home. I will not be a slave again. Ti-Jean may kill us all if he wants—Haiti is his private property."

"What're you talking about, Manman?" Odilon gasped, defiant. "How can Ti-Jean kill us all? He'll kill many, but in the end, Haiti will stand firm. The survivors will emerge victorious."

"I believe that too," Thérèse added, her usual bravado shining through as she tried to recharge her energy, ready to face the danger and stumble on toward Anwodo.

Casting around in the fatal darkness, they found an old trail along the north bank, beneath the cover of a dense cacao grove. Taking long, purposeful strides, they threaded their way down the path. The dew from the thick yellow cacao leaves drenched their clothes, soaking them to the bone. Crippled by fear, Cécile collapsed several times, and each time, Odilon and Thérèse halted to steady her. Yet with every new explosion, her fiercely determined resolve to get home blazed even stronger.

It was still dark when they entered Anwodo at five-fifteen. In the distance, the echoes of war and its explosions chilled the early morning air—sounds that lodged a knife in Cécile's heart, sending her into a state of panic. Odilon and Thérèse struggled to calm her. Between midnight and dawn, eternity seemed to stretch on, making it the longest and most harrowing night of their lives.

The entire village slept as the trio hobbled in. No sprawling dogs snored on the doorstep of Makonmè Anasé, their neighbor. No cats scampered after rats on the roof; no breadfruit fell from the nearby cacao field. Hens roosted silently like owls on the mango branches. Even the newly hatched chicks in the makeshift outdoor kitchen did not chirp. They were sound asleep, enjoying the warmth and protection of their mother's feathered wings.

Nature seemed frozen; the only noise disturbing this silent world was the creak of the latch as Odilon gently lifted it to open the door. In the background, the distant aerial bombardments could almost be heard, though they gave the neighbors a moment to catch their breath. No one was truly asleep—they were simply cowed by the shockwaves of the bombs, which could be felt even in Anwodo.

"*Mezanmi, annou leve kanpe!* We can't let Ti-Jean kill us!" Anasé, the next-door neighbor, shouted loud enough to be heard in the forest nearby.

"You're right, Makonmè Anasé," Odilon murmured in the quiet of their house. "Don't let the assassins destroy you." He gently helped his mother lie down on her sprawling lower bunk bed.

"Bathe her forehead with alcohol," Thérèse suggested.

"I'll do that," Odilon replied. "Go outside and talk to the neighbor. I think she's been waiting for us, maybe for quite some time."

Yawning, he went to the old silver chest to retrieve an alcohol-tinged liquid—a brown mixture of *kleren*, lavender water, and wildflowers stored in an old Barbancourt bottle, an ancient family heirloom passed down through three generations. Cécile's grandmother had used it to break fevers in the dead of night when her mother was ill. Before Manman Anasile died, she made Cécile promise to protect the bottle and never destroy it.

Cécile kept her vow and became known throughout the entire section for the bottle's healing powers, often using it on the village children. Soon, everyone wanted a splash of Cécile's magic waters.

Anakreyon sent two of his henchmen one night to steal the bottle, but as they approached the courtyard, a large, dry leaf suddenly smacked one of the intruders squarely on the forehead. Terrified, they bolted, leaping off the trail and vanishing beneath the banana grove. This unexpected event not only glorified the bottle's supposed magical powers, but also elevated Cécile's status, as she was believed to control its power.

Soon, without realizing it, Cécile became an indispensable figure in the battle between good and evil. It was no surprise that earlier in the night, the houngan in Nan Jean-Louis couldn't begin the ceremony until Cécile arrived. However, on that New Year's Day, neither the Divine power of the bottle nor the ancient *lwa* from Africa invoked earlier were strong enough to prevent the carnage about to unfold in the Northwest Province.

Odilon poured some of the liquid from the bottle, bathing his mother from head to toe, urging her to sniff it so the alcoholic fumes would clear her head—just as she used to do with the children when they were sick.

When Odilon stepped outside, he found the entire village awake, people gathering, uncertain of what to do next. Should they join the resistance against the invading army? No one had moved earlier during the aerial bombardment, as there had been an unspoken agreement to follow the RRF's orders.

But after hours of indiscriminate bombing, with the memory of the dead from the first campaign still fresh, the villagers realized they were defenseless against the bombs. Their only choices were to flee to the mountains or fight. To Odilon's relief, they all chose to fight, though it sent a chill through Thérèse. She, too, hoped for victory, but not at the cost of losing the man she loved.

A defense committee for the section was quickly formed. All men and women of fighting age were chosen to create a civil defense brigade, armed with weapons seized from Anakreyon's fleeing police. These arms had been found in a cache buried behind his mansion the day he fled for safety. Still, the brigade agreed not to act until they had a clearer understanding of the situation.

Seeking information, an elderly woman turned up the volume on her radio in the midst of the crowd so everyone could hear Olivier Zebeda's voice. Rebel Radio had announced that he was about to make an important statement. Within seconds, the entire village fell into a silence deeper than the night itself. Thérèse clung to Odilon, her eyes brimming with tears, war anxiety etched into her face.

"Chérie, it's okay... we'll be alright," Odilon murmured, wrapping his arms around her waist in a comforting squeeze, though he was equally afraid. Haitian men, however, don't show fear in front of their women. In the tropics, men follow the old saying: they are made to suffer in silence, while women are made to feel the pain.

"Brave people of this great province, Commander Zebeda has an important message for you!" the announcer's voice roared over the airwaves. The crowd fell silent, eager to hear the message.

"Compatriots," Zebeda began, "shortly after two o'clock this morning, the criminal regime in Port-au-Prince launched a major assault on our entire province. As I speak, we are under attack by air, sea, and land. This attack follows a grisly pattern of repeated strikes, but this one is different—it's well-coordinated and decisive. Their goal is clear: to finish us off. But we will not run. We are responding head-on to their diabolical onslaught! In the RRF, we understand our historic mission. We cannot turn our backs on it, even if it means sacrificing our lives. This mission is deeply rooted in our revolutionary convictions and our unwavering commitment to rid this country of tyranny so that freedom and democracy may finally take root.

"If they want a people's war, we will give them one! Valiant people of Gros-Morne, Bassin Bleu, Bombardopolis, Jean-Rabel, Môle Saint Nicolas, Port-de-Paix, and all outlying areas, I command you to stand firm. Join our combatants in their heroic mission of resistance. Valiant people of Haiti, let's unite, speaking with one voice to denounce Ti-Jean and his criminal accomplices!"

"*Viv Ayiti Libere!*"

"*Viv Papa Dessalines!*"

"*Viv Charlemagne Péralte!*"

"*Libète ou Lanmò*, we'll be victorious!"

Zebeda's message struck a deep chord in the hearts of the villagers of Anwodo, fueling their unwavering determination to resist the enemy at all costs. And they were not alone; every city, town, and village in the Northwest rose up in defiance. Zebeda's loud call to arms, however, placed the people on a direct collision course with the Haitian Army. By now, the army had labeled everyone in the province—children included—as potential enemies, prepared to kill anyone who stood in their way.

Yet, Zebeda's call for mass insurrection seemed more like a desperate cry. Its consequences could prove dangerous for everyone involved. RRF intelligence had long known that a government attack was imminent, but there was little they could do to stop it. They barely had enough time to fortify their defenses or evacuate the population, particularly the young and elderly, as they had done in the first campaign in Bombardopolis.

A people's war, however, does not mean exposing the most vulnerable to enemy fire. The RRF wanted to move the most at-risk civilians deep into the mountains, behind rebel-controlled lines, out of the reach of government forces. In fact, three days before the attack, the RRF high command had unanimously agreed to do just that. But they hesitated, fearing the evacuation would cause unnecessary panic, as they didn't know exactly when the attack would occur.

They were also concerned about managing another mass exodus, doubting they had the logistics to handle it. Moreover, they feared appearing weak in front of a population that stood steadfastly behind them, ready to make the ultimate sacrifice. In the end, their failure to act led them to gamble on the timing of the next attack. But they had grossly underestimated the government's decision to launch a final assault on New Year's Eve.

By ten a.m. the next day, heavy fire raged across the province. Swift boats launched an amphibious assault in coordination with special operations forces, who parachuted deep into rebel territory. The bombing was relentless, and ground operations appeared to be successful in the initial phase.

Within hours, the town of Môle Saint Nicolas in the Far West was seized, allowing government forces to establish a link with Bombardopolis, which they had already captured during the first failed campaign. This strategic move had positioned the army to advance rapidly toward Jean-Rabel, where Ricardo's rebel forces were stationed. Still, the RRF controlled Mare Rouge Height and the surrounding valleys. To the south, Isabelle and her fighters were forced to retreat, abandoning Gros-Morne for higher ground, deep beneath the green foliage, two kilometers outside of town, just north of the Pendu River.

Above them, farmhouses along the mountain ridge were engulfed in blazing fires, sending huge columns of smoke into the sky. From a distance, it appeared as though the peasants were burning the fields in preparation for spring planting.

The government's strategy was clear: destroy every house on the outskirts of town, denying the rebels any potential sanctuary that could later be used as staging areas for counterattacks. The hawks in Port-au-Prince had learned from their past mistakes and were determined not to repeat them.

By the time government troops entered Gros-Morne, the rebels had already fled, leaving the streets deserted. Most of the residents had also evacuated, fearing brutal reprisals. They remembered what had happened in Bombardopolis during the first campaign when General Lacroix's squads fumigated every house, killing all inside. The act earned him the grim nickname "The Great Fumigator." Jubilant soldiers streamed into town, searching door-to-door for any hidden rebels.

As the army's tanks and trucks rolled north, the soldiers encountered an unexpected roadblock, three hundred yards from the south bank of the Pendu River. The lead truck struck a powerful explosive device, sending the vehicle flying, its shattered pieces scattering like debris adrift in space. The convoy came to an abrupt halt, and more than two hundred soldiers, spooked and panicked, leaped from their trucks, firing aimlessly.

Fifty yards off the main highway, behind a cactus hedge, a shirtless giant of a man lay atop a chestnut mule, a Kalashnikov rifle slung across his back. Barefoot and dressed only in blue trousers rolled up to his knees, he lay low on the animal, almost motionless. From the saddle, he pulled out a conch shell and blew it three times, loud and clear.

More than fifty armed civilians emerged from a coffee field bordering a courtyard near the road, poised for a charge. In response, the infantry soldiers quickly took aim at the courtyard. A bullet struck a young combatant in the face, sending him to the ground. His body convulsed in protest, trembling like a fresh-caught minnow tangled in a net.

An army captain led the charge toward the courtyard. The man on the mule signaled his comrades to remain still, not to retrieve the young fighter who lay face down, blood pooling beneath him. Then, as calm as ever, the mule rider drew a Colt Dragoon revolver. He steadied the barrel, took careful aim at close range, and pulled the trigger.

The shot sent the captain spiraling backward, his body landing over a cookfire beneath an avocado tree in the middle of the courtyard. Soldiers scrambled for cover, retreating under a barrage of bullets back to the main road. The mule reared up, frenzied, nearly breaking its reins. The shirtless man clung to its mane, and with his free hand, fired into the air, scattering the advancing soldiers. Regaining control of his mule, he bolted into the coffee field, with the other combatants retreating behind him, too outnumbered to fight.

A chubby young woman rushed out of a nearby house, shouting, "Marco!" Her arms outstretched.

The wounded man lifted his bloody head, trying to face her, defiant against the odds. But his strength failed, and he collapsed, his forehead sinking into the blood-soaked dirt. The girl, glancing over her shoulder, grabbed his arms, trying to pull him up, but his body was limp, weighing her down. Straining, she dragged him into the coffee field, where they disappeared from view.

The pursuing soldiers halted at the edge of the courtyard, then returned to their trucks and sped north toward the river, leaving other field commanders behind to clean up the carnage. The RRF strategy was to retreat when fixed battles were unwinnable, leaving behind civil brigades to harass the advancing troops. The man on the chestnut mule was later revealed to be Yvon Zapa, a fearless guerrilla commander and leader of the region's civil brigades.

From her distant mountain hideout, Isabelle watched in horror as column after column of trucks, loaded with government soldiers, raced toward Bassin Bleu, the next town deep in the Northwest. She radioed Joséphine, stationed in Bassin Bleu, who quickly dispatched a rebel unit south to destroy a key bridge six kilometers away, at the entrance to the La Pierre basin. The bridge, about six hundred meters long, spanned Trois Rivières, the largest river in the Northwest, feeding the fertile coastal plain of Lower Moustique.

The army's plan had been to use the bridge for a grand entry into the heart of the Northwest—something the hawks in Port-au-Prince were eager to accomplish. But when the bridge fell into rebel hands, its destruction sent plumes of decimated concrete into the air, thundering down like a storm. The triumphant mood of the war planners in the Haitian capital, who had launched their New Year's offensive just hours earlier, quickly crumbled with it.

The decimation of the bridge brought the jubilant advancing government troops to a grinding, devastated halt. As long lines of military trucks were stranded on the south bank of Trois Rivières, the soldiers ran into a steady stream of bullets. The RRF was taking the fullest possible advantage of the thick cover provided by coffee fields on the mountainside. Meanwhile, the dusty, narrow highway offered no safety for the panic-stricken soldiers, whose trucks attempted a U-turn but failed miserably by rolling off a cliff, causing a stampede that resulted in dozens of dead and wounded soldiers. Many of them were taken prisoner by the RRF fighters, who forced the army to retreat all the way back to Gros-Morne, twenty kilometers to the south.

Confidence grew among the rebels on the southern front. Joséphine and Isabelle each sent a message to Zebeda, assuring him that their positions were holding firm, though they were unsure for how long. Rebel commanders sensed that the army would not withdraw from the province until it had achieved its objectives or been defeated on the battlefield—something the rebels no longer believed could be easily accomplished, even with the strong popular resistance behind them.

The scope of the government offensive, the impressive display of weaponry and the decisiveness that empowered army commanders confirmed to the RRF high command that the war would drag on until the army suffered total defeat, or total victory was achieved. Following Zebeda's orders, Arthur Auguste, commander of the northern front, had dispatched two-hundred fighters from their elite units across the rugged mountains, taking a back road to reach the southern front, based four kilometers north of Pendu River, right outside Gros-Morne. That reinforcement allowed Isabelle and Joséphine to send some fighters from Upper Moustique, a mountain chain dominating the Jean-Rabel Valley and Lower Moustique, to reach the western front – where Ricardo was facing the same dilemma the women had faced earlier in Gros-Morne.

But this muscle-flexing and military maneuvering did little to ease the pressure off the RRF, for the war was not confined only to outlying areas – it was lodged deep in the hearts of the resistance movement in Port-de-Paix and Saint Louis. Both towns were under a ferocious air, sea, and ground offensive that showed no signs of stopping. Huge columns of army soldiers landed near the beach resort of Nan Chalet, two kilometers north of downtown Port-de-Paix, where they seized control of the northern half of the city while engaging rebel forces in fierce firefights all over town.

In Port-de-Paix, the resistance was equally fierce, despite the relentless aerial and artillery bombardments the rebels endured throughout the day. By nightfall, they had successfully penetrated the government line. Just a few meters away, on the hilltop of Morne-aux-Pères, Jean-Michel had carved out a corridor around the foothills on the eastern edge of the city. Rebel fighters used an old trail hidden beneath the foliage to reach the village of Bodin, two kilometers north of the army's military base. There, they opened a new front to the north, putting the army on shaky ground by forcing it to split its forces, which eased the pressure on Jean-Michel near the city center. At six p.m. on New Year's Day, he issued an emotional call for total and popular warfare.

The strategy now was to recreate the February 1802 battle in Port-de-Paix, where General Jacques Maurepas decisively defeated the French forces led by General Jean Humbert. The issue with this strategy was that the RRF no longer held the strategic high ground and, worst of all, was forced to fight on the army's terms—with vastly inferior weaponry. Like Maurepas, the RRF had the unwavering support of the local population, but unlike him, who had retreated to a hilltop and evacuated the population while turning Port-de-Paix into a smoking ruin, the RRF had only fortified the city itself, neglecting the surrounding areas.

The RRF boasted some of the best field commanders, much like Maurepas had with François Capois (then a young captain), Poitevien, René Vincent, Jacques Louis, Placide Lebrun, Nicolas Louis, and others along with a valiant battalion from Saint Louis du Nord led by the legendary Prudent. However, unlike Maurepas, the RRF placed too much emphasis on urban warfare, rather than relying on the mountain gorges that had proven so effective during the battle of 1802.

The hawks in Port-au-Prince were keeping their fingers crossed. They knew it was never going to be easy in Port-de-Paix, as well as in Saint Louis. But as long as they could maintain their foothold in both towns, they believed their chances of success were still very much alive.

In Saint Louis, the situation was most alarming. The town had been under unyielding bombardment during the day, reinforced by fresh troops arriving non-stop, either by swift boats or helicopters that parachuted them deep behind rebel lines. The residents woke up on New Year's Day in total shock, breathlessly watching government soldiers patrolling part of their town. Weary soldiers with rifles took position a few meters south of Ti-Riviyè in the northern fringes and were met with fierce resistance.

For weeks, the RRF prepared for that battle. Every house in the north entrance was a fortress. Wet sandbags mixed with concrete, reinforced by long trenches, made it almost impossible to penetrate the center of Saint Louis du Nord. Despite unforgiving, unappeasable aerial bombardments, the call for resistance was greeted with such stoicism that astonished helicopter pilots were forced to withhold their fire as they watched, from the air, a sea of people on the streets braving death by artillery fire to the mounting cries of *"Vive Haiti!"* and *"Abas* fascism!".

By nightfall, the army, still holding its position at the northern entrance, found itself in a precarious situation. Cut off from its base, the infantry division was left vulnerable to a potential rebel onslaught. Its deep incursion into the RRF's two main bastions of resistance was seen by military analysts as daring at best, and reckless at worst. However, the army's ability to maintain a presence by nightfall—despite heavy losses throughout the day—was enough to give the hawks in Port-au-Prince the confidence they desperately needed to rally their base. They had begun to detect the insurgency's military weaknesses.

The battle dragged on through the night and well into the next day, without any interruption. To avoid the carnage from the trenchant, adamant bombardments, Zebeda ordered a massive evacuation, taking almost the entire population of Saint Louis to safety behind the mountains, leaving only fighters and volunteers to meet the invading army. The scene was shockingly repellent on the edge of Vertus, where piles of dead bodies lay on the roadside. The smell of rotting flesh, ghastly wounds of the dying, and lurid pallor of their skin were of a revolting nature. The urge to resist reached an immeasurable pitch.

Zebeda now faced the toughest fight of his revolutionary life. He must beat back this latest attack, or face a crushing defeat, which would have dashed any hopes for a speedy win in this civil war. But on New Year's Eve, Zebeda refused to think of the dreadful consequences that might result from an RRF defeat in Saint Louis du Nord, strategically the heart of the resistance.

It was the place where the entire RRF high command expected to proclaim, *en grande pompe*, the triumph of their movement and the beginning celebrations of *le grand soir de la révolution*. The whole country fixed its eyes on this legendary town that refused to back down in the face of appalling crudity and utter inhumanity. The RRF high command knew its task was huge, for the heart of Haiti beat at the center of Saint Louis. The dream must live on, no matter its total cost or toll.

For now, however, these grand dreams would have to remain just that—dreams, drifting further from becoming reality. The possibility of realizing them plunged even deeper into doubt when disturbing news from Port-de-Paix reached Saint Louis around eleven o'clock on January 4th. The entire RRF high command was thrown into shock: government forces had breached rebel lines just below the foothills of Morne-aux-Pères, only meters from the city center.

After two days of bombing and shelling, reducing the area along the south entrance to ashes, an amphibious landing at the southern edge of the bay of Port-de-Paix forced Jean-Michel Desquiron to once again split his forces, to block and destroy the army's new front, south of the city.

The war escalated, and the military balance appeared to be shifting. About half of Port-de-Paix was now under government control, including the city's airport and the strategic northern and southern entrances. The RRF still controlled the downtown district, the strategic army barracks on the southern edge's hilltop, the main suburb on the eastern side of the city, and more importantly, all the hinterlands.

Fighting raged on without any hope of subsiding. The army's strategy was to put pressure on both Saint Louis and Port-de-Paix, forcing rebel commanders to fight a conventional war—a war that the hawks in Port-au-Prince were convinced would favor the army, as they had the logistics to sustain it, while the RRF did not.

The RRF had underestimated the army soldiers' will to fight to the bitter end. Despite heavy casualties being inflicted, the army suffered few desertions; and its ability to transport fresh troops to the front left no chance for a pause in the fighting. This would have eased the pressure on the RRF and allowed them to regroup. At the same time, the western front was dealt a major blow when Ricardo conceded the key town of Jean-Rabel, the last town the RRF still held in the Far West.

The army launched a powerful ground assault on the town, leaving Ricardo and his fighters with only two options: fight and risk annihilation by a vastly stronger force, or escape. Conventional wisdom suggested the latter. Despite the army having cordoned off the entire town, the rebel forces managed to escape without losing a single fighter.

Meanwhile, confidence within the army ranks grew. For the first time, commanders believed they could break the backbone of the resistance. Military planners in Port-au-Prince expressed cautious optimism about their progress but remained tight-lipped, avoiding public statements. Instead, the pro-government press celebrated each town recaptured from the rebels, plastering images of captured fighters on their front pages—a clear attempt at psychological warfare aimed at demoralizing the RRF's popular base.

A major assault on the northern front pushed the rebels south to the village of Bonneau, two kilometers from Anse-à-Foleur. The fall of the city sent chills through the hearts of rebel commanders, who had until now considered the northern part of the province the most secure. However, when Arthur Auguste sent his best fighters to reinforce the southern front in Gros-Morne, the security of Anse-à-Foleur and its hinterlands was left largely in the hands of defecting soldiers under Colonel Baltazar. Panicked by news of the army's advance, these soldiers fled in droves, abandoning their posts without even packing their belongings. In Bonneau, however, the RRF gained significant support from hundreds of local volunteers, who vowed to die, if necessary, to repel the army's advance.

In the battle for Saint Louis from the north, the village of Bonneau became so strategically important to the RRF that Zebeda dispatched some of his best-trained elite commandos, along with hundreds of volunteers from Saint Louis, to reinforce the resistance and take the initiative against the army, which was now stationed just a few hundred meters downhill near the fishing community of Méyans.

Located five kilometers north of Saint Louis du Nord, Bonneau sits on a hilltop that separates the coastal valley of Cap-Rouge to the south from that of Méyans to the north. To the east, vast coffee plantations stretch across the mountainside, and dense tropical undergrowth enhances the forested atmosphere, providing excellent cover for guerrilla operations should the RRF decide to utilize it.

However, to the west, a massive cliff juts sharply from the shoreline, making it perilous for passing vehicles. The lone, dusty highway runs along the mountainside, just a few feet from the cliff, where any mishap could prove catastrophic for military convoys. A safe passage through this route would almost guarantee a swift approach to the very doorstep of Saint Louis. Between Bonneau and the northern entrance to Saint Louis lay the Rivière Des Barres Basin, a shallow coastal plain that lacked the relative sanctuary the rebels might otherwise find in the protection of mountain gorges.

Bonneau, the only link to Saint Louis from the north, was crucial for both sides. The military needed to secure it to advance south, while the rebels drew their line in the sand, vowing to defend the village to the last fighter. The road leading south was mined and booby-trapped, with columns of fighters hidden deep beneath the dense foliage, waiting for the perfect moment to strike. Several attempts by the army to move southward were brutally repelled by tenacious rebel fighters, responding by unleashing hails of fire on army soldiers, forcing them to retreat like wild *touloulous* into their holes. Determined carpet-bombing by the army's air forces did little to dislodge them.

A stalemate dragged on in the northern front, frustrating the military planners in Port-au-Prince, who had hoped to establish their first solid link from the north by connecting their infantry division in Saint Louis with their new base in Anse-à-Foleur. Time was not on the army's side, as they were camping in hostile territory. Meanwhile, the RRF's southern front was barely holding, and the western front had already lost its urban centers, forcing a retreat all the way to Lower Moustique, where Ricardo hoped to create a buffer to block the army's northward advance. He was determined to make a stand along the southern bank of Trois Rivières. If this last line of defense collapsed, a ground assault on Port-de-Paix from the southwest hinterlands would be almost inevitable.

At this critical phase of the war, the RRF swiftly lost its initiative, reduced to fighting on the army's terms. Despite enjoying widespread popular support and a growing number of volunteers from across the country, the RRF faced significant disadvantages. Its lack of air support, shortage of armaments, and tactical immobility left it in a precarious position, putting the rebels at a dangerous disadvantage.

Chapter 26

Sunday, January 26th was as dangerous, hellish, and uncertain for the villagers of Anwodo as the first day of the assault on Saint Louis. The war had entered its fourth week, and what had initially promised to be a swift, decisive victory for the hawks in Port-au-Prince was now becoming a prolonged conflict. Desperate for an end to the fighting, people clung to hope each day, though it remained as elusive as ever.

For the first time since that dreadful New Year's Day, the guns in Saint Louis fell silent, though no one knew why. Both sides remained firmly entrenched, and, although the firing had ceased, no one dared to venture outside.

Anwodo had become a ghost town, nearly deserted as most of the inhabitants fled to the relative safety of the mountains. But Odilon's family chose to stay. Cécile was resolute, refusing to move to higher ground. She made it clear she would rather die in her own little house than sleep in the open, surrounded by uncertainty.

That Sunday morning, she lay abed, awaiting the wave of bombings to begin. Odilon stood outside, preparing breakfast as he did each morning. These simple folks needed to recharge their bodies to withstand the dreadful day ahead. Rushing inside, Odilon offered a small plate to his sleepy mother.

"*Manman*, won't you please get up? I made *boukousou*. They're hot, and you might want to try them," he encouraged her, setting a plate of *cassava* bread on the little table next to Cécile's bunk bed.

"What time is it, my son?" she sighed, peering at the food.

"About ten o'clock…I'm not sure," he replied.

"I have fifteen minutes past ten," clarified Thérèse, who sat on the *nat* combing her tangled hair – wearing the nightgown she had purchased at the flea market in Ti-Riviyè on Christmas Eve.

"Is the bombing over today?" Cécile yawned.

"I was down by the Ti Toto windmill," said Odilon. "Many people waited for the bombs to drop, so they could go out about their business. No one knew when to leave." He reached into the small silver chest and pulled out a cup, pouring some coffee to enjoy with his freshly baked *boukousou*.

His mother awakened with a start. "Odilon, why did you go that far away? Don't you know it's dangerous?" growled Cécile, windmilling in a sleepy stretch, longing to get up, grounded in place by fear. She then sank back down into bed.

"*Manman*, I had to try my luck. There's hardly anything left to eat in this house. If we don't do something soon, we'll starve. In Vertus, I saw people wandering the streets like zombies, searching for whatever scraps they could find. It's chaos down there. Those who didn't flee to the mountains say they'd rather die fighting with the RRF than hide in their homes and be killed by bombs. There's almost nothing left to buy. I had to fight my way through the crowd just to get a little dried fish—paid three *goud* for three small ones," Odilon said. Thérèse listened to his words with dismay.

"If something doesn't happen to stop this war, we're going to die," said Thérèse, worried sick. Snagging her hair on the comb didn't help any.

"*Manman*, get up! The *boukousou* is getting cold and dry," begged Odilon.

Cécile sat up, ate what little was on her plate, and slowly made her way outside to get more food. In moments, she rushed back in. "Kids, hurry! Go outside and tell me why all those people are standing in the middle of the road, down by Anakreyon's house!" she screamed.

"What people are you talking about, *Manman*?" Odilon pushed through the front door to hurry outside, Thérèse following close behind.

"Don't you see?" Cécile yelled from inside.

"Yes, I do *Manman*. Why are they there? I walked by a while ago. It was quiet, and I didn't see anybody. Let me go and find out."

"Odilon, would you please stay away? You don't know them," begged Cécile, fearing for her son. "What if they're from the government?" Thérèse disregarded Cécile's last statement and followed right behind Odilon.

As they reached the giant mango tree separating the courtyard from the main pathway leading to the gathering crowd, Odilon stopped, grabbing Thérèse's hand, turning around to give a final reminder to his mother.

"*Manman*, how many times have I told you not to worry? Yesterday, you said it was a wonderful idea to create the committee for defense of the village…saying that we must be on constant alert. Finish your breakfast; we're just doing our job!"

Cécile fell silent, recognizing the harsh truth in her son's words. Meanwhile, a group of angry villagers poured into the area, fueled by a rumor that the old chief had been spotted in Ti-Riviyè, making his way back home. Enraged, the crowd destroyed the remaining vestiges of his estate. Odilon, rifle in hand, took charge once again, instructing the group to stay on guard. Others in the crowd, some from distant parts of the section, brandished machetes as their weapons of defense.

After four hours of waiting, the crowd realized that the hated Anakreyon was nowhere to be found. They dispersed, though the fear of his potential return lingered in the villagers' minds. To calm the unrest, Zebeda sent rebel fighters to the village—not to block the old chief's return, as the RRF knew Anakreyon wouldn't be foolish enough to try—but to reassure the villagers and help them focus on the real threat: fending off the advancing army.

Even so, Odilon was not to be deterred, considering the chief was his own personal enemy, someone he would love to lay his hands on. He yearned to challenge him, meeting him face-to-face, looking him straight in the eye – forcing him to publicly admit to the murder of his brother. Once guilt was evident, he would smash in the chief's ugly face with the butt of his rifle, turning him over to the angry mob to finish him off.

Leading as usual, Odilon took Thérèse and twenty people from the section on a wild goose chase for the chief. The small group searched every corner, finding no trace of the old chief. But later in the afternoon, responding to a local tipster, they found themselves at the chief's main advisor's hideout. This was Alphonse Jean-Baptiste, the former "little man to the chief" – now an accessory to murder.

The once-feared village elder trembled when he was dragged from a deep hole inside the trunk of an old fig tree, hidden in thick underbrush across a shallow ravine. The massive tree, concealed near an abandoned windmill behind the coffee fields of Nan Banman, close to Thérèse's parents' home, was known to only a few. Desperate to save his own worthless skin, he had chosen to hide there, willing to live in a tree to avoid capture.

The advisor's eyes glazed over with terror, displaying the cowardice of a tyrant. Filthy and drenched in sweat, he smelled like wild goat's pee. His uncombed hair, brackish and bushy, gave him the appearance of a wretched street punk. The half-torn, odorous, wrinkled black jacket he wore over patched blue jeans gave him the appearance of an ancient werewolf, like the one legend claimed had once lived in this remote part of the countryside. Barefoot and with a long, drooping beard, he only reinforced the mob's belief that he was nothing more than a filthy, evil old man.

As he was dragged beyond kicking and screaming out of his hiding place, he came face-to-face with Odilon, who led the crowd with an air of utmost authority. A young boy in the crowd, swinging a tree branch, struck Jean-Baptiste in the head. As he fell, he knelt, pleading for his life before Odilon.

"String him up!" cried a lively woman, expressing everyone's thoughts.

"No," Odilon muttered, breathing heavily. "That gives him an easy way out. He must confess his crimes before he dies."

"What happened to your magic pipe, old man? Why doesn't it save you?" shouted an angry Thérèse. "Do you think we respect you anymore, murderer?"

Reduced to a whimpering child, Alphonse made no attempt to respond, staying tight-lipped and facing no one—resigned to his fate. Once one of the most feared men in Anwodo, he now faced the harsh truth: people knew what he had done.

"Tell the crowd you're an accomplice in my brother's death," Odilon snarled through clenched teeth. He could now vividly recall seeing Alphonse lurking in the shadows of the chief's compound the night his brother died—he had even told Thérèse about it. She had been shocked, though she already knew Alphonse was an informant for the chief.

Alphonse remained silent, his head bowed low, nearly touching his knees, staring at Odilon's feet. Not long ago, he had begged the chief to spare this peasant's life, pleading for restraint from the authorities. But now, his own time had come.

"Life has its major twists and turns, doesn't it?" Odilon challenged him. Still, Alphonse did not respond. Nor did he raise his head to face the angry crowd. Odilon then walked away, allowing the crowd to take him on.

Two large men held him by the arms, tying his hands behind his back. Dragged all the way there, he was led to the avocado tree outside of the old chief's compound. This was the same tree where Odilon, from its upper branches, had seen Alphonse sit with the chief near his dead brother – lying in a pool of blood – while three murderers pondered what to do with the body.

"If you admit your guilt now…I'll set you free," Odilon decided. He did not really want to show mercy, unsure what the mob would do. Some of the men started to cradle their rifles, obscene smiles all around.

Alphonse said nothing, showing no attempt to face the men – who formed up an execution squad. Four of them made a line, quickly mounting their rifles into position, twitching index fingers on the triggers.

"I can't watch this, Odilon…it's too much," cried Thérèse. Burying her head under Odilon's loose t-shirt, she covered her ears with her hands to avoid hearing the discharge when it reverberated against the surrounding hills.

Standing up in a last show of defiance, unwilling to die on his knees, Alphonse braced his back against the avocado tree while the bullets pounded onto him. As his head slumped over, his eyes crossed and glassy, blood poured from his chest, mouth, and ears, streaming down his filthy clothes.

Satisfied, the crowd cheered, grateful to see this monster dead.

"I know it's tough to watch an execution, *cherie*. But I needed the courage to face the death of a man who participated in the murder of my beloved brother. I'm sure he would've done the same thing for me," stated Odilon. His vengeful eyes followed as the dead man was carried away from the tree and dumped into a hole. He was then covered with forgiving sod.

The crowd dispersed as Thérèse, who walked in a state of shock, latched onto Odilon's arm as they rushed to get home before nightfall.

"I'm struck by the fact that he said nothing, even when you gave him a chance to save his skin," Thérèse choked, a lump in her throat. They strode under the cacao trees to reach the deserted compound's courtyard.

"I have to admit he was courageous, but for the wrong reasons," responded Odilon.

"What do you mean by that?" Trembling, she could not forget the way Alphonse's corpse stared at them accusingly, with its crisscrossed eyes.

"I mean, he kept his word to Anakreyon right to the end. He never revealed where the old section chief was hiding. That was going to be my next question if he'd admitted his guilt. He was just an underling—my real target is Anakreyon. You could see he was terrified, but he didn't beg for his life. I believe he was strong in the way he faced death… I just wish he hadn't sided with the Devil."

As the sun sank behind the mountains, the two young lovers knew they had to quicken their pace. The sandy trail ahead began to narrow, fading under the weight of encroaching darkness. It was dusk. Around them, the green foliage blended with their shadows as they walked hand-in-hand, their strides quickening beneath the towering breadfruit trees. Above the overhanging branches, the sky stretched, distant and streaked with shades of pink and red, tinged by thin clouds dissolving into the eerie approach of twilight.

As they entered Anwodo, the chirping of crickets, the booming of peeper frogs, and the occasional crowing of roosters signaled the official arrival of night. But with the dreadful sound of exploding bombs echoing in the distance, the villagers knew it would be another night of terror—almost unbearable. Each blast sent searing arrows of fear through Thérèse's stomach.

Odilon was inside the gate when Cécile called out. "My son, where in the world have you been? M. Noel from Bwa Chandèl came three times to offer you a job. I told him to come back tomorrow…I didn't want to say 'no' to him!"

"We got caught up in helping people whose houses were destroyed by the bombing…we lost track of time," explained Odilon as Thérèse leaned against him. They stood in front of Cécile with their heads bent, arms linked, deep in a lie. They could not tell the truth, fearing it might upset the aging wise woman, triggering a heart attack. For the moment, the truth was better left unsaid.

"You know I don't work for Noel. Remember what he did to me last time? I worked two days for him under horrible conditions, and he paid me nothing."

"I remember, my son. But I kept thinking there's nothing to eat, and I saw an opportunity for us to earn some much-needed cash. Besides, I believe M. Noel is wise enough to pay. Anakreyon is no longer around, and he would be foolish not to pay you. The committee would bury him alive," Cécile replied.

"I think your mother's right, Odilon," said Thérèse.

The tropical dusk, in one rushing move, faded to darkness while they were talking. So, they went inside to prepare for yet another night of psychological torture caused by the ceaseless sounds of war.

The night went as it had come, noisy and appalling. The sounds of war showed no signs of subsiding, even as the sun began to rise behind the mountains. Chilling automatic gunfire mixed with powerful blasts of explosions reduced the little village of Anwodo, and the whole province for that matter, into something like a burning field. And for Odilon, his lover, and his mother, it was pure Hell on Earth.

#

The government offensive had now entered its fifth week, and the intensity of its resurgence after a day of relative calm left no doubt in the people's minds: the hawks in Port-au-Prince were pressing hard for a victory by or before Three Kings' Day. Traditionally held on January 6th, the holiday had been postponed twice by the government, hoping the rebels' defeat would justify a military parade. This year, it was set for the third Wednesday in February.

The insurgents were equally determined not to let that happen. Zebeda was pushing his military and revolutionary skills to the max. He knew it would be the biggest task of his life. Any weakness on the battlefield could impair victory. But along with the rest of the RRF high command, he had dedicated everything to making the war sufficiently bloody enough that the army would have no other choice but to retreat.

In Port-de-Paix, Jean-Michel was under tacit orders to use any means at his disposal to prevent a government takeover of the city. Things got bloodier along the frontlines near Bodin, just north of Port-de-Paix, on Three Kings' Day. Several columns of rebel fighters swooped down overnight from various directions, reinforcing a weakening rebel position along those lines. The RRF fighters had managed to push government soldiers to the northern edge of the city where they had landed on New Year's Day.

It was one o'clock in the afternoon when Jean-Michel's black, bulletproof jeep pulled into Capois La Mort Square in the city center, across the street from the National Bank. He drove, and four well-armed security guards sat in the back. Echoes of heavy artillery fire boomed loud and clear, for the frontline was right along the north bank of Port-de-Paix River, only meters away from the city's main northern entrance.

With one swift motion, the guards flung the doors open, their AK-47 assault rifles at the ready, shielding Jean-Michel as he strode out in full glory. Standing straight, proud, and upright, he fingered his bushy growth of beard, a trademark black beret planted on his head. He wore night-deep sunglasses that circled his chubby, oval-face, gazing straight ahead. There, he saw a large crowd of RRF supporters mixed with well-armed volunteers camping across the street, starting to chant revolutionary slogans when they saw him.

Glancing at the next street, oblique from the square, he saw it was empty, virtually deserted. Not saying a single word, he appeared fearless, confident, and utterly revolutionary. Spirits soared as he beamed an awesome smile, waving to the crowd. Leaving the jeep stationed near the square, he did not cross to meet them. Instead, he walked northward – on his way to the frontlines. His security guards, every man in full combat gear, followed him. No assault rifle was draped around his bull neck, but his usual pair of sidearms were strapped around his waist. His well-worn, wrinkled leather boots crackled with every step he took, like Zebeda's.

Heavily armed fighters patrolled every street corner. Deep trenches and large pits of sandbags were visible at every street entrance, strategically located to create multiple layers of fortifications to deter the army soldiers, should they manage to break into rebel lines and move southward across the southern bank of the river.

The night before, unbeknownst to Jean-Michel and his entourage, an elite commando from the army had set up snipers on the rooftops of several buildings along the government-controlled northern bank. Their mission was to knock down every rebel appearing on the horizon. As he headed for the last block before reaching the river, one of the snipers fired from a building on the hill of Morne-aux-Pères. Bullets struck Jean-Michel on his neck and chest. The impact knocked him to the ground.

Two of his security guards returned fire, providing cover as the others shielded Jean-Michel's body, moving him from the open riverbed—an effective no-man's land. Retreating under fire, they managed to carry him two blocks to safety, where they urgently radioed for help.

Several rebel fighters from a nearby street corner rushed to the scene. Jean-Michel lay prone in the arms of his guards. His olive-green shirt, soaked in blood, was removed, used as an improvised bandage to alleviate the flow of blood oozing from the bullet wounds. One had struck him at the base of his throat.

Though losing consciousness, Jean-Michel was still alive. An elderly woman who knew him rushed to his side, crying out in disbelief. She had often served him coffee at the small restaurant she ran across from City Hall. Pulling a bottle of rubbing alcohol from her purse, she gently sponged his face and head. Five minutes later, a blue minivan screeched onto the scene as a paramedic team tumbled out. The blaring horn, screeching brakes, and squealing tires underscored the urgency of their mission to save Jean-Michel's life.

His comrades froze in total shock as he was placed on a stretcher, carried away under the disbelieving eyes of the dazed rebel fighters and other onlookers gathered around. Inside the van, Jean-Michel lay motionless, while the medical team struggled to revive him. Silent terror descended on the people in the van. Suddenly, the shaken voice of its driver broke the silence.

"*Kolangèt*, this is…too real to be true!" he cried out, smashing his hands against the steering wheel. His sorrowful brown eyes welled with tears.

To the medical team in the van, Jean-Michel was a messianic leader—an untouchable, invincible revolutionary saint sent to bring salvation to the people of the Northwest. Caring too much to accept the tragic reality of his condition, they refused to acknowledge the possibility of his death. The impossible had to be done to save him, and to achieve that, they needed to keep the news under wraps. The psychological impact of Jean-Michel's death, even in normal circumstances, would almost certainly lead to the total collapse of the resistance in the city.

"Is he still breathing?" the driver asked warily, his eyes red and watery, drowning in anguish that choked the voice deep in his throat.

"I…really don't know," answered the man in the back holding Jean-Michel's head.

Face swollen beet-red with rage, he used a wet rag to clean up the man's long, straight beard, sticky with blood trickling from his nose. His neck appeared to be broken. Something had to be done quickly to save his life. Reaching the missionary hospital in La Pointe was their goal; but to do that, they had to cross enemy lines. They drove east to the edge of a swampy lake, taking the same trail the rebel fighters used on New Year's Day to open up the Bodin Front and relieve Jean-Michel from heavy bombardments near the city center.

The afternoon sun slanted low over the decaying streets and bomb-struck houses when they drove through Cathedral Square on their way to reaching the lake's edge. They headed east toward the wealthy suburb of La Coupe, passing several blocks of bombed-out houses. No one knew how many innocent men and women had lost their lives beneath the rubble. But every two or three blocks, a lone little house stood intact, miraculously spared from the savagery of war.

After fifteen minutes of intense driving, they reached the lake, lying still against the backdrop of a dense coconut grove on the eastern edge of La Coupe. A few huts dotted the area, home to local fishermen. The driver sprang from his seat, rushing past hollow trees to retrieve a canoe docked beneath a mango tree in the middle of an empty courtyard. A lone young girl, sucking her thumb and twirling her hair, watched in fascination as he pushed the canoe to the back of the van. Three men exited the vehicle, carefully carrying Jean-Michel on a stretcher, which they then folded and placed inside the canoe.

"Where are you going with Papa's boat?" yelled the girl.

"Shhhh," replied one of the men. "We'll bring it back."

Two of the men got in the canoe, one on each end, while Jean-Michel lay in the middle. They used a forked pole to push through the mangroves, determined to make it to La Pointe, their only hope of saving Jean-Michel.

As they poled through the swamp, each gigantic push forced the bottom to burst upward in a gurgling sound. Floating past hollow trees in the middle of chirping swallows, dozens of bird nests, and then the emptiness of the open water, they finally left the swampy side of the lake behind them. The north bank was now just a few feet off, but it felt like a world away.

Exposed to enemy fire as they made their final push to reach the other side, they felt a cool dark breeze coming through, sending chills through their veins. All was quiet except for the war noises echoing in the distance and the splash of the poles sloshing through the murky water.

Five minutes later, they emerged safely on the deserted north bank. No rebel soldiers awaited them, and no fishermen cast their nets along the shore. Moving quickly, they lifted Jean-Michel by his shoulders and legs, carefully placing him back onto the stretcher. Ahead lay acres of banana fields, and they had to cross them to reach the hospital. With mounting terror and careful not to jostle the stretcher, they finally made it.

Zebeda, flanked by Dr. Duchaud and a group of surgeons, greeted them upon arrival. Olivier Zebeda had come down from Saint Louis, determined to test his own resolve. Though his heart held no fear, he knew well the dire consequences of war. But this was the first time someone so close to him had been struck down by the brutal realities of the conflict.

Jean-Michel was gently placed onto the operating table as Zebeda and a group of comrades anxiously waited in the hallway. The towering revolutionary paced back and forth, unable to stand still, repeatedly checking his watch. Two hours later, Dr. Duchaud emerged from the operating room, his pale face haggard, resigned. From the doorway, he called to Zebeda, who quickly rushed to his side, already expecting the bad news.

"He didn't have a chance," Dr. Duchaud confirmed, his voice breaking as he struggled to maintain his composure. "We fought against the odds to save him, but he simply lost too much blood."

Zebeda said nothing, collapsing into Dr. Duchaud's open arms. Tears carved dirty lines down his sun-weathered cheeks. The other commanders in the hallway, realizing their hero was gone, remained composed. This was not a time for mourning; it was a moment to prove their revolutionary courage. They brushed away their tears, determined to suppress their emotions.

Following Zebeda and Dr. Duchaud into the room, the commanders gave the revolutionary salute to their fallen comrade, who lay lifeless on the operating table. Jean-Michel's face, serene in the stillness of death, seemed to smile, as if confident his comrades would carry on, and, most importantly, that Haiti would survive.

In that room lay Jean-Michel Desquiron, who had vowed to sacrifice his life for the freedom of his country. A true Marxist and a patriot to his core, he remained committed to his promise until his final moments. He lived as bravely as he died: fearless and uncompromising.

No one knew for certain what went through his mind in those last moments. Struck down by bullets, he fell silently to the ground— no scream, no cry, no tears. He had always told his comrades that death didn't matter to him; life did. And for him, the most precious life to protect was Haiti's, the country he loved enough to give his own life for.

The rebel commanders moved closer to the table, singing *La Dessalinienne*, then gave Jean-Michel a final military salute. One by one, they bent down to kiss his forehead. Zebeda then ordered the body to be wrapped in the red-and-blue Haitian flag and taken to rebel headquarters deep in the mountains for a formal burial.

Chapter 27

"He was a man of great courage with unmistakable purpose, entirely committed to a just cause and motivated by the highest of principles. His life was short, but full of accomplishments. Of course, like all human beings, he had his own strengths and weaknesses. How can we not miss his cheerful smile in times of success, and his sorrowful attitude during moments of failure? His critics, especially his enemies, will say that he lived a surreal life, vacillating between the imaginary and the real.

"But his uncompromising stand against tyranny speaks for itself. We can only say that history will prove his critics wrong, for like our forefathers in 1804, eradicating social injustice in Haiti is a non-negotiable issue between us in the RRF, and the neo-colonialists at the service of imperialist dictates," reported Zebeda on Rebel Radio. His voice wavered, struggling to push forth his revolutionary charisma.

"Who's he referring to?" Thérèse asked Odilon as they climbed the mountains along the mud-clogged trail near Nan Banman. They were on their way to finding whatever they could to stay alive in the war-ravaged zone. They took their little radio everywhere with them, constantly searching for news from the front. Swinging under an old mango tree, they could see how it dominated the endless flora of green, lush banana groves filling the valley below, as yet untouched by the war.

"I don't know. Remember, we tuned in at the middle of the speech," replied Odilon. Leaping over a branch, he raised the radio above his head to get the best frequency, so no words from Zebeda would be missed.

Their leader concluded his address with these solid remarks, "Jean-Michel Desquiron, a man of uncompromising brilliance and stubborn honesty, is gone – but not forgotten – he will live on in the lives he's touched, and in our memories. Comrade, your unexpected departure leaves an emptiness that will be extremely difficult, if not impossible, to fill. Just like Jacques Soleil, Raymond Jean-Francois, and Rony Lescouflair to name a few…you've joined the long list of martyrs for this great cause. My dear brother, you are from now on, just like your predecessors, a star that will forever shine in the firmament."

A twenty-one-gun salute followed this short speech, along with the Haitian National Anthem.

"Odilon did you hear that?" screeched Thérèse, frozen in total shock. The radio dropped out of Odilon's shaking hands.

"Yes, I think I'm having a nightmare. I guess…Zebeda knew what he was talking about," he muttered, shaking his head in disbelief.

"What was he talking about?" inquired Thérèse, her already red eyes filling with moisture – like a banana leaf overflowing with morning dew.

"He talks about so many things. I can't remember them all. But he always reminds us that war is an ugly business. He says the conflict is forced upon us."

"That's true. Remember the day at the square? The RRF didn't come 'til after the police started to shoot people. You can see how the government is dealing with the Northwest. They'll surely kill everyone standing in their way." She paused, twirling her longest locks with her little finger. "You know something?"

"What is it, *chérie?*"

"Until this war, I didn't know that those with money and power could be so cruel in this country. I thought it was only Anakreyon and his people. Now, I know better. Odilon, I refuse to think about the people who've lost their lives. It's like an earthquake that never stops shaking. Even if the war ends soon, I don't think I'll ever be able to return to my neighborhood. It will be too painful."

"I don't think your folks in Port-au-Prince will return, Thérèse."

"Oh yes! They probably will. That is, if the government wins."

"Are you sure?" Odilon seriously doubted the likelihood of this.

"I'm almost certain. I live there, and I know how they think. They have no sympathy for people like us. Every time someone of our kind walks into their store, they become suspicious. They don't trust anyone who's poor. Sometimes I feel like telling the customers not to come anymore."

"And you kept your mouth shut…"

"Odilon, I had to. I needed the job."

Odilon said nothing. Thérèse leaned on him as they walked down the muddy trail. It had been raining cats and dogs the night before. Their clothes flapped as they sluggishly walked between and beneath the giant banana leaves where the fresh morning dew lingered. Along the trail, they passed several empty houses with sealed thatched doors and no signs of life.

"Odilon, nobody lives in these homes anymore."

"I guess the people fled to the mountains. They're not too scared of war, but they're afraid of dying from hunger," said Odilon. Now, he was so thin that he seemed to disappear when he turned sideways. His already frail frame had withered even more since the war began, and if he didn't get more food soon, he would surely die of malnutrition.

Like the tinkling of bells from far away, they heard strange voices rising from across the valley, stopping for a moment to get a better grasp of the situation. They managed to pinpoint the direction the voices came from, but the banana fields on both sides of the trail prevented them from seeing who made the sounds.

They paused, unsure whether to continue along the path or follow the sound of the voices. Suddenly, stomping footsteps echoed behind them. Spinning around, they saw the boy they had saved from drowning in the river basin a few weeks earlier. His skinny brown cheeks gleamed as he flashed them a dazzling smile. He had thought about his rescuers every day since that dramatic moment, and now his small hands were overflowing with freshly baked *cassava*.

"How wonderful to see you again!" exclaimed Odilon, eyeing the young man's food.

"I'm so happy to meet you again. It's a dream come true!" declared the boy, stepping off the trail to get away from the sticky, muddy pathway.

"Where are you going?" asked Thérèse.

"Home," replied the boy, pressing his bare feet against the fallen banana leaves to wipe off chunks of mud stuck on his skeletal legs.

"Don't you live over that hill anymore?" Odilon urged, wondering if his grateful mother stored a supply of food they might wish to share.

"Yes, I do. But I came from the riverbed, where people are trying hard to buy some *cassava*, when I heard voices. I was hoping it might be you guys. As I looked closer, I couldn't believe my eyes. It is you! Or perhaps I am only dreaming?"

"You said they're buying *cassava* in the riverbed…a new market there?"

"Not really. Many people in this valley are dying from hunger. There's nothing to buy since the war began. So, merchants moved here to get away from the bombs. As you know, the flea market in Ti-Riviyè is destroyed, along with the bamboo trees."

"We need to go get *cassava*, too," stated Odilon.

Turning toward Ti-Riviyè, they pushed into the banana field. Halfway through the trees, Odilon heard a familiar sound— something slithering beneath the dry banana leaves—and quickly ordered Thérèse and the boy to stop. For twenty seconds, they stood as still as stones, trying to pinpoint where the sound was coming from.

"Look, Odilon," Thérèse whispered, pointing at a drooping, rotting avocado tree just five feet away.

"What is it?" the boy asked, edging closer to hide behind Odilon.

"Shhh!" Odilon muttered, signaling to them to be quiet. Emerging from the leaves, a seven-foot-long, brown-mottled snake slithered toward them, raising its head and narrowing its eyes.

"It's a *landomi*," Odilon warned. "We need to run—now. Follow me."

Odilon took two steps backward, with Thérèse and the boy close behind. They sprinted through the dry leaves, zigzagging until they outpaced the snake. Frustrated, it vanished behind the avocado tree once more.

The trio didn't stop running until they reached the open, sandy banks of Ti-Riviyè, crowded with half-starved people trying to buy *cassava*. Thérèse, still shaken by fear of the snake, collapsed to the ground, struggling to catch her breath. The boy, clutching his cassava tightly, was far less terrified. Having lived nearby, he was more accustomed to episodes like this.

"Hold my *cassava*…I'll get some more for you," he ordered.

"I don't think you can squeeze your way inside. This desperate crowd will crush you," warned Odilon. He squatted down in front of Thérèse, caressing her face with his palms to calm her down.

"Don't worry, I did it before," declared the boy, laying his *cassava* on Odilon's lap and vanishing among the crowd.

"Wait a minute!" cried Odilon, "I didn't give him money!"

"Odilon….can't get that nasty snake off my mind," admitted Thérèse.

"We're safe…I bet that snake was as scared as we were."

"I thought you said it was a *landomi*? How come it crawled around in broad daylight? It's a night creature. It should've been asleep in its hole."

"Maybe the war disturbs everything, including the animals. There aren't many mango trees left that are blooming. It's going to be a long, hot, miserable summer for those of us who survive this war."

Fifteen minutes later, the boy waltzed out of the crowd, three hot *casavas* in his intrepid little hands - giving the lovers a big smile as he proudly handed them to Odilon.

"How did you pay for them?" asked Odilon.

"I didn't have to," the boy replied.

"How come?" asked Thérèse, now in full control of her senses.

"One of the venders is my uncle. I told him who needed-"

"What did you tell him?" Odilon asked, not allowing the boy to finish his sentence.

"I told him my mom needed some," said the boy, pleased with himself.

Soon, they left the improvised marketplace as the heat and humidity became unbearable under the tropical sun. The boy headed east toward the hill to go home, while Thérèse and Odilon turned west, making their way back to Anwodo.

"Be careful, okay, little man? Go straight home," yelled Odilon. "And don't stop to pet any snakes!" Laughing, they all waved goodbye – hoping to get home safely.

#

Later, as nightfall crept through Anwodo and the crickets' songs filled the moonlit valley, Odilon and Thérèse stood on their front porch, gazing at the starry sky.

"Chérie, it feels peaceful tonight, doesn't it?" Odilon said, wrapping his arms around Thérèse's waist.

"It does," she murmured. "But don't trust it. The war's still raging somewhere in the province. Every time it's this calm, it means something terrible is brewing," she added, kissing Odilon's shoulder.

"Son!" Cécile called from her bed, where she was nursing a sore knee.

"Are you alright, Manman?"

"Yes, but I forgot to tell you: Makonmè Anasé came by twice this morning, looking for you. She said it's important. Go see if she's there."

"Yes, Manman, but I don't think she's home. I don't see any light from her windows. I'll check anyway."

Odilon held Thérèse's hand as they walked the path to Anasé's front door. After just one knock, the door cracked open.

"I thought you weren't home. I didn't see any light," said a startled Thérèse.

"Yes, I'm here. I ran out of gas, so I couldn't light my lamp. If something doesn't change soon to end this war, we're going to die from a lack of supplies."

"I have a sense the war is coming to an end…not in our favor," sighed Odilon, his voice stretched dark with emotion beyond his years. He did not want to admit it but was hoping deep inside that he was wrong.

"No, don't say that!" Thérèse pleaded, gripping his arm. "Can you imagine what that means to the rest of us?"

Anasé cleared her throat to get their attention. "The reason I came looking for you twice this morning is because of the rumors I've been hearing. The news isn't good, and I didn't want to tell your mother," she admitted, lowering her voice so Cécile wouldn't overhear from next door.

"What did you hear, Makonmè?" Both Odilon and Thérèse were fascinated and edged closer to listen. Any news was good news to them.

"I'm sure you know what happened to Jean-Michel in Port-de-Paix," Anasé's voice dropped a full octave, weary with wartime dread.

"Yes, we did," replied Odilon. "We learned that from the radio this morning."

"What you heard was the *troket, chay la dèyè* – the tip of the iceberg."

"What?" peeped Thérèse; she shook in mounting horror.

"Rumors spread this morning that the RRF has abandoned Port-de-Paix, and government soldiers are in full control, going house to house to find collaborators."

"Are you sure of this rumor, Makonmè?"

"I don't know…I'm not sure, but the people who came up from Port-de-Paix this morning told plenty of horror stories."

"*Kisa?*" bellowed Odilon, "How could it be?"

Hollow screams reverberated through his heart, mind, body, and soul, flooding his wounded psyche with a torrent of intense pain. The prospect of moving from hope to despair, from joy to sorrow, and from relative freedom to a doomed future terrified him. Odilon had spent twenty of his twenty-five years as a deprived human being, a disregarded soul who, like the other village boys, crossed into manhood without even realizing it. Since his brother's death and the brief taste of revolutionary freedom, with its darkest, most nightmarish elements, Odilon felt something take hold of him—something fully known to grown men but lost on mere boys. In that moment, he felt jaded. Old. Afraid.

"How can I survive as a man, fulfilling my duties as a concerned and productive husband, if the revolution doesn't triumph? How can I accomplish the beautiful things I want to do with Thérèse?"

These thoughts plunged him into a deep, unshakable melancholy, setting him apart from the others. Feeling like a tragic figure, he lowered his head and fell silent, leaving Anasé and Thérèse to ponder their next move if Saint Louis were recaptured by the government—or worse, if Chief Anakreyon regained control of their section.

The darkness concealed his mood as he leaned against the door, seemingly asleep, his withdrawal unnoticed. But from nowhere, for no discernible reason, voices of hope began to echo in his mind, returning with a vengeance, like ghosts from the village forest creeping into his consciousness. "The revolution lives!" the voices cried. Yet, crippled by fear and uncertainty, Odilon struggled to escape the weight of his despair.

The grim reality of an impending defeat made him see his fellow oppressed villagers as dead leaves, blown aimlessly through the trees by howling winds. But as he listened more closely to the voices of hope, he forced himself back to reality. Despite the unforeseen obstacles ahead, he knew he couldn't live in a state of uncertainty, like dust blown by desert winds. He needed to live as an honest citizen, claiming his rightful place in the long march of humanity, aware of the limitations of his life.

"Odilon, wake up, wake up!" Thérèse hissed. "We have to go home."

"What time is it?" he asked.

"How do I know?" Thérèse answered. "I only know one thing."

"What?"

"It's late – we need to get home. Besides, we have to be up early."

"What for?"

"Didn't you hear what Makonmè Anasé said?"

"No…"

In the still of the night, as the nascent moon rose over the hill, they left the neighbor's house, following the short path home. But Odilon's unusual mood that night captured Thérèse's attention.

"Odilon, what was wrong with you tonight? You're usually the leader of our political conversations. But tonight, you let me and Makonmè do all the talking and planning, while you fell asleep."

"*Chérie*, I'm sorry…I was tired." Refusing to admit his fear, he lied, not knowing what might come should Chief Anakreyon make a comeback.

"Odilon, Makonmè told us that government troops are in La Pointe, moving north to reinforce those fighting in Ti-Riviyè. Rumor has it Anakreyon will return!"

"*Chérie*, stop that nonsense. Anakreyon return? He'd have to kill everyone here. If we let him return, he'll transform this section into a cemetery."

"Odilon, that's why Makonmè and I think it's time to activate the plan. We're going to mobilize our committee tomorrow…first thing."

"I agree."

Hearing only the sound of snoring as they entered the house, they set up their small mat, laying down two layers of cotton bedsheets to protect themselves from leeches. Finally, they crossed their arms beneath each other's heads, like two innocent doves, and fell asleep without changing their clothes. A long day lay ahead, and they needed the rest.

#

At five a.m., the sun was still hidden behind the mountains, far from rising. The air was dark and hot, reminiscent of long, hazy August nights when the sky would come alive with shooting stars, leaving blazing red trails across the heavens. During those nights, children in the village would race to their parents, awestruck by the streaks of light cutting through the darkness, becoming prime witnesses to the time of the falling stars.

The valley slept, except for the farmers leading their herds of cows and goats to nearby streams for an early meal before another long, hard day of working the soil. Inside Odilon's small house, however, everyone was awake and alert, including Cécile—though for different reasons. She was unaware of the decisions made the night before. Her early rise was solely due to her morning rituals, which she followed unless pain kept her confined to bed. But the unexpected wakeup of her "children" and their unusual eagerness to hit the road puzzled her.

"What's going on? Are you two up to something? Why are you rushing outside? It's not even six o'clock yet!" she complained, yawning at the edge of her bunk.

She cradled a water cup in one hand and held her toothbrush, with a drop of Colgate toothpaste, in the other. She was about to pull the latch on the front door to head to the cacao trees, where she sat on her *biyot* each morning to brush her teeth before having her usual breakfast of *boukousou*, peanut butter, and ginger tea.

"*Manman*, we're up for a long walk this morning," replied Odilon, hitching up a loose rope belt around his sagging pants. Thérèse stood behind him, wearing clean overalls and a pair of light-blue tennis shoes, looking like a Haitian princess ready for a tropical expedition.

"Why and where is this walk?" asked Cécile, suspicious and quite anxious.

"The committee is marching to Fond Philippe," answered Odilon. "We're going to hunt Anakreyon down. Rumors say he was spotted in that area with a group of armed men. We're going to try to stop him before he gets here."

"Kids, be careful! You know what you're getting into. Anakreyon is a vicious man, not easily thwarted. I'm sure bullets will fly, and you'll both be right in the middle of it. Remember the old saying: 'Snakes that want to grow stay in their holes.' You'd better be careful. This is the last thing I need on a day that hasn't even started yet," Cécile groaned, resigned to the fact that she couldn't stop the determined lovers from going about their mission.

"We're aware of the risks, *Manman*," sighed Odilon. "But we're taking them now, before it's too late. Can you imagine Anakreyon and Fosia back in this section, to once again rule our lives?" He finished, laying a gentle kiss on his mother's floppy, wrinkled cheek to reassure her that they would be just fine.

"Who's taking care of the animals since you're leaving early?" Cécile asked, hands on her hips. "Don't you sweet-talk me; they need to be fed!"

"Don't worry *Manman*. I've already done that while you were asleep. By the way, your soup is ready in the kitchen."

"Be careful, kids." Sighing, the old lady could only pray for them.

"We will!" chorused the lovers, closing the door behind them and heading out to pick up Anasé, on their way to join the committee.

Cécile watched with apprehension through splintery cracks in the wooden window as the young lovers faded away in the morning dew, trailing off into the darkness.

Odilon's blunt words, used to justify his involvement in the plan to stop Anakreyon, had pierced Cécile's core. Though logical and patriotic, they filled her with fear. Her hands trembling, she dropped her toothbrush into the sloshing cup of water on the table and went back to bed. Unable to sleep, she lay face down, hoping and praying that the day would not be fatal for her only son and Thérèse.

Back outside, the lovers met up with Anasé, who had been waiting for them. Hiking up the hill, Odilon used a conch shell horn to summon the valley committee members, letting them know they were ready for the long march. As he blew his shell, people streamed from everywhere, rushing to the hill to join them. Happily, even a reserve unit from the RRF came along to accompany the marchers.

By six a.m., their ranks had swelled as they passed through other villages in the rural section. By the time the sun rose, hot and capricious, lingering behind them, they had already crossed a dozen streams and climbed several rugged hills. As the rising tropical haze gradually replaced the cool morning dew, the revolutionary-charged crowd showed no signs of distraction from what they considered their sacred mission: to eradicate fascism and the sadistic practices that had long lurked, unseen, in their midst.

Odilon hiked at the head of the band, displaying no traces of fatigue. From time to time, the last words Cécile exchanged with him before their departure haunted him. He struggled to repel the depression that he had suffered the night before – no longer able to bear the treatment given to people like him in his beloved rural section. The more he thought about it, the more he felt resolute in his determination to never again be regarded as a dry, dead leaf, blown by the winds and destined like maize to wilt in the sun.

Suddenly, a deep male voice boomed from behind. "Kanpe!" shouted a heavyset man with a round, boyish face, a straw hat perched on his head. Lines of sweat traced salty paths down his cheeks. Gasping, the crowd stumbled to a halt.

"What was that for?" Odilon demanded, waking up from his trance.

"We can go no farther. It's too dangerous. Anakreyon lives across the hill, in that village," the man stated, stepping forward to lead the group. They now stood midway up a low hill dotted with tall breadfruit trees swaying gently in the breeze.

Across the hill was a small village, perched on a ridge and overlooking a windy upland valley where a mysterious, swampy lake lay dormant. No one could be seen going in or out of the village. There was no sound of barking dogs or crowing roosters, and certainly, no meowing cats. The stark structures of the huts resting on a mountainous ridge and the rugged scenery they projected were enough to convince Odilon that whoever had lived in that village must have only used it as a temporary residence.

For a moment, no one uttered a word. Everyone looked hypnotized, gazing at the lake below, silently becoming conscious of the bizarre landscape surrounding them. Scratching his head, Odilon remembered the strange wilderness his father had always talked about when he was a kid – the place where inexplicable things occurred: werewolves stalked in broad daylight, owls and hawks intermingled to hunt prey, water streamed northward, *simbi* swam in deep river basins, and fig trees trembled without any windstorms.

The marshland, with its dense green vegetation surrounding the swampy lake, made it nearly impossible for the people to tell where the ground ended and the water began. Suddenly, a massive black snake, resembling the water moccasins of the Florida Everglades, erupted from the wet muck—a gigantic creature that sent large mats of breadfruit leaves rippling across the surface of the lake.

Thérèse froze – Odilon thought she made a most beautiful statue. "What the *hell* is that?" she whispered to him, caught in a sideways turn.

"Shhh, quiet," he whispered back, drawing her to his side.

The heavyset man ordered everyone to move downhill with steady caution. "It's dangerous... a lot of strange things are happening around here. If you hear or see anything mysterious, don't panic. Just keep moving," he instructed, his voice commanding the full attention of the crowd.

"I'm not afraid," Odilon muttered to Thérèse. "If I was, I would've stayed home...I had that choice."

"Odilon, the man is right. Just because someone is being cautious doesn't mean he's a coward," she answered, as most of them started to climb downhill.

Frightening sounds of gunfire erupted from small houses across the ridge. The people who reached the foothill scampered back up again to join those somewhat hidden in the undergrowth, while the RRF unit – supported by the volunteer civil defense brigade – moved into position.

They returned fire with such speed that within minutes, the gunfire from the village was silent. But the lake at the base of the foothill made it impossible to reach the village. As they had still not seen who was shooting at them, the RRF commander ordered the people to halt their march, taking cover behind the thick vegetation to avoid enemy fire. At that point on, there was no doubt in anyone's mind that the invisible beings in the village were none other than Anakreyon and his henchmen.

"We're going to walk around the lake, to get to the other side – while using caution," said the heavyset man, who knew the area. Everyone followed him in stark silence to the opposite side of the hill.

They skirted the swamp and emerged behind the village fifteen minutes later, encountering no one as they entered the tiny makeshift encampment. Yet, signs of life were everywhere: rustic tables with dominoes set for play, huge pots of rice cooking over open flames, clotheslines strung between tree branches, and doors left wide open. Despite searching every inch, they found nothing.

Odilon dropped to the ground in anguish, slamming his head against the dirt. "How could Anakreyon have gotten away? Where was he?" he screamed.

"There they are!" shrieked a woman who had searched downhill, spotting the old chief and about a dozen of his armed guards fleeing beneath the coffee trees. The RRF unit unleashed a torrent of bullets in their direction. The chief's men tried to return fire but were quickly overpowered. They dropped their weapons and scattered under the thick cover of the green foliage, leaving Anakreyon to face his fate at the mercy of Odilon's furious people.

As before, when executing the chief's main informant, an irate mob marched up to the old chief. Like a dead leaf in the wind, the coward's whole body shook. "Please, don't hurt me," he begged for his life – still in his torn pajamas.

He was barefoot, filthy, and reeking after his long time in hiding like a coward. His tangled hair stuck up in wild tufts, entwined with dry leaves, giving him the look of a wild man—a predatory *malfini*. His fingernails and toenails had grown long, perhaps intended as his last line of defense. Emotions ran high as the crowd surrounding him seethed with rage and hurt, their senses overwhelmed. They glanced at one another, waiting to see who would make the first move to lay hands on the chief.

Anakreyon's eyes glazed over, like a wild mongoose trapped in a cage—desperate, like the snake it once battled, wanting to crawl out of his own skin. By the swampy lake, the former chief was forced to confront the dramatic downfall of his wretched life. In a blur, he realized he was truly hated, abandoned by his closest allies, and left to face his fate—alone.

"I beg you, don't shoot me," he croaked, his voice like that of an endangered toad, pleading for mercy.

"I didn't know you were such a coward," said Odilon, facing him with an unbelievable thirst for revenge. But the old section chief did not answer. Instead, he turned to the RRF soldiers, seeking a last-minute pardon.

"Besides my brother, how many people have you executed in this section?" Odilon questioned.

The chief did not answer, ignoring Odilon while trying, once again, to exact a pardon from the RRF fighters. Infuriated, Odilon yanked a guava stick out of Thérèse's hand, lashing a heavy blow against the chief's forehead. He was knocked down, rattling noisily on the ground, rolling against the banana trees as he tried to crawl into the lake.

"Don't forget he's a werewolf…we'll lose him if he goes in the water!" cried out a woman in the crowd. Odilon then grabbed Anakreyon by his legs, scooping him up and turning him over to the angry crowd.

With manic glee, someone in the group snatched a stick from a nearby cookfire, while another fetched a can of gasoline. Within seconds, the chief was set on fire and burned alive – his body thrown into the swampy lake, to be eaten by caimans.

"Justice is served," Odilon growled, heaving a sigh of relief.

"The chief is dead…his henchmen won't return," declared a visibly shaken Thérèse, understanding the power of social justice.

Lost in their own musings, the revolutionary crowd climbed back over the hill to avoid crossing the dangerous swamp. It was now late afternoon, and the desire to get home before sundown and leave this ghost-infested area was their top priority. To lighten their moods, the people marched in a single file, singing revolutionary songs, crossing stream after stream to reach the north bank of Ti-Riviyè, where the group then dispersed.

Chapter 28

Jean-Michel's death dealt the RRF its greatest setback since the war began. When news of his passing reached the frontlines in Port-de-Paix, rebel fighters dropped their weapons in disbelief. It was a devastating blow to their cause. While some fighters took it as a reason to deepen their revolutionary resolve, the majority were paralyzed by the loss. As a result, Port-de-Paix became a no-man's-land. Government soldiers seized the moment, pushing the RRF back to the southern edge of town. Meanwhile, to the southwest, Ricardo Alcindor attempted to reclaim lost territory but was forced to abandon the strategic western front, leaving government forces free to move without fear of rebel reprisals.

For the first time in weeks, all was quiet on the western front – a sharp contrast to the Port-de-Paix region, a few miles to the north. Although the guns were silent, an agonizing calm hovered over the landscape, creating the sad, macabre aura of a burial ground. Beneath the somber cloud-filled sky, in the midst of a tropical haze, the shallow plains looked like a weather-beaten zone devastated by the fury of a hurricane. Trees were torn down, banana fields flattened, houses crushed, and rivers polluted from torn human flesh blending with bloated bodies, floating downstream.

Paradise Found had become Hell Itself. Gone was the magnificent view of a luxuriant yucca field from the mountainsides, gone was the spring grass that lay dormant like a green carpet over the valley floor, and gone was the crystal-clear water that once ran from nearby ravines, shining and sparkling like diamonds in the sunlight. Only victorious government soldiers could be seen patrolling the desolate roads and the main highway leading north to Port-de-Paix. It was a moment of great optimism for the hawks in Port-au-Prince. But Ti-Jean remained cool and reserved, staying above the moment, leaving his associates to beat the drums of war.

After hours of fierce street fighting, the rebel presence in Port-de-Paix began to dwindle. Government soldiers patrolled the town center and controlled both entrances to the city. Still, the rebels held on, putting up a ferocious and heroic resistance for five days. But by the fifth day, their supplies started to run dry. The RRF headquarters in Saint Louis were unable to resupply the southern front, as Port-de-Paix had been cut off from the rest of the province once government forces secured the main entrances. Meanwhile, artillery bombardments rained down relentlessly on rebel positions in the south of town.

Ricardo Alcindor, in a shrewd move, managed to infiltrate the city – a desperate attempt to reverse the tide. But his reinforcement proved no match against the sustained bombardment from the army's air force. Facing obliteration, Ricardo withdrew all rebel forces from the city in the middle of the night, using the thick blanket of the coffee fields along the foothills on the eastern edge of the city, leading the rebels to their original headquarters in the mountains near Saint Louis du Nord.

The fall of Port-de-Paix solidified the government's position in the province and dealt a psychological blow to the RRF movement. It left Olivier Zebeda facing a fait accompli, making him feel as though he were standing on the edge of a cliff. For the first time, Zebeda was forced to consider the possibility of defeat in both his military and political strategies. He was facing enemy forces on all sides, and each passing hour pushed his political future into a more precarious position. Now, he had to single-handedly defend the town of Saint Louis. Ricardo, in the process of retreating from Port-de-Paix, was unable to enter Saint Louis to assist him. Isabelle and

Joséphine, keeping government forces at bay on the southern front, could not move beyond the perimeters of their control. Arthur Auguste could not take away any of his forces from their strategic positions in and around the village of Bonneau. And any deployment from the northern front could be fatal for Zebeda in Saint Louis.

The morning after they seized control of Port-de-Paix, General Lacroix, confident of victory, raised the stakes on the rebels. He made it clear on Radio Nationale that Zebeda had only two choices: surrender or die. He promised an armistice for rebel fighters who laid down their weapons, while simultaneously announcing harsh punishments for die-hard combatants and any civilians who collaborated with them.

But Zebeda was not yet surrounded. He still controlled Saint Louis and all outlining villages to the east, creating an effective triangle that stretched all the way to the RRF headquarters deep in the mountains. Despite sustained artillery barrages on rebel positions around Saint Louis, the revolutionary forces in the town grew defiant, holding on against the odds and ready to fight to the last man alive.

Along the frontlines around town, rebel fighters and army soldiers traded insults, sharpening their military and ideological positions to stand ready for the final showdown. The rebels threw slurs, comments, and obscenities at the government troops along the frontlines in Ti-Riviyè.

"*Fuck* you, slaves of Ti-Jean and his imperialist patrons!"

The soldiers shouted back, "*Fuck'n* commies, shut up!"

Olivier Zebeda now had to face up to the realities of the war and the truth. How could he reverse the situation, turning things around to his advantage as it was the month before? Steeped in his beliefs and goals, he was ready to face this latest challenge with extreme caution. An indisputable revolutionary leader, enigmatic in his glory, relaxed in his demeanor, yet strong as a rock, he was never afraid to deliver his boldest thoughts and beliefs to his comrades.

As the tropical night descended on Saint Louis, with the distant rumble of artillery fire echoing in the air, Zebeda withdrew from the frontlines to the nearby forest of Anwodo. There, he met with his entire high command, whom he had summoned the day before to discuss strategy in a war that was worsening daily for the RRF leadership. On the banks of a small stream running through the forest, Zebeda faced his comrades.

Squatting on large banana leaves spread over a carpet of green grass, with sand-polished pebbles nearby, the commanders gathered to listen. Zebeda, dressed in military fatigues with his black beret resting on his knees, knew his task that night was more challenging than ever. This night was different from previous ones in their fight for freedom. His thoughts were focused on the positive aspects of the war, not on surrender. He was a bold, legendary leader who did not conform to the standard mold.

As he sat before his colleagues, Zebeda was ready to tell them that he was destined to uphold his revolutionary ideals until the end. Under a cloudless, moonless sky, chilled by uncertainty, he needed to use all his persuasive skills to reassure them that the truth was still on their side and that they must not be intimidated or give in to their enemies. He not only had to reaffirm their faith while praying for peace, but he also had to convince them never to deviate from their paths. He had to reestablish himself as the leader worthy of their trust—the man with the will to do whatever must be done to complete the mission they had barely started.

Joining the RRF military high command for that historic meeting were Dr. Duchaud and Daniel Achille, the two most important ideologues of the revolutionary movement. Ricardo remained calm, appearing strong and confident as he glanced at the moonless, starry sky. In reality, he was deeply concerned about the recent turn of events. Arthur Auguste sat next to Zebeda, who was flanked by Isabelle and Joséphine. Arms and legs were crossed; Kalashnikovs lay on their laps. A small Coleman lamp brought light to the dark forest.

A huge poster of Jean-Michel was carted in for the meeting. Holding this picture in his right hand, Zebeda tossed his beret on the ground, standing up in one fluid motion with his steadfast gaze fixed to address his fellow revolutionaries.

"Comrades," he began, "none of us believed we would come here to discuss the situation we find ourselves in. None of us thought it even remotely possible that Jean-Michel was not going to be with us, within the few, short weeks since the war began. But, despite the grim realities we face today, and despite the uncertainties that lie ahead, I continue to have unyielding faith – because I know that the people of Haiti will never again allow themselves to be zombified – like the walking dead!

"I have faith because our military forces are still very much intact. I have faith because I'm convinced that our movement is spearheaded by some of the best and brightest minds in Haiti. And while we may be the front forces leading the charge on the ground, we are by no means the only players in this fight. Our struggle has never been an isolated one. It is part of a global struggle to eradicate ignorance, hatred, tyranny, and neo-colonialism from the Earth.

"Because of our tireless efforts, our people can now clearly see the difference between right and wrong, between changes that would better their lives, and changes that would destroy them. And because they can see the difference between revolution and reaction, it is now almost impossible to reverse the goals of the Haitian people."

He paused for a moment, as if trying to catch his breath. His comrades, heads down, seemed unable to face their leader. A deathly silence reigned, disturbed only by the chirping of crickets in the foliage. Then, he continued.

"Let's remind ourselves about what we're up against. We're fighting a chimera with multiple heads. Often what we see is just the tip of the iceberg. Nearly seventy years of blatant imperialist influence has caused Haiti to be the victim of four major aspects of foreign domination: military, ideological, cultural, and economic.

"Let's not forget the logistics and military aid provided by foreign nations that support the Haitian government. Let's not forget a never-ending propaganda campaign against revolutionary ideas carried out by a *bourgeois* and reactionary media. Let's not forget the foreign influence over our educational system. Let's not forget the takeover of our economy by foreign investors.

"Comrades, we've been fed propaganda from the *bourgeois* press about national reconciliation as the quintessential solution to all of Haiti's problems. Let's face some reality here and be frank with ourselves. Reconciliation is a mutual agreement between two parties that are at odds with each other. Reconciliation can only be accomplished with a shared understanding that we must get rid of the obstacles standing in our way.

"Many obstacles keep us from living in peace and harmony. In the case of the masses, this aim has been difficult to achieve because they have no political clout, even though they are the backbone of our society. Although they represent the labor force, they have been put down and oppressed by the ruling party. Since the birth of our country, the masses have been forcefully discouraged from participating in any realistic process that would move Haiti forward."

Isabelle's eyes turned red and moist. She feared what would come next. She was fighting to hold back tears.

"The ruling party, however, also has many obstacles to overcome," Zebeda continued, "First, it needs to relinquish a substantial amount of the control and privilege it has amassed for nearly two-hundred years. It has to cease being a crippled *bourgeoisie* at the service of foreign nationals. In other words, it has to become its own master, playing the major role in the industrial development of Haiti. But no such desire has risen from its mindset. Within this *bourgeoisie*, there may be elements motivated by a genuine nationalistic urge to propel their actions toward the creation of a national industry, with all the necessary elements to sustain it. However, they are so few in numbers, their feelings will remain just that: positive feelings overshadowed by a materialistic society with the tastes to live as *bourgeois*…forever.

"Comrades, history teaches us that fighting direct colonialism is often easier than waging a struggle against entrenched neo-colonialism. Under classic colonialism, people are driven to resist in order to restore their wounded pride and reclaim their hard-earned freedom, which was taken by a foreign power that dictated every aspect of their lives. This alone is enough to galvanize significant elements across all levels of society to rise up in arms.

"In the case of Haiti, a country with such a glorious past, the need to purge foreign influences from our state bureaucracy could not be more urgent. So, it's easy to understand the reasons behind the concerted national support during the struggle against the American military occupation of Haiti at the turn of the twentieth century.

"But the reemergence of the indigenous state immediately gives rise to a neo-colonialist domination, totally committed to upholding the interests of the departing foreign forces. This subordination is rather apparent, for it paralyzes and cripples the growth of most, if not all, productive forces. The appearance or reappearance of native faces in the leadership of the country, including the army, has paved the way for a semblance of newfound freedom, which is in fact more illusory than real."

The forest floor was heavy with a somber quiet as the military commanders listened, their faces etched with fatigue and resignation. Zebeda's voice, though steady, carried the weight of grim inevitability as he is poised to declare that the time had come to confront the impossible. Shadows flickered across the trees, mirroring the dark thoughts that clouded their minds. Eyes that once held the fire of ambition now stared blankly, struggling to reconcile with the harsh truth of their situation. The silence was palpable, broken only by the occasional shuffling of restless feet, as the finality of their leader's words sank in, each commander grappling with the weight of retreat.

"Furthermore," he pressed on, "in the new era of a global economy imposed by donor countries, this economic and political tutelage is a heart-breaking death sentence for the masses. So, the *nouveaux riches*, in spite of the level of their nationalistic feelings, cannot in any way, shape, or form, carry out their historic mission. In other words, the local *bourgeoisie*, because of these constraints, cannot lead the country in a struggle for total independence from foreign domination. It smothers the emergence and growth of any productive force. To be blunt, it cannot become a national *bourgeoisie*.

"An understanding of these factors renders our position as a revolutionary force all the more important. Our struggle is a national liberation struggle, a direct force to recover our freedom and real economic and political independence. No matter what the consequences are or will be in the future, our liberation struggle is justified – because only this force can guarantee our national liberation. This will never happen as long as Haiti is under the economic and political influences of imperialist countries.

"Having pointed out these factors, we must not forget or deviate from our predestined mission." Turning inward, Zebeda's eyes misted over. He thrust his head downward, attempting to hide his emotions. He paused for five seconds, took a deep breath, and regained self-control. Watching with equal emotion, his heartbroken comrades kept an unbroken faith in their leader.

"Brothers and sisters in arms," he continued, "new realities sometimes require new tactics and strategies to sustain a protracted revolutionary war. In the face of major attacks by the enemy, in the face of relentless bombings, and in the face of a mounting death toll, the only thing we can strategically do is to organize a strategic withdrawal of our forces to our headquarters in the mountains.

"I know this is a hard pill to swallow, but this is why we are revolutionaries. Whatever the appearances may be, we're a lot closer to achieving our goals than we were a month ago, and the enemy knows it. They only control the main towns but won't dare to venture outside city limits. A strategic withdrawal will allow us to return to the cities whenever we think the time is right to resume our fight.

"We will never surrender our cause, our principles, or the hope of the masses, including the faith they have put in us. We will continue our work to unseat the fascist regime in Port-au-Prince. As long as we remain an unbroken force, Ti-Jean and General Lacroix cannot assume that the war is over.

"So, comrades, I'd like for us to take a hard look at what I have just described, and also at what I have just proposed before we make our final decision."

Not one word was spoken. For three long minutes, the rebel commanders remained frozen, refusing to look each other in the eye. What they were considering was too shocking to be true. Then, in a blur, the silence *de mort* was broken by the ragged voice of Joséphine, who scrunched in closer to make her point.

"Comrades, I don't have the will to abandon the people in town. I was planning to die with them if I have to. Furthermore, I'm certain I won't have the stomach to digest the reports of the mass slaughter that will take place as a result of our withdrawal. Can we please give it a last try?" she pleaded. "Maybe things will start turning to our advantage."

"Joséphine, 'abandon' is too strong a word," responded Daniel. "This struggle is our life, but we need to pursue it with wisdom and caution. I know there'll be reprisals as a result of our retreat, but the greatest hope we can push into the hearts of the masses is that of knowing we're still alive. As long as we're alive, the revolution lives; and this prospect will haunt the enemy forever. We cannot afford to play into the enemy's hands or commit an apocalyptic suicide. We'd become tarnished as historic figures if we were to fall into their trap. Revolutionary romanticism isn't meant to be blind stoicism.

"Additionally, a revolution cannot be fought solely through the barrel of a gun. Armed struggle is a means to an end, but those who lead revolutions to victory always anchor their goals in pragmatism."

As Daniel spoke, he stroked his mustache and wrapped his arm around Joséphine's shoulders, pulling her closer to console her. At his gentle touch, Joséphine's tough generalissimo facade crumbled, and she began to sob as long-held tears streamed down her cheeks.

"I think the biggest, most immediate threat to our revolution, after we retreat," Daniel continued, "will not be from the enemy, because he's clearly defined. Our biggest challenge will be keeping the masses focused when those career Marxists *de salon* start masturbating over our setbacks, and when the self-proclaimed ideologues from the so-called progressive press start editorializing our withdrawal through their artificial progressive newspapers, offering possible alternatives to resolving the crisis.

"They have long been rebels without a cause. They're nothing more than Marxist non-revolutionaries, whose ultimate aim is to share power with the enemy while using the masses as stepping-stones to reach their desired goals. Through the multiple media they control, they've only given us token support – out of fear of losing their 'revolutionary' credentials. But deep inside their souls, they pray every day that our movement will not succeed. They are hypocrites!

"Those Marxists turned button-down technocrats are far more at ease when sharing power with the reactionaries, in any power-sharing arrangement, than they are in sharing power with us. They would forfeit their role to lead in a heartbeat rather than assume any form of responsibility. Their aim is to be loved by everyone, friends and foes alike."

"How can someone claim be a Marxist militant, and at the same time enjoy reactionary legitimacy?" Isabelle demanded, who up to that point had been quietly sitting on her banana leaf. "Only those who do nothing can enjoy such illusory admiration. But their purposeful interference and confusion could prove damaging to our cause."

"You know, Isabelle," said Ricardo," those phony revolutionaries you just described still have an eye on the revolution if it triumphs. In the event of a revolutionary entry into Port-au-Prince, they will be quick to position themselves as qualified technocrats to hold bureaucratic posts and head diplomatic missions around the world, traveling aimlessly and living lavishly off the people's sacrifices, while making sterile speeches at international forums."

"True enough," emphasized Dr. Duchaud, "Those guys are fake revolutionaries. You can see how they supported General Lacroix."

"Yes," added Zebeda. "But what the enemy really wanted was for us to capitulate. They wanted us to lay down our weapons, or use them against our own officers, who would've surely opposed, for good reason, any capitulation with the same fury they used to fight their enemies. By doing that, we would've created our own self-destruction. We knew better than to capitulate!

"However, as I said earlier, our fight to rid Haiti of its enemies is not an isolated one, coming from some remote corner of our country. Through the progressive media, the world has been made aware of our fight for freedom. I believe that our great motivation and our will to resist have already made inroads deep into the hearts of many oppressed people around the world. I'm convinced that due to the strength of our courageous men and women, our movement has grown steadily, both in strength and sophistication."

Zebeda paused to assess the situation. It grew deathly quiet. They all knew that they faced an inevitable conclusion. Their leader, in an awkward and agonizing gesture, drew back for a moment, gazing up at the stars. He could not look anyone in the eye.

"Now," he continued, regaining his composure, "It's time to vote on this major decision. Anyone who opposes the withdrawal, please raise your hand." No one so much as moved. With that one act, the first phase of the war ended.

The next night, under cover of darkness, the RRF withdrew to its original headquarters, deep in the mountains. A division of the retreating forces came across Bèbè Le Tyran as he attempted to join government forces near the city of Port-de-Paix. He was executed on the spot. That last symbolic act marked the conclusion of the first dramatic phase of the people's struggle, in its utmost and explicit desire for change.

As the news of the RRF retreat spread like wildfire, striking without notice, Haiti sunk into an intolerable state of depression. Cities became ghost towns as people barricaded themselves inside their homes, waiting for the passage of winds of terror and death, while hoping that their fury would not engulf them.

Meanwhile in the Northwest, Zebeda ordered all divisions of the rebel army to rendezvous in the rocky foothills on the eastern edge of Anwodo. There, they formed two columns of military formations, marching on to their headquarters – an act they could not have envisioned some two months earlier.

In a world of darkness edged by a vague horizon of uncertainty, Olivier Zebeda, the man who had risen to the role of revolutionary hero, paced up and down the middle of a coffee field—motionless beneath the mountain ridge, untouched by civil strife, yet offering the perfect setting for a surrealist world. This was a place where lovers embraced at noon with the delirium of midnight; a region steeped in superstition, where children carrying water jugs shivered in morbid terror at the thought of werewolves as they passed through on their way to the river; and a realm where houngans waited for days, seeking a chance to commune with Gran Bwa, the god of the forest.

Zebeda leaned against a cashew apple tree, a lone hero soul-searching and struggling to regain control of his inner emotions. He was losing his true self, fighting off the invasion of depression and nostalgia creeping into his body. Here, long after the echoes from the bootsteps of the last retreating fighter faded away in the darkness, he was still below the mountain, confronting his personal demons.

Head bent down, arms wrapped around a branch, with his sidearm strapped below his belly, Zebeda's broken stare was that of a dazed child leaving behind a roller-coaster ride. That ride had taken him to the giddy heights of revolutionary fame, to the uproarious and defining moments of the war, to the dazzling splendor of a high noon, to the "shock and awe" hours in the battlefields, to the unexpected setbacks, to the death of his dear comrade, Jean-Michel, and ultimately, to the humiliating retreat from everything that had once fostered and bolstered his flamboyant image as a saintly, messianic king reigning from the gilded throne of revolutionary politics.

Reviewing the brief moments of glory in his beloved native land, Zebeda sought refuge within a bittersweet melancholy that crept into his mind, infiltrating the bottomless depths of his soul. But beneath the waves of dire uncertainty rushing ahead, his patriotism stood firm, never wavering. Only this strong sense of patriotism kept him from drifting into the remote, lost seas of despair. Zebeda knew his mission had been aborted. Only through the assurance of staying alive, along with the unequivocal support of his revolutionary comrades, could he guarantee that the people of Haiti would someday be free. Dying in battle would have to wait for another day.

With his goals firmly in mind, Zebeda regained his composure. He had successfully defeated the demons and the gloom, while re-embracing his revolutionary romanticism. Loosening his grip on the cashew apple tree branch, he strolled into the still of the night, a rejuvenated man, to rejoin his colleagues – who were already on the mountaintop. Up there, they entered their headquarters with firm conviction, to wait for the right moment to continue their predestined mission.

Chapter 29

The front door creaked open, startling Odilon from a fitful sleep. He lifted his eyes above the shafts of sunlight penetrating the cracks in his small nat. Stretching and scratching his head, he rolled over but saw no one. Thérèse was not by his side. Her pillow of Spanish moss and the blue sheet they used as protection against the thriving community of bedbugs lay in crumpled, wrinkled folds. Her slippers sat beside the bed. But her colorful parasol, white overalls, blue-black glasses, pink brassiere, and the pair of blue tennis shoes she had placed on the old rocking chair in the corner the night before were all gone.

Startled, Odilon got up and glanced over at the bunk bed. It was empty. Cécile, his mother, and Thérèse, his most cherished companion, were nowhere to be found. The bed was neatly made, wrapped in a flowery cotton bedsheet, with two red pillowcases covering the pillows where Cécile slept every night.

"This is weird! Who opened the door? Was it the wind?" he muttered, leaning forward to push the front door further open. He looked across the courtyard—nothing, no one, *nadie*. Stepping back, he slipped his skinny legs into a pair of old, frayed blue jeans, grabbed his machete, and ventured outside. Fumbling for a moment, he paused to latch the door, then decided to head east.

The earth trembled beneath his feet with each step over the wet, dew-covered grass. Though Odilon was deeply focused on finding his loved ones, he couldn't help but notice that the village was deserted. Yet, in his troubled, war-torn mind, this barely registered. The sounds of conflict had ceased, but the roosters weren't crowing. No village children were by the ravine, brushing their teeth or washing their little naked behinds as part of their morning rituals. The sky had turned gray, the songbirds were silent, and the domestic animals had vanished. The smell of burning grew stronger with each step. The valley was unnervingly still—no barking dogs, no meowing cats, no distant sounds of exploding bombs.

Unaware that he strolled alone in a standstill world, quivering with fear, he floated like a thin, wan ghost parading in the sunlight. He wandered sheepishly across the valley floor, glancing around, but found no one. Tired of floundering like a lone, wounded animal, he made his way back to the house, totally confused but hopeful that somehow Thérèse and Cécile might have returned. It was wishful thinking.

As he reentered the village, he was greeted by the same eerie solitude he had left behind an hour earlier. He didn't go into the house. Instead, he slumped onto the front porch, head hanging low, his back against the wall, while his heart raced. Feeling wretched, he pondered his next move. Then he spotted a folded piece of paper tucked under the door. With a cry of delight, he snatched it up and opened it.

"Odilon, join us in Nan Banman by my mother's house under the cacao trees. The fumigators are in town," Thérèse had written in her fractured French.

Blazing with sudden anger, Odilon turned ice cold in frozen terror. "Why didn't they wake me up? Why would the fumigators…is the war over? What happened to the RRF? Why did they leave me alone?" Like a lone ship adrift in his surprise and sorrow, he sank onto the porch, crumpling the paper in his hands.

Reality began to creep into his fragile being, making him feel like a zombie surfacing from its trancelike state. He began to comprehend what was happening in the world around him. The war might be over, but the village was empty. No farmers went about their morning routine of feeding the animals, no early birds were heading to the flea market in Ti-Riviyè, and no pilgrims traveled to their sacred missions at the Catholic chapel behind the mountains. His world was a dry, motionless, soundless, empty existence. He had been abandoned by those he loved and trusted.

Instead of heading east to join his family in the mountains of Nan Banman, he sprang to his feet and began making his way west, toward Saint Louis.

"Before I die, I need to know what happened to those people," he murmured into the soulless emptiness.

In a flash, his war-ravaged body surged with energy, driven by a renewed sense of revolutionary bravado. He was ready to face whatever reality awaited him, even if it meant paying the ultimate price to learn the fate of the residents of Saint Louis.

Rather than taking the risky country road into town, he slipped through the sugarcane fields that blanketed the green valley floor, careful to avoid detection. *Atansyon pa kapon* (being cautious doesn't make you a coward). He saw, sensed, and heard nothing as he navigated the fields, finally reaching the edge of the war-torn town. As he pushed through the cane, the sporadic crack of gunfire echoed in the distance. Still, he saw no one. He moved cautiously, inching down a low hill that served as the buffer between rural Saint Louis and the town proper.

Banana fields, dotted with small houses and mango trees, lined the northern edges of town, providing Odilon with the cover he needed to reach the gates of the main highway, which led to both the northern and southern entrances. As he moved, he began to hear what sounded like the tortured cries of people in distress. Creeping between bombed-out houses, he reached an abandoned two-story mansion along the dusty highway, nestled in a courtyard shaded by tall, drooping mango and bushy lime trees. He slipped into the courtyard, hiding behind the lime trees to avoid detection.

The agonizing sounds grew louder as he approached. Were they ghosts? Werewolves? Shuddering, he knew he was close to people in grave danger but didn't know who they were, where they were, or what threatened them. Terrified, he crept beneath the lime trees until he reached the back door of the mansion, a once-imposing structure now crumbling with age. Built in the late nineteenth century by a wealthy Persian merchant hoping to leave his mark on the Arab community during the booming coffee trade, the mansion had long been abandoned. In the courtyard sat a deep, open well, thick with green algae and slime, where froglets, snakes, and palmetto bugs poked their heads above the surface.

What remained of the once-elegant colonial windows were rusty frames, their shutters flapping in the tropical breeze. The wooden back door was long gone, but thick undergrowth sprouting through wide cracks in the floor provided cover for the rear entrance. Layers of spiderwebs and tall grassy weeds invaded every corner of the ancient dwelling. Everything but the skeletal structure had crumbled away.

On the inside, fragments of fancy mosaic tiles, Persian rugs, and crystal chandeliers were visible, almost a century after being abandoned by the owner. Superstition kept people away; no one tried to take over the mansion, as rumors spread that ghosts and other evil spirits held court inside, even in broad daylight. Inside the grounds of the sprawling estate, generations of animals survived on their own. Donkeys, horses, cows, pigs, hens, ducks – all these lived, reproduced and died, feeding on each other and the large reserve of vegetation packed within the compound. It was a haunted zoological garden, one that people were afraid to visit.

Somehow, Odilon remained undeterred amid these scary newfound surroundings. But his sudden presence provoked a loud reaction from the startled animals. Dogs barked, cats meowed, donkeys brayed, cows mooed, pigs oinked, frogs croaked, snakes hissed, ducks quacked, roosters crowed, and songbirds squawked, clicked, and chirped. And the wild horses were jumping, snorting, and neighing – animals on the verge of a strange frenzy. But that day, Odilon was in no mood to interpret the voices of animals he had disturbed. Were they real, or merely magical figments of his troubled and superstitious peasant's imagination?

The overbearing sounds of gunfire mixed with the passing military vehicles from the main street recaptured his attention. His immediate goal was to get a view of the main street. Avoiding the animals, he went through the dilapidated mansion, wending his way to the second floor – where he stood silently behind the walls separating the front balcony from the old master bedroom. There, through an open, shattered glass window, he peered outside.

He could not believe his eyes. At every intersection, the dusty main street was filled with columns of people hogtied against one another. Heavily armed soldiers guarded them. These prisoners were all men, standing motionless and resigned to their fate, sweltering like dogs in the ninety-degree tropical humidity.

Swollen, bloated dead bodies scattered akimbo, bloody arms and legs like tree branches, littering the roadsides. The front walls of nearby houses were streaked with fresh blood and gore, evidence of multiple hideous murders committed the previous night. Every few minutes, a truckload of dead bodies snorted past – right there in downtown Saint Louis, the Town from Hell! Odilon was desperate to know where the trucks were headed. He crawled downstairs, going back to the now friendly-seeming courtyard. This time, no animals appeared, and he heard no sounds. The creatures took shelter in the vast courtyard, and the complaining ghosts and werewolves were silent.

He headed back outside, using a narrow alleyway behind piles of craggy rubble that led him to a hilltop overlooking the town. As he observed from a safe distance, the trucks drove along a corridor between the rocky riverbed of Ti-Riviyè and the trenches that the RRF had built during the war to reach the shorelines, where they were emptied into mass graves…with prisoners being forced to bury their dead.

Horrified, Odilon's heart shriveled into curds of fear. He had found what he was looking for, but no longer wished to view the gruesome scene. Then, he started to clamber away from the area until he could no longer see the shorelines as it disappeared behind the mango trees. Shuffling across the valley floor like Bawon Samdi, god of the cemetery, he was lost in the prairie of death. Shaking like a torn, dead leaf, he was on the verge of losing his sanity – blown to pieces by the winds of remorse. His nightmarish state shoved him into a melancholy of no return, as he wandered lost and without direction.

Breathless, exhausted, he returned to his empty village and collapsed at his front door. A few minutes later, he regained a measure of self-control. By then, he remembered the note – realizing that he could be responsible for the death of his loved ones if he did not make his way to Nan Banman.

#

"I don't think Odilon would be so naïve as to remain in the house…" mused Thérèse, scratching her head and biting her nails.

"If we don't see him in the next hour, I'm going to die!" Cécile cried out in anguish, pulling a handkerchief out of her blousy dress pocket to blot out the salty tears streaming down her brown, wrinkled face.

A worried pair, they sat on the front porch of Thérèse's parents' tiny home, made of thatch and covered with dry palm leaves. Strips of palisades, tied together by three long sticks, formed the front door. The only sign of wealth was a small, solid-silver latch used to lock it. Inside, the one-room house was furnished with a rustic bed, and the mattress and three pillows were made from hand-sewn blue fabric stuffed with Spanish moss collected from oak trees on the forest floor. Aside from the door latch, there was no silver chest, no cabinets. A multicolored plastic rug covered the lone table, which was placed in the right corner near the door. Eating utensils were wrapped in a blue tablecloth to protect them from the dust of the dirt floor.

In the corner next to the table sat a large clay jar filled with cool spring water from the river, used for cooking and drinking. Just below the ceiling, an open attic stored dried maize, green bananas, and mangoes—goods that were loaded onto the back of a small mule and sold at the marketplace near Ti-Riviyè, the family's only source of income.

Outside, a wall-free kitchen with a thatched roof was held up by four sturdy wooden poles rooted in the ground. There was no stove, only three large rocks forming a fire pit, where chunks of dry wood were used as fuel for cooking. A *korosol* tree and a young *mangfransic* mango tree stood on the opposite side of the kitchen, providing much-needed shade from the tropical heat. Around the courtyard, pigeon-bean plants grew among maize, okra, and yucca, forming a small garden where children ran naked in the afternoons, playing hide-and-seek.

But this little house sat at a particularly strategic position on the mountaintop. To the rear was a deep gorge. During the war, the rebels made it into a staging area. The front yard offered a stunning panoramic view of Ti-Riviyè Valley, exposing anyone or anything going up or down the main trail.

#

That day, the breathtaking view from the mountaintop was lost on Thérèse and Cécile, who stood anxiously on the front porch. Their hearts leapt at every hint of movement from beneath the banana leaves near the trail. The usually stunning valley vista meant nothing to them. The wave of death and destruction sweeping through Saint Louis had spread to the surrounding areas, clouding the minds, bodies, and souls of all who lived in the Ti-Riviyè Valley.

Thérèse's mother remained in the kitchen, preparing rice and beans for their two unexpected guests. Inside the house, her father and three brothers—all in their twenties—were piling heaps of dried corn in preparation for the spring planting. Though Thérèse's brothers no longer lived in the house, having married and settled nearby, they brought their children daily, ensuring the warmth and love of the family home never faded.

It was one of the grandchildren, a boy of about six, playing near the mountain ridge, who spotted Odilon making his way through the trees along the foothill—drenched in sweat and straying off the trail. His loved ones, unaware, waited nervously as he struggled upward, heading straight for them.

"Odilon!" the boy cried out with such excitement that the echo carried all the way to the mountaintop, astonishing the anxious people.

"Where did you see Odilon?" screamed Thérèse, rushing to meet the boy.

"There he is, coming up under the mango trees," he answered, throwing his small hands into the air and jumping with joy.

Thérèse raised a hand to her forehead, shading her eyes for a clearer view. "Chéri, why did you do that to us?" she hollered, spotting him resting against a rock. Exhausted and hungry to the core, Odilon only wanted to recharge before making the final push up the mountaintop to the house.

He didn't answer her but sprang off the rock and made his way toward her. When they met below the mountaintop, they collapsed into each other's arms, laughing with sore relief. Cécile, watching from above, burst into joyous laughter. Soon, everyone in the courtyard joined her. Thérèse's mother abandoned her wooden spoon in the pot of rice and beans and ran toward them. Her father and brothers, who had been piling corn inside, rushed outdoors. They all converged on the mountaintop, watching as Thérèse helped Odilon climb the final stretch.

Most of his strength had trickled away like water during the rugged climb, but now, surrounded by people who loved him, Odilon felt no anger toward his mother or Thérèse for leaving him behind that morning. Safely on the mountaintop, away from danger, he tried to grasp everything that had just happened to him.

"Tell me…where were you?" Thérèse repeated.

"I can't speak – I'm too tired," he mumbled.

As he pressed on, Odilon finally realized how foolish he had been to put himself in harm's way. He should have headed for the mountain as soon as he found Thérèse's note. He wished that what he had witnessed in Saint Louis was merely a hellish dream, a horrible nightmare from which he had wandered in and out. He prayed that the RRF soldiers were still fighting, the Haitian Army had been obliterated, the haunted house didn't exist, Saint Louis hadn't become Hell on Earth, the dead were alive, and those who had been arrested and bound together had morphed into a tropical hurricane that wiped out all the criminals.

He wished, too, that Saint Louis and Anwodo were intact, full of happy people going about their lives, that the revolution had triumphed, and that the mass graves near the shore were only figments of his imagination. But they were real—he couldn't shake the horrors he had witnessed. Those incredible scenes had left deep, indelible scars on his war-weary mind.

Thérèse wrapped his arms around her neck, pulled him to her waist, and helped him up the mountain. Odilon's fragile body was quickly rushed inside and gently laid in bed. The celebration halted, giving way to uncertainty and anxiety. A plastic bowl of warm water was brought in, and Cécile poured seven drops from her famous healing bottle—the one she always carried when traveling—into the water. She stirred it with her hands, fetched a clean towel, soaked it, and dabbed it on Odilon's forehead.

Gran Bwa was invoked, as well as Metrès Ezili, the most powerful of the African gods, to bring comfort to Odilon. After fifteen minutes his condition stabilized, and he fell asleep – a resting prince in the arms of his faithful servants. Only the voice of a Rebel Radio announcer would wake him from his slumber.

This voice was none other than Zebeda's. He wanted to reassure the masses and the world that he and his whole movement were alive and strong, simply waiting for the perfect moment to come down from the mountains. In a long, emotional speech, he reviewed the bloody moments they had recently suffered. After twenty minutes of in-depth analyses of the current state of the movement, Zebeda concluded with some emotional remarks:

"The RRF will never relinquish its revolutionary right to accompany you on your final journey to freedom. Do not be discouraged. Do not lose hope. Keep your eyes on the heavenly prize. Remember my first speech at the square…I reminded you then that the road to true independence has many setbacks. What's happening today is one of them. It may prove hard to swallow, but that doesn't mean the end of our fight. As long as we're alive, we will never change course, because we know we're on the right one.

"Only those who quit will miss the Promised Land. Remember, we are a resilient people, and it was our resilience that earned us our independence in 1804. We are a people with a glorious past. As passionate lovers of freedom, we cannot and must not allow ourselves to be swayed by reactionary propaganda. In 1804, we emerged victorious after thirteen years of bloody warfare with the French. We instantly became a sanctuary, a sacred refuge for those in our grand family of the Americas fleeing the horrors of slavery.

"To those seeking freedom from colonialism, Haiti was a beacon for revolutionary ideas. With open arms, we offered help in any way we could, even if it meant sending our sons and daughters to the trenches to fight and die alongside them. Countless names come to mind of those who visited us to share ideas on how best to destroy the poison of colonialism. The concept of Pan-Americanism has deep roots in Haiti. Leaders like Francisco Miranda, Simón Bolívar of Gran

Colombia, José Martí of our sister island Cuba, Farabundo Martí of El Salvador, and Augusto Sandino of Nicaragua all looked up to us as a shining example in their quest for political independence.

"That's why we must never forget that we are not alone in this struggle. But it's heartbreaking to see what the traitors in control of our country have done to our motherland. Today, other nations question whether Haitian intelligence has been reduced to the humiliating condition of conformism. Many of our best and brightest have long rejected the idea of patriotism, driven solely by greed, trading their inherited dignity, rejecting the basic principles of human decency, and becoming puppets in the service of the enemies of the masses.

"But things have never stayed that way. Throughout our history, our nation has produced great men with unblemished brilliance, who didn't hesitate to put their intelligence and even their lives at the service of our deprived masses. Antenor Firmin, Jacques Stephen Alexis, Adrien Sansariq, our own Jean-Michel Desquiron – to name a few – are all part of this honored category. Their bravery and heroism will always be our guiding light on the difficult path that lies ahead. We would be traitors, killing them twice if we abandoned our cause, the revolution for which they died. We will never leave behind our struggle to eradicate fascism from our homeland!

"Courageous people of Haiti, keep the faith. The RRF is with you to the end, whether that finality is bitter or sweet. Our strategic withdrawal is but a detour on the bumpy road to freedom. When everything is said and done, we will not only remember the horror of our enemies, but also the indifference of those who pretended to be our friends but stood idly by and did nothing."

"*Viv Haiti! Kenbe Djanm! Pa Lage!*"

That was to be the last time they would hear from Zebeda and the RRF. But for Odilon, surrounded by his loved ones, lying face up on that small bed, it was all he needed to hear. Zebeda's words were the natural healing force, the therapeutic boost Odilon was waiting for to land back on his feet. In fact, Thérèse's family was also invigorated by the words.

The entire valley, the whole province and the rest of the country – except for those involved with the government, of course – heaved a sigh of relief, as now they knew they had not been abandoned when the RRF had retreated to the mountains. Even nature responded favorably to Zebeda's speech. The clotted grey clouds vanished, as the tropical sunshine reappeared. Dark green leaves shining from the valley floor, lazy, and serene floated and bounced under the cool sea breeze of the tropics. Daylight once again came to the hearts and minds of the fear-stricken people of the Northwest. No matter what happened, life must go on.

Rising, Odilon rubbed the sleep from his eyes, stretching his arms, and spread them outward like the Haitian eagle – ready to fly into a universe of uncertainty. Rejuvenated, an awesome smile swept over Thérèse's face. She leaned against the bed, catapulting into an explosion of joyous laughter as she watched the wing-like movements of Odilon's arms and shoulders as he stepped outside into the courtyard.

"I'm so lucky to have a man like you in my life," she muttered, hurrying to join him outside. Her family was glad to see Odilon up and around too.

To Thérèse, her man was far more than a lover. She could not envision herself living without him. To her, he was a frantic brother, a one-of-a-kind human being with a brave heart, having a firm but positive attitude to confront the unwelcome circumstances of life. Odilon was an indispensable teacher who taught her how to smile, to love, to struggle, to suffer, to live, to believe in herself, and to ultimately overcome and triumph over all the vicissitudes in life.

From inside the little house, Cécile raised her head, flashing a smile at everyone. "My son is back!" she gladly announced. The family smiled at her in return.

Outside, the two lovers sat under the *korosol* tree, contemplating a renaissance of activities in their surroundings.

"*Chérie*," said Odilon, "you haven't told me why you left me in the house."

"We didn't abandon you! You told us to go, you'd join us when you got up. I had no reason to believe you wouldn't come," Thérèse replied lovingly, caressing his face with her warm, thin fingers.

"Are you sure I told you to go?" Odilon asked, puzzled. "I don't remember saying that – or even talking to you."

"*Oui, chéri.* What makes you think I would lie about something so serious? Makonmè Anasé came early this morning, around four o'clock. She told us that we needed to leave right away. By the time we walked outside, there was no one left in the village. I went back inside and shook you awake. You rolled over and asked what was happening. When I explained, you told us to leave and said you would join us. I thought you wanted to make sure everything was secure before leaving; but for our safety, you told us to go," Thérèse said, softening her voice.

"I must've gone back to sleep. I was really exhausted, if you remember. So, what did you do when you didn't see me coming?" Odilon inquired.

"As we got on the road, we saw a lot of people going in our direction. It looked almost the same way during the night of the first bombing. I thought you were behind with them, since you'd told us you were coming.

"By the time we got to the bottom of the mountain, and we didn't see you, we became very scared. The road was empty. Everyone was gone. I helped *Manman* Cécile climb up, and I took my brothers to go with me back to Anwodo. On the way back, I was praying to see you coming up the trail. We went all the way back to the front door. We knocked, looked inside, and called your name. There was no reply, and you were gone. I couldn't find the note I left you, and so I fell into the arms of my brothers. I began to cry. I cried all the way back here, to wait for you."

"I must've been talking in my sleep. I don't remember you saying anything…did hear a bang from the front door. That's what woke me up. But when I went outside, I saw no one. I went around and around, going stir-crazy. I searched the whole valley, going home to find the note."

"So, what did you do after you read the note?"

"I…ummm…folded it in my shirt pocket…rushed up here."

He was becoming skilled at lying. Odilon couldn't tell her about his horror story in the city: about the voices of people in distress, the haunted house filled with invisible ghosts, the animals that mysteriously disappeared, hundreds of men tied-up against each other like living zombies, truckloads of dead bodies buried in mass graves, and the blood stains spilled along the front walls of houses.

"I won't tell my story to anyone as long as the military is in town. If one day the revolution triumphs and I am alive, I'll be glad to tell it," he thought to himself.

They got up, exchanged longing smiles, and started descending downhill with their arms intertwined. They paused for only a moment to inhale the heady fragrances of the wild citronella and other deciduous species of shrubbery, evergreen hollies guarding both sides of the trail leading down to the valley floor.

"When was the last time you were here in this section?" Thérèse asked Odilon, not unlike a teacher questioning her student. He admired her "take charge" attitude as she squeezed his hand – surely, she would make a great *Manman*!

"Let's see, I think it was a year ago. I was on my way to Bassin Joseph, to do a job for a farmer from Saint Louis," Odilon responded, rediscovering for the first time in weeks the natural exuberance of his charming, delightful, attractive Creole *marabou*.

Her hair was dark, thick, long, a bit wavy, glistening as she moved languidly – combed into a pair of perfect braids with a blue barrette on each end, enhancing her girlish face. Breathtakingly seductive, her full lips were coated with glassy rouge lipstick. When she gave her throaty, sexy laugh, her straight white teeth sparkled in the sun.

After taking a bath to wash away the sweat and grime from her long and hectic morning walk, she felt refreshed. Exuding the scent of lavender water perfumed with sweet basil that she had rubbed on her body, she was able to talk, smile, and laugh with ease. Her long, straight nose accentuated her vibrant personality. It was framed by deep brown doe-like eyes, long eyelashes, and bushy eyebrows. She had put on a pair of large, ornate Creole-hoop earrings that perfectly complemented her flawless face, framed by a sensual chin, adding the final touch to her majestic appearance as a Creole queen.

This "queen" wore a knee-length, flowery blue dress, unzipped slightly below her ample breasts, which were cradled by a white brassiere. Though she had a slim waist, her full hips and firm buttocks, supported by her long, smooth legs, gave her a sizzling voluptuousness that men wildly craved.

Her flip-flop sandals forced her to lean on Odilon as she took careful steps along the rocky trail. As they made their way down from the mountain ridge, Thérèse suddenly stopped, yanking Odilon against her as she rubbed her ample breasts onto his chest, caressing his neck, surging his sexual appetites into full bloom.

Odilon pulled Thérèse off the trail, landing with her beneath an avocado tree amidst okra plants and tall, bushy maize. There, the little man and his buxom woman hastily stripped, consumed by uncontrolled, passionate love that seemed as if it could last forever— or at least until the first rooster crowed, signaling sundown's arrival. Then they would need to hurry back to Thérèse's mother's house.

That afternoon, pleasure mounted its peak – but did not come without a price.

Chapter 30

Odilon, Thérèse, and Cécile remained in Nan Banman for a week, waiting for the security situation in town to stabilize. However, after the week was up, Odilon no longer wanted to stay. He could not bear the pain of waking up each day to find himself, his mother, and Thérèse dependent on her family, especially when their financial situation was comparable to those living in extreme poverty.

Encouraging news soon arrived. People who had been in Saint Louis reinforced Odilon's desire to go home, as most people fleeing the night of the RRF retreat had already returned. The valley was now full of life. The flea market by the riverbed swelled with merchants, street vendors, and buyers looking for bargains. The village of Anwodo breathed with life, again. By the village square, children were jump-roping, chatting, and playing hide-and-seek. In Saint Louis, apart from the bomb-struck buildings, few signs of the war remained. The bloodstains had been erased with water hoses, wielded by caring folks and neighbors. Almost all vestiges of the war-ravaged environment were gone, including the death squad fumigators, the sandbags, the trenches, the armored vehicles, and the continuous psychological torture from the reverberation of exploding bombs in the distance.

While Port-de-Paix, Gros-Morne, and Jean-Rabel were still being militarized, and rumors of "fume squads" spread around, Saint Louis was vacated. No sign of military occupation could be found. The army had withdrawn to the sleepy village of Villasso, three kilometers from the southern fringes, a measure they considered necessary to maintain control of traffic in and out of town. Their true aim was to prevent the return of insurgents from the southern gorges, trying to sneak back into Saint Louis. In its downtown area, the shopping district was back in full force, but the main marketplace was only half full. Many of the "market movers" were nowhere to be found, presumably having perished in the war. This included fishermen, butchers, *machann pisket*, legumes vendors, soothsayers, dreamcatchers, charm executioners, troubadours, private prostitutes, and the famous balladeers who performed near the northern edge of the marketplace.

An unspoken consensus prevailed: "No one should cry, for crying won't bring deliverance". The people of Saint Louis wanted to withhold their once-shared emotions, pains, and humiliations, betting on their shared hopes that someday a more favorable wind would blow their way.

Meanwhile in Anwodo, Odilon and the rest of his family were home, beginning to resume their former routines. One night, shortly after supper, Odilon watched Thérèse running toward the bushes. When she reached the cacao trees, about ten feet from the house, she bent down on her knees – spending several minutes throwing up. Odilon sped to her side, looking all around to see if anyone else was watching.

"Thérèse, what's wrong?" He rocked her in his arms to comfort her.

"I don't know. I'm feeling dizzy, nauseous, and weak, especially in the morning and at night…around this time," Thérèse answered, her voice feeble as she leaned on Odilon, who slapped his forehead when the realization hit like a thunderclap.

"Do you think you're pregnant?" Odilon asked, grinding the words.

"I don't know. I hope not."

"Let's go back in the house, *chérie.*"

"Odilon, wait."

"*Chérie*, you're getting me scared. The last thing we need is a baby."

"Odilon, why do you say that? Wouldn't you want to have a baby that…looks like you and me?"

"*Chérie*, don't get me wrong. The most precious gift is a child, the fruit of our infinite love. But I've always wanted that baby to be happy…that we're able to take care of our child. We struggle every day to make ends meet. If we have a baby now, our whole family will suffer."

"I have faith. God will lead the way…"

"Which god are you talking about, Thérèse? The same God that did nothing as innocent people were massacred by our government?"

"Odilon, I don't want to get into that right now. Anyway, it's getting late. The mosquitoes are eating me alive. We need to get back in the house."

Odilon frowned as he led Thérèse past Cécile's small garden. But when they neared the front door, Odilon released her arm, gripping her by the waist as if they were returning from a romantic interlude.

"Look at you guys – two beautiful *kolibri* on a honeymoon walk," smiled Cécile, laughing at the two lovers as they came into the house.

That night, Odilon went to bed with serious issues buzzing in his mind: the uncertainty of tomorrow, the scare from the last one hundred days of war, a bleak future that was becoming bleaker by the second, his mother's frail health, the daily struggle to bring food to the table, and most importantly, his future with Thérèse – which he now dreaded to the core.

He never questioned his deep love and respect for her, but he had been living in constant fear of getting her pregnant. What a fool he had been, having unprotected sex! He had not wanted to spend their food money on protection. The reality he disdained was at last a certainty. Odilon dreamed of seeing his passionate relationship with Thérèse bear the fruit of a child, but under the proper conditions – a baby through whom the reflections of both he and Thérèse were apparent – clear, vivid, unequivocal, unmistakable. However, he could not bear the thought of raising a child only to offer him the same precarious, unpleasant, and miserable future that the village's children were facing.

Unbelieving in miracles, unlike Thérèse, to him it was no "misfortune" that he was raised as a poor boy, whose future was to become a sharecropper, an exploited peasant, a deprived human being, a "nobody" destined to grow, live, work, and die in poverty. Now that he comprehended the complexities of class division within society, he fully grasped the fact that his upbringing, wrapped in misery, poverty, and humiliation, was predestined and could not have been altered.

Putting his own flesh and blood through such an existence was cruel to a child that never asked to be born, he thought. But how could he refuse, denying Thérèse, the woman he loved, the bliss, the *joie-de-vivre*, the obsessive desire that all women have for an infant to breastfeed, to spoon-feed, to cuddle and play with like a toy from the exotic boutiques at the fashion district near downtown Saint Louis?

While he brushed away these painful thoughts, straining to chase them out of his mind, an idea suddenly popped into his head. "I'll become a baggage handler on one of the buses carrying passengers between Port-au-Prince and Saint Louis." With that last hopeful and cheerful thought, he fell asleep.

Early in the morning, the father-to-be was already up, rejuvenated by his newfound objective and fresh hopes of finding an alternative to his old, boring, day-labor jobs, which were getting harder and harder to find.

Hope eases pressure, suppresses anxiety, and controls stress. *L'espoir fait vivre*, as they say in Haiti. The hope of getting a job earning pretty good cash, almost daily, warmed his heart, stirred his soul, and temporarily changed his mindset, vision, and prospects about life. In an instant, Odilon seemed to have made the right choice for someone who had no formal education with any specific skills.

The route from Port-au-Prince to Saint Louis was often filled with expatriates from around the globe, their suitcases packed with dollars and euros. Each visit to Saint Louis had a purpose. Some came to buy beachfront properties with large verandas or extended thatched bungalows offering breathtaking views of turquoise waters. Others sought to purchase rich farmlands from the lush plains, or to party endlessly in the beachside nightclubs of the dusty, booming town. But this latest rush to Saint Louis—and the entire Northwest—had nothing to do with the usual quest for pleasure. Fear, anxiety, and a desperate need to know the fate of their loved ones drove this new wave of returnees.

Gazing through the holes beneath his thatched window, Odilon observed the serenity of night lifting and fading away in the green foliage.

"Where are you going this early?" asked Thérèse, who had been watching him, remaining silent until she saw him put on his clothes to leave.

"Oh, I forgot to tell you that I have to meet the guys in Bwa Chandèl for a *konbit*. We're starting early," Odilon quipped, hurrying to avoid further questions. He snuck outside, but Thérèse followed him.

"Odilon, since when do you wear your good clothes for a job on the farm?" she questioned. Eyes snapping with anger, hands on her hips, she sent him a scathing glare down to his toes – standing tall under her yellow nightgown. She was determined to find out about his early morning venture.

"Okay, *chérie*. I'm sorry for lying…didn't want to let you know, but it seems I have no choice. An idea came to me last night after you fell asleep. I want to find a job on one of the Port-au-Prince to Saint Louis buses. I need to make it to the station, so I can speak to the drivers," he grimaced with guilt. Edging closer, he pulled Thérèse into his arms and started stroking her hair.

"You mean…you were going to leave us in the house and go to Port-au-Prince, without letting us know?"

"How could I do that? Do you think I want to kill my mother?"

"That's not what I meant…you need to watch your actions a little closer."

"*Chérie*, don't say that! You make me feel irresponsible. I'm not moving to Port-au-Prince! I'm just going to the bus station to see if they'll give me a job. Please, go back inside, *chérie*. You know I love you. I'm late already. I'll be back in a short while."

Odilon released Thérèse, ducking under the *mangfransik* mango tree to watch her go back inside. She stepped up to the front porch, leaning against the half-open door to watch her soulmate as he turned around, heading down the narrow trail and fading to dimness in the darkness behind the cacao grove.

Dressed like a city boy and resembling a popular folk singer, Odilon was ready to begin a new chapter of his life. Refreshed by the lavender water he had poured on himself after his morning bath, the hopeful peasant hit the trail with optimism. He jogged along the sugar-sand road, tweeting like a robin, a *kolibri*, or a cicada in the morning dew, eagerly awaiting the sunrise. He wore a long white tunic with blue horizontal stripes, complete with lower pockets to jam his hands into as he moved. To feel more upbeat, he slipped on new socks inside his second-hand blue Adidas tennis shoes and his nice pair of khaki pants—recently bought by Thérèse at the Ti-Riviyè flea market.

It was still dark when he reached the mango grove on the edge of town. He was fearless and nonchalant striding along the bushy, narrow path. No rumors of werewolves or early morning ghosts could scare him off his course. The high-pitched sounds from the bus horns in the distance made him even more upbeat as he switched speeds, from jogging to flat-out running, pushing himself to reach the bus station in the northern entrance near Ti-Riviyè on time.

Within minutes, he was at the bus station. But most of the buses had already left by the time he arrived. There were some *tap-tap* being loaded with merchants going to Port-de-Paix, and a lone bus stationed on the opposite side of the dusty highway, facing south. It was getting ready for the long trip to Port-au-Prince.

The main highway linking Saint Louis to Gonaives, the most important city in the Haitian heartland on the road to Port-au-Prince, was rocky, dusty, or muddy, depending on the season. A road not yet built, it was no better than an old trail from the wild, wild west, long ago written off by those in charge of public works.

Ironically, the Northwest Province produced many influential politicians, well connected to the highest echelons of government after government. But no one had ever come close to presenting a plan for building the infrastructure. Politicians vacated the place, returning only once in a blue moon, especially during the holidays, in helicopters or inside their window-tinted, four-wheel-drive SUVs — just to fill the exotic, sandy beaches and party like thieves all night long.

Few bridges could be found in the province's main highway, while many streams and rivers crossed it along the way. After a heavy downpour, rivers would overflow their banks, leaving lines of buses and other vehicles stranded until enough water receded so they could continue their journey. Down by the sandy riverbed, impromptu marketplaces were set up by the locals to satisfy the needs of stranded passengers, while earning some cash in the process.

Therefore, the road from Saint Louis to Gonaives was precarious at best, and perilous at worst. Skilled drivers were needed to maneuver the buses down that hectic, dangerous road. It took three-and-a-half hours to make the torturous trip from one end to the other on a fifty-mile highway. From Gonaives to Port-au-Prince, the trip became less treacherous as the road was built, paved, and in some areas more or less maintained. This second leg of the route was a ninety-mile trip, usually completed in two hours' time. In the face of harsh reality, the buses from Saint Louis had to leave early in order to make it to Port-au-Prince at a reasonable time, and no bus could make a roundtrip in one day.

Odilon was lucky to find one bus driver to speak with that morning. As he approached the bus, the driver stood by the front door, talking to two passengers who brought in oversized luggage – instructing them about the extra charge for going over the limit. Two baggage handlers hung out in the back, loading the bus while talking to the passengers getting on. Odilon waited, several feet from the driver, understanding this was not the time to approach someone for a job.

Hands crammed inside his bulging shirt pockets, he was optimistic about his prospects that morning, although his optimism lowered somewhat as a tinge of anxiety moved in. A few minutes later, the misunderstanding between the passengers and the driver was resolved. The driver, back in his seat, honked the horn and stepped on the accelerator. He was sending the last signal to passengers and baggage handlers to be ready for departure.

Odilon knew the time was ripe to make his move. "Good morning, sir," he said, casually strolling up to the driver with a broad smile on his face.

"Are you going to Port-au-Prince…do you need a ticket?" questioned the driver, lighting up a cigarette.

"No, sir," Odilon stammered, temping down his nerves. "I was watching your workers loading up the bus. I saw they have a lot of work. I'm asking if you could use an extra helper. I can handle baggage," he continued, heart racing a mile a minute.

The driver moved his head back, dragged on his cigarette, and slowly released the smoke from his mouth. "What's your name, son?"

"Odilon Joseph."

"Where d'you live?"

"In Anwodo, near Bwa Chandèl."

"Are you sure you can do this job?"

"Don't judge me by my physical appearance; it can be deceiving. I'm a very hard worker, and I'm ready to prove it." Grinning mysteriously at the young peasant, the driver sucked another long drag from his cigarette.

"Listen, we're getting ready to leave. You can start work on our next trip, which is this coming Thursday. Be prepared to spend the night in Port-au-Prince, because we don't do fast turnarounds. You get paid every Saturday morning…one hundred *goud* per week. Whatever else you make from the passengers is yours to keep."

"Thank you, sir!" It was all Odilon could do to keep from screaming. He was overjoyed. He got the job! Turning around, he prepared to go home.

"Hey!" the driver called to him. "I forget to tell you: employees are to be here at four in the morning."

"Yes, sir! I'll be here," Odilon replied, grinning from ear to ear.

Crossing the busy street, he took the same trail he used to get into town, weaving around merrily in the mango grove. He could not hide the enthusiasm on his face when he arrived home twenty minutes later to deliver the good news to Thérèse. Cécile, not an early riser, snored in bed when he strutted into the courtyard.

Thérèse was in the outside kitchen, making coffee, but her eyes were glued on the main road leading into town. At Odilon's appearance, she raced from the kitchen, wearing her yellow nightgown and floppy slippers, her hair was loosely wrapped with a red and blue kerchief.

"You're back already!" she exclaimed, beaming at him.

"Oh yes, I am. I told you I wasn't going to be late," he stated, practically crowing as he kissed Thérèse, letting it linger in the air.

"How did it go?"

"Fine. I got a job…I'm starting Thursday, early in the morning."

"Are you kidding?" Her laughter could be heard all the way to town; she was so relieved. The soon-to-be father had a job!

"No, I'm not. It's a tough job, no doubt. But I think this is much better than pulling weeds out of other people's farmlands."

#

"Odilon, it's so dark at three in the morning," Thérèse complained and gave a languid sigh, strolling with her man to Saint Louis – where he had to report to work.

"When the buses leave, stay with the merchants by the riverbed near the bus station until daylight before going home," Odilon cautioned, holding his lady's hand as they hurried to reach the bus station near Ti-Riviyè.

"You know something?" her sexy voice trilled, soft as melted butter.

"What?"

"I've been thinking a lot lately."

"About what, my love?"

"About our future…our baby-to-be, how long it's going to take for us to afford our own place, even if it's only a hut on the edge of town."

"Thérèse, I've been thinking about the same things. But if there's something I've learned from what we've been through, it's patience. Who dreamed the revolution would be aborted? We may be condemned to die in poverty, but if we have a child, we must do whatever it takes to spare him the tough life we're stuck living."

Describing their ordeals and their hopes to each other, they crossed the yucca fields, the banana fields, and finally the mango grove – without any awareness of them. Only the bugling sounds of the blaring buses across the main highway brought them back to reality. They stood for a moment, gazing into each other's dark, red-rimmed eyes, under what was left of that famous, humungous old bamboo tree, now shattered at its base and splintered by artillery bombardments during the war.

Thérèse did not want to let go, not because she doubted his love, but because she was afraid. Hesitant and scared to death, she worried about Odilon embarking on new tasks and entering a whole new world in a brand-new city.

"That's okay, *chérie*," he sighed, nibbling on her delectable lips.

Thérèse said nothing, eyes misting over. Four a.m. barged in; the bus horns blared with increasing intensity, signaling employees to report to duty.

"Stay safe, be safe, *chéri*! Remember, I love you…I'll never stop loving you!" The expectant mother snatched ten *goud* out of her purse, stuffing it into Odilon's pocket, while handing him a little brown sack – containing a traditional Haitian peanut-butter sandwich, a couple of bananas, and two cans of *Kola Couronne*.

"*Chérie*, don't worry. I'll be all right. Please, take care of my mother. Remember, I love you…far more than I can ever say."

Snatching a sob in her throat before he heard it, she watched him cross the street to join his bus, remaining nailed to the spot with anxiety. After a long moment, Thérèse decided to follow their plan, heading to the riverbed a few yards from the bus station. Once there, she took her place among the gathered merchants, preparing for another hectic day. Chatting with them to pass the time, she saw it was way too dark to go back over the hill alone.

She patted her slightly protruding belly. "Little one, you have a good man for a father," she breathed, happier than she had been in several years.

#

"You've never been to Port-au-Prince before, Odilon?" asked a coworker. The bus had just left Saint Louis, fast approaching the fishing community of Villasso, bumping and grinding along.

"No," replied Odilon. "This will be a wonderful new experience for me."

379

"It sure will, Port-au-Prince is a big, big city," stated the coworker, coughing into his hand. A head cold was insufficient reason to call in for a sick day.

"You know my name…what's yours again?" Odilon asked.

"Evans Philippe. But you can call me Evans. The other gentleman that works with us is Delama Oriol. Everyone calls him Mr. D. He's not like us, as you can see. He's a deeply religious man…always carries his Bible. When it's this quiet, when everyone's asleep, that's when he reads it…muttering to himself, too."

"Did he ever try to convince you to join his church?"

"Every day. But I don't pay attention to him. There's a whole world out there to discover…I'm too young for a bunch of old-fogey stuff!"

Laughing, Odilon peeked out the window to observe the spectacular dawn unfolding outside. As the darkness melted away, the crepuscule faded into an inevitable daylight. A morning breeze made the banana leaves on both sides of the rocky highway flutter like giant butterflies in the wind. Yet, as night gave way to broad daylight, the scars of war remained: bombed-out houses lined the roadside, bloated corpses of animals decayed on the pavement, entire banana fields lay destroyed by artillery, and heavily armed soldiers patrolled the highway—the war's most chilling reminder.

Odilon was somewhat used to these things. He got up, stretched his arms, yawned, and raised his eyebrows. He inched closer to the window to get a better view of the gruesome reality of war.

"Odilon, get back to your seat! It's too dangerous," Evans whispered, lowering his voice to avoid being overheard. But the passengers enjoyed a deep morning snooze, packed in sardine-style, sitting on the hard wooden seats.

"What you're seeing will be like that until we pass Gros-Morne. They're stopping vehicles at every checkpoint, to search for suspected rebels. Before the war, it took us three-and-a half hours to get to

Gonaives. Nowadays, it's a long and miserable five hours on the road, while being bugged by those slobs."

"*Oui*, I understand. But why's it too dangerous to look outside?"

Grumbling and sighing, using his head cold to cover what he said, Evans hunched closer to Odilon. "These officers don't want people to look at them. When we get to Port-de-Paix, they'll come inside to inspect. Don't pay attention. Get busy. Even if there's nothing to do, look busy."

"This is insane, I thought the war was over…"

"Shhh! You're-" he coughed, "too loud. You don't know who's sitting next to you. You can't trust anyone. Last week, I watched in petrified horror as they shot three men near the bus station in Port-de-Paix."

"What did they do?" A shiver played across Odilon's spine.

"Nothing. The officers said their mission is to 'zombify' the province. So, they expect everyone to act like zombies. You're not allowed to look them in the eyes. You don't ask questions. You just do what they tell you."

"But Evans…the men must have done…something?"

"I told you; they did nothing wrong. They were getting out of the bus, and they didn't hear the order to stay inside. Two officers moved in, started hitting them with their rifle butts. The men tried to explain. That made the officers even angrier. They dragged the men out of the bus, led them near an old, crumbling wall across the street from the station, and shot them. Thrashing around, they died…instantly."

"What did the other passengers do, Evans?"

"Odilon, what could they do…we all watched like morons."

Before the first rays of sunlight emerged from behind the mountains, the bus had already pulled into the Port-de-Paix station. It grew quiet as the passengers waited motionless, like children from a nun–run catholic school, for the military police to board the bus. The pair of coworkers ended their conversation – hushed as mute Haitian barn owls.

Odilon watched out the window. Within a moment, he was shocked as he saw the courage, resilience, and sharp determination of the people of Port-de-Paix to go on with their lives. In the middle of bomb-ravaged homes, dirt-piled streets, and cratered narrow alleyways, life seemed undeterred. In this blatant misery and gruesome oppression, the scars and the fear appeared, at least on the surface, to have been replaced by a powerful determination to survive.

One police officer entered the bus, moving swiftly to the rear. "How many people are on this vehicle?" he demanded.

His stern, round face was barely visible behind fathomless dark sunglasses, and a green cap with a white cross sat tilted forward on his head. Muscular yet short, he stood five feet tall. His olive-green shirt, taut and tucked into wrinkled, blood-stained brown pants, completed his menacing appearance, like that of a 'madman,' exuding a mean, vicious, and aggressively cruel demeanor. Clutching a clipboard and a red pen to write his report, he wanted to remind everyone on the bus that the men with iron fists—the mythical monsters and disguised *tonton macoutes*—were back to stay in the province. But no one answered his question; he hadn't addressed it to anyone in particular.

Odilon, sitting in the back row, appeared calm, fearless, not displaying any nervousness. But deep inside of him, the anger was unbearable. His heart nearly burst with his passionate hatred for those who inflicted heavy pain on the masses. That hatred soared higher as he kept eyeing the policeman's shiny sidearm; the brutal, short man paced up and down the aisle like a ferocious tiger, checking every row while looking for suspected rebels. Finally, Odilon shut his eyes in anguish.

"Who are the workers on this bus?" asked the supposed police officer.

"We are," answered Odilon and Evans in unison.

"And why didn't you answer earlier, when I asked for the number of passengers on this vehicle?" the officer growled, spitting between his clenched teeth, an angry werewolf ready to go on the offensive.

"We didn't think you were talking to us…personally," replied Evans. Odilon said nothing, struggling to control his anger.

"And what is your name?" the officer asked.

"Evans Philippe."

"And you?" the officer directed at Odilon.

Odilon hesitated, taking a deep breath. He might have become known in these parts as a minor revolutionary leader. "My name is Odilon…Marrette." He lied once again, fearing that his name might be on the officer's 'blacklist'.

"You said your name is Odilon…right?"

"Yes, sir."

"From what rural section?"

"Ummm…I don't know, sir. I only know I'm from the village of Remoussin, between Rivière Nègre and Rivière Lakay."

"Hey, wait a minute. Who do you think you're talking to?"

"A… policeman?" He drew out the word, twisting it into something that sounded like 'ape policeman.'

"I don't like your attitude…you might be the Odilon on my list."

Evans, who sat next to Odilon, kept pressing on his foot in a desperate attempt to keep him quiet. Odilon understood. But how could he not answer, since the questions were directed at him?

"You said your name is Odilon, right?" the officer asked again, raising his voice in anger as he smacked the clipboard against Odilon's seat. Everyone on the bus, some of whom had seen this stuff before, froze in terror.

"How many times do I have to answer? Yes, I am Odilon," he firmly stated, facing his possible death calmly, keeping his voice low and unbowed.

"This is a sign of defiance! I allow no one to talk to me that way!"

Odilon opened his lips, ready to reply. But the angered policeman did not give him a chance. He jumped on him, grabbed him by the neck, and dragged him down the aisle and out of the bus. The bus driver, alerted by Evans, having no clue about what was going on in the back, leaped out the front door to join the police officer in order to plead for Odilon.

The bus had two compartments, like most buses in that part of Haiti. The driver's section was separated from the passenger side, allowing the driver and his associates to ride under cool air conditioning, free from the dust, noise, and haze of the tropical heat that passengers sitting in the back section had to endure. To add to that, the driver was busy that morning flirting with his concubine, a grocery merchant from Saint Louis traveling to Port-au-Prince. Evans had to knock on the glass window separating the two compartments whenever he needed the driver's attention.

"Please, officer, tell me what's wrong!" the driver pleaded as he reached the policeman – fearing that his new bus worker was about to be thrown in jail, or worse, executed on the spot like the three men murdered a week earlier.

"Your *bèfchenn* is a rebel, a fuck'n communist," the short man replied, alerting other officers nearby. Six of them soon joined in. Odilon was roughly hurled to the ground, while two officers pinned him down, pressing their mud-smeared boots on his face and legs. They were every inch the same as the animal executioners at the city's butchery.

"Please, officers. You know me! The boy is my employee. Do you think I would hire a communist for my bus? Please, I know his parents. He's a totally quiet, respectful boy," the driver pleaded again. "I begged his parents to let him work! They'll never forgive me if something happens to their son," he sobbed, in full begging posture on his knees. The driver had never spoken to Odilon's parents, of course. He simply had to do something to remove his new worker from the grip of these savage hawks.

"What's his name?" quizzed the officer-in-command.

"Odilon Marrette," the enraged, short policeman replied, scrutinizing what he had scrawled on his pad.

"Please, give him another chance!" the bus driver woefully beseeched.

The officer-in-command took two sharp, military steps backward, raised his walkie-talkie to his mouth and radioed police headquarters. "I've got someone in custody by the name of Odilon Marette…verify his status," he said. In an almost caring manner, he jerked the driver up from his knees in a sign of reassurance.

"No…he's not on the list," a deep voice crackled over radio static.

"Release him," the officer-in-command ordered.

As soon as the heavy metal boots were lifted from Odilon's head, the driver helped him to his feet and led him back to the bus. Wincing in great pain, Odilon returned to his seat. Meanwhile, the driver retrieved a black, mid-size purse from his compartment, took out two hundred gourdes, and folded the money into an envelope. After sealing it tightly, he slid the envelope into a deep pocket on his shirt. He then exited the bus, signaling to the seemingly helpful officer-in-command.

"Officer," he said with a relaxed grimace. "Can I talk to you for a moment?" Carefully, he softened his voice in total obedience.

This officer, a slim, tall man with a dark complexion and gold teeth pegging his smile, moved smoothly toward the driver – ordering his crew to return to duty. He knew what the driver needed, as they both pretended to be involved in deep conversation. They walked together, passing some street vendors, crossing the street and lastly making their way to the outer back of the bus. The driver then pulled out the envelope, sliding it neatly into the officer's outstretched hand.

"Thank you," the officer-in-command mumbled with a grin. "You don't need to worry…I have you covered…go on about your business."

"Thanks, sir."

The driver got back onto the bus as the corrupt policeman faded into the crowd of travelers, street vendors, and grocery shoppers to get to his office, a small police station on the edge of the street corner.

These officers mainly ignored the profound contempt the masses in Haiti held for them. Many people "understood" that injustices must be committed daily for greedy policemen to find ways to supplement their meager salaries. Aggressiveness, intimidation, and the constant threat to arrest, beat, or even kill, made these "law enforcers" into the new gods of Haiti. They would do anything for money, including flattering, executing, trading their own inherit dignity, even betraying their family, neighbors, close friends, coworkers, and ultimately *Haiti Chérie*.

They cultivated no patriotism, no sense of nationalism. From the rural section chiefs' offices to the largest state bureaucratic machine, Haiti has always been for sale, selling its beautiful Creole women, sandy beaches, rich farmlands and all of its natural resources to whoever had the cash to pay for it.

"Odilon!" yelled the driver from his open compartment door. "Come to me for a minute."

"Yes…" rasped Odilon, whose swollen tongue made it difficult to speak. With Evans's help, who supported him by the shoulders, he managed to make his way to the driver. People on the bus were terrified, watching him limp past. His face was bruised, swelling scarlet from the blows he had suffered from the policemen, who had kicked his head and pushed it into the unyielding dirt. His shirt was torn and dirty, his pants, socks, and tennis shoes smeared with grungy yellow mud from the officers' boots. Traces of blood seeped from his nostrils. His eyes were swollen and red, but he was not crying. A man should not cry in the face of adversity, he believed.

With some difficulty, he got to the bus driver. "I'm sorry, sir, to put you through that ordeal…this morning," Odilon stammered, feeling embarrassed. He could taste wells of blood forming in his mouth and wondered how bad he looked.

"There's nothing to be sorry for, son," the driver said gently, holding up Odilon's chin to study his face. "When we reach Gonaives, I'll take you to the dispensary for a checkup. It was a mistake on my part, not teaching you the rules. I'm sorry, but it's a jungle out here. We can only pray for a miracle to free this country. This stuff can happen anywhere along the road, right up to Port-au-Prince. Just remain quiet whenever an inspection is taking place," the driver commanded.

"Thank you, sir," Odilon wheezed.

"Mister, don't let him do any work," the driver added.

"Yes, sir," replied Evans, steering Odilon to the back of the bus.

Odilon was reeling from a second, more delayed shock. Just when he thought he had jeopardized his job and humiliated his boss irreparably, life's tangled twists and turns surprised him. The bus driver had not only saved his life but also preserved his hopes and dreams—his job prospects, his potential future, and his aspirations of becoming a father. What else might this intriguing new career have in store?

Chapter 31

The bus driver, a tall, light-skinned fellow with a boyish face and the charms to match it, was a former religious activist for the Catholic Church. He had quit his activism after discovering secret documents linking the Church to the Haitian government in passing out the names of innocent civilians to the central authorities in Port-au-Prince.

His name was Albert Barlatier, and his years of activism made him a well-known and popular man. He was a fellow of thirty-seven years of age. Most people called him "Ti Rouge," for he was not rich. In Haiti, people of his complexion were called "*blanc*" only if they are from well-off, traditional mixed-race families.

Barlatier was muscular, athletic, and helpfully jovial. His combed-back hair was brownish and wavy, not unlike a white man's hair, and he liked to stroke his hair as he talked to people – putting across the image of an impressive, dignified person. He was beardless, but had a dark mark on his face, right below the right side of his nose. Due to his pleasant, boyish appearance, women tended to be attracted to him. They succumbed to his charisma and fine, sweet-talking manners. In every town, major village, and city, from Port-au-Prince all the way to Saint Louis, this popular bus driver enjoyed some concubines. He was stroking one of these "fine ladies" in the front driver's compartment when Evans alerted him about Odilon's ordeal.

When the bus finally left Port-de-Paix, and the shallow bay of Lower Moustiques on the south bank of Trois Rivières dwindled in the distance, a sense of normalcy resumed inside the bus. Sweet

Caribbean music played, easing the passengers' minds away from the unbearable reality of dust streaming in through the windows, and the mounting haze competing with the sunrise looming on its horizon.

Groaning softly in the back of the bus, where the baggage handlers sat, Odilon showed his most positive face to his colleagues. Sitting calm and collected on his hard wooden seat, he was in agony, but did not show it. A man must never display his weakness. After all, he thought, considering those who did not make it through the war, this was a small price to pay if his ordeal opened the eyes of any undecided people about the true nature of this brutal regime. That last thought managed to chase away the pain, the nightmare, the shame, and the horror ravaging his gentle heart.

"Are you feeling better?" Evans asked, as he patted Odilon's face with a wet rag soaked in salt water to assuage the hideous swelling.

"I'm okay," Odilon answered with a repressed smile. It did little to hide his true state of mind – he was outraged, in spite of his silence.

"There's nothing I can say to help ease the pain. But hang on, my friend. This hellish life will come to an end…someday." Evans continued to pat Odilon in the back, as unseen tears began to fill his eyes.

"You talk funny. You're not from Saint Louis…are you?" asked Odilon, who only wanted to reassure Evans that he would be okay.

"No, I'm not from Saint Louis – my father came from there," Evans replied with a smile. "I talk funny? At least I'm not missing some teeth!"

#

Indeed, Evans's Creole was rather vague. Twenty-six, his complexion was notably bronzed and handsome. He was rather tall per Haitian standards, about six feet high, with East Indian features. Straight in the front, his hair tended to be a bit wavy in the back. He had a nice oval face, with a strange, white birthmark on his chin. To keep his "pretty face" smooth, he carried a pack of razor blades so he could shave twice a day – once in Gonaives and once in Port-au-Prince. With familiar strokes, he would shave every hair from his face, including any trace of a mustache or sideburns.

He had such large ears that his friends called him a rabbit. No matter how hot it got in the tropics, Evans wore a blue jacket, a pair of blue jeans and a white pair of tennis shoes. He never pulled his pants up to his waist. He did not use a belt either, leaving his pants to fall midway to his flat behind – exposing his underpants to the ladies who might wish to see them.

"You said you're not from here. So, where are you from?" Odilon asked, throwing a repressed smile that quickly gave way to a painful laugh as he inwardly mourned the condition of his teeth, which were not in the best shape.

"I'm from the Bahamas, the town of Spanish Well on the island of Eleuthra." Easing down next to Odilon, Evans tried to keep his minor head cold away from the pain-ridden younger man.

"You don't look quite Haitian to me."

"Why? Is it because of the way I speak?"

"No. I mean, look at your hair. It's different from everyone on this bus." Pointing at the passengers, Odilon glanced at their way to give weight to his words. "Look for yourself," he added.

"My mother...was from Guyana." Evans reciprocated.

"Where is that?" Odilon, being uneducated, had little geographical knowledge.

"In South America, near Venezuela. She met my father in Eleuthra. Dad was a musician, a *troubadour* singer from Saint Louis, who made his living off temporary contracts that he signed with tourist resort owners along the coast of Eleuthra. When I was three, my family moved to Freeport, the most beautiful town on the island of Grand Bahama. Life was great there. Dad made a lot of money playing in nightclubs."

"What about your mother? Did she work?"

"No, she was a dressmaker. Things were going splendidly until one day she left to visit relatives in Guyana and... never returned."

The bus worker turned away, his eyes misting over as he stuttered. The mysterious disappearance of his beloved mother had shattered his father. Evans was only five at the time but could still recall his mother's dignified posture, her long straight hair, ebonized complexion, and the moments she bickered with his dad. He fondly remembered the sweet, unforgettable times they spent together on luxurious retreats at Paradise Island near Nassau in the Bahamas. His father, devastated, had sunk into a deep depression, abandoning everything—including his music career, self-esteem, personal ego, and will to live. The only thing keeping his father anchored was Evans, in whom he saw a mirror reflection of his wife.

"So, what did your father do when your mother didn't come back?"

"Dad became mentally ill...he was chronically depressed."

"What's that?"

"He was sad all the time, didn't want to do anything but cry and lie in bed."

"Why didn't he go to Guyana to look for her?"

"I don't know, man. Every time I question Dad about this, he never gives me a direct answer. After two years of living in chronic melancholy, one Saturday morning he moved us to Jacksonville, Florida. Life was harsh at the beginning. Dad was unable to hold a steady job. So, he returned to being a folk musician, taking me wherever he went, including nights spent in strip clubs." To give Odilon an idea of his background, Evans continued his story, which turned out to be riveting.

Tall and muscular, with an imposing gaze that attracted a lot of fans while they toured the Bahamian nightclubs, Evans' father never remarried. He lived his life as an unconventionalist, a Bohemian from the tropics who roamed the coasts of Florida, taking his *troubadour* music wherever he could. For two years, father and son entertained the northeastern coast of Florida, from Daytona Beach to Saint Augustine. Using the Historic District near Downtown Saint Augustine as a staging area, their two-man band garnered followers, locals and tourists alike, from all over the South. On the green lawn of the lighthouse near the town of Palm Coast, they were called the Black Gypsies – based on the banjo and acoustic guitar they played as they performed.

Later, they settled in the town of Green Cove Springs, on the west bank of Saint Johns River – fishermen by day, catching a good haul along the Saint Johns River Bridge, to sell in the nearby fish market. At night, they played folk music at a small bar near the riverbank, heavily frequented by tourists ferrying via steamboats from across the river, in search of wild adventures. Each of the *troubadours* wore a coat with a large belt about his waist, long, pointed shoes, and a large straw hat, making them resemble a pair of medieval *jongleurs*. These two folk musicians attracted tourists from nearly everywhere, including patrons from the wealthy World Golf Village on the International Golf Parkway.

"Life got pretty good again, right? Say, how did you come to Haiti?" Odilon asked, bitterly showing his teeth through a repressed smile.

"Life was okay for a while. But everything changed on a rainy Saturday morning, when I was driving Dad's Oldsmobile down a road called Route 16 – taking my girlfriend to work. I lost control on the slippery highway. The car spun and whirled around like a twister, taking several other cars with it. Police arrived, and they immediately arrested me."

"Why?"

"I was driving with a restricted license. They took me to the Saint Augustine police headquarters. On investigating my background, they discovered that I was an illegal immigrant…I had to be turned over to Immigration, as I was unable to produce documentation that I was an American citizen. Since I didn't have records showing where I came from, within a few days I was shipped to Port-au-Prince, Haiti, a country completely foreign to me."

"How sad! I guess life is tough outside of Haiti, too. How did you survive in Port-au-Prince? Did you know anyone there?"

"No. But I was surprised to meet a lot of young guys like me who were born in other countries. Life was pure hell in the beginning, man."

For days, Evans roamed the streets of Port-au-Prince, begging, panhandling, and sleeping in public parks to survive. He spoke flawless American English, but had no formal education, no skills other than playing music in folk rallies with his father. Yet, he was street-smart, and a shrewd survivor. His rusty Creole and painful struggles to blend into the hectic life of Port-au-Prince did not break his morale or his will to move upward. Every two days, he would go to the central office of Haiti's telephone company, calling his father in Florida to reassure him that he was alive and well.

He became acquainted with the complex nightlife in the city: its cafés, bars, and nightclubs. To keep off the dangerous streets, he became a pimp at a little bar near the Port-au-Prince harbor, protecting a young prostitute from Saint Louis against the perilous, often fatal life of those who live in the shadowy underworld. It was there that he decided to explore other ways to survive in Haiti. Following the advice of the prostitute, he went and got a job on one of the provincial ferry buses.

The pimp life had taken its toll. It earned him great money for sure – made from the raw exploitation of someone forced to sell her body to survive. Before going off to work as a baggage handler, he made a promise to the prostitute that he would return to rescue her from that degrading lifestyle. He would merge his life with hers, and like dandelions they would magically sprout, grow, and blossom to reproduce, while they rebuilt their lives.

Chapter 32

Shortly after three in the afternoon, the bus pulled into Port-au-Prince's Penn Station. A horde of people stormed out, as street vendors mixing with taxi drivers solicited the passengers, who were trying to get to the streets.

Recent rains had left the fractured, paved streets clogged with a fresh layer of dark mud and litter on either side of the bus. From the back, Odilon watched as waves of people navigated the muddy street—wrangling, negotiating deals, selling, buying, and panhandling—while columns of cars sluggishly maneuvered through a heated traffic jam. He was amazed; everything was bigger, more rushed, and more sprawling than he had ever seen.

"This is nothing like Saint Louis…" he muttered.

"Hey Odilon," called out Evans. "Stand on the ground and be ready to handle the baggage when I hand it down. You must do this with care. Some passengers are intimidating and pushy. Don't let them make you crazy!" Evans pulled the baggage out; impatient passengers were ready to eat Odilon alive if he could not immediately give them their belongings.

"I'm trying, I'm trying! But they want it now!" said Odilon, overwhelmed.

"Don't worry, my friend. You'll get used to it. You're being baptized today," laughed Evans, as Odilon struggled to keep up the pace.

"Wait," Odilon panted. "I need to check the names. Hold off for a second," he furtively begged.

"Delama, can you give Odilon a hand? We're facing a total revolt from the passengers!" The other baggage handler had met them there at the station.

"I'm busy too, can't you see?" spat the fatigued Delama, carrying his Bible in one hand while writing on a passenger sheet with the other.

Reeling from the bruises he suffered during the Port-de-Paix incident, Odilon displayed remarkable courage as he dutifully performed his tasks. Although he moved slowly, he managed to mask his pain with forced smiles as he handed luggage to each passenger. Fortunately, his ordeal ended within an hour as the last of the passengers departed, leaving the bus empty and allowing the workers to retreat indoors for a much-needed respite.

Their bodies and clothes drenched in sweat, their faces smeared with a mix of street dust and grime, the workers were desperate for a cool breeze to breathe a sigh of relief. Across the street, the driver joined colleagues from other regions, sharing jokes about their travails on poorly maintained roads, their wild adventures, and the children they had left behind. Their lives bore a striking resemblance to those of American truck drivers navigating the interstate highways across the United States.

Back on the bus, Odilon was starving, but had no strength to put food in his mouth. Twice he reached for a banana in the little brown sack Thérèse had given him. But his hand quivered each time, and so he pushed the sack away, exhausted. Evans sat next to him, spreading one arm across the wooden railing and folding the other under his head, resting on the seat in search of a little comfort.

"Hey, Albert, you said you were going to Pétionville – are you still going? I want to know before I leave," Evans shouted through an open window at the driver, who chatted with his colleagues outside the bus.

"Yes, and I need your help…don't leave yet," the driver replied, raising his hands to form the "stop" sign.

"What do you mean by 'leaving'?" Odilon asked Evans.

"Well, I have to go home!"

"I thought we were supposed to sleep on the bus."

"Who told you that, Odilon?"

"No one told me anything. But that was what I thought."

"No one sleeps here, not even the bus! It's too dangerous."

"You mean it's not safe to spend the night here?"

Odilon turned cold…arms crossed, two fingers on his lips, in deep thought.

"What's wrong, Odilon?"

"Nothing."

"Don't tell me…you don't have anywhere to go…?"

Odilon did not reply. Instead, he turned his back on Evans – peering out the windows to watch the wave of activity going on outside the bus. He had been hoping that the street vendors would not go home, the gas station across the street would remain open, the taxi drivers would spend the night stationed on the corner, and the buses would not move.

"Where am I going to sleep? How could I ask Albert for another favor?" He was thinking. Odilon believed he would lose respect among his colleagues if he were to ask for help again. He did not want to be a burden, deciding to spend the night near the bus station. "The night will be short. If it doesn't rain, I'll be okay," he thought.

"Do you have an address, Odilon?" Evans asked, turning to face him.

"Yes…I do," he grunted manfully.

"Give it to Albert, so he can drop you off on the way to Pétionville."

"I'll do that."

"Sure. Say, kid, what's the address?"

"Listen, Evans, I don't want to lie to you. I don't have an address…but I don't want you to tell Albert."

"Why?"

"I can't. I'm too ashamed."

"There's no need for you to be ashamed." Sighing, Evans had figured Odilon was in such a pickle. But the kid obviously did not want any charity.

"Yes, there is. What will he think of me? I want a job, not favors. Please, don't tell him."

"Odilon…where are you going to sleep?"

"Don't worry. I'll stay here."

"You can't; this area's deserted by midnight. It will be very dangerous around here. People disappear every day in this city." Evans grabbed up Odilon's little sack lunch, to carry it for him. "You'll come home with me."

"Where do you live?"

"Not far from here. In the morning, Albert will pick us up from there, as he always does for me."

"Do you live with your parents?"

"No, I live alone in a small studio apartment…Remember I told you I have no parents here."

"Chop, chop! Come on guys, let's go. I'll drop you home on the way back," the driver yelled. "By the way, son, do you have an address?"

"Yes, he does," replied Evans, pre-empting him before he opened his mouth.

Once the driver was fully aboard, they set off along the Pan-American Highway, passing by the seaside park of Bicentenaire. Odilon watched in astonishment as numerous ships, including a US Navy vessel, docked in the harbor. To his left, an exotic tropical garden burst with hibiscuses, lilies, and red roses, complemented by multicolored pentas and Mexican heather. The brilliant lime-green lawn, well-kept and bisected by marble walkways, featured wooden benches crafted against the backdrop of a giant fountain. Lovers strolled along, embracing and kissing. At the far end of the park, university students were engrossed in completing their homework assignments.

Despite his pain, Odilon was almost in a state of awe. "Listen…Evans, are there two different kinds of Haiti?" he questioned his newfound friend.

"What…why?" Evans replied.

"This area has no comparison to where we just come from."

"You mean the bus station?"

"Yeah."

"Well, this is the reality of Haiti. In one minute, you're in Hell. The next minute, you think you've entered Heaven's gates!"

"This is funny, Evans."

"Don't let the gorgeous appearance fool you. It's just a façade."

"I know."

"This is the downtown district we're passing through. Do you see those beautiful stores, and the horde of people going in and out of them?"

"Yeah," sighed Odilon, trying to sound relaxed and happy while experiencing mind-numbing pain. "What about it?"

"Most of them are window shoppers, not real buyers. Haiti is a country of bluffers. See how they're dressed up, to the teeth?"

"Yeah." Frowning, Odilon only hoped his own teeth would be okay.

"It is…part of a comedy designed to manipulate gullible people. Most of them are con artists. Be careful who you talk to – and where you spend your money."

The bus switched to Rue Pavée, heading east to Pétionville, the exclusive suburban town where most of the Haitian elite lived. But as the vehicle rolled in front of the National Palace on its way to the fashionable district of Lalue through the Champs De Mars, Odilon's jaw dropped with indescribable astonishment. He was witnessing for the first time the great monuments – the imposing statues of Haiti's independence heroes.

"Evans, I never knew the National Palace was so big. No wonder these people are willing to kill millions to stay in power!"

"That's the biggest contradiction you can see, the minute you set foot in Haiti. The difference between the super-rich and the deprived masses is so huge, the major question is: how long can this awkward balance survive?"

"Zebeda was right about everything he told us. There isn't only one Haiti. There are two: one is for the rich and one is for the poor," Odilon pointed out.

Laughing in relief, Evans said, "When I first arrived, I was shocked."

"But…why did you end up in Haiti?"

"I did tell them where I was from. In prison, they tried to send me back, but the Bahamian authorities refused to accept me, stating that I was born in 1975."

"What in the world does that mean?"

"I was born after the country gained independence from Britain. Therefore, I'm not a true Bahamian. Besides, I left there when I was five. Anyone born after Independence is not considered Bahamian, if he or she has foreign-born parents. And you must be eighteen to become a citizen."

"But how did they end up sending you here?"

"Because of my birth certificate. It says my father is Haitian and my mother is Guyanese. So, I was given two choices."

"What were the choices?"

"To go to Haiti, or Guyana – the country of my mother. But I barely remember Mom…she disappeared when I was little. I grew up with my Dad, and for a long time I ignored the Guyanese side of my heritage. Haiti…was the perfect choice."

"Were you aware of the problems here?"

"I knew about the misery. Sometimes Dad talked about it…so I was pretty well prepared. Haiti may be a poor country, but I'm not behind bars. Freedom of any kind is much better. When you're in prison, they treat you…like a criminal!"

They both laughed at that absurd old joke, and Odilon finally spoke. "Evans, I think you made the right choice."

"Without a doubt! I knew my life was going to be harsh. Even if Haiti was a rich country, I would've seen hardships…didn't know anyone…had no money."

"That's true."

"Listen, Odilon. Just because a country is rich doesn't mean everyone lives a good life. There're millions of people in the United States living in poverty. Thousands of people camp on the streets, sleeping in public parks, or under bridges near highways."

"What are…highways?"

"A highway is a major road, usually double-sided, where vehicles are allowed to go faster than in residential zones."

"I didn't know there were people living in poverty in America. I really thought they were all rich…I guess poverty is everywhere."

"In wealthy countries, there are better opportunities. You can go to school, learn a trade, and make a difference in your life. That's why many Haitians succeed in the United States. They're hard workers."

"Thank you for opening my eyes. I guess I still have plenty to learn about this complicated world. Say, could you hand me a banana out of my bag?"

#

Night had fallen on Saint Louis, and in the village of Anwodo, darkness tightened its grip. Heavy gray clouds obscured any sliver of crescent moonlight, shrouding the valley in darkness. An unusual tranquility settled over the cozy hamlet, the muddy walkways keeping children from playing in the tiny square, as their cautious parents forbade it. At sundown in the tropics, legends of kid-eating werewolves kept everyone indoors.

The silence was only broken by the distant, infrasonic chirping of crickets. Inside Odilon's small house, however, Thérèse and Cécile lay awake with eyes wide open. Sleeping early was avoided, as it often led to nightmares, and these days there was much on their minds. The two women, engulfed in sadness and anxiety, found themselves reflecting on Odilon's life—his earnestness, his passion for his beliefs, his moments of joy and gloom, and his boundless courage in facing uncertainties. These thoughts prevented them from succumbing to their fears. Yet, the night was particularly unsettling as Odilon was not at home. Worse still, they had no idea where he might be spending this eerie night, alone and separated from them.

Cécile, as usual, lay abed in her pink nightgown – quite alert. Faint, flickering light from the gas lamp filled the room, while the partners in solitude desired to stay up late to talk about their greatest possession, now slipping away from their lives.

Thérèse had fixed the floor up as if Odilon was going to sleep there. His pillow, his pajamas, his white sheet, and his sandals were each laid out with care on the *nat*. Thérèse wore her nightgown; without her brassiere, her lush, swollen breasts were on display. She sat cross-legged on the *nat*, while a small mirror lay on her lap as she performed her nightly bedtime ritual of combing her hair into small dreadlocks.

Cécile and Thérèse felt trapped, squeezed between hope and melancholy, and happiness and anxiety. "Oh, I miss him," sighed Cécile, folding two hard pillows under her head to bend forward, in order to see Thérèse while they talked.

"I can't describe how I feel. It's like a big chunk of my body has been stolen from me," murmured Thérèse, dabbing on a little hair grease and then smoothing it in.

"I can't wait 'til tomorrow, to see him." Odilon's mother settled onto her pillows, but do as she might, nothing was conducive to sleep.

"Tomorrow, rain or shine, I'll be at the bus station to wait for him."

With that pleasant thought, they found the strength they were looking for to brave their lonely night.

Chapter 33

In Port-au-Prince, meanwhile, the night was just beginning for those who embraced a nocturnal existence. These frontier men and women—adventurers at heart, flushed with liquor—partied until sunrise. For them, the night always felt too short, and their revelry grew wilder as the hours passed. Yet ecstasy inevitably turned to bitter chagrin as the harsh light of dawn brought their festivities to an end.

Evans took Odilon to his one-room studio apartment near a nightclub on the south side of the city. It was tucked away in a two-story building on a backstreet, accessed through a narrow alley. Located on the top floor, the studio afforded Evans a perfect view of the activity near the club. Inside, the blasting-hot salsa music shattered the general peacefulness, resonating loud and clear.

Evans' place was modest, with Spartan, inexpensive furnishings: a twin-sized iron bed draped with a red sheet, a small wooden table a few inches from the doorway, an overflowing laundry basket tucked into a corner, and an old, yet regal-looking, unstained wardrobe beside the table. Despite these humble elements, the room was spotless. Evans, a clean young man who dreamt daily of striking it rich by playing the Haitian Lotto, maintained meticulous order. Everything was so neatly arranged that it captured the attention of any visitor, reflecting his existential reality.

Odilon sat in one of the two wooden chairs at the table, like a tired bird—exhausted and beaten after a horrendous day. With legs crossed and an aching hand supporting his bruised chin, he longed for bed but felt too dirty. Dust caked his face and neck from the long trip, and swelling from the beating in Port-de-Paix marred his cheeks, nose, and an eyebrow. His thoughts wandered to home, to his wary mother and anxious Thérèse. How were the two most precious people in his life coping in his absence?

Evans went to take a bath in the small shower compartment outside his room. While waiting for his return, Odilon was nearly lulled to sleep by the music from the bar across the yard; but every time he began to doze off, visions of Anwodo invaded his dreams. Minutes later, Evans reappeared, wrapped in a long purple towel, water droplets streaming down his hair and face. "The water is cold, Odilon," he commented, humming along with the tropical melodies from the bar.

"I don't mind," Odilon replied. "Cold showers are normal back in Anwodo, where we use water from a stream, and it's quite refreshing." Adjusting to an upright posture in the chair, he gave Evans a weak, painful smile—the discomfort was nearly overwhelming.

"You'd better hurry. We'll have to go to the bar to eat," said Evans, checking his watch while hastily donning his clothes.

"I'm hungry, but I don't feel like eating…just don't have the strength," sighed Odilon, hurrying outside to take his bath. Following him, Evans called out, "Hey Odilon, here's a bar of soap and a towel."

"Thanks. I thought there was soap in the shower," he replied, lowering his voice as he entered the small shower compartment.

Ten minutes later, Odilon resurfaced. His face looked almost normal; he was refreshed by the cool water and the sweet perfume from the Palmolive soap that he used to cleanse his frail body from head to toe.

"Where are you going... you've put on nice clothes?" Odilon asked Evans, who was dressed in clean blue jeans and shiny white tennis shoes, paired with a yellow t-shirt featuring red horizontal stripes that cleverly exposed his muscular biceps. His hair glittered under the stark fluorescent light, the ultra-sheen hair grease transforming him into the very image of a Caribbean nightclub *chulo*.

"Man, my job on the ferry bus is only a job, something I do to survive. But since I was little, I've always been a nocturnal bird, like the Haitian owl. My nightlife is just beginning."

"So…where are you going?"

"You hear the music across the yard, can't you?"

"Yes, I can."

"That's where I'm going; and I'd like to take you, too."

"Me?"

"Yes, you. Is anyone else here?" What a rube this man is! Evans thought.

"You must be out of your mind! I love the music, but I have no strength for pleasure, especially after such a horrible day."

"Odilon, you know something?"

"What?"

"If I didn't have a passion for music, I'd be dead by now."

"How's that?"

"Music is my biggest cure for the blues. You see that bar? Thanks to it and some of the people working there, I can call Haiti home. When I went there the first time, I knew nobody…now it's my second home. I really want to take you there, so you can meet someone who's dear to me."

"But I don't have good clothes, don't look like a city boy…like you. And also, my face is swollen…" Odilon patted it, but it was not too bad.

Evans inched over to the wardrobe, pulling the door open. "I think we're about the same size. Here, pick whatever you like. I know it's been a rough day…I promise, we won't stay long."

Odilon reluctantly donned a red burgundy shirt, not changing his pants. Although the shirt was too big, its long sleeves camouflaged Odilon's small body. Tucking it in, he felt that his demeanor as a country boy was adequately suppressed.

Five minutes later, the boys were ready to fly. As they went to the door, there came a sudden knock. "Who the *hell* is that?" Odilon cried, freaking out.

"I don't know. Let me see. Who is it?" Evans asked, rather curious.

"It's me, Boss Joseph."

"Oh! You got me scared," replied Evans, opening the door.

There stood an older man in his late sixties, with greyish-white hair and two missing front teeth. Bobbing and weaving, he braced against the doorframe. His speech slurred, and he appeared drunk. "You know you didn't pay this month, don't you?" the man said, mumbling the words as he spoke.

"Yes, I do, sir. I went to pay the other day, but you weren't there; and you told me not to leave the money with your wife."

"Oh, I see. But do you have it now?"

"Sure…wait a second."

Evans took out his wallet from his pants, removing five Haitian *goud* and handing them to the man, who was anxiously waiting. Once he was paid, Boss Joseph soon faded into the dirt alley behind the building.

"That man looked…weird," Odilon commented.

"He is weird. His house is on the front street, the first one in this narrow alley. His wife runs a small grocery store in the front compartment. They're the only ones in the whole yard who have a telephone and an official subscription with the electrical company. They've turned these private services into a big business."

"How's that?"

"They charge anyone who wants to make a phone call three *goud* for ten minutes if it's local, and fifty *goud* for a long-distance call. They also provide electricity to everyone in the yard."

"And how much do they charge for that?"

"Everyone pays five *goud* per month for the juice."

"And they don't get caught…?"

"I don't know, and I don't care. But it's not only done here. This business is all over Port-au-Prince. Haitian authorities are ridiculously corrupt. They charge a decent fee and then turn a blind eye. This country sucks, man!"

While they were chatting, the boys did not realize they had already crossed the empty field carving the courtyard away from the small bar. But when a sweet, slow romantic *bachata* song started blaring over the stereo speakers, the two partygoers were amazed to discover they had reached the front door.

A strong, tall, well-built gentleman greeted them. He was a *grimo* with a tattoo on each upper arm. In the still of the night, he wore dark-tinted spectacles and a dual-tone straw hat, fit for an American cowboy. He also had on a white jersey t-shirt, a chunky silver belt, and tight blue jeans tucked inside his cowboy boots. As the club's bouncer, his job was to screen everyone coming in. Above all, he was checking for weapons.

"Hey Evans, whassup?" chortled the man in American English, giving him a breathtaking, hard-squeezing macho hug.

"Nothing much," Evans replied in English. "I'm struggling, but fine." Evans grinned, presenting Odilon to the giant man. "This is my new best friend and coworker, Odilon," he told the bouncer.

"Hey, Odie!" crowed the man with a beaming smile. "My name is Jean," he continued, swiftly turning to Evans. "Listen, your *chica's* inside. She's been waiting for you, and she's hot under the collar, know what I mean?"

"Let's go in, 'Odie'. Talk to you in a bit, Jean," Evans said.

"No prob, bro!" Jean nodded. "Have a drink on me!"

As Odilon and Evans opened the double doors, stepping down to reach the counter, the music grew louder, but also sweeter. A thrilling *compa-love* was being played. Odilon felt out of place. It was not because of the music. Though a country boy, he was accustomed to traditional, mainstream Haitian music. He felt ill at ease because this was the first time he had found himself in such a glamorous setting, far different from the rustic *djouba* he was addicted to.

Odilon turned around at the bar, gazing in curiosity across the dance floor. There stood a Dominican girl in a Mexican outfit, holding a cup of famous Haitian Barbancourt. She twisted, stirred, and whirled to the beat of the sweet *compa*-love, wearing a special garment called a *hupil*, made of cotton with rectangular stripes sewn together lengthwise. Moving languidly, two other women joined her on the dance floor. One was a Puerto-Rican, with reddish curly hair. She had a *queechquemitl* draped over her lithe body, her head poking through one of its corners. The bottom corners were left hanging, front and back. The third woman was a slim Haitian of fair complexion, who wore a special skirt, a *manta* made out of a long, woven rectangular cloth, wrapped around her hips and tucked in at one corner.

All three were tonight's prizes, and since this was Mexican Night, everything from Mexico was being honored. Odilon and Evans leaned against the counter to get a better glimpse at the beautiful ladies on the dance floor. Watching in awe, Odilon was intimidated by this exotic display of human beauty. But Evans, who was used to these sights, turned around, ordering two piña coladas from the barman. Odilon's wide eyes swept over the women, who were chatting and smiling in the middle of the dance floor. Were these three "ladies of the evening"? If so, he saw that prostitutes could indeed be most beautiful, fascinating, and charming.

At the far corner of the bar, a group of ogling tourists eagerly watched the trio of feminine prizes. Four of them moved to the dance floor, pulling the Haitian woman aside. These wild adventurers were out to devour any Creole *chica* from the tropics, whether she was a prostitute or an altar girl coming from the parish priest.

"*Non!*" screeched the young woman, only in her mid-twenties, wrestling free from the grips of these savage hawks.

"Ah, Rosita, *donne-moi une petite chance!*" said one of the men, lowering his voice like a sneaky fox, showing squinted eyes in a shrewd tactic to catch his prey. He was short and muscular, with a bald head and a tiny, red drooping brush of pointed beard on the tip of his chin.

"Get away from me," the girl scolded." I can't sleep with all of you!"

Odilon tapped Evans on his shoulder to direct his attention to what was happening with the young woman. With his index finger, he pointed at the scene.

"Hey, what the fuck do you guys think you're doing?" Evans grunted, moving in to pull the prostitute away from the grip of the aggressive tourists.

"*Chérie*, did they hurt you?" Evans gently asked the young woman, whose face was coated in heavy makeup in order to heighten her Creole charms.

"No, they didn't. You know in this business, one needs to be careful with these wild men…they will tear me to pieces, if I let them!"

"Listen, I have a friend I'm proud to present to you," Evans said with a frown, pushing the smiling young peasant forward.

In shock, Odilon and the young woman froze upon seeing each other.

"Roseline?" Odilon gasped.

"Odilon?" the prostitute returned. Both began to tremble, out of emotion and astonishment.

"What are you doing in here, Roseline?" Odilon asked, eyes brimming with tears. "This cannot be. I am mistaken – no, I am not!"

Roseline was too abashed and mortified to utter a word. She fell into Odilon arms. Teardrops sprung out of her big black eyes, welling down her cheeks. Normally a cool customer, unshaken by anything, Evans turned pale upon witnessing this scene – he had no idea the two of them knew each other.

"I'm so stunned, I can't talk…I'm so ashamed," muttered Roseline. No one knew her real name before, not even Evans, her *chulo*. Everyone called her Rosita, and this Mexican-sounding name suited her perfectly, as she worked in an environment where most women carried a Spanish name.

Roseline bent her head down, blushing in humiliation. "How will I ever regain my dignity in front of the people in Saint Louis?" She was thinking. Squirming, she wanted to bolt away, in disbelief. Unable to handle the situation, she needed to escape.

Odilon, still reeling from sheer stupor, could not find the words to reassure Roseline that he would not tell anyone in Saint Louis about her deplorable existence. In shocked horror, he could not stop searching Roseline, examining her transformed, used, exploited, and ravaged body.

As streams of tears rolled down her cheeks, they washed away most of the makeup coating her face and lips. The real Roseline emerged, exposing a gaunt appearance that even Evans found difficult to comprehend. The firmness and glow of her once girlish face had vanished, giving way to paleness and ugly wrinkles. As Odilon looked across her chest, he could only see a deep depression. Gone was the firmness, the ladylike perkiness of her lovely breasts.

Roseline, before she came to Port-au-Prince, was every bit as charming as Thérèse – with a Creole elegance that moved any man's heart. Now her magnetic smile, her innocent gaze, and her tantalizing buttocks had evaporated. Her once shiny, steady, secure, and unyielding legs were covered by pantyhose. Her exuberance, Creole beauty, and tropical charms were gone, consumed by the harsh, hellish existence of those who live in the shadowy world of drugs and prostitution.

She bent her head down in guilt. Odilon quickly understood. He inched over, holding her by the shoulder. "That's okay, Roseline. Don't worry, I'll never tell anyone that I met you here. Besides, how can I tell my folks I was here, too?"

"I think we should go to my apartment," Evans proposed. "Roseline…Rosita, you're coming with us. Don't worry. I'll tell the boss you're not feeling well." Leaving them for a moment, Evans went back to the bar counter.

"Hey, Mr. Pierre, Rosita's going to bed for a while. She's…feeling dizzy," he told a short man serving rum behind the counter.

"What am I going to do if she leaves? Look how many people are here tonight. This is the busiest night of the week…these men are here for her," the man replied, lost in total disappointment.

"Don't worry, Mr. Pierre. I'll make sure she gets a two-hour rest…she'll be back good as new." Evans said. The bar manager, a lecherous looking man in his mid-forties, glared at Evans over the rim of his owlish spectacles.

Coughing, Evans returned to join Odilon and Roseline.

"Listen Evans," Roseline said, "before we go to your place, could you please wait outside for a couple minutes? I need to go get something from my room."

Roseline released her hand from Odilon's, slid over to a back door and slunk the rest of the way to her room, located just a few feet away from the main building, on a dirt alley in a large rooming house partitioned into several jail-like cells that the bar owner used to "house" his prostitutes.

Each room was furnished with a twin iron bed and a tiny dresser in which the occupants kept their meager belongings. Roseline got to the door, pulling the key from her purse, and unlocked it. Diving forward, she collapsed in a sobbing heap on her bed. After a while, she got up, pulling out the drawer of her small dresser, and yanking out a little Bible. Stepping back to the edge of the iron bed, she perched on her knees, shaking as she started to pray.

#

Meanwhile inside the bar, the party atmosphere continued. An army of prostitutes and pleasure hunters flanked the dance floor, dirty dancing and explicitly displaying many forbidden moves encouraged by the Haitian *compa* music. At the edge of the bar stood a small group of male Canadian tourists, intoxicated by Haitian rum, waiting with growing impatience. Nothing was on their minds but the Creole body of Rosita, which was nowhere to be seen, and they were tough customers.

Evans began to worry. So did Odilon, who stuck his head through the window blinds in hopes to see Roseline's figure coming out from the dirt alley. He saw nothing but heavy rain drops pelting and smearing the windowpane. Thirty minutes had crept past since Roseline left, promising to return in just five minutes.

Meanwhile, under mounting pressure from the tourists behind the counter, Mr. Pierre stormed through the French doors splitting the bar and dance floor. "Where the *hell* is Rosita?" he asked, hitting his hands in exceeding displeasure.

"I don't know, sir," replied Evans.

"You don't know?" Mr. Pierre roared. "Didn't you tell me she only wanted to lie down for a little while?"

"Yes, I did, sir. She said she was going to her room to pick up something. I'm…getting worried," Evans replied, as Odilon looked on.

"Why don't we go find her? You know her room number, don't you?" Odilon asked Evans. He was having a hard time moving past finding her so haggard, old, and feeble-looking under her makeup.

Before Evans could say "yes", Mr. Pierre gave him a blunt order. "You need to go find her now, or you lose all privileges in here."

The stakes were too high. Evans did not have any time to lose. He loped out into the now harsh downpouring rain. Grateful that he was not trying to sleep outside of the bus station, Odilon followed close behind. A few seconds later, they reached the front door of her building, which was unlocked. Drenched and dripping, they went in, shedding water along the way – tiptoeing down the empty hallway leading to Roseline's room. The door was locked. Evans gave a gentle knock. There was no response.

"Rosita…" Evans called, lowering his voice to avoid disturbing the other prostitutes, who might be at work with clients. Evans left Odilon at the door, checking the one kitchen in the rooming house to see if Roseline was there. She was not. Just when they were about to leave in disappointment, Odilon detected a steady trickle of purple liquid seeping out beneath Roseline's door.

"Evans," he called, freezing in place. "Look," he whispered, pointing his index finger at the dark stain that was growing on the cement floor.

Fearing the worst, Evans moved to break in. Odilon stopped him. "You can't do that. We can be accused of hurting her, or even declared prime suspects if something…happened to her."

"But what do we do? She's not responding."

"Let's get the bar owner. He must have the key…he owns these people."

"Let's go," affirmed Evans. They walked outside, braving the heavy downpour. Soaked and wet, they pushed their way between the intoxicated partygoers shaking their bodies on the dance floor and moved toward the counter. "Mr. Pierre, come, come," Evans wheezed.

"What's going on?" he asked in a bullish rage.

"Please, come. We need to show you something," Evans replied as the disgruntled bar owner loomed menacingly over him and Odilon.

"Can't you see how busy I am? And where's Rosita?"

"Sir, that's precisely what we want to talk about," Evans explained.

"I'm too busy! I can't follow you," Mr. Pierre said, pointing at the line of rowdy Canadian men – ready to eat him alive for their rum.

"Sir, we went over there and searched the place. We called to her, and she didn't respond. But we saw trails of blood trickling from under her door…"

"You saw *what?*"

"Just what I said, Mr. Pierre."

The barman dropped everything and followed them, griping and yelling all the way. By the time they arrived at Roseline's door, the pool of blood had begun to form puddles. Mr. Pierre jerked out a large set of jangling keys from his pocket, sticking his master skeleton one into the keyhole. As they squeaked in, Odilon and Evans clasped their hands over their eyes, not wanting to view the terrible sight.

Mr. Pierre pulled the tiny door open; he threw up his hands in disbelief and vast disgust. The boys' worst fears were confirmed: Roseline lay face up, lifeless in a pool of coagulating blood. A four-inch knife handle stuck out of her stained, besmirched chest. Her eyes were closed, as if she were asleep.

Her strong, dark, wavy hair was matted in clumps with blood. Piteously, her cheerful Mexican outfit was carefully draped on top of the tiny bed. No bloodstains could be detected on it. Instead, she wore her favorite pink nightgown, the hem of which floated in the air from the breeze of a small, rotating floor fan.

There was no physical struggle in her final moments. A note found atop her Bible, placed next to her Mexican outfit, revealed that she had taken her own life.

"Dear Evans and Odilon," the note read, "Perhaps you will never forgive me for what I did. I will be gone by the time you read this note. But I wanted you to know that I couldn't accept my life – full of shame, humiliation, and exploitation. When I came to Port-au-Prince, I was full of hope. So were my parents and my brothers and sisters back home, who counted on me to lead them out of poverty.

"After many unsuccessful attempts to find a job in one of the factories by the airport, I ended up here, hoping to earn some quick cash and return to Saint Louis to open up a small grocery store.

Instead, I could only attain this small room and a few *goud* in exchange for my body, my hope, and my dignity. Having sex with crude strangers every night was not easy for me. But tonight, the humiliation was too much. When I saw you, Odilon, I was ashamed, too ashamed to continue to go on like this.

"Evans, please forgive me, my love. Although I never admitted it, you were the only one who gave me comfort. Please, don't stay here…there's no future. Tell the other *chicas* not to give up the struggle; I have always admired their courage.

"Odilon, please don't tell Thérèse, my parents, or the rest of my family. Keep it secret, like when we promised each other at the square not to let our parents know about how we were going to follow Zebeda to the mountains. My time has come, but you must keep the faith. Haiti will be better someday, and its beautiful children will not have to sell their bodies…and souls…like I did.

"Remember, don't give up. I'll see you on the other side, in Heaven.

"Love, Roseline."

As Odilon read the handwritten note, scrawled in cramped Creole, Evans listened, overwhelmed by grief. Mr. Pierre was also shocked—not by Roseline's death, but by the loss of his prized "Rosita," the best offering he had for his clientele craving Creole young women. Like a flickering fluorescent lightbulb extinguished in the aftermath of a major windstorm, she would be difficult to replace.

Chapter 34

Six months after the tragedy at the bar, Odilon was still reeling from the loss of Thérèse's best friend. The inability to express or share his grief, sorrow, and overwhelming guilt—especially for not being the one to break the news to Thérèse or Roseline's parents—was tearing him apart.

Roseline's last words and the image of her lifeless body wrapped in a flimsy nightgown, floating in a pool of her own blood, haunted him every day. Keeping that secret was too much of a burden for him to bear. He began to develop symptoms of anxiety and depression. Simple tasks such as getting up in the morning, taking the animals to the open field for their daily grazing, doing easy household chores, and waking up in time for work were starting to be too much to undertake. Twice he missed the bus because he overslept, and Thérèse, now in the last stages of her pregnancy, could no longer be his helpmate.

Odilon's chronic gloom, his nightmarish state, and his fading hopes of solving his financial problems were steadily wearing him down, leaving him sick and vulnerable. Desperate to maintain his faith that the RRF would one day descend from the mountains and free Haiti from misery, he no longer believed he would live to witness the triumph of revolutionary ideals. Nor did he think he'd be there when Zebeda stepped up to the microphone before thousands of jubilant supporters to unveil his grand plans for the nation.

As the days drifted by, Odilon sank into a haze of bewilderment, filled with ambiguity and hopelessness. Adding to his misery was the realization that he was not going to fulfill his dreams of providing Thérèse the luxury of having their own place, her autonomy, her pride, her wishes, her joy, her independence, and the ultimate reward, the dignity of being her own person. All that seemed to be fading, gone with the rains. His dreams, his hopes, his relentless perseverance, his positive attitude, all were wallowing in a sea of precariousness and despair.

One morning, he woke at dawn, as usual. It was Saturday, his day off—an ideal excuse to stay in bed. But the night had long ceased to offer rest, only an endless nightmare he endured, waiting for release from his haunted existence. As the crowing roosters signaled the inevitable arrival of daylight, he got up, stretched his thin arms, and scratched his frizzy hair. Moving to the silver chest in the corner, he poured cool water into a cup. After spreading toothpaste on his toothbrush, he silently trudged outside, careful not to disturb the others still asleep.

His daily routine had begun. He brewed coffee for Thérèse, hot ginger tea for his mother, and to make breakfast complete, he fixed peanut butter sandwiches. He wrapped these in a clear plastic bag that he folded under a large cover-plate – a delicious repast, one fit for royalty. Heady fragrances from the ginger tea filled the air. Moving like molasses, he took his animals to the open field.

An hour later, he returned home to find his folks still sleeping, snoring peaceably in their respective beds, even as bright rays of sunshine slipped into the room through cracks in the thatched windows.

"What's going on here?" His voice was hollow as he murmured. "You seem to forget what's happening today."

"Odilon, what time is it?" Thérèse asked, waking and struggling to sit up, shifting her position in the bed. Her pregnant belly, swollen beyond its limits, only deepened Odilon's anxiety about the baby's imminent arrival. Thérèse finally managed to sit, her legs spread wide for balance. Meanwhile, Cécile remained fast asleep, snoring as if lost in another world.

"I have to go to Saint Louis, later," Odilon said.

"What for? Didn't you get paid yesterday?"

"Yes, I did…I'm going to see my friend Evans."

"I thought you told me he lives in Port-au-Prince?"

"Yes, he does, but he sometimes spends the weekend with his relatives in Saint Louis. Do you want to come with me?"

"Odilon, I can barely move. I don't want to put you through the predicament of watching out for me. Besides, I have to urinate so often."

"Okay, at least I won't be late."

Seizing the chance to visit his friend in town and enjoy some 'alone time' together, Odilon set off down the path to Saint Louis an hour later, with Thérèse's watchful eyes following him as he walked away.

#

The last remnants of the morning dew evaporated, and the green foliage regained its full coloration, floating in the lazy, cooling tropical breeze. Jogging along the rocky walkway on that Saturday morning, Odilon felt his confidence returning. He had not felt this way in weeks. When he looked across the sweet potato fields plotted between single mud houses in the valley, Odilon sensed that he was, at last, recapturing a positive note against his prior airs of adversity.

The innocent smiles of children running free on their way to the river, the cherubic bliss they displayed as they intertwined and laced the "apricot" mango trees, soothed Odilon's inner self – making him crave to view his future in a positive frame of mind. He dreamed of his own child-to-be joining the frolickers, looking so dear, so naïve, so innocent while flying like a *kolibri* chirping under the clear-blue tropical sky.

When he reached the edge of Anwodo, he glanced across the foothill. The frantic promenade of some adventurers, lovers, and hunters in the meadow below attracted his attention. He jogged down to get closer to them, but half-way down, he remembered he could not stay too long away from home, from his "controlling" Thérèse. So, he climbed right back up, continuing his journey – which led him to a goat-grazed hillside, where the path narrowed to a little walkway taking him all the way to a small courtyard. A little brick house roofed by thatches stood in the middle of the courtyard, adjacent to a huge, spreading almond tree.

A few children wandered around the tree, gathering ripe almond fruits freshly fallen from the branches. The moment they spotted Odilon, they dashed inside, disappearing into the dull emptiness of the house. A scrawny teenage girl hurried onto the front porch, casting a sideways glance as if investigating. Her gaze fixed on the far end of the yard, she seemed to overlook Odilon, though he stood just inches away.

"*Bonjour*, Micheline!" Odilon called out with a grin.

"Oh, you got me scared!" screeched the girl, flapping her hands on her chest as if trying to measure her heartbeat.

Odilon laughed. "Is Evans here?" he asked.

"Yes, he is. Let me get him for you," replied the girl, scampering back inside.

Odilon waited by the porch for a while. After a few moments, Evans strolled out, yawning, barefoot, naked from the waist up, and wearing brown trousers.

"Look at your hair, man…you're a punk," Odilon laughed. "Did you just wake up?"

"No, man. I've been up…was still in bed," Evans yawned, stroking his hair in acknowledgement. "I don't care…anymore, Odilon," he added.

Evans had been staying there since the death of his "Rosita" – refusing to set foot in his Port-au-Prince apartment. The vivid memories of making love in her room were too much to endure. Unlike Odilon's, his grief did not disintegrate into melancholy or chronic despair. But for the first time since he arrived in Haiti, Evans questioned his future. Conditions in Haiti could not offer hope for people like him. Being born in a foreign country rendered his prospects for a better tomorrow remote. Life is toughest for those who live on the fringes of society.

"What's going on?" Evans asked, regaining his composure.

"Nothing, man, I just wanted to see how you're doing," Odilon replied, his hands stuffed into his pockets. He moved closer, wary that others on the front porch might overhear their conversation.

"You know, Odilon?"

"What?"

"I've been thinking about quitting my day job. It's becoming too difficult to handle. Every time the bus reaches Port-au-Prince, all I can think about is Rosita. Even though she lived 'the life' as a prostitute, she was an amazing person with a good heart. Besides my father, she was the only one who taught me how to appreciate life. It's... funny... how the same life she told me never to give up on... she took in the blink of an eye."

As they talked, they ended up under the spreading almond tree.

"You know, Evans. I've been thinking of quitting baggage handling, too. But for a different reason."

"Why…is it the humiliation that comes with the job?"

"No, it's far less humbling than what I used to do. My problem is that I was hoping to be able to save enough money to rent a small house before our child is born. The baby is weeks away, and I'm not even close to making that a reality."

"Odilon, what do you have in mind? You can't quit now and return to the farms, cleaning fields for next to nothing in pay."

"That's not what I have in mind. I've been watching this town carefully…there's a huge construction boom underway. From Port-de-Paix to Saint Louis, all you see is houses being built. I'm going to try my luck there. If I get a job, I'll be able to stay in this neighborhood and not have to be away when the baby is born."

"That's a great idea, Odilon! If I can get a job in construction, I'll stay here permanently…it will help me a lot in getting rid of my problems."

Indeed, Saint Louis was fast becoming a renovated town, only a few months after the tragedy of a rebel war that had trucked away many of its inhabitants. Now, signs of the war were all but gone — except for the deep psychological scars affecting the population, especially with the strong military presence staying outside of town. This was a harsh reminder that Zebeda was no longer their hope for a better future. On the brighter side, a surge of money coming from expatriates living in Florida and the Bahamas was helping to change the social and economic dynamics of the region.

The quest for survival forced the deprived masses to concentrate on making enough money for food, not on the RRF, although they believed that the rebellion was their ultimate salvation. Along the main dusty highway between Port-de-Paix and Saint Louis, new construction sites popped up like gigantic mushrooms in the grassy morning dew. The two friends in adversity had discovered their consolation in nourishing the dream of finding a secure job in the midst of the housing boom.

A few weeks later, they found work doing manual labor for a construction company in town. Things were starting to look up for Odilon and his friend. For the first time, they began making real plans for the future. Every Friday afternoon, Odilon's pockets were filled with enough money to open a savings account at the regional bank in Port-de-Paix. Following Evans' advice, he purchased a small vacant lot on the outskirts of town near Ti-Riviyè, where he planned to build a two-bedroom house.

Odilon began to learn the importance of strategic investment. In five months, he managed to secure a few plots of land in the valley of Ti-Riviyè. He also managed to convince Thérèse to stay in Anwodo until they could save enough money to build their small home. Meanwhile, the baby was born – a boy, the perfect image of the two lovers. Thérèse seized this "golden opportunity" to start her own business. She built a modest grocery stand at the flea market near Ti-Riviyè, selling lots of groceries, from rice and beans to *kola* and cornmeal. With her profits, she started buying farm animals to solidify her new position in the village as a businesswoman.

Things began to come together. Evans rented a small two-room house on the outskirts of the southern entrance to town, paying far less than what he had shelled out for the tiny studio in Port-au-Prince. Also saving his money, he hoped to secure a decent spot in the harsh reality of Haiti. He rarely set foot in Port-au-Prince and stopped going to nightclubs – needing a complete break from his former lifestyle. He enrolled in night school to learn French and to polish his halting Creole.

His biggest nightmare was the death of his Rosita/Roseline, which continued to torment him. This was worst at night when he could hear her voice telling him how much she missed him. But he was fighting to move beyond this. He now lived in Saint Louis, away from the hectic Port-au-Prince life, and his future had never been so bright and promising.

For a while, both young men's problems seemed to have all but disappeared. Like every oppressive society, however, life for the disenfranchised is always a precarious endeavor, shaky like houses built off the ground. Since the RRF had retreated to its mountain headquarters, the police presence had been a constant nightmare in town, harassing the population, arbitrarily arresting innocent civilians and torturing people suspected as collaborators working for the RRF. Besides the police's oppressive tactics, the Haitian military presence was never far from any population center in the Northwest Department. Outside of every town and village, columns of soldiers lined the road, setting up checkpoints leading in and out of town.

While the hawks in Port-au-Prince claimed victory in the Northwest and then bragged about peace and stability in the region, to its inhabitants, it was a different story. People felt their province was nothing but an occupied territory. Like civilians everywhere, they started complaining about their ordeals, their constant fear. Some youngsters even began to openly express their desire for the RRF to return in order to shield them from what they perceived to be a hellish, nightmarish condition. The construction boom in town only benefited a small group of people— those who had relatives in Miami and elsewhere with the money to invest.

In Saint Louis, underground cells had already been established and a clandestine committee for the defense of the town was formed. Leaflets had been circulating at night. Young people in town were now in open defiance to the authorities. To the general population, however, especially the older folks, this new wave of agitation was received with muted lips. The memory of the last carnage was too fresh in many minds. They had good reasons to be cautious. The hawks in Port-au-Prince saw this latest wave of opposition as a golden opportunity to activate a plan that had long been in the works. They wanted to bulldoze Saint Louis du Nord once and for all and redirect La Rivière des Barres to where it once would have been.

One bright Friday morning, Saint Louis du Nord awoke, fully alive yet as anxious and hopeful as any other town in the region. The clear blue sky spread endlessly, presiding over a cool breeze that caressed the evergreen trees in the nearby hills. Nothing out of the ordinary stirred. The main highway leading to both Anse-à-Foleur and Port-de-Paix was packed with travelers, pedestrians, horseback riders, and commuters. Shopkeepers and street vendors were on high alert, ready for another profitable day. All over town, the sound of breaking bricks from construction sites echoed with force, annoying many town dwellers who had grown weary of the disruptive noise. It was, indeed, the beginning of another gorgeous day in the tropics.

That day, Odilon and Evans were working at a construction site in the suburban area of Soufò, building a two-story house just two blocks from an all-boys' Catholic elementary school. Thérèse had taken the day off for a doctor's appointment at a clinic not far from Odilon's site.

By eleven-thirty that morning, news reports out of Port-de-Paix confirmed an imminent military move against Saint Louis. In fact, travelers and merchants returning from Port-de-Paix claimed to have seen large columns of military vehicles rolling north, passing by the missionary hospital of La Pointe on their way to Saint Louis. All *tap-tap* going south in the opposite direction were forced to turn around. Frightened passengers jumped off the commuter vehicles and fled to the mountains.

As the army convoy reached the edge of the Saint Louis River, military commanders halted their advance. Leading the operation was Lieutenant-Colonel Ferdinand Desroches, a chubby man infamous for his ruthlessness. Although he encountered no resistance—and despite being a Saint Louis native—he was determined to execute his mission with an unexpected zeal that he believed would guarantee him a promotion once the operation was over.

Backed by tanks and other armored vehicles, he ordered several infantry divisions to move into town while helicopter gunships hovered overhead. On the southern edge of town, they started rounding up young men of fighting age and tied them against one another like cattle in a ranch. As the army soldiers moved to the marketplace, it was total bedlam. Buyers and sellers dropped their belongings and fled in several directions. A group of young peasants from Bwa Chandèl ran east, passing through the large courtyard down in the property of the Catholic Church building, skittish as they headed toward the mountains. As soon as they reached the hilltop, they were spotted by low flying helicopters which unleashed hails of artillery rounds, forcing the young people to retreat into town. In the melee, several of them were struck by bullets coming down on them like sheets of rain.

Those who fled to the north and west suffered the same faith. What the army was trying to do was to morph the town into a huge cage, circling it on all sides to obliterate everything, and everyone onsite. Large explosions rocked the town from all directions. Fire mixed with the dark ballooning grey cloud rising into the air, replacing the bright turquoise skies of the morning. A large cluster bomb struck a passing vehicle near the fishing village of Villasso. This had sent the car spinning off the ground, dumping it into a deep-wooded ravine, killing all its passengers. Fishermen along the green cove near the mouth of the Saint Louis River ran for cover. It looked as if the people of Saint Louis had not suffered enough from the previous war-inflicted pain.

After meeting no resistance, Lieutenant-Colonel Desroches decided to orchestrate a bloodbath. An hour later, the town came to a virtual standstill. Businesses closed, traffic halted, streets emptied, and residents went stir-crazy as people strained to find a safe refuge. Long lines of young men tied against one another were seen being forced to build trenches outside of town to dump dead bodies.

Darkness descended in a blur, coming down like a judge's hammer. What appeared to be a clear-blue sky ruling over a bright sunny day a few hours before, now resembled the nightmarish specter of hell on earth. To the frightened throngs, midnight had once again arrived at noon. Each wave of artillery bombardment carried charges of fire and rockets that shook the ground in full fury, blowing off rooftops, collapsing buildings, uprooting trees, and wiping out every single house that was targeted.

People were flushed out of their homes by infantry troops who threw grenades to force them out of their hiding places. Some of them attempted to put up some resistance, but they were quickly subdued by the overwhelming fire power unleashed upon a defenseless population whose only crime was to demand fair living conditions, equal protection under the law, and a right to education.

Then, a sudden downpour mixed with heavy wind gusts moved in as if Mother Nature wanted to wash away the blood-stained walls and the corpse-filled streets. For about an hour, there was a deathly silence. The buzz from the helicopter gunships seemed to have disappeared. Survivors used the cover from the rain to try to flee. Lines of the sudden destitute were seen making their way toward Latiroli, on the shorelines near the southern edge of town, desperately trying to reach the island of La Tortue. A ferryboat adrift in the town harbor, swamped with terrified passengers, struggled for more than two hours in the choppy waters before the captain finally managed to dock. Other moored ferryboats bobbed wildly, resembling loose corks or apples on the water.

#

After five hours of relentless pummeling, the army withdrew, leaving behind countless piles of destruction and misery, reviving harsh memories the residents thought they had overcome. Survivors, one-by-one, crawled out of their hideouts to assess the damage.

On the steps of the Catholic church overlooking the marketplace near the town square, where they had all received the sacrament of baptism, scores of frightened children, newly created orphans, quivered with unchecked fear – screaming for their lost parents. Left to fend for themselves, these bewildered children could not comprehend the full horror of hatred. Their weather-beaten faces exposed their malnourished bodies, which jutted out bonily beneath their ragged and tattered clothes. Sustained bombing had reduced the marketplace into a toxic dirge, including the make-shift grocery stands, countless items of merchandise, hundreds of animals, and the blind *troubadour* singers, who were unable to escape before the carnage started. They were all swept into oblivion.

#

When the first wave of bombing began, Odilon and Evans ran from their construction site to the clinic, where Thérèse and the baby were waiting. Together, they took refuge along with hundreds of other people in a public school building next to the Catholic church. Later, as survivors began to emerge from their hiding places, they also left their shelter, drained and shattered.

Their souls melted in their tracks as they surveyed the destruction. The bombing had stopped, and the rain and the wind subsided, but it was still drizzling.

"Thérèse, I think you need to go back inside. It's still too unsafe for the baby to be out here," Odilon removed his thin jacket to cover and protect his son.

"Odilon, you're right. When you guys are ready to go home, you come to get me," mumbled Thérèse, weary and scared as she navigated through a crowd of survivors coming out from the shelter.

"Never seen anything like this before," Evans declared in total shock.

"Me, neither," responded Odilon. Anxiety overcame him. He could not stop thinking of his mother, stranded alone in Anwodo in a small, vulnerable house.

By five-thirty that afternoon, unable to contain himself anymore, Odilon got Thérèse and the baby and headed east toward the rolling foothills. Evans, unable to get to his apartment on the southern edge of town, went along with them.

It was still too dangerous to venture beyond the town's perimeter. Rumors spread that the army was still stationed a few meters below the southern bank of the Saint Louis River.

They could not believe their eyes when they reached the hilltop – horrified by the utter devastation below. Saint Louis was in ruins, with a third of the town devastated by the pummeling. Heaps of bicycles, motorcycles, trucks, and buses crammed atop one another, creating a massive junkyard. Through the gutted houses and mud-clogged alleyways, groups of stragglers, exhausted and hungry, roamed in a desperate search to find food and shelter. A safe refuge had to be found for them before nightfall.

Evans, being the tallest of the three, held the baby while Odilon, who knew the way, took the lead – with Thérèse holding onto him. They trudged in complete silence, determined to make it home before darkness, through a sea of dead human beings, farms and domestic animals littered around them. Some houses on the hillside, miraculously, were still standing. But they were vacant and without rooftops. All of a sudden, Thérèse screamed, bursting into tears.

"I just…stepped in…something. It feels…soft," she shuddered, eyes wide as saucers.

"Don't panic! We'll be home soon," promised Odilon, pulling Thérèse toward him. They pressed on. Some fifteen minutes later, they reached the edge of the hill. They searched the valley below, but the village of Anwodo was nowhere to be seen. Instead, there was a vast area filled with knocked-down trees, flattened cottages, and tall grasses, everything bent flat, as if a giant roller had bulldozed it.

"Where is…Anwodo?" Thérèse whispered.

"I don't know. Maybe we took a wrong road…"

"I think that's what happened," muttered Evans, holding the baby close to his body. "We should turn around," he continued, unable to contain his emotions.

"Anwodo is…gone," Odilon mumbled in disbelief.

"Odilon, how can you say that? How could this be?" cried Thérèse.

"I don't know. But isn't it what we're seeing now?" Odilon pointed to the ravaged landscape, finally crying out in utter devastation, "*Manman!*"

Fearing the worst, they began to move downhill in slow, studied silence. Their hearts were pounding in rapid pulsations by the time they reached the foothill, looking out across the ravine. They saw nothing but a silent, giant empty and desolated space stretching into infinity before them. The landscape offered nothing, no hope – only an eerie reminder of what had once been the village of Anwodo. The hawks in Port-au-Prince had made good on their threat to extirpate the population of this rebellious region. The cacao groves, the cashew nuts, the orange trees, the mango groves, the avocados, and the *kowosol* trees were gone, crippled by exploded bombs, except for a handful of stragglers.

"It's…like a giant marshland I've seen in Florida. The only difference is the smoke and the destroyed houses." Evans remarked in awe, gripping the baby tight to his chest.

Forming a human chain, they crossed the flooded ravine, struggling against the powerful current. They made it safely across, treading in sadness down what once had been a red-dirt road winding between the banana and yucca fields. They found a tiny walkway. Wet and muddy, it led them to where the village of Anwodo had stood several hours earlier.

As they entered the site, the walkway vanished, dissolving into a river of mud and blood. The people, including Cécile, were gone. Only a few uprooted trees remained as the last proof that once, there had stood a vibrant village called Anwodo, inhabited by people with good hearts.

"*Manman!*" Throwing his head back, Odilon screamed at the tops of his lungs, hurling himself onto the muddy ground. Thérèse reached out to grab his hands, pulling him against the branches of a fallen mango tree.

Evans drew closer to Odilon. "Let's not lose hope. Maybe the people took refuge in another location," he coaxed, still holding tight to the baby. "Staying here is not going to help. We need to start looking," he asserted.

"But where?" begged Thérèse, groping around in utmost disbelief.

"Anywhere, everywhere! And Odilon, you need to be strong. In this moment of crisis, no one will pay us any special attention. If your mother is to be found alive, it's up to us to make it happen. So, my friend, let's get up. Look around you, it's getting late," Evans declared. Thérèse pulled Odilon up to his feet, helping him balance.

They could not go back to Saint Louis – it was too dangerous. Besides, sounds of automatic gunfire could be heard in the distance, which indicated a resumption of the bombing to come. Keeping their pain to themselves, Thérèse, Odilon, Evans, and the baby trudged on, managing to make it over the mountains to Nan Banman, where the people had suffered little effect from the bombing. Thérèse's parents' house stood firm there, having survived the carnage. Its location, high on the mountaintop and framed by towering trees, may have saved it. Consequently, it felt like Heaven on Earth when they arrived, before a steady, normal tropical rain began to fall.

But darkness had already descended on the devastated region, and Odilon could not sit, rest, or lie down. His feet were cold, wet, and swollen from wading through the flooded terrain. His neck, back, hips, and stomach hurt – his entire weather-beaten body ached, from head to toe. Adding to this misery was the evidence of a growing dysfunction between his brain and the rest of his body. He was having trouble with rationalization. The one person on his mind was *Manman*, for whom he was ready to sacrifice everything, including his life, to find her.

Everyone crammed into one room, talking about their latest ordeal. Odilon heard and felt none of it – the agonizing murmurs of the people around him, the cries of the baby yearning to be breastfed, the voice of Evans trying to reason with him, the touch of Thérèse desperately trying to comfort him, and the rumbling of thunder rocking the sky in a new torrent of rain. Pacing up and down to find relief from his screaming nerves, he could create no room to maneuver. He tried to cry, but with no strength. Finally, trapped in a corner sitting on the dirt floor, he spent a sleepless night yearning for daybreak so he could resume his search for his beloved mother.

The next morning at dawn, Odilon was up. The bombing had stopped. He left Thérèse there with the baby, going out with Evans. They searched every inch of the valley, every river, every ravine, every corner of Saint Louis, and every mass grave. They found no trace of Cécile or any of the inhabitants from Anwodo. They spent the entire day looking for Cécile and some other folks from the village who perhaps might have been able to tell them what had happened. As dusk approached, they retook the road back to Nan Banman, passing for a last time through the flattened village of Anwodo in the hope of finding some clues as to what had happened to Odilon's mother. They were not so lucky. All they could see was a raised landscape full of childhood memories that was too harsh to relive. So, they walked east. Just below the mountain, they met Dieudonné, the boy whose life was spared thanks to Odilon near the river basin in Ti-Rivyè as he was about to drown. His eyes were red. He looked desolated and terrified. He was walking in the opposite direction.

"Where're you going Dieudonné?" Odilon asked.

"I don't know."

"Where are your parents?"

"I don't know. Lovinia told me she saw police came into the village and asked everyone to come out for their own protection. The people came out, but they were taken to Nan Figue."

"Then what happened?" Odilon and Evans demanded in unison.

"I don't know. Lovinia said they heard shots fired."

"Go up to Nan Banman to Patekrè's house, Dieudonné. Tell Thérèse we're coming. It's too dangerous to go back to Anwodo," asserted Odilon.

They waited a few minutes, watching the boy hiking over the mountainside and then they made a U-turn back into town toward Nan Figue. At the edge of Anwodo, an old man spotted them.

"Odilon!" The old man called to him. "You need to flee. I thought you were dead. They got your name on a list and collaborators came three times looking for you. You're lucky you're still alive. The village people were not. And if you want to make it to tomorrow, I wouldn't advise you to stay in this area. Go, and go now."

At that moment, he had gotten what he was looking for. Cécile was no more, swallowed by the savagery of war and outright hatred. He started hitting his head against the ground as his body was shivering.

"Odilon, I understand, but we need to get out of here before we become the newest victims. For the sake of your wife and your baby, we need to get out of town."

"No, I'm going to stay here until they come and kill me, too."

"Don't be so selfish. You can't look for an easy exit. I know you don't mean it. You love your wife and your baby too much to allow yourself to be killed by the criminals."

With great stoicism, Evans steadied his friend as they walked in complete silence to Nan Banman. Once again, Odilon was questioning the existence of God. For him, this latest catastrophe was not only too harsh to accept but also incomprehensible for a population so resilient, so devoted to life, despite enduring one tragedy after another. By now, he saw his path clearly: the only way forward was to take his wife and baby and leave Saint Louis for good, in a desperate search for salvation. But where would they go?

Chapter 35

At the first grey light of dawn, all three quietly left Thérèse's parents' cottage. They walked in silence down a trail leading to the heart of the valley, avoiding the main path and instead taking a narrow walkway hidden beneath thick yucca fields.

The narrow path led them to the edge of town, where they encountered no one. It was still dark, and a dusk-to-dawn curfew was in place. They stopped beneath a large mango tree near Soufò, waiting for the right moment to cross the main street. Soon, they spotted a tall man on a mule, his ebony face blending into the darkness of his jacket. The man halted upon seeing them. Odilon's heart sank, fearing they were about to be caught by the police.

"Where are you young people going at this hour? The man asked. His voice seemed buried in the depth of his throat.

"We're going to the hospital of La Pointe. The baby is very ill," Thérèse explained.

"Be careful. About a dozen of police officers are stationed by the marketplace at the entrance of Main Street. The wild dogs have never been so wild."

The man struck his mule, which bolted off in a cloud of brownish dust. After hearing the man's assurances, they rose and began walking in sync with the changing atmosphere. Avoiding the marketplace, they followed a narrow alley that wound down to the shoreline. In the dim morning twilight, Evans took the lead, guiding them with the thin beam of a flashlight, carefully steering clear of the morning dew clinging to the sea grape leaves.

Minutes later, they reached the seaside section of town, greeted by the blustering wind and crashing waves on the sandy beach. Evans switched off his flashlight as they arrived, the dim glow of the sea just enough to illuminate their path. They moved together over a mosaic of grey and white pebbles, their world silent and deserted, disturbed only by the occasional lines of seabirds flying overhead.

They headed south along the sandy shores, carrying sandwich bread, peanut butter, and distilled bottles of water they had purchased for the baby two days earlier. Wrapped snugly in a homemade quilt for protection against the cool, rushing winds, the curious baby poked his little button nose out, smelling the sea breeze. Thérèse had placed her infant in a knapsack, strapping it to her back to free her hands and make the march more comfortable. They were three hesitant, lonely pilgrims, preparing to undertake an endless pilgrimage.

At daybreak, they reached the sugar-sand shores near the village of Lapointe, where fishermen cast their nets into the turquoise water. They spoke to no one, pressing onward as they rolled up their pants to wade through the river mouths flowing into the ocean. By ten o'clock, they arrived at a massive wooden shipyard along the seaside, just two kilometers outside Port-de-Paix. The three travelers were searching for a legendary sea captain named Michel Peleah.

Peleah was a notorious captain, famed for his daring trips on the high seas, braving wind gusts, rainstorms, shark-infested waters, and the US Coastguard, to deliver illegal immigrants to the shores of Nassau, the capital of the Bahamas. Bahamian police could only see a boat filled with green bananas, according to the legend, which had it that Peleah owned a white stick, given to him by Agwe, the god of the sea, with the power to turn humans into vegetables in the eyes of the Bahamian authorities.

When Odilon, Thérèse, and Evans arrived at the shipyard, Peleah had already completed one hundred and fifty-two successful trips. With such an impressive track record, his popularity soared. In every coastal town, from Port Magot in the north to Port-à-Piment in the south, there wasn't a single person who didn't know of him or have a family member who had traveled with Michel Peleah. But this self-styled 'crusader' was far from being an ordinary seafarer—though few were aware of this.

Though he became an overnight celebrity, a San Salvador to thousands fleeing the poverty-stricken region, his peers saw him as nothing more than a ruthless sea pirate—his cruelty rivaling that of the *flibustiers*, the seventeenth-century pirates who prowled the northern seaboard for prey more than five hundred years ago. Peleah took pride in calling himself a modern-day buccaneer, a name he adopted after the French pirates who lived on the island of La Tortue where he was born, just off the coast of Port-de-Paix.

Peleah was a soft-spoken man, rarely refusing to allow passengers onboard. But when he sailed the high seas, he was said to turn into a ferocious sea monster. When bad weather threatened his ship, people were thrown overboard to ease the boatload. And the green bananas seen by the police of Nassau Bay were actually real, since the boat was often half-empty by the time it arrived in Nassau. The remaining passengers, scared out of their wits, hid underneath the deck, out of sight of the Bahamian police. Only a few select souls in the province knew the true nature of these crimes on the high seas.

Odilon and company had no clue about this ugly practice. Nor did hundreds of Peleah's would-be passengers swarming the city of Port-de-Paix, walking along the narrow streets right under the noses of corrupt police officers, profiteers on his payroll. When they arrived at the shipyard, he was in town, enjoying the favors of a local mistress. They were greeted by one of his two lieutenants, who asked them to wait. They ambled a few feet away under the sea-grapes, sitting down to gaze at the huge swelling surf, while enjoying the splashing, foams and rolling sounds of the breaking waves.

"You know how to swim, Odilon?" Evans chuckled, in a serious tone.

"I'm not a professional…I can manage to stay afloat," Odilon replied.

"Listen, guys. What're we going to tell Peleah?" Thérèse asked, her voice heavy with anxiety.

"Let me do the talking," Evans said, motioning for their silence. "You stay quiet. As I told you last week, my father knows him from Freeport in the Bahamas. He used to come in every Sunday for breakfast. My father called me last week to say he had arranged for Peleah to take me to Nassau."

"But, what about us?" Odilon and Thérèse cried in alarmed chorus.

"I'll…ask him to let you onboard," Evans said, smiling to reassure them.

Fifteen minutes later, Peleah arrived. Tall and thin, he wore glasses on an almost beardless face, save for a tuft of grey-white hair beneath his chin. His kinky afro, with reddish traces around his forehead, was typical of mariners from La Tortue, his main base of operations. He presented the very image of a *kinkyjoe,* a rugged islander, with grey eyes, a freckled face, and black tennis shoes worn without socks. His short khaki pants exposed his red, hairy legs, while a tropical, flowery, short-sleeved shirt completed the look. Three long gold chains hung around his neck, and heavy gold rings adorned each of his hairy fingers.

Michel Peleah, like most of his fellow sea captains, was a rank womanizer – said to have fathered sixty-three children – scattered from Miami to the Bahamas, and in Haiti. His vaulted position as a sea captain, and a projected aura of innocence, gave every woman who slept with him "easy" justification, as he looked so harmless and slight, his slender physique camouflaging the demons dwelling within.

"How are you, kids?" he beamed, casting a deceptive smile on Odilon, sending a cursory glance over the other people eagerly awaiting his arrival.

"We're fine," Evans replied, praying that he did not sound nervous.

"What can I do for you?" Peleah chuckled. "Or, you for me?"

"My name is Evans Philippe. My father sent me…he said he has already talked to you," asserted Odilon's good friend.

"Yes, he told me your story. I'm really sorry for what happened," Peleah responded with a thin, halting smile. "Listen, you came a bit early, but right on time – tomorrow, at two in the morning, we set sail."

"Are you sure?" cried Evans, as Odilon and Thérèse gazed on in disbelief.

"Unless we run into a storm, we'll be in the water first thing in the morning."

"But, Mr. Peleah…I have a…little problem."

"What is it, Evans?"

"I brought my friends with me. We've been through so much together. They were the ones who saved me when I was truly in trouble. They gave me food when I was hungry, provided shelter when I was homeless…"

"I understand; you need no further explanation. Bring them along with you. The departure point is near the village of Bodin. You won't see me, but I will instruct my aides to allow you in. By the way, what are your friends' names?"

"Odilon and Thérèse."

"Perfect. See you onboard, guys."

"Thank you," they replied in one voice as Peleah disappeared behind them, heading onto the dock.

Turning, Odilon ducked back under the sea-grapes, reflecting upon this latest move – standing with bowed head, locked into a collision course with history. Once more, he had to bitterly face the undying pain, the unbearable sorrow, the patriotic guilt, the loneliness, the love, the hate, and the fear of uncertainty that lay ahead. By leaving Haiti this way, he was unsure whether or not he was actually a traitor. After losing so much, wouldn't it be wiser, braver, more patriotic, and more revolutionary to join Zebeda in the mountains, instead of fleeing the country that he unconditionally loved? Racked with spiritual pain, his mind foamed high like the sea, in raging turmoil.

Odilon knew he was not a coward, a rat, or a thief in the night. But he could not feel anything but uncertain. He glanced across the shoreline, seeing a horde of people trying to escape – ready to give-up everything including their lives to get out of Haiti – knowing then that the enemies of his country had won at least another round in this protracted struggle. That dug into the deepest portion of his soul, but he suffered in silence. He feared Thérèse and Evans would misunderstand if he shared his feelings. That night, as moonlight glittered over the sandy shoreline, Odilon's concern for the future deepened as he prepared to face the unknown.

However, his main reason for retreating beneath an old sea-grape tree was to avoid being swept away by the vast ocean of people pacing up and down the seashore, desperately waiting for their chance to board the ship. Their gaunt and careworn faces betrayed what they would otherwise hide deep inside their souls. Night voyages on the high seas have never been easy undertakings, especially for desperate escapees, reluctantly gambling their lives on a rickety ship, braving miles of shark-infested waters, the sadistic whims of sea captains, hunger, dehydration, and the raw humiliation awaiting them at the hands of immigration officials.

A lone barefoot man in his mid-thirties, whose khaki pair of pants were rolled up to his knees, stood motionless a few feet away from Odilon, gazing at the ocean waves and the white, cresting sea-foam – much like the frosting on top of a carrot cake. Hands shoved into his pants, he was haggard, worn out, and thoroughly exhausted. His invisible eyes burrowed into the shadow of his brow; his bony cheekbones jutted upward in his angular, wrinkled face. All this made him seem like a frightened child after a hair-raising ghost story.

"Hey man, why're you staring at the water?" Odilon called out to him.

But the man did not say anything back. Instead, he turned around, curtly acknowledging Odilon; and near the corner of his mouth grinned a slight, subtle smile. He then walked away, fading into the long shadows of the crowd.

That bunch was getting rowdier by the hour. One-by-one, they came pouring in from every corner of Haiti, each carrying a distinct story they would rather die than tell virtual strangers. Down the beach where Odilon sat, a heavy-set, short woman whose name was Louisinette strolled past while hopping like a kangaroo. She soon erupted in violent outbursts, claiming she had lost her five-year-old son. She cried out that he went astray while she was buying fresh cassava from a street vendor at the improvised marketplace created for the refugees—right at the entrance of the beach resort of Nan Chalet, near the northern fringes of town.

An army of volunteers gathered up, lickety-split, to locate the lost boy. After one hour of searching, he was spotted at the far southwest point of the beach, where the refugees' encampment ended. A man with a hairy face, wearing a long robe without pants, held the boy's hand. They turned south, as if leaving the beach camp. The weird-looking man had one white, stringy hairline on his forehead, and a pair of stud earrings in each ear. His bushy eyebrows hardened, making him look like nothing but a vicious werewolf – ready to eat the child.

Two brave men in the crowd jumped on this stranger. Petrified by the rage of the thronging mob, the strange man fell to his knees, begging for his life, asking for mercy, claiming to believe the boy belonged to some family in town. He was only taking him to the nearest police station, for safety purposes. After fifteen intense minutes, a middle-aged woman in a white maternity outfit with blue leggings, who also wore a pair of camisoles, darted forward, raising her right index finger and turning around to face the curious crowd.

"Let him be," she commanded, sending the crowd scattering and then motionless in a blur. She trained her harsh, domineering voice on the groveling, spooky stranger. "You may go, but don't ever come back here!" she snarled.

The man rose in one second to his feet, fleeing like a kangaroo rat lost in a cactus bed. Bored now, the crowd drifted away. The horror-stricken boy, with a wary, suntanned and sweaty face, seemed bewildered under the weight of so much attention. He was reunited with his anxious mother, vanishing into the crowd. Later that afternoon, rumors spread that the strange woman was none other than Camélia, a well-known *manbo* from the village of Boukan Carré, near the town of Bassin Bleu in the southern edge of the province.

Chapter 36

Just before two a.m., near the shores in Bodin, the scene was chaotic. The main boat, about thirty feet long and fifteen feet wide, was anchored two kilometers offshore. Meanwhile at the seaside, a horde of people wrestled like bears for a chance to get onboard a lone lifeboat, used to transport the refugees to the main vessel. Three muscular seamen attempted to bring about a sense of order by reading a list of would-be passengers and checking off their names before allowing them into the lifeboat. They were overpowered by the furious crowd – determined to get to the main ship, whether dead or alive.

A brief distance away, Odilon, Evans, and Thérèse watched the scene unfold with much apprehension. They had been standing there for hours, with no chance of boarding the lifeboat.

"I don't think we have a chance," Odilon murmured, shaken; so was Thérèse, who still had the baby strapped to her back tight in a knapsack.

"You guys wait here. Let me go speak to whoever's in charge before it's too late," said Evans, rolling his pants up to his knees, wading through the saltwater to fight his way to the man in charge. "Listen, my name is Evans…my friends and I already got the approval from Mr. Peleah to get on," he shouted, straining to be heard over the chaotic voices of the angry faceless crowd.

"I didn't get any word from Mr. Peleah… but tell your friends to come with you. You'd better hurry, we're leaving in fifteen minutes.

After this trip, there won't be another," replied a short man, his matching set of gleaming gold front teeth shining in the moonlight.

Evans ran right back to Odilon and Thérèse. "Let's go now! The captain told me this is the last trip to the main vessel."

Thérèse struggled to stand up in the middle of feeding the baby, who was crying for milk. "Odilon, I'm very scared. I think we need to take a second look at what we're about to do. Why don't we let Evans go…we can try to do it properly next time?" Tears ran down her cheeks, for mounting terror had almost crippled her.

Odilon held Thérèse firm in his arms. "*Chérie*, I agree with you. I think it's too risky for you and the baby. Go home to your parents in Nan Banman. Let me go. If something happens, it will only be to me, not you, not the baby. I don't think I can put you two through this ordeal," Odilon soothed, but he too was crying.

"No way!" yelled Thérèse. "I'm not going to Nan Banman and leaving you to face this alone. Without you, my life is meaningless."

"Let's go, guys. We don't have much time…we need to get in the water now, before we lose our opportunity," Evans called, hoping to be heard.

"This is it!" roared the captain. "We can't accept any more people."

"Wait!" yelled Evans. "I have to go get my friends, remember?"

The worried travelers were the very last ones to get on the lifeboat. Odilon witnessed in horror the hopeless agonizing cries of those left behind. Five people alone drowned, attempting to reach the main vessel, their bodies washed ashore by the rolling waves. Was this a prelude to what was to come?

As Peleah's master ship drifted away from the mainland, the reality of the refugees' deprived conditions began to set in. The rowdy noise, the pushing, the shoving were slowly replaced by the unbroken sound of crashing waves and the wet winds that whipped and flapped the sails of the vessel. Then it became deathly quiet.

Inside the ship, life was miserable. By the captain's order, no one was allowed to stay on the deck. One hundred and ninety-three people were crammed below, with scanty food and water. Down there, Odilon felt trampled by the weight of confusion and the haughty will of the sea captains. Like a wild mongoose trapped in its hole, he longed for the sun to come to his rescue, liberating him from this nightmarish dilemma.

Glancing over the crowded boat, Odilon came to realize that finding a spot on this craft was one thing, surviving the passage was quite another. Head bent down, he brooded in deep thought, pondering how long he was going to remain cooped up in what seemed to be a floating beach hut rather than a sea-going vessel. Thérèse, who leaned into him, was consumed by the morose atmosphere. She said nothing as the ship pushed against the timid waves and as the wind flapped its sails about.

After one hour of sailing, Odilon left Thérèse for just a moment, managing to squeeze up the hatchway in a desperate try to escape confinement. For a moment, he pretty much got his wish. Through cracks in the hatch, he watched the morning twilight fading in the horizon – contemplating with awe the stars shining in the firmament against the backdrop of the dim-blue darkness of the universe.

Then, in a stunning slow motion, the faint glow in the distance began to blossom, morphing the sky into a grey-seeping mist, wiping out the fluorescent glow of the stars, erasing their entire luminescence. In a dramatic shift, the sun shot out its orange beams over the ocean waves. But that swiftly faded, giving way to a golden glow striking the foamy ocean white caps, setting them to glitter in a spectacular show. Odilon's ocean world had entered a new dawn. It was finally daylight.

"This might be what it was like on the slave ships," he mused.

By the time they reached the seashores of La Tortue, the sun had already pushed its way from behind the cottony slate-grey clouds, rising above the horizon to cast its yellow glow on the vessel deck.

But it was still dark in the belly of the ship, where the refugees crammed together like paper wads in a bottle. The sea captains had sealed the hatch to foil any passengers who wanted to escape. Thérèse, who again leaned on Odilon's skimpy arm, groped for the tiniest traces of comfort to fall asleep.

But the concentrated stench below the deck, mixed with the fetid, overcrowded conditions, gave her no spell of relief. Evans bent his head down, blushing in embarrassment. A feeling of guilt overwhelmed his body. He did not want to face Odilon and Thérèse in these dark hours of uncertainty.

"Why did I bring them here?" he grumbled to himself.

Meanwhile, the vessel docked near the village of Nan Figué, a small fishing community nestled on a tiny inlet squeezed between some rocky headlands, which offered a perfect estuary for the illegal boat. This village was framed against the backdrop of a barren landscape, on the mouth of a treeless, low hill coated with light tropical undergrowth. A line of thorny acacia trees spawned a natural buffer between the foothill and the western fringe of the village. And to the north, clusters of royal palms and towering almond trees offered the illusory picture of an oasis sprouting in the midst of a sandy desert.

They spent four hours near that village, without going ashore. Claiming insecurity, the vessel's crew ordered everyone not only to remain in the ship's belly, but also to remain silent – avoiding suspicion from the village authorities. Few people believed it. Most of the passengers concluded that if Port-de-Paix looked the other way, what could a tiny village like Nan Figué do to a renowned chieftain like Peleah? Therefore, the captain's order did nothing to alleviate the fear and misery occurring below the boat's deck, in a sea of growing confusion and chaotic Hell.

Yet somehow, by midday, Evans managed to sneak out of the hatch and reach the outside after befriending one of the crewmen with his earnest, sweet-talking style. Upon stepping onto the deck, however, the harsh glow of the sun's rays struck him like steel pilons, pounding into his head and face. The heat seared him, just like cassava grilling in the countryside.

To ease his burning skin, he took advantage of the midday low tide, sliding down a knotted rope and grabbing a canister with his left hand. He filled it with salt water, using it to rinse his face. But the water quickly evaporated, leaving countless grains of salt that badly itched his burning, rose-reddened skin.

Still sprawled, panting on the deck, he realized that the deplorable conditions in the belly of the ship were far worse than the punishing sunshine. He begged the crewman to let him retrieve his friends from their hellish situation. But the man refused, insisting that they would be leaving any minute. Once the vessel set sail, everyone would have to go back down, including Evans.

The sea was calm, almost motionless—but just a few meters from the docking ship, a narrow fringe of mangroves formed a stunning saline shrubland, a kind of mangrove swamp that provided an ideal habitat for seagulls and other seabirds. Evans tried unsuccessfully to convince the crewman to use the vessel's lone lifeboat to retrieve water from around the mangroves. He argued that the water there was brackish, having observed a couple of small brooks streaming down to the semi-enclosed body of water, creating the appearance of an estuary. Fifteen minutes later, they set out to sea, with the captain assuring the refugees that they would soon reach the town of Cayòn, about six kilometers to the south.

As they departed, Mother Nature showed some empathy for the weary refugees. Voluminous dark clouds emerged, blocking the sun's sharp, deck-piercing heat. A cool, pleasant ocean breeze swept through, so refreshing that the crew captains ordered the vessel's hatch open, allowing fresh air to filter inside. As the sailors left the estuary and sailed into open water, a much larger and denser mangrove forest greeted them, offering a stunning glimpse of the marine ecosystem of northern Haiti.

Here, in this part of the country, the *Rhizophora mangle* (commonly known as red mangroves) found along the northern seaboard and around river deltas were impossible to overlook. The symbiotic relationship between the mangroves and the marine life here could not be underestimated. While marine biologists called them red mangroves for their tangled, ruddy roots, locals referred to them as 'walking trees' due to their constant movement on the water's surface. Their overhanging, bushy branches served as breeding grounds for rooks, and in these rookeries, exotic seabirds like roseate spoonbills and white pelicans were plentiful. Among the coastal mangroves, the rare blue-footed booby stood out—a dazzling seabird with webbed, bluish feet and white-feathered streaks on its pale, cinnamon-brown head. With its brown-painted wings, this bird was most striking for its clumsy-looking walk and its goofy-shaped body when stationary.

As the ship neared the mangroves, Odilon managed to sneak his head out of the hatch. He gazed in deep admiration at the clustered colonies of pelicans, their elastic pouches snapping up red snappers— the rosy-pink fish so popular in Haiti. Awestruck, Odilon called to Thérèse and Evans to come and see the pelicans, which waited for a group of snappers to gather in the shallows before diving from above, scooping up the fish in their bills.

Thérèse, too dazed to move, sat with the baby on her lap, breastfeeding him. Seeing her pale face, Odilon had to admit that a rickety boat was no place for sightseeing. Yet, she would have been amazed if she knew the rich biodiversity beneath the mangrove's surface—a sanctuary for marine species like sheepsheads, shrimp, snooks, oysters, and snappers, as well as countless nursery areas for shellfish and crustaceans.

With responsible and democratic leadership, these mangrove zones could have been used to develop commercial fisheries, vital for strengthening local economies. Perhaps, someday, this might prevent desperate civilians from risking their lives on the high seas. Instead, governmental neglect, coupled with deforestation and beach erosion, threatened the continued existence of these beautiful native species.

Shortly after 5:30 a.m., the vessel reached the town of Cayòn on the southwestern edge of the island, the last stop before heading north to the Bahamas. Just as the passengers hoped to get on deck to buy bottles of water, a last-minute change in the itinerary shattered their plans. The crew announced that they could no longer dock, as the island authorities would arrest them. So, they pressed on, sailing out into the open sea.

As with all illegal trips to the Bahamas, safety was not considered a priority. Aside from the lone lifeboat tied to the rear of the vessel, there were no life jackets, no safety guidelines, and no crew members explaining to the passengers what to do if trouble arose on the roaring, tempestuous ocean.

When they left the island, the weather was perfect, with a clear blue sky reflecting on the turquoise water. A cool tropical breeze swept through the vessel, making it feel more like a vacation cruise than an overloaded, decrepit, illegal boat. It was so calm that the captains allowed some passengers to come up to the deck, providing a brief escape from the dangerous and unsanitary conditions below. Odilon and Thérèse seized the opportunity to escape the chaos, joining Evans on the deck to chat with several other passengers.

By the time Odilon reached the deck, the vessel had traveled far from the island of La Tortue, also known as Tortuga, leaving him with only a faint glimpse of his beloved homeland, slowly disappearing before his eyes. Breathless, he stood motionless against the vast expanse of the endless sea.

"I'm scared," said Thérèse, leaning against Odilon as she tried to burp the baby after breastfeeding him.

"I am, too," he replied, squeezing her hand. "Right now, I feel absolutely powerless," he confessed – gazing deep into her eyes.

Turning at a sudden noise, they both gaped across the deck in total shock to find a transformed Michel Peleah. He was wrapped in a loose white robe, wearing blue-blacker spectacles, with an Afghan turban draped across his head.

"Evans," Odilon whispered. "Do you know this man?"

"Quiet, that's Peleah," he replied, lowering his voice and pushing Odilon and Thérèse further away, so he would not hear them. They moved behind the crowd, which poured out onto the deck in search of fresh air.

"This man is just plain weird…he wouldn't even talk to me when I approached him a bit ago. I heard some folks say earlier that he's…possessed. They saw him throw two live roosters into the sea," Evans whispered.

"Look how red his eyes are. Maybe he's still being possessed," Thérèse muttered.

Peleah now sat in an armchair, his feet resting in front of two women massaging his lower legs. A gleaming, sharp machete lay across his lap, and he smoked a thin-reeded pipe. He seemed like an out-of-control tyrant, intoxicated by alcohol and drug-induced euphoria. No one dared speak to him, except for the obedient women tending to his legs. He maintained a three-foot radius around himself with a small umbrella, calling it his 'free space,' allowing only the other captains to enter if they needed his advice.

Meanwhile, to create a sense of normalcy in the midst of mounting madness, a bevy of bustling *troubadour* musicians scrambled up from below the deck, loaded down with their drum-style instruments. A short, skinny man led the group, playing the role of lead singer and acoustic guitarist.

A pudgy woman singing in the background was playing a *guiro*, a Latin-American percussion instrument, while shaking her hips to the sweet Caribbean beat. A young boy of about fifteen skillfully shook a maraca, one of the instruments most preferred by Haitian peasants.

The total chaos of two hours earlier was soon replaced by an improvised ballroom on the high seas. Peleah appeared to be pleased by this event – he began to stroke one of the women's breasts, laughing and dancing to the beat of the band in his loose robes.

Odilon could not believe his eyes, watching in disbelief as half-a-dozen young women danced and pranced around cabaret-style, like in the Lower Port-au-Prince nightclubs.

"I can't believe this! They think they're on a cruise ship!" he groaned with a broadening grin, throwing his head back to laugh it all off.

Before long, pigeon beans and rice were served. But Peleah received a warlord's treatment – eating roasted white fish topped with tomato salsa, drizzled with a balsamic glaze fit for a pirate chieftain. Odilon ate nothing. The last vestige of his appetite had gone south, as the crude smell from the ocean floor and the ambiguity of what lay ahead settled into his fragile body.

"These people…are insane," said Thérèse with a wan, lilting laugh, raising the baby to her shoulder, patting his back to put him to sleep.

"I don't think so," explained Evans. "It's a better way to get your mind off a desperate situation," he added.

"I'm not surprised at your answer, Evans. That's your escape from reality. I bet you're dreaming of Port-au-Prince," Odilon guessed with a sigh.

"Man, you know how I feel about those days…they bring me nightmares each time they invade my memory, especially that dramatic…."

Odilon stopped him, quick to change the conversation. He had not yet told Thérèse about what had happened to her good friend Roseline, and he was not going to tell her under these circumstances.

"This music reminds me of when I attended the *djouba* every Saturday night at the Andre Hall in Vertus, near the bamboo tree," he reminisced, pressing his foot against Evans' leg.

Getting the veiled message, Evans turned around, closing his mouth and moving away to the middle of the crowd – recovering from his thoughtless blunder.

Fifteen minutes later, an old, bald-headed man with a steel-grey mustache emerged from under the deck, carting a large banjo on his shoulder. He took up position near the rest of the musicians and began to play. In that instant, the *troubadour* band was finally complete. The dancers went wild as the party ballooned full-blown.

Peleah could not resist. Within minutes, he was on his feet, legs spread and arms outstretched, moaning like a bull in heat. His women responded in kind, sticking their humongous buttocks in the air, while Peleah's three-foot radius zone was violated right under his nose; but he was too intoxicated to notice it.

The party dragged on until the wee hours of the morning, while the weather cooperated. The clear-blue sky of earlier in the day was festooned, decorated with a dazzling array of stars, their leader being the bright, sensuous full moon. Thérèse, earlier in the evening, had retreated under the deck to rest with the baby. Odilon and Evans took turns checking on her.

#

For two days, they proceeded at full speed, navigating the middle of the ocean, surrounded by nothing but an endless sky and a vast expanse of salty water. Odilon felt as if the planet had shrunk to his own little world: a group of determined refugees crammed like down feathers into an illegal ship that seemed to sail aimlessly through the Caribbean Basin. The only other creatures they saw were small colonies of dolphins, occasionally leaping by, their beak-like snouts breaking the surface and their curved bodies rising joyously in the dark-blue water.

On the third day, Odilon was relaxing on the deck when he noticed a shore bird flying past his head. "Finally, we're close to land!"

he shouted, racing below deck to tell the good news to Thérèse. But his joy proved premature. Another day passed, and the anticipated land was nowhere in sight. To make matters worse, since the sighting of the bird a change in the weather entered the picture.

It was eleven a.m. when the sun, in a rushing blur, disappeared—replaced by sudden darkness and a steady increase of westward wind. Soon, the gale grew gusty, and the waves swelled skyward, shaking the vessel. Everyone above was ordered below, leaving only the crew captains to wrestle with the wind as they struggled to maintain control over the choppy water and the slippery deck.

The sea churned, swelling with white heaps of foam. Amid increasingly powerful gusts of wind and thick sheets of rain, the ocean turned violent, with wind gusts and waves surging to heights of over one hundred feet. A succession of swirling curves formed as waves crashed over the boat's bow. In an instant, the sky darkened to a deep grey, and billowing clouds engulfed the horizon. The storm briefly quieted for five or six minutes, only to return with even greater fury—waves advancing like giant rollers, pounding the ship from all directions.

By now, despair swept through the refugees. A sense of resignation that death was imminent grabbed hold. Sobbing mothers buried their children under their arms. Clusters of families bunched together like grapes, preparing to face the inevitable. Dozens of people lost consciousness, their internal organs churning inside their bodies.

Most of them envisioned a capsizing boat. Their faces dulled, atrophied by fear and hopelessness, frozen in shock, they watched breathlessly as their hopes, their dreams, and ultimately, their lives dissipated in a blizzard of wind, waves, and rain. Many were throwing up, expelling small amounts of food mixed with bile and blood.

Women and children shrieked into the gale, accompanying the frightening high-pitched screams of the captains on deck. These latter souls also cursed aloud at the monster waves and squalling winds, forcing the vessel to slant sharply low on one side, sending a chilling sensation into the hearts of the refugees.

Thunder growled with a deep, bass rumble, and lightning flashed across the sky, but the refugees were too dazed to notice. Fear and seasickness had taken their toll. Most of them were like zombies, even when conscious. A tremendous gust unleashed its fury against the ship's mast, snapping its rake—forcing the luff and base to bend backward, while the upper part, completely broken, dangled by the moorings.

Terrified, Odilon tore off his shirt to wipe the sweat from Thérèse's face, drenched with fear that their fate was sealed. Holding her tight against him, he also gripped their son, lying in her lap and sleeping like an angel. Thérèse was not crying, but her fright mixed with nausea from seasickness was obvious.

"Whatever will be…will be," she moaned, feebly rejected by life. Odilon said nothing, struggling inside with wretched guilt for having caved in to Thérèse's insistence that she board the vessel with him.

"Oh God," Odilon muttered, "Let me die, but give them life."

He was ready now to brave death, overcoming his fear of the unknown, preparing to be reunited with his loved ones, who had been swept away by the hideous circumstances of their poverty-stricken lives.

Nevertheless, Odilon clung to the faint hope that a miracle might occur, that the angels of the sea would intervene to save their lives. But that hope was quickly dashed by the dreadful rumbling of the re-emerging thunderstorm, the raw twilight, and the hopelessness reinforced by the swearing crew captains and his own powerless situation. He sat, listing back and forth like a defeated rooster after losing a cockfight. Pulling his feet up, he felt like a trapped zombie, led by his captors.

Two hours later, the huge mass of swirling wind that had been throwing water over the beleaguered boat's deck miraculously stopped. The storm was over. It seemed as if the sea monsters had gone into hibernation. All was motionless and still. There were no salty breezes, and no more wild waves could be seen. However, half of the refugees were close to death, either from hunger, the unsanitary conditions, or the sheer dread of death itself. Half-human and half-zombie, they were losing their basic instincts of human decency, their self-consciousness, their pride, their dignity, and their sense of *raison d'être*. They were too weak, too beaten by the weather to find the strength to even grasp their own surroundings.

The vanquished monsters of weather left the refugees with a glimmer of hope, but not with the assurance that their lives had been permanently spared. Land was still nowhere in sight. They did not know where they were, and the ship bobbed about in the dormant water, for the wind had knocked out its wings. The crew captains were left powerless, having no means to guide a wingless boat to land.

Peleah, who had barricaded himself within the lone cabin below deck, reemerged pale, sick-looking, and horribly bruised. He used a white t-shirt to make a distress flag, ordering one of his crew members to climb a wing-pole to install the flag. Four days floated by; they remained adrift in the water. On the fifth day, they detected a cruise ship at a great distance. They waved and shouted, but the ship did not stop.

After floating aimlessly for another two days, they woke one morning to find the boat beached on the shore of a desert island. Using the lone lifeboat, they transported people ashore, discovering that it was a tiny, deserted Bahamian isle, about one hundred miles north of the island of Inagua. Peleah rejoiced, even though they were virtually stranded. As a Machiavellian sea captain, he was already contemplating his departure.

Odilon and many of the others were skeptical, despite assurances from the captains that they would safely make it to Nassau. They spent twelve days on the island, eating crabs, fish, and wild *malanga*. Throughout those days, the crew managed to repair the broken sails.

This brought hope to the refugees, although the crew never gave an official departure time.

"We will set sail soon," Peleah mysteriously chanted. It made Odilon suspicious, wondering what his real plans were.

On the thirteenth day, Odilon, Thérèse, the baby, and Evans were asleep when they were awakened by the sounds of people yelling along the shore. Jumping up, Odilon could only see that there was a full moon, and the sea was calm.

"Don't leave us!" screamed the people as they tried to swarm the vessel. Near the lifeboat, Peleah stood with four of his bodyguards, armed with M-16 rifles, pointing them at the angry crowd charging to get at them. They shot in the air to intimidate the surging throng, which was immediate but only somewhat effective.

Undaunted, a burly two-hundred-and-fifty-pound man with wire-rimmed spectacles and a bushy mustache forged ahead. Half-naked and chesty, eyes spitting fire, he was an enraged tiger.

"We cannot be afraid of these thieves!" he bellowed, urging the crowd to take on Peleah.

In a dramatic standoff, Peleah ordered his guards to point their guns at the crowd, but to refrain from pulling their trigger. He knew he could not kill everyone without being killed. Those who love to kill are always the biggest cowards.

Odilon was quick to understand what they were up against. "We have to get out of here alive," he said to Evans, who stood next to him – ready to take on Peleah. Thérèse was speechless, mindlessly cuddling her inert baby, alive despite the fact that most other infants on the ship had already succumbed to dehydration.

The two friends calculated their next move – determined as the rest of the crowd, but wondering how they could overcome the insane, roguish, rascally Peleah. Just then, a bare-boned skinny old man who walked bent-over dropped to the ground.

"We're doomed!" he squeaked out in an agonized voice. "Peleah planned this…he knew we were going to die here. That's what he does every time he's in difficulty at sea!"

"What does he always do?" queried Odilon, inching closer to the old man, who lay face-down on the ground. Too weak to get on his feet, he raised his hand, pointing at the vessel. "If we let him go, he's not coming back," he sighed, collapsing.

"Odilon, we need to make a move now!" cried Evans.

"But how?" replied Odilon.

"Look behind you. You see these empty buckets?"

"Yeah."

"We're going to fill them with sand."

"What for?"

"Shhh…you're talking too loud. We'll push through the crowd with the buckets. Everyone is so headstrong; they won't pay attention to us. We're going to try to reach the front of the line."

"I see what you mean…it's a dangerous plan, but it will be fatal if we let him get away without us. The nearest land is too far away, and no other boats…"

"Understand where I'm coming from?"

"Perfectly well, Evans. But I also understand something else."

"What?"

"We're doomed if we let him take us onboard with his armed bodyguards. We'll be thrown overboard at gunpoint, once we're out in the ocean."

"Odilon, please don't try to attack those maniacs. You'll be dead in a heartbeat!" cried Thérèse, who struggled to suppress her fears.

"*Chérie*, don't worry. We'll be all right…stay here with the baby," Odilon soothed his Thérèse. The move they were going to make could be fatal, but he was not about to dwell on it.

With tons of kisses, he managed to console his lady; but trickles of sweat trailed down her worried face. As the boys reached the middle of the crowd, she tried to move forward and join them, but her legs buckled. Falling, she caught herself, deciding to remain safe with the baby. Within seconds, the boys reached the front line.

A tall man saw them. Realizing what they were doing, he pulled them aside. "Two unarmed men against four with guns? You'll be dead on arrival. We need to overwhelm them. There are more empty buckets left…I'm going to get five guys to fill them. When you see me coming with the other men, follow us…we want to surprise them, not get shot," the man explained as he was swallowed up by the crowd.

Odilon and Evans fidgeted, waiting for him to come back. As soon as he returned with the others, Odilon stopped them. "They'll suspect something if they see a bunch of men with sand-buckets getting close to them. Let's spread out, attacking them simultaneously with great speed," he said. Agreeing, they got ready.

As they edged to the buffer separating the crowd from Peleah, who was trying one more time to fool the people, a guard shot in the air menacingly. Odilon charged him anyway, in a concerted rush with the others. Shots rang out – one man fell, and it was Odilon, struck on his right shoulder. But their plan worked. The courageous men threw sand at the guards' faces. It took the milling throng mere seconds to grasp things; they blocked the guards to protect the sand throwers. Gobs of grit stinging their eyes, the water-wading guards attempted to swim away, but were swiftly subdued. Peleah was grabbed by dozens of hands, mauled horribly by an angry mob ready to tear him to pieces. He and his blinded henchmen were pulled over to the sea-grapes along the shores, tied up with their shredded clothing and left to rot on the deserted island.

Meanwhile, Odilon lay spread-eagled on the ground, bleeding profusely, fully alert but quiet. Evans ripped off his shirt, tightly wrapping the bullet hole in Odilon's shoulder, praying to God it would stop the bleeding.

Thérèse grew hysterical, crying for help – but feeling powerless and horrified. Barely able to breathe, dehydrated and pale, she was beaten by the surging tides of despair. No tears streamed down her dried-out face, while she needed to cry, scream, rail, and take her own last stand against the odds. Struggling to hold her squirming baby, which was fussing due to the hullabaloo, she raced to Odilon's side, licking his face to blot out the sticky blood and sand covering his forehead and cheeks.

"No, don't…it sort of feels good," Odilon sighed, reaching for her.

Six men moved in and carried him to the lifeboat, where he was hurried to the main ship. Everyone boarded the ship, and Odilon was kept on the deck. His eyes half-closed, he was laid on a cardboard box covered by a blue carbon sheet. Gasping for breath, he lay motionless, maintaining a weak pulse.

Drifting seaward, the vessel entered the ocean, the island fading from sight. Finding an inhabited place to land was the top priority. For the many people onboard, Odilon had become their hero, even in his agonized state. They were only able to escape the deserted island due to his courage. Gathering, the grateful people organized a candlelight vigil to pray for him on the deck. And as the sun rose from the horizon, as the vessel set sail to no known destination, Thérèse crouched on the deck, tearfully caressing Odilon's forehead while trying to make sense of their latest misfortune. Adversity drew its arrows ever closer to her heart. No matter – she realized that beyond the certainty of death, there are no guarantees in this life.

Once again, she was reminded that the road to freedom and independence so many of us dream of is often a long and treacherous one. Only a strong will can ever lead us to a better tomorrow. However, behind our desire for authentic change lies the central motivation for living. The longing to live in a just world, free of oppression, exploitation, and humiliation is what propels disenfranchised and marginalized people to a powerful determination toward social equality. It is unfortunate that the existential maladies of our time lie beneath an obsessive quest to only own more property.

This compulsive desire to take over, rule, and dominate brings with it a dangerous, red-hot thirst to crush opposition, to kill without mercy – anything in order to shoot all the way to the top.

Fighting for social justice has never been an easy task, especially in those places where basic human rights are suppressed. While many of us resist unjust forms of subjugation, too often we find ourselves pinned down by fear of the unknown. Although we may grasp the need to engage in the battle for democratic governance, we tend to be limited by our acute understanding that the lengthy road to that desired end can be wretched, painful, and potentially fatal. So, we remain passive to many forms of inequality, which are taking place all around us. Our passiveness toward iniquity is rooted in a daily struggle that never ceases to go on inside of us. It is the struggle between an instilled false sense of the security of independence, and the price we must pay to reach true social, financial, and political freedom.

Thérèse and Odilon were not immune to this struggle. Within the boundaries of their own understanding of this complex world, they truly desired to make a difference. As he lay motionless by her side, and as the breaking waves pushed the crowded vessel into unknown waters, one question puzzled her to the core: why is life one emergency after another? Not being aware what her next move would be, she was hoping and praying for a miracle, but not expecting one.

Elsewhere, Evans and a group of men guiding the vessel strove like titans to make it to a place where Odilon could be safe. They did not know where they were, but one of the men stated loudly that he was convinced pushing northward would eventually take them to the Bahamian island of Exuma.

The day crawled by, but land was nowhere in sight. Every few minutes, Thérèse took Odilon's pulse, her sole method of checking on him. To pass the time, she told him stories, as if he was in a position to respond. On the second day, around eleven a.m., a crewman detected land in the distance. Getting excited, everyone cheered. Some thought that the place was none other than New Providence, the main Bahamian island that houses the capital city of Nassau. But as they sailed closer, and the land was fast getting larger, this expectation was lowered. The site they had discovered was none other than Haiti, and the town of Môle Saint Nicolas was not far offshore.

"This is Haiti!" exclaimed one of the men.

"Haiti…" groaned Thérèse, wiping sweat off Odilon's brow.

"Yes," he uttered unexpectedly.

Everyone was in shock – their hero was conscious! Odilon's surprising words poured refreshing, cool waters of hope into the minds of Thérèse and Evans. They rushed him to the lifeboat, merrily carrying him ashore. But when they stepped onto the white sandy beach, the open seaside was virtually empty. Only a small sampling of fishermen could be seen in the distance.

"Odilon, *chéri*…talk to me," Thérèse begged, imploring him to not give up the fight. "Hold on, *chéri*, hold on! This isn't over yet; you're a strong survivor. We can make it. We'll have our life together. We'll raise our child the way you've always wanted it. We'll stay here in this town, building a new life, away from the bad memories of Saint Louis. Please…please, Odilon, *la vi mwen, zantray mwen, nòm dous mwen, pa lage mwen*," she pled, eternally pledging to him, moving the baby closer to his father. Surely, the presence of his son would keep him alive!

Odilon raised his eyes, smiling at Evans, who was standing next to him while he held Thérèse's hand. "I'm at peace…I know I'm in Haiti," he rasped, voice shaky and weak, moving his lips slowly. "I just didn't wish to die on foreign soil. You both know I was never a coward…but my time has come to depart from this Earth. There's no doubt in my mind that you will be all right. Evans will help with our son. I have a firm conviction that this is by no means the end of my existence; through you and our boy, I will live on. Don't cry over my death, which should've come in the frontlines along the RRF resistance fighters.

"But with Zebeda still in the mountains, and because of you, the baby, and Evans, I know the final chapter in the fight to liberate my country has yet to be written. Go make new friends, meet new people, build new alliances, preach the renewal of justice, and always take a strong stand for what you really believe in. Haiti will not live on, if we're not ready to die for her."

With these final words, he leaned forward, kissing Odilon Jr.'s forehead, squeezing Thérèse's hand and casting a strangely lingering smile at Evans – as if to say, "Goodbye, but not forever, my good friend."

Looking straight ahead, he closed his eyes and walked into the sunset, unafraid at last.

Glossary of Haitian / Other Non-English Terms

Abas: "Down with."

Acapella: Singing without instrumental accompaniment.

A fait accompli: An accomplished, irreversible deed or fact.

Ah, Rosita, donne-moi une petite chance: "Oh Rosita, give me a little chance!"

Arriviste: Recently arrived, as to power.

Atansyon pa kapon: Being careful doesn't mean being a coward.

Avanse, nou pap domi isi ya, n'ap kontinye: "March on, we're not sleeping here, we need to keep on walking."

Ayiti Kiskeya: Ancient name given to Haiti by the native indigenous people.

Bachata: Slow, romantic style of music, developed by Haiti's poor folks.

Badji: The altar of the houngan.

Bal des enfants: Sunday afternoon parties for teenagers.

Bèfchenn: Baggage handler.

Biyòt: A hard piece of wood used in the mentioned part of Haiti, on which women sit across their kitchen stoves to cook.

Bonjou mon fwè: "Good morning, my brother."

Bonsoir: "Good evening."

Bon teint: Staunch

Boukousou: Traditional bread made out of cassava flour.

Bourgeois: The uncaring, petty middle classes.

Bourgeoisie: A social order dominated by the *bourgeois*.

Bouzen: prostitute

Bracero: Spanish for farmhand or other worker.

Café-au-lait: Coffee with milk and a skin color description.

Calabash: A gourd good for holding water.

Carte blanche: Free reign.

Cavalier: Gallant or chivalrous man.

Charmant: Charming

Chicas: Girls, rowdy young women.

Chulo: The Spanish word for a pimp.

Clairin: Traditional Haitian rum.

Coiffure: Special hairstyle.

Compa-love: Style of Haitian compa or kompa music.

Compradò: Bourgeois buyers.

Conquistador: Spanish conqueror.

Cuisiniers: Cooks

Dechouke: Uproot

Décolleté: Low-cut neckline.

Dekou: Pitch dark at night.

De mort: Of death.

De salon: Of the high life.

Djouba: Night time festivity in the countryside associated with Zaka, the god invoked for a good harvest in agriculture.

Dokounou: A traditional cake made out of ganger and sweet plantain stuffed in a piece of a banana leaf held together by a dry, tied leaf.

El comandante: The commander.

En avant: "Let's go."

En grande pompe: With great pomp.

Envokasayon Soley: The invocation of the Sun – a popular song in Voodoo initiation.

Et les nouvelles: "And the news; is there any news?"

Européenne: European

Fòk nou leve konpe: "We need to rise up."

Fòn pran Anakreyon: "We will go get Anakreyon."

Fritay: Fried food

Gendarme: Police officer.

Generalissimo: Commander in chief.

Goud: Haitian currency.

Grandon: A powerful farmer.

Grimo: A dark type of Haitian mulatto.

Haïti Chérie: Beloved Haiti.

Haute-couture: High class or culture.

Houngan: A male Voodoo priest.

Impresario: Producer of entertainment.

Je suis là, oui, chéri: "Yes, I'm here, honey."

Jistisye : An enforcer.

Joie-de-vivre: Joy in living

Jongleurs: Medieval entertainers proficient in juggling, acrobatics, music, and recitation.

Kalalou gombo: Okra, a vegetable with a slimy component.

Kanpe: "Stand up."

Karako: A loose-fitting garment for women and children.

Kenbe Djanm: "Hold firm!"

Kinkyjoe: English-Bahamian slang for a black man with red-tan hair and skin tone.

Kisa: "What?"

Kleren: Traditional rum.

Kolangèt: "Fuck it."

Kolibri: A Haitian songbird.

Konbit: Cooperative, agricultural work.

Konpa: A music genre, a slow meringue, originated from Haiti in the 1950s.

Korosol: Sour-sop or guanabana, a tropical fruit with edible pulp and a sizable seed. It is related to custard apples.

Kote lwa nan Lafrik Ginen yo: "Where are the African gods?"

La Dessalinienne: The name of the Haitian National anthem.

La diablesse: The devil wife.

Lafrik Ginen: Guinea, Africa.

La mère patrie: The motherland.

Landomi: A variety of nocturnal snakes.

Latifondistas: Major large landowners.

La vi mwen, zantray mwen, nòm dous mwen, pa lage mwen: "My life, my everything, my sweet lover, don't leave me."

Le grand soir de la revolution: The great eve of the revolution.

Les grandes dames de Port-au-Prince: The affluent ladies of Port-au-Prince.

L'espoir fait vivre: "Hope keeps you going when you have nothing else."

Libèté ou lanmò: Liberty or death.

Li gen lwa: He/she is now being possessed.

Lwa: The spirit of Voodoo.

Loggia: A roofed open gallery.

Machann pisket: Ambulant merchants selling minnows in bunches.

Madras: A special fabric used to make tropical or summer clothes.

Main de fer: Iron hand.

Maître à penser: Leader or ideologue.

Malanga: A tropical edible plant, a vegetable whose roots are eaten like yam.

Malfini: A very popular Haitian hawk.

Manbo: A Voodoo priestess.

Mamselle: Miss

Mangfransik: A variety of mango

Mango *Djon*: One of the mango types in that part of Haiti.

Mango *monben* and mango *minvil*: Delicious types of mangos.

Manman: Mother

Marabou: Black woman with a spotless, smooth, milk-coffee tan.

Mesdames et Messieurs: Ladies and gentlemen.

Mèsi bondye: "Thank you God."

Mèt Bawon Samdi: Master of the cemetery.

Mèt Minuit: Master of midnight.

Mezanmi, annou leve kanpe: "Friends, let's rise up!"

Mezanmi, n'an trave oui la a: "My friends, we are in trouble."

Mon amour: My love.

Mulâtresse: Mulatto girl or woman.

Mulatta: Female of mixed black-and-white race.

Mulatto: Male of mixed black-and-white race.

Nadie: No one.

Nouveaux riches: Newly wealthy upper-class.

Nat: A mat made out of dry banana stem straps.

No hay un paso atras. Nou pap fè yon pa kita, yon pa nago: "Not one step backward."

Nombre: Name

Oui, nou konnen: "Yes, we know."

Pa Lage: "Don't give up, keep up the fight."

Pantas and Mexican heather: Tropical and sub-tropical flowers.

Parvenu: Relative newcomer to a social class.

Pichónes de Haitianos: Children of Haitian descent born in Cuba.

Piskèt: Minnows or tiny freshwater and saltwater fish.

Pit an wen, koman-w ye: "My child, how are you?"

Pour le meilleur et pour le pire: For better or for worse.

Queechquemitl: An ancient Mexican garment used by indigenous women.

Raison d'être: motivation or reason for living.

Rara: Haitian rap-style music.

Restavèks: Children in forced servitude.

Rezistans: Resistance

Romancero: Loverboy or Don Juan.

Roy: A vegetable stew made out of malanga roots, a cocoyam popular in Haiti.

Sang mêlé: Someone of mixed blood.

Sapoti: Sapodilla, a tropical fruit that looks like a potato on the outside for its brownish skin; it has very sweet flesh.

Sa se trokèt la, chay la dèyè: "This is just the tip of the iceberg."

Simbi: Spirit or goddess of the water. She is part of a group of names from Haiti's African ancestral roots; according to legend, she controls the underwater world.

Soley, Kote ou ye, n'ap cheche-w: "Sun, where are you, I'm looking for you?"

Soukèt lawouze: Rural police.

Soup joumou: soup made out of calabas squash.

Soutane: Religious cassock.

Tafiatè: A drunk or a heavy consumer of tafia, the Haitian traditional rum.

Tanbou: A tall Haitian drum.

Tant: Aunt

Tap-tap: A pick-up truck or minivan converted as a jitney; used in local transportation.

Tonton macoutes: A Haitian paramilitary force created in 1959 by dictator François 'Papa Doc' Duvalier.

Touloulous: Caribbean crabs.

Tout zanfan peyi d'Ayiti yo: All the children of Haiti.

Vèvè: Symbols associated with the lwa. They are usually drawn at the beginning of a voodoo ceremony.

Vive: "Long live"

Wounsi: Second-in-command after the houngan.

Zanfan peyi d'Ayiti yo: The children of Haiti.

Zenglendo: Bands of paramilitary death squads.

Zouk: A music genre sounding almost like Konpa; originates from the French Antilles.